RaeAnne Thayne

The
Sea Glass
COTTAGE

HQN

ISBN-13: 978-1-335-04516-4
ISBN-13: 978-1-335-08149-0 (International Trade Paperback Edition)

The Sea Glass Cottage

HQN
22 Adelaide St. West, 40th Floor
Toronto, Ontario M5H 4E3, Canada
www.Harlequin.com

Printed in U.S.A.

Whenever I am asked to provide acknowledgments and a dedication to my book, I am overwhelmed with gratitude for all those behind the scenes who have a role in bringing to life my initial raw idea to a completed book my readers can hold in their hands. As always, I am deeply indebted to my editor, the wonderful Gail Chasan (and her amazing assistant, Megan Broderick); to my indomitable agent, Karen Solem; to Sarah Burningham and her hardworking team at Little Bird Publicity for tirelessly helping spread the word about my books; to Lisa Wray and her marketing team at Harlequin; to my assistants, Judie Bouldry and Carrie Stevenson, for keeping me on track; and to everyone else at Harlequin—from the art department for their stunning covers to the copy editors, sales force, production team and everyone else I may have failed to mention.

As always, I owe the deepest of debts to my hero of a husband and our three children, who have somehow managed to put up with my deadline craziness for more than sixty books. I love you all dearly.

Finally, this particular book would not have been possible without three cherished friends who helped me see the possibilities: Jill Shalvis, Marina Adair and Joan Swan. I can't thank you enough for all your help!

To our newfound family, Shane, Ryan and Brad. Our lives have been changed forever by your willingness to open your hearts.

The
Sea Glass
COTTAGE

1

OLIVIA

She could do this.

Olivia Harper approached the nondescript coffee shop across the street from her apartment in the Lower Queen Anne neighborhood of Seattle.

The place wasn't necessarily her favorite. The servers could be rude, the food overcooked and the coffee rather bland compared to the place she preferred a few blocks east. The ambience at the Kozy Kitchen wasn't particularly cozy, or "kozy," either, for that matter, featuring cracked vinyl booths and walls that had needed a new coat of paint about a decade earlier. The Kitchen, as those in the neighborhood called it, was too tired and dingy to attract many hipsters, with their laptops and their slouchy knit caps and their carefully groomed facial hair.

Right now, it was perfect for her needs. Olivia stood outside the door, ignoring the drizzle and the pedestrians hurrying past her on their way to somewhere far more interesting and important than this run-down diner.

Every instinct inside her cried out for her to rush back down the street, race up the three flights to her apartment, climb into her bed and yank the covers over her head.

Any normal person would feel the same in her situation, especially after enduring a life-changing event like she had experienced five days earlier.

Her reaction wasn't out of the ordinary. In the five days since she had witnessed a horrific assault at another diner, the nightmares still haunted her, so vivid she had awakened every morning smelling spilled coffee, blood and fear.

She closed her eyes, still hearing the screams of the barista, the enraged yells of the junkie senselessly attacking her, Olivia's own harsh, terrified breathing.

She could feel the floor tiles under her knees and the cushions of the booth pressing into her back as she huddled on the floor, trying to make herself disappear.

Until that experience less than a week earlier, Olivia had blithely gone through life with absolutely no idea what a craven coward she was.

If she had ever thought about it, which, quite honestly, she hadn't, she might have assumed she would be the kind of person always ready to step up in the face of danger. Someone who could yank a child out of the way of a speeding car or dive into a lake to rescue a floundering swimmer or confront a bully tormenting someone smaller than him.

Someone like her beloved father, who had given his life to save others.

Instead, when her moment to stand up and make a difference came along, she had done absolutely nothing to help another human under attack except crouch under a table and call 911, all but paralyzed by her fear.

Shame left a bitter taste, even five days later. She hated remembering that she had done nothing while that junkie had fired a gun in the air then used it to pistol-whip the barista again and again.

Olivia had wanted desperately to run out of the coffee shop and find help but she'd been afraid to do even that, not sure if he had more rounds in his weapon.

The attack had seemed to last hours but had only been a moment or two before the barista herself and another customer, a woman approximately the age of Olivia's mother, had finally put an end to the horror.

That customer, just walking into the otherwise empty coffee shop, had sized up the situation in an instant and demonstrated all the strength and courage that had completely deserted Olivia. Instead of hurrying out of the coffee shop to safety, she had instead run to the barista's aid, yelling at the junkie to stop.

Startled, he had paused his relentless, horrifying random attack and had eased away slightly. That had been long enough for the barista, battered and bleeding and crying in pain, to pick up a carafe of coffee and throw it and its piping hot contents at him.

Olivia could still hear his outraged yell and the shouts of a neighborhood police officer who had finally responded to her call, ordering everyone down to the ground.

In five minutes it was over, but Olivia had relived it for days, especially coming face-to-face with the stark realization that she was a craven coward.

Steve Harper would have been ashamed of her.

Amazing, the lengths a person could go to deceive herself. All this time, Olivia thought she was strong and decisive and in control.

In certain areas of her life, maybe. Hadn't she moved away from her hometown in Northern California to go to college twelve years earlier and never looked back? That had taken strength. And she had built her own social media marketing company in her own time, working nights and weekends until she now had clients across the globe.

Of course, she was terrified to take the leap and make her side hustle her full-time job. She still put in long hours handling information technology for a medical conglomerate because the pay was good and the benefits amazing—even though her ex-fiancé worked in the administration for said conglomerate and made her life unnecessarily difficult, simply because she had broken off their engagement six months earlier.

She was constantly running from any situation she found emotionally threatening.

"Are you going in?"

A man was holding the door for her, she realized. He was about her age and not bad looking in a slightly rumpled, professor sort of way.

She started to take a step inside after him but fear froze her in place. She couldn't do it. Not yet.

"I'm waiting for someone," she lied.

"Here's a crazy idea. You could always wait inside, where it's dry."

He smiled, his brown eyes friendly and with a glimmer of interest.

"I'm good," she mumbled.

He shrugged and let the door between them close with a disappointed sort of look.

Yeah, she was a coward when it came to dating, too. She had one serious relationship in college that had ended by mutual agreement. Then she'd become engaged to the first guy she dated out of school, until she realized neither one of them loved the other. They were simply together for convenience.

She had convinced herself that a mildly enjoyable relationship was the safer choice. What if she loved someone passionately, fiercely, and then lost him suddenly, as her mother had her father? Sixteen years later, there were times Juliet still seemed shattered.

So many things could go wrong. A car accident. A plane crash. A heart attack.

A burning building where a man might run inside to save people, despite his daughter begging him not to do it.

Olivia shoved her hands into her pockets against the damp Seattle afternoon. Nothing would take the chill from her bones, though. She knew that. Even five days of sick leave, huddling in her bed and mindlessly bingeing on cooking shows hadn't done anything but make her crave cake.

She couldn't hide away in her apartment forever. Eventually she was going to have to reenter life and go back to work, which was why she stood outside this coffee shop in a typical spring drizzle with her heart pounding and her stomach in knots.

This was stupid. The odds of anything like that happening to her again were ridiculously small. She couldn't let one man battling mental illness and drug abuse control the rest of her life.

She could do this.

She reached out to pull the door open, but before she could make contact with the metal handle, her cell phone chimed from her pocket.

She knew instantly from the ringtone it was her best friend from high school, who still lived in Cape Sanctuary with her three children.

Talking to Melody was more important than testing her resolve by going into the Kozy Kitchen right now, she told herself. She answered the call, already heading back across the street to her own apartment.

"Mel," she answered, her voice slightly breathless from the adrenaline still pumping through her and from the stairs she was racing up two at a time. "I'm so glad you called."

Glad didn't come close to covering the extent of her relief. She really hadn't wanted to go into that coffee shop. Not yet. Why should she make herself? She had coffee at home and could have groceries delivered when she needed them.

"You know why I'm calling, then?" Melody asked, a strange note in her voice.

"I know it's amazing to hear from you. You've been on my mind."

She was not only a coward but a lousy friend. She hadn't checked in with Melody in a few weeks, despite knowing her friend was going through a life upheaval far worse than witnessing an attack on someone else.

As she unlocked her apartment, the cutest rescue dog in the world, a tiny, fluffy cross between a Chihuahua and a miniature poodle, gyrated with joy at the sight of her.

Yet another reason she didn't have to leave. If she needed love and attention, she only had to call her dog and Otis would come running.

She scooped him up and let him lick her face, already feeling some of her anxiety calm.

"I was thinking how great it would be if you and the boys could come up and stay with me for a few days when school gets out for the summer," she said now to Melody. "We could take the boys to the Space Needle, maybe hop the ferry up to the San Juans and go whale watching. They would love it. What do you think?"

The words seemed to be spilling out of her, too fast. She was babbling, a weird combination of relief that she hadn't had to face that coffee shop and guilt that she had been wrapped up so tightly with her own life that she hadn't reached out to a friend in need.

"My apartment isn't very big," she went on without waiting for an answer. "But I have an extra bedroom and can pick up some air beds for the boys. They've got some really comfortable ones these days. I've got a friend who says she stayed on one at her sister's house in Tacoma and slept better than she does on her regular mattress. I've still got my car, though I hardly drive it in the city, and the boys would love to meet Otis. Maybe we could even drive to Olympic National Park, if you wanted."

"Liv. Stop." Melody cut her off. "Though that all sounds amazing and I'm sure the boys would love it, we can talk about that later. You have no idea why I called, do you?"

"I… Why did you call?"

Melody was silent for a few seconds. "I'm afraid there's been an accident," she finally said.

The breath ran out of Olivia like somebody had popped one of those air mattresses with a bread knife.

"Oh no. Is it one of your boys?" *Oh please*, she prayed. *Don't let it be one of the boys.*

Melody had been through enough over the past three months, since her jerkhole husband ran off with one of his high school students.

"No, honey. It's not my family. It's yours."

Her words seemed to come from far away and it took a long time for them to pierce through.

No. Impossible.

Fear rushed back in, swamping her like a fast-moving tide. She sank blindly onto the sofa.

"Is it Caitlin?"

"It's not your niece. Stop throwing out guesses and just let me tell you. It's your mom. Before you freak out, let me just say, first of all, she's okay, from what I understand. I don't have all the details but I do know she's in the hospital, but she's okay. It could have been much worse."

Her mom. Olivia tried to picture Juliet lying in a hospital bed and couldn't quite do it. Juliet Harper didn't have time to be in a hospital bed. She was always hurrying somewhere, either next door to Sea Glass Cottage to the garden center the Harper family had run in Cape Sanctuary for generations or down the hill to town to help a friend or to one of Caitlin's school events.

"What happened?"

"She had a bad fall and suffered a concussion and I think some broken bones."

Olivia's stomach twisted. A concussion. Broken bones. Oh man. "Fell where? Off one of the cliffs near the garden center?"

"I'm sorry. I don't know all the details yet. This just happened this morning and it's still early for the gossip to make all the rounds around town. I assumed you already knew. That Caitlin or someone would have called you. I was only checking in to see how I can help."

This morning. She glanced at her watch. Her mother had been in an accident hours earlier and Olivia was just finding out about it now, in late afternoon.

Someone should have told her—if not Juliet herself, then, as Melody said, at least Caitlin.

Given their recent history, it wasn't particularly surprising that her niece, raised by Olivia's mother since she was a baby, hadn't bothered to call. Olivia wasn't Caitlin's favorite person right now. These days, during Olivia's regular video chats with her mother, Caitlin never popped in to say hi anymore. At fifteen, Caitlin was abrasive and moody and didn't seem to like Olivia much, for reasons she didn't quite understand.

"I'm sure someone tried to reach me but my phone has been having trouble," she lied. Her phone never had trouble. She made sure it was always in working order, since so much of her freelance business depended on her clients being able to reach her and on her being able to Tweet or post something on the fly.

"I'm glad I checked in, then."

"Same here. Thank you."

Several bones broken and a long recovery. Oh dear. That would be tough on Juliet, especially this time of year when the garden center always saw peak business.

"Thank you for telling me. Is she in the hospital there in Cape Sanctuary or was she taken to one of the bigger cities?"

"I'm not sure. I can call around for you, if you want."

"I'll find out. You have enough to worry about."

"Keep me posted. I'm worried about her. She's a pretty great lady, that mom of yours."

Olivia shifted, uncomfortable as she always was when others spoke about her mother to her. Everyone loved her, with good reason. Juliet was warm, gracious, kind to just about everyone in their beachside community of Cape Sanctuary.

Which made Olivia's own awkward, tangled relationship with her mother even harder to comprehend.

"Will you be able to come home for a few days?"

Home. How could she go home when she couldn't even walk into the coffee shop across the street?

"I don't know. I'll have to see what's going on there."

How could she possibly travel all the way to Northern California? A complicated mix of emotions seemed to lodge like a tangled ball of yarn in her chest whenever she thought about her hometown, which she loved and hated in equal measures.

The town held so much guilt and pain and sorrow. Her father was buried there and so was her sister. Each room in Sea Glass Cottage stirred like the swirl of dust motes with memories of happier times.

Olivia hadn't been back in more than a year. She kept meaning to make a trip but something else always seemed to come up. She usually went for the holidays at least, but the previous year she'd backed out of even that after work obligations kept her in Seattle until Christmas Eve and a storm had made last-minute travel difficult. She had spent the holiday with friends instead of with her mother and Caitlin and had felt guilty that she had enjoyed it much more than the previous few when she had gone home.

She couldn't avoid it now, though. A trip back to Cape Sanctuary was long overdue, especially if her mother needed her.

"Thanks again for letting me know."

"I'm so glad I called. The minute you find out anything about Juliet, let me know."

"I will. Thanks."

After she ended the call with Melody, Olivia immediately called her mother's cell. When there was no answer there, she dialed Caitlin's phone and was sent straight to voice mail, almost as if her niece was blocking her.

She glared at the phone in frustration.

Left with few other options, she finally dialed the hospital in Cape Sanctuary. To her relief, after she asked whether her mother was a patient there, she was connected almost instantly to a room.

"Hello?"

Her mother did not sound like herself. Usually Juliet's voice was firm, confident. She wasn't exactly brusque, merely self-assured and determined to waste as little time as possible.

Today, Juliet's voice was small, hesitant, almost… Frightened.

With her own emotions frayed from the week she'd had, Olivia was aware of a subtle thread connecting them for once, as unexpected as it was unusual.

She was frightened, too.

"Mom. What's going on? Is it true you were in an accident?"

"How did you find out?" Juliet asked.

Not from you or from Caitlin, she wanted to answer tartly. The two people who *should* have told her hadn't bothered to pick up the phone, had they?

Otis came running over with his favorite toy and sat at her feet, happily chewing.

"Melody called me, saying she'd heard bits and pieces and knew you had been injured. Apparently you had a fall. Are you okay? What happened?"

"It's the stupidest thing. I'm so embarrassed."

"I don't think the word *embarrassed* needs to enter the conversation here. You're hurt. You had an accident. You didn't break a bottle of pickles at the grocery store. Did you fall off the roof?"

Juliet released a breath. "I was up on a ladder, trying to hang some baskets I had just potted to the hooks in one of the greenhouses, and…something went wrong."

Olivia frowned at that momentary hesitation. "Something?"

"The ladder buckled or it wasn't set up right in the first place. I don't know exactly. To be honest, everything's a bit of a blur. Of course, that might be the pain medicine talking."

"What were you doing up on a ladder? You're the boss. Don't you have people to do that?"

"We're shorthanded. Don't get me started." Juliet's voice sounded somewhat stronger. Talking about the garden center she loved must have helped take her mind off the pain and fear.

"I spent three years training Sharon Mortimer to be the assistant manager under me and she decides two weeks ago to take a job running the nursery at a box store in Redding. Can you believe it? Where's the loyalty?"

She didn't want to deal with the garden center's personnel issues right now, when her mother was lying in a hospital bed. "What are the doctors saying?"

"You know doctors. They only want to give you bad news."

"What did they say?"

Juliet sighed. "Apparently I have a concussion. And I broke two ribs and also my right hip. That's the side I landed on. They were afraid my wrist on that side was broken as well where I tried to brace my landing, but it seems to be only sprained."

How far had she fallen? Good heavens. It sounded horrible. "Oh, Mom."

"It's not as bad as it sounds," Juliet assured her. "I was only on the ground for a few minutes before one of my customers found me and called paramedics. And they were there right away. So handsome."

Juliet seemed to be drifting away again.

"What are the doctors saying about your recovery? Will you need surgery? A cast?" Olivia pressed again. She had no idea how a broken hip was treated.

"Dr. Adeno, that nice new orthopedic doctor, was just here and she wants to do surgery tomorrow. I still haven't decided if I want to go through with it."

Olivia rolled her eyes. "It's not like Botox, Mom. It's not about whether you feel like it or not. If you need orthopedic surgery, you don't have many options. Not if you want to walk again."

"She says I'll be in the hospital three to five days and need four to six weeks of recovery. I can't be away from the garden center that long! The whole place will fall apart, especially without Sharon."

Everything always came back to the garden center. Why was she so surprised?

After Steve Harper's tragic death, her mother had stepped up to run the business that supported her family and had surprised everyone—probably most especially Juliet herself—by being great at it.

Olivia had tried not to resent her mother's long hours as she had immersed herself in learning the business.

She had never been gifted with the green thumb of her father, or her older sister. Steve and Natalie had bonded over their time in the garden. Nat had loved playing in the dirt while Olivia much preferred digging into a good book.

"This couldn't have happened at a worse time." Juliet suddenly sounded close to tears.

"Spring growing season."

"Right. Our busiest season of the year. And that traitor Sharon deserts us for stock options and a better 401(k). What am I going to do? I can't have surgery tomorrow."

Again, her mother sounded frightened and Olivia had no idea how to handle it. Juliet was one of the most together people

THE SEA GLASS COTTAGE

she'd ever known. Hearing this vulnerability in her voice disturbed her almost more than the accident itself.

"I'm sorry," she said gently, not knowing what else she could say.

"I wish you were here."

The small, frail-sounding words came out of nowhere, almost as if Juliet didn't really know she had uttered them.

Olivia stared into space while she felt something odd and sharp tug at her chest.

Her mother needed her. For once, Juliet wasn't the invincible almost-fifty-three-year-old widow running a successful business and raising her teenage granddaughter on her own. She was an injured woman who needed help and didn't know how to ask for it.

In the end, that was all that mattered. Olivia reached for a piece of paper, already mentally going through the list of things she would have to do in order to take extended emergency family leave from her job, close up her apartment and head out of town.

"I'll come down for a few days," she said instantly, without giving herself time to panic. "I'll be there as soon as I can make the arrangements."

"Oh. Oh no," Juliet said quickly, as if coming to her senses and realizing what she had said. "I know how busy you are. Anyway, what will Grant say?"

Grant was her ex-fiancé. Though he was an executive at her job, he wasn't directly over her department and had nothing to say that mattered. At least he hadn't in the six months since they broke up. "Don't worry about me, Mom. This is an emergency. I can take some time."

"Oh. I hate to be a bother. I feel so stupid."

"You're not a bother and you're not stupid."

What kind of weird universe had she slipped into where *she* was the one giving her mother counsel? That wasn't the natural order of things. Usually Juliet didn't need Olivia or anybody. After Olivia's father died, her mother had tried very hard to prove that to the world.

"I'll get down there soon as I can."

"I'll be fine, honey. I promise," Juliet continued to protest. "Don't come. Do you hear me?"

Before Olivia could answer, Juliet switched gears. "Oh. I need to go," she said. "Caitlin just came in."

Of course her mom needed to go if Olivia's fifteen-year-old niece was there. She almost insisted her mother hand the phone to Caitlin so Olivia could yell at her for not calling her the instant she found out about Juliet's accident, but she had a feeling Juliet would refuse, ever protective over the daughter of the child she couldn't save.

"All right. I'll talk to you tomorrow."

"Don't come down, honey." Her mother suddenly sounded far more like herself, her voice brisk and in control. "I mean it. We'll be fine. I may not be able to get around for a few weeks, but I can supervise operations at the garden center just fine from a wheelchair. I'll call you later in the week. Bye. I love you."

"I love you, too," she started to say, but by then, her mother had already hung up the phone.

Olivia sat for a moment, her dog happily chewing his toy at her feet and full-on rain splattering the window now.

She was half tempted to listen to her mother and stay right here in Seattle, especially after Juliet had just bluntly told her not to come. But then she thought of Juliet's frightened voice and knew she couldn't stand by. For once, her mother needed her. If that meant Olivia had to bury her own anxieties and juggle work and clients to make it happen, she could do it.

2

JULIET

Juliet Harper ended the call to her daughter, aware even through her fuzzy, painkiller-addled brain of the usual funny catch in her chest that always showed up when she talked to Olivia.

Their relationship seemed so...wrong. She always ended up saying the wrong thing, doing the wrong thing.

Every time she spoke with Olivia, she had the best of intentions, determined this would be her chance to heal whatever was broken in her interactions with her daughter.

Instead, she would end up bumbling her way through a conversation, never saying what was really on her mind or expressing how much she loved and admired Olivia for all she had overcome.

She knew what was at the heart of it. She had failed one daughter so miserably and was desperately afraid she would screw up with the other one. The great and terrible irony in the whole situation was that her very fear was the main thing in the way of forging a warm and loving mother-daughter relationship with Olivia. The one she yearned for with all her heart.

"Who was that?" Caitlin took a sip from the soda she had brought up from the hospital cafeteria after Juliet had made her granddaughter go down and find something to eat.

Why couldn't her interactions with Olivia be as easy as those with Caitlin?

"Your aunt Olivia. I asked you to call her. Why didn't you?"

"I sent her a message," Caitlin said, her tone defensive. "Maybe she missed it."

"I told you to call her, not message," she said. Caitlin always did things her own way and had since she was a baby. When other children would stack two or three blocks together, Caitlin would use them like percussion instruments. Instead of playing with dolls, she had dressed up the wriggling cats and tried to have tea parties with them.

She shifted in the hospital bed in a futile effort to find a more comfortable position.

Everything hurt. Who knew that one stupid decision, to climb a ladder without someone there to hold it for her, as she always insisted for her workers, could have such devastating consequences?

She should have known. She wasn't stupid, though nobody would know that by the traumatic events of her day.

The pain meds were wearing off. Instead of asking for more or surrendering to her discomfort, Juliet forced herself to focus on her granddaughter.

She looked so much like her mother, with Natalie's blond hair, bold eyebrows, stunning hazel eyes. Where Natalie had favored layers and big curls, like the style of the day when she was a teenager, Caitlin wore her hair short in an almost elfin cut. She dressed in her own unique style.

"Olivia must have got my message. Otherwise she wouldn't have known you were hurt."

"She only knows because Melody Baker called her. She and Olivia were tight as could be when they were in school. Always together. If you saw one, the other one was close behind. Kind of like you and Jake Cragun."

Caitlin made a face. "We're not together that much."

Both of them knew that wasn't true. Their neighbor had been Caitlin's closest friend since grade school.

Caitlin had girlfriends, too, good ones, but Jake was her BFF, her confidant.

Juliet had always thought it was so sweet, the way the two of them were always talking a mile a minute to each other. When they weren't together, they were texting each other or sending memes back and forth.

They had supported each other through some pretty tough things. Despite her young age, Caitlin had been a rock to Jake when his mother died of cancer three years earlier.

Juliet felt a pang when she thought of her dear friend Lili-anne, who kept a smile on her face even when she lost her hair and when the grueling effects of chemotherapy treatment kept her on the couch for days afterward.

"How's your English homework? Did you finish the essay you needed to write?"

"You're in a hospital bed and you're still going to nag me about my homework? Really, Mimi?" Caitlin said. She always called Juliet that, from the days when Caitlin had been learning to talk and instinctively tried to call her Mama, since Juliet had been her primary caregiver most of her life.

"It's my job to worry about your homework." Juliet frowned as she tried to adjust. Pain clawed at her and she couldn't hold back a moan.

Worry furrowed Caitlin's brow. "Right now, my English

homework should be the last thing on your mind. For once, can't you just rest and focus on yourself?"

Juliet wasn't completely sure she knew how to do that. She had been taking care of those she loved all her life, from the time her own mother died when she was fourteen and she had to help her father raise her younger sister.

She hadn't minded. She loved her family, loved cooking nutritious meals and keeping house. Marrying Steve right out of high school and slipping into life as a full-time mother and wife by accidentally getting pregnant on their honeymoon had seemed a natural transition.

And then, after all those wonderful years of marriage, Steve had been killed and she had been left to handle everything. The garden center. Sea Glass Cottage. The girls, with Natalie in and out of jail and treatment centers as she battled her addictions and Olivia slipping further and further away, like a freesia blossom bobbing on the breakers, being carried out to sea by a riptide.

She was trying. Exercising more, eating better. She had lost some of the stress weight she had gained after Steve died and she wanted to think she was more fit than she'd been her entire adult life, especially after her doctor told her regular exercise was one of the best ways to slow the progression of her condition.

What would happen now? Would she regain all the weight while she recovered from her injuries?

Had this stupid fall ruined everything?

The questions seemed to rattle together in her brain like dry seeds in a gourd.

"You should rest while you can," Caitlin said, fluffing her pillow and adjusting the blanket.

Sleep did sound lovely. In sleep, she could push away all the fears and worries and unfinished tasks she didn't make it to that day.

"What about you? Do I need to arrange a ride home for you? It will be dark soon."

"I could take the bus if I had to, but I don't because I'm staying here. The nurse told me this chair folds out to a bed, so I will just sleep in the room with you in case you need anything."

"No. Absolutely not."

"Why? It's just one night."

"Because you have school tomorrow. How do you think you'll do on your history test on two hours of sleep in an uncomfortable hospital chair?"

"I'm planning to take a sick day tomorrow. You need someone here when you have surgery."

She almost told Caitlin she had asked Olivia to come home, but suspected her granddaughter would not be thrilled at the information. For some reason, Caitlin didn't seem to like her aunt right now, though they had been de facto siblings for most of Caitlin's life and certainly since Juliet took full custody of her granddaughter after Natalie's death, when Caitlin was not quite three.

Yet another thing Juliet couldn't fix. Pain lodged in her chest, this time having nothing to do with her broken bones. She had tried to dig out the root of Caitlin's anger toward her aunt, but this was one thing the girl wouldn't share with her.

Oh well. It probably wouldn't be an issue. She doubted Olivia would be able to come home. Her daughter was far too busy and successful and *happy* in the life she had created away from Cape Sanctuary. It was for the best anyway.

"I will call one of my friends to be here during the surgery. Maybe Stella or Jane could come while I'm in surgery. I understand that you might not want to stay at Sea Glass Cottage by yourself tonight. Let me call Henry and see if he can pick you up and let you stay at their place tonight."

Caitlin lifted her chin. "Stop worrying about me. I don't

need a ride and I don't need a babysitter because I'm staying here tonight."

Some part of Juliet was grateful for her granddaughter's loyalty. Caitlin could be the sweetest thing, affectionate and helpful, eager to please.

She could also be as stubborn as a mule with a canker sore.

"You have school tomorrow," she repeated. "You can't stay here all night. I appreciate the offer, honey. Truly I do. I'll be okay. I can press a button if I need a single thing and the nurses will be here soon."

"How are you going to stop me?"

She narrowed her gaze at the defiant tone, so familiar. When she spoke like that, she looked and sounded just like her mother had in the last few years when Nat had been so troubled. Slipping out at night, going to wild parties, coming home drunk or stoned.

She had learned some bitter lessons through the experience of being Natalie's only remaining parent in the last three years of her oldest daughter's life. She wasn't about to make the same mistakes: passivity, inertia, acquiescence. Forget that.

"Young lady," she said sternly. "You are still a minor and I am still your grandmother, not to mention your legal guardian. I might be in a hospital bed but that doesn't make me completely helpless. You are not staying at this hospital tonight. I will make that clear to the entire medical staff if I have to. You don't have to stay with Henry and Jake if you don't want to. I can call another of your friends. Maybe Emma or Allie. It doesn't matter to me. You choose. But you're not staying here."

Caitlin looked slightly shocked at her fierce response. "I just don't want you to be alone."

"I'm in a hospital full of people who will be coming in and out at all hours of the night to check my vital signs and take my blood and roll me this way and that. By the time they release me, I'll be desperate for some alone time."

Caitlin still looked as if she wanted to argue, but before she could, a knock sounded at the door.

"Come in," Juliet called, grateful for the interruption.

It wasn't a nurse with another dose of pain medicine, as she was hoping. Instead, Henry Cragun and his son Jake pushed open the door.

"Hey. You up for visitors?"

Juliet fought the urge to pull the hospital blankets over her head. How ridiculous, when she was injured and in pain, that she could worry about vanity right now, but she hated the idea of Henry Cragun seeing her like this.

Wounded, frail, broken.

Old.

She sighed. While she didn't particularly want Henry here, perhaps he and his son could talk some sense into her stubborn granddaughter.

"Hi," she said, aware she sounded slightly breathless. With any luck, Henry would merely assume she was in pain. He could never guess that lately she always felt this way whenever he was around.

While Jake went immediately to Caitlin to give her a hug, Henry headed to her bedside. He was carrying a vase full of flowers, big lush pale pink peonies she knew probably came from his garden. They looked feminine, almost sensual in the hands of such a tough, hardworking man.

"Those are gorgeous," she managed, her voice squeaking. "Thank you."

"You're welcome." He set them on the table beside her bed, then gave her a long look. "Oh, Juliet. What have you done to yourself now?"

She felt old and clumsy and stupid. "I broke the cardinal rule of ladders and now I'm paying the price."

"I hear you had quite a nasty fall."

29

"She has two broken ribs, a concussion and a broken hip," Caitlin offered, ever so helpfully.

Juliet felt like an ancient old crone.

Henry winced in sympathy. "You never do things halfway, do you?"

"I'm fine. Don't worry about me. Surgery tomorrow and a few weeks of recovery and I'll be good as new."

He raised an eyebrow, clearly doubtful, and she wanted to throw a pillow at him. She was trying to be optimistic here. She didn't need a hospital room full of Debbie Downers.

"I hope that's the case," he said. "What time is surgery tomorrow?"

"We're not sure yet," Caitlin said.

"I haven't decided if I'm having surgery."

It was a stupid position and she knew it. Of course she had to have surgery. She had a broken hip that needed to be repaired. She had no choice, and no amount of trying to exert a little control would change that.

"I hope you know that Caitlin is welcome to stay with us until you break out of here. Even after, if you need to go into a rehabilitation center."

She was an old lady with a broken hip who might need to go into a nursing home to recover.

Could her life hit a lower point?

"Thank you. I was hoping you'd say that. There you go, honey. You can stay with Henry and Jake for now. I'll compromise. You can take a sick day tomorrow to be here during my surgery as long as you email your teachers to find out what homework you might have."

Her granddaughter pouted but apparently didn't want to argue in front of their neighbors and friends.

"What can we do to help?" Henry sat in the visitor's chair, entirely too close for Juliet's comfort. Of course, anywhere he chose to sit in the room would be too close for comfort.

That was the awful pain pills talking, she told herself, but she knew it was a lie. Over the past few months, she had developed a completely ridiculous attraction to the man.

She couldn't be attracted to him. He was her friend. One of her closest. His late wife had been one of her dearest friends.

She needed to focus on that and not on the way her pulse seemed to jump whenever he was near and her insides felt shaky and weak.

She cherished his friendship too much to ruin everything. Not only that, but he was eight years younger than her, and as a local landscape designer with a thriving company, he was one of her best clients at Harper Hill Home & Garden. She couldn't lose sight of that.

"I don't know yet, to be honest. Right now, I can hardly think straight. I just want to make it through the surgery tomorrow and then I'll focus on how to make it through the next few months."

He reached for her hand, his skin warm and a little rough from his work as a landscaping contractor.

"I would tell you to call me if you need anything, but I'm pretty sure you won't do that, will you?"

She wanted to lean into his hand, into him, and let him take care of everything. That was one of Henry Cragun's defining traits. He came across as a strong, capable man who could handle any crisis, from a leaky faucet to a woman who hadn't had an orgasm with someone else in years.

She didn't lean into him. Instead, she slipped her hand away to play with the edge of the hospital blanket. "I don't think I need help right now, but thank you. I have good employees." At least the ones who were left. She felt the betrayal all over again of losing Sharon.

"Well, keep me posted, then. I'll be around."

She found more comfort from that than she probably should. "Thank you."

31

A knock at the door heralded more visitors.

"You're a popular person today."

"Yeah. And all I needed to do to win the popularity contest was fall off a ladder."

He smiled as the door opened and Lucien Hall, her longtime neurologist, walked in.

Juliet could feel panic swelling in her along with the pain. Oh no. She should have anticipated this. Lucien treated her disease and was one of a very small number of people who knew about it.

If he said anything, even dropped a hint, her secret would be out and everything would change.

"I'm sorry to interrupt. I was here visiting another patient and received a text from Dr. Adeno, letting me know about your injuries. I just saw you a week ago. What happened?"

"She fell off a ladder and broke two ribs and her hip. And she has a concussion," Caitlin said, giving the doctor a curious look. Juliet's heart dropped. It was clear her granddaughter was wondering what kind of doctor Lucien was and what reason Juliet might have had for visiting him.

Lucien gave her a look that was part disbelief and part admonishment. "What were you doing up on a ladder?"

"Hanging flowers," she said. "I'm fine. I'm sure Dr. Adeno gave you the full report. How are you? How's Jorge?"

Lucien had recently married his partner in a beautiful seaside service, and Harper Hill Home & Garden had helped with the flowers.

"He's wonderful, but don't think you're going to change the subject that easily," he said.

Juliet tried not to panic. She couldn't have a conversation right now with him while Henry, Jake and Caitlin were there.

To her vast relief, Henry seemed to pick up on her distress. He glanced at the teenagers.

"Come on, kids. Let's let Juliet and her doctor talk. We can grab some dinner then head over to Sea Glass Cottage and pick up some things for Caitlin so she can stay in the guest room."

Caitlin looked reluctant to leave her grandmother. "Are you sure you don't want me to stay?"

"I'm fine. I have nurses to take care of me. Don't worry."

"I'll call you later, to make sure you're still okay."

"Is there anything we can bring back to you later tonight? Anything from home you might find comforting?" Henry asked her, so much gentleness and kindness in his eyes that she suddenly wanted to cry.

She couldn't lose his friendship. It was too precious to her, like a rare flower that only bloomed once every hundred years.

He leaned in and kissed her cheek, and she again fought the urge to throw her arms around his neck and let him take care of her.

"Thank you for the peonies. I can't believe you remembered they're my favorites."

"You're welcome," he said, his voice gruff. "Don't fall off anything in the night."

"I'll do my best."

She felt that same complicated mix of gratitude and tenderness as Henry ushered his son and her granddaughter out of the hospital room, leaving her alone with her neurologist.

"So. Talk to me," Lucien said in his no-nonsense voice. "What were you thinking?"

"I wasn't," she admitted.

"You shouldn't have been up on a ladder. You know that, right? I warned you that the new medication we were trying might cause dizziness."

She shifted on the bed. "Yes. It's been worth it. I haven't had any symptoms."

"It's too early in the trial to know if that will continue. You know that, right? You have multiple sclerosis, Juliet. You can't pretend you don't. Yes, you're lucky enough that your symptoms have been mild so far, but no one can predict what might happen."

"I feel strong and healthy, except for the broken bones," she muttered.

"You know that may not continue forever, though. We can keep the symptoms at bay a long time but possibly not indefinitely."

She knew. She knew entirely too well. She woke up each morning wondering if today would be the day she would suddenly develop vision problems or her hands would go numb. With each muscle pain or spasm, she worried this was the beginning of a steep decline.

At the end of each day, she said a prayer of gratitude that she'd been able to make it through another day where she could keep up with the demands of her life.

Dr. Hall's voice gentled. "You need to promise me that next time you're prescribed a medication that may cause dizziness, you don't climb up a twenty-foot ladder to hang a flower basket, got it?"

"I promise. It was a mistake. One I'm paying for dearly."

"Dr. Adeno says she wants to operate tomorrow."

"That's the plan."

"You'll be in excellent hands. She's a very good surgeon."

"Nice to know."

"If I have your permission to talk with her, I'll give her a call to discuss co-treatments. Some of the medications you're on for the MS might impact your healing process."

"Yes. You can talk to her. Thank you."

He squeezed her hand. "Good luck tomorrow. I'll check in while you're still an inpatient and have my office schedule you for a few months from now so we can check in."

After he left, the room seemed blessedly empty, but she knew it wouldn't last. More nurses and technicians would be in to poke at her.

Juliet was exhausted suddenly. She longed to curl up on this bed and forget everything. Her pain, the accident, the burden of her MS diagnosis that she had carried alone every day for the past four years.

The bouquet Henry had brought her stirred the air with its luscious smell, and she closed her eyes, focusing on that scent and trying to picture the showy blossoms with their intricate layers of petals until she fell asleep.

3

OLIVIA

"Only another hour now, Otis. Can you believe we made it this far? We got this, right?"

The little dog in his crate on the back seat snored, which she decided to take as his answer.

She was so tired. It had taken her several hours to make all the arrangements at work, tie up loose business ends and pack up her car. She hadn't been able to hit the road until about ten the previous night and had been driving for twelve hours, stopping only to catch an hour or so of sleep in the parking lot of a twenty-four-hour grocery store.

She had stopped for gas and to let Otis out a few other times. Other than that, she had been behind the wheel.

The scenery here was lovely as she headed south along the coast toward home. Still, she couldn't help wondering if she was making a terrible mistake.

Her mother was in an accredited hospital with trained care-givers. What exactly could Olivia provide that they couldn't?

What could she do in Cape Sanctuary besides get in the way? She wasn't good at dealing with sick people. The sight of blood made her queasy and she didn't have a lot of patience for sitting around in a hospital room.

And heaven knew, she was helpless at the garden center. The last time she had tried to help out during a visit home shortly after graduating from college, she had ended up killing an entire table of vegetables by using the wrong fertilizer before one of the other workers stopped her.

"My mom is hurt and she wants me there. I owe her," she said out loud. "You understand, don't you, Otis?"

Her dog, awake now, gave his sweet bark, as if he fully agreed with her. That was yet another reason she adored his face. He had become her sounding board, her confessor, her personal secret keeper.

"You don't think it's crazy, do you? I mean, she's my mom and she's hurt. And I love her. And going home to help for a few days is the right thing to do."

Otis thumped his tail and circled his crate a few times.

"Yeah. I'm glad you agree. Thanks, bud. Good talk."

The dog scratched at the floor of his crate and circled again, a clear indication that he needed out for a bit. Though painfully close to her destination, Olivia decided she could use the break as well to stretch her legs.

She picked a well-lit convenience store just off the highway and used her credit card at the pump to fill up before walking Otis around the side of the building, one hand on the canister of pepper spray on her key chain and the other tightly gripping the dog's leash. He wouldn't be a lot of protection but she found comfort from his presence anyway.

So far on this trip, she had managed to avoid too much crowd anxiety by paying at the pump and hurrying in and out when she needed to refill her coffee or use the restroom. It helped that she was driving overnight, when most sane people were sleeping. The morning was well underway now, though, and the convenience store parking lot was quickly filling up with commuters. No one looked threatening, she told herself, lifting her face to the sun and rotating her shoulders to ease some of the tension there. She couldn't spend her entire life in fear because of one moment she couldn't take back.

After a quick trip inside, where she held on to her pepper spray the entire time and hurried back to the car as soon as possible, she and Otis hit the open road again. For the rest of the journey, they made good time. When they were about half an hour from Cape Sanctuary, she had stopped again to use the restroom from all the coffee she'd been drinking and to give Otis some water when she suddenly realized she should probably have a plan for the dog once she arrived in town.

She certainly couldn't take him to the hospital with her, especially when she didn't know how long she would be there. As he had never been to Sea Glass Cottage, she didn't want to simply abandon him in a strange house.

On impulse, she dialed Melody.

"Hi. I was just thinking about you," her friend said. "How's your mom?"

"She had an okay night. I talked to her this morning and found out her surgery is scheduled for eleven. That's why I'm calling. Any chance you could do me a favor?"

"Sure," Melody said instantly. "Anything. Do you want me to go sit with her during the surgery?"

"Thank you, but what I actually need is a dogsitter for a few hours while I head to the hospital myself. I was going to drop Otis at Sea Glass Cottage, but Mom and Caitlin have cats and he can be kind of a wuss when it comes to felines. I'd like to give him the chance to get to know them first when I'm there to referee. Do you mind watching him while I check on her?"

"Like, right now? As in, you're in town?"

"Almost. I'm about twenty minutes out."

"Did you drive all night? You must be exhausted!"

She wasn't as tired as she'd expected, fueled by caffeine and adrenaline, but she had a feeling that wouldn't last.

"I'm okay for now."

"After we spoke on the phone yesterday, I didn't think you were going to be able to make it back."

"My mom needs me," she said simply. "I'm sorry I didn't tell you, but I was so busy making arrangements I didn't think about it until I was on the way. I didn't want to call you at 3:00 a.m."

"You know I would have taken your calls. Day or night, hon."

Oh, she loved Melody. She had dear friends in Seattle but she wasn't sure any of them were of the call-me-day-or-night variety. "Thank you."

"We're happy to dogsit. The other boys are in school, but I still have Charlie home with me and can promise you, he would love to play with a dog. Ours is kind of a party pooper."

"Thank you. Otis is very well behaved and loves children, I promise. You're a lifesaver. I have no idea how long I'll be at the hospital. It might be several hours."

"No problem. We don't have anything on our schedule today."

"I owe you. I'll be there in about fifteen minutes."

"Perfect. That gives me time to get out of my yoga pants and into some real clothes. See you then."

Olivia ended the call, grateful all over again for the priceless gift of old and dear friends. Melody had been her rock during those difficult years after Steve Harper died and Natalie went off the rails.

Olivia wanted to think she had been the same to her in return when Melody's mom had died after years of alcohol abuse, but she was almost certain the ledger would never be equal.

As she drove into town, her skin started to prickle, memories flashing across her mind like a fast slideshow.

Her dad used to love breakfast there at the Huckleberry Café on lazy summer mornings, always ordering pancakes with extra of their eponymous syrup.

The small beachside park reminded her of her father trying to teach her and Nat how to surf. She could almost taste the salt of the seawater, feel the cool Pacific surrounding her, hear the laughter of her older sister.

Those lush, abundant flowers hanging in baskets from the lampposts throughout town probably came from the Harper Hill nursery. Every year, her family would gather one evening and pick the most luxurious baskets from their vast selection then load them into one of the nursery delivery trucks to deliver to the city office for the seasonal display.

Her dad was always so delighted at being able to do a little something to beautify their community.

He had loved Cape Sanctuary. That was the main reason he had become a volunteer firefighter, so he could give back to the neighbors and friends he loved.

The sleepy little beach town hadn't changed much. It was a bit out of the way for a huge tourist influx but visitors still managed to find it in the summertime, coming in droves to enjoy the towering rock formations offshore, the impossibly green forests, the fairy-tale cottages surrounded by gardens and wind chimes.

It really was a beautiful setting. Too bad her memories marred the serenity of it.

When she drove past the site of the old McComb building, long since rebuilt, she noticed a new restaurant sign hung out front.

Her father had died there. He had given his life for the town he loved, an event that had been the single defining moment of her life. She would never be able to bring herself to go into that restaurant, even if people told her it served the best food in town.

She pushed away the memory as she turned down a road and approached Melody's trim house, several blocks from the ocean.

It was a two-story cottage, really, probably less than a thousand square feet on each level, but charming, like something out of a Disney movie or a fairy tale.

Rosebushes lined the walk and cheerful blue shutters provided a stark contrast against the pale, weathered shake siding.

She pulled into the drive and turned off the engine to her crossover hybrid. "Here we are, Otis. We made it in one piece."

Her dog flopped his tail against the wall of the crate. He grew even more excited when she came to the back and opened the door of the vehicle to clip on his leash and let him out. She held the leash with one hand and carried the crate with the other, in case he needed to retreat inside his happy place while he was visiting strangers.

"I need you to behave yourself now," she instructed him. "It will be okay. You'll see."

Otis looked doubtful and she picked him up for a quick hug. "I know how nervous you get around new people. But if I can come back to town and deal with my mom, you can spend a little time with people you don't know. I'll be back in a few hours to get you."

The dog gazed at her with a trust she found humbling. In the three months since they had adopted each other, she was astonished at how important Otis had become to her.

Melody came to the door before she even had time to ring the doorbell.

"Oh. I'm so happy you're here." Her friend hugged her tightly, and for a few lovely moments, Olivia hugged her back, feeling some of the anxiety that had simmered just under her skin begin to ease.

She cherished her friends in Seattle, she thought again, a community of caring, intelligent, funny men and women. But there was something as comforting as warm socks about being with her childhood best friend, the woman who had always known her best. It seemed to settle something deep inside her.

Melody had lost weight since she'd seen her last and she had new circles under her eyes, but her smile was bright and genuine.

"You must be so tired."

"I'm all right," she said. "Juliet wanted me here. So I'm here."

"I'm so sorry she's going through this. Your mom is so fiercely independent. This must be torture for her."

"I can only imagine. I'm sure she's driving the doctors and nurses crazy."

"You're probably in a hurry to get to the hospital. Don't worry. We'll have a chance to catch up."

"Thank you. This is Otis. He's usually a sweetheart, though a little shy."

"Excellent. Charlie and Thor, that's our golden retriever, will be glad for the company. They're playing in the back right now."

"Otis can be a nervous Nellie. He might not want to even come out of his carrier," she warned.

"We'll be gentle, I promise. He'll be okay, Liv. We don't torture fur babies around here. My boys are careful."

She was being ridiculous, she knew. Otis was just so dear to her, her first creature since she'd become an adult. She hadn't had a dog in years, not since her dad's beloved border collie died of old age a few months after Steve's death. She'd forgotten how dogs could reach in and grab hold of a person's heart.

"Thanks." She hugged Melody again, wondering if the weight loss was from a diet or if she had stopped eating after her idiot husband walked out on her. "I love you tons. You know that, right?"

"Yes." Melody eased away, her eyes suspiciously bright. "I'm really sorry about your mom. But on a purely selfish note, I'm so glad you're home for a few days."

She was the *worst* friend. She should have come home the moment she heard Rich Baker had walked out on his family. Melody hadn't told her; she'd had to hear the news from Juliet, who had sounded heartbroken.

As soon as she hung up after hearing the news from her mother, Olivia had called Mel and they had cried together for a good hour on the phone. She had tried to stay in touch since then with video chats and funny texts and even a few care packages of things she thought might cheer her up.

In retrospect, she was ashamed she hadn't done more. Squeezing even a weekend out of her schedule to fly down would have meant more than all the floral bouquets or bath baskets or luxury linens she could have sent.

"We'll catch up. I promise. As soon as I get my mom settled, we'll find a babysitter for your boys and we'll head to The Sea Shanty, where we can drink margaritas all night and tell each other everything."

"That sounds perfect," Mel said with a rather watery smile. "I've missed you."

"Same, times a million," she said, giving Melody another hug.

"You'd better get out of here and head to the hospital so you can catch your mom before surgery."

"Yeah." She hugged her dog one more time then set him back in the safe zone of his carrier and headed for the door.

"I'll call you as soon as I know anything," she promised.

"I'll be waiting."

Melody stood at the top step of her cottage, waving as Olivia headed down the sidewalk.

She had just reached her vehicle and opened the door when a shiny blue pickup truck pulled up into the driveway next to her.

Not her business who else might be visiting Melody, she told herself as a man climbed out of the driver's seat.

For just a moment, their gazes met, his curious and maybe a little suspicious, and Melody felt as if someone had dumped a bucket of salt water over her head.

It was Cooper Vance, Melody's older brother.

Lean, tough, dangerous. Gorgeous.

A hundred memories suddenly chased each other across her

mind, tumbling and rolling, leaving her off balance and feeling a little dizzy.

She was only tired and overcaffeinated, she told herself. That was the reason she felt that seismic jolt of awareness.

When she was barely a teenager she used to have such a crush on him. In one of those weird twists that often happened among neighbors close in age, his sister had been *her* best friend, while *her* sister, Natalie, had been his.

She used to think he was hotter than all the guys in her favorite boy band mixed together.

He gazed at her without any trace of recognition. Big surprise there. She had only been fourteen the last time she saw him, gawky and awkward, with an overbite, braces on her teeth, frizzy, overprocessed hair and no figure to speak of.

He had moved away from Cape Sanctuary, joining the military as an elite special forces pararescue trooper. When Natalie died of an overdose, he had been stationed overseas and hadn't been able to make it back for her funeral.

Somehow their paths had not intersected in all the intervening years. If she were smart, she would figure out a way to keep them from ever intersecting.

The man was trouble.

She had known he was back in town. Melody had mentioned it a few months ago in an email, something Olivia had registered vaguely as one of those interesting details that wouldn't have much impact in her life. Why would it? She was busy with her life in Seattle and rarely came back to Cape Sanctuary.

And then her mother had mentioned Cooper a few weeks ago, telling Olivia she had run into him at the grocery store. The conversation had been typical Juliet.

"He was so kind," her mother had said, always looking for the good in people. "He insisted on loading all of my groceries into my trunk like I was some old lady. I always liked that boy. Your father did, too. It didn't matter what his background was, how difficult his home life might have been, that his dad was in prison and his mom was a drunk. He always worked hard and looked out for his family."

Yes, Cooper was perfect in Juliet's eyes. Olivia had a sexy dream about him that night, she remembered now, and could feel her face heat at the memory.

She frowned and would have climbed into her car and driven away except this was Cape Sanctuary and that sort of rudeness just wasn't acceptable.

He offered a polite smile. "Hi. I'm Cooper Vance, Melody's brother."

"I know."

He looked apologetic. "Sorry. I haven't been back in town very long and I'm still trying to remember faces and names."

He gave her a closer look. "Olivia? Is that you? Good Lord. How long has it been?"

So long. And not long enough.

"A few years. Mel told me you had moved back to town."

He shrugged. "The fire chief job opened up here and I was looking for a change. The timing seemed right. I can't believe I didn't recognize you. I obviously wasn't looking closely enough. You look like your mom and...you have Nat's eyes."

Grief twisted across his features and she felt a pang of sympathy. She missed her sister, too.

People had been saying she resembled her mother and her sister most of her life. She didn't see it. Natalie had been tall, willowy, gorgeous, with long wavy blond hair and compelling, classically lovely features.

Olivia felt like the awkward clone rendition of Natalie, as if the mold that created them had been slightly damaged by the forging progress and was starting to wear out. They shared the same high cheekbones, the same hazel eyes, but Olivia had never reached Nat's height and her hair wasn't quite as vibrantly blond.

It was also annoyingly frizzy, until she'd grown tired of trying to straighten it and just adopted beach waves or messy buns.

Most important, Natalie had carried herself with an assurance Olivia had never felt.

Would Olivia have grown into her skin a little better if her father hadn't died so abruptly and if Natalie's life hadn't spiraled out of control shortly after? She didn't know. She only knew that by the time her sister died, Natalie had no longer looked like the classic beach beauty. Her hair was dry, falling out, and her weight had dwindled so much that her bones showed and her skin had become sallow and loose.

Cooper hadn't been there to see it, of course. He had been off saving the world. He and Natalie had been best friends, but when she had needed him most, Cooper hadn't been anywhere around. If he'd stayed, maybe he could have stopped that downward spiral. None of the rest of them could.

"I didn't know you were back in town."

"Yes. Barely."

"Your mom and niece will be so happy to see you. Have you stopped by the hospital yet?"

"On my way now. I only stopped to see if Mel could babysit for me."

He looked surprised. "You have kids? I had no idea! How many? How old?"

"One. Otis. He's about three, at least according to his veterinarian, but I can't be sure."

He smiled slightly and she ordered her stupid hormones not to react. "None of the human variety?"

She thought she would by now. She'd been with Grant for four years, engaged for two, and they'd talked about possibly having one and adopting another child or maybe even siblings out of the foster system.

That had been her one regret when she broke off the engagement.

"No. And I understand you don't, either. Mel likes to talk about you."

His sister was justifiably proud of Cooper, who had been a hero before he left town and who continued that pattern in the military, from what she heard.

"How's your mom doing? That was one hell of a nasty fall."

"You were there?" That didn't really surprise her. Cape Sanctuary had a small paid staff of emergency medical technicians and EMT-paramedics. Most of the volunteer firefighters were also trained as EMTs, as her father had been.

"I was on the ambulance that responded. It was scary for the first few minutes, until she regained consciousness."

"Unconscious! Nobody told me she was unconscious."

"She fell pretty hard. We were worried about a spinal injury, so it took us a while to stabilize her. Your mom was a trooper, though. Asking about the guys' families and when Lindy Melendez was having her bridal shower."

"Yeah. That's my mom."

Everyone loved Juliet Harper. If her mom ever decided to run for mayor of Cape Sanctuary, she would be a lock.

"Well, thanks for helping her."

"It's part of the job," he answered with a smile that left her feeling dazed.

She was sleep-deprived from driving all night, worried about her mother and stressed about leaving her doggy. That was the only reason for her ridiculous reaction. She certainly wasn't still pining over her best friend's older brother, no matter how gorgeous the adult version of Cooper Vance might be.

"I guess I'll see you around," he said, with another of those lethal smiles.

She nodded, which was all she could manage, climbed into her vehicle and drove away, vowing to do her very best to make sure she saw him first and prevented that from happening.

4

COOPER

Olivia Harper.

Cooper watched her drive away in a little silver SUV, feeling as if he were the one who had fallen off a ladder.

How many years had it been since he had seen Olivia? He couldn't remember. It even might have been before he left town for good. Melody had mentioned her a few times over the years. He remembered Melody telling him when Olivia graduated from college, when she got a job in tech somewhere in the Pacific Northwest, when she started her own social media company.

She'd been engaged a few years ago, he remembered now. And then Melody had told him she'd broken off the engagement sometime later.

Other than those few shout-outs from his sister, he hadn't really dwelled on her much. If he did, he had thought of her as Little Livie, Natalie's baby sister and his own sister's best friend.

In his mind, she still had pigtails and braces and walked around with a book in her hand most of the time.

She wasn't that girl anymore. The Olivia he just encountered was still small in stature but she wasn't gawky and awkward anymore. His reaction to that one brief slash of smile still seemed to ricochet around his chest.

She wasn't for him, Cooper reminded himself. She was only here temporarily to visit her mother and she would be leaving soon to return to her life in Seattle.

He, on the other hand, was here for good. His sister needed his help and he had vowed to her and to himself that he would do whatever necessary for Melody and her boys. They had to be his focus, not this instant, unexpected reaction to Olivia Harper.

He pushed her out of his mind, grabbed his toolbox and headed up the steps to Melody's house. One of them needed fixing, he noted. He would add that to his to-do list.

Before he could knock on the door, his youngest nephew raced around the corner of the house, Melody's big, goofy retriever right behind him. "Hi, Uncle Cooper! Did you bring your dog?"

He always loved listening to Charlie, who had trouble with his *R* or *L* sounds, so called him Coopah and used words like *bwing* instead of *bring*.

"No. Jock was sleeping when I left and I didn't want to disturb him."

"That's okay. Because guess what? We're dogsitting!"

"I heard that." He studied the boy and the dog. "Weird. He looks just like Thor."

Charlie giggled. "This *is* Thor, silly. The dog we're supposed to be dogsitting isn't here yet."

"I think it is, since its owner just left."

"Oh! I want to go see!"

Charlie raced up the steps to the porch of Melody's small two-story house. "Mom! Hey, Mom! Where's the dog? Is it here?"

His sister came around the house holding a tiny trembling

purse pooch cradled in her arm. "Hey. Keep it down. He's nervous enough already."

"Oh. Sorry." Charlie spoke in what he probably thought in his five-year-old wisdom was a whisper but was loud enough to rattle the windows.

"This is Otis. He's not sure about us yet."

"He's so cute! Hi, buddy. Don't be afraid. We're nice. Except for Will and he's still at school." He beamed at the dog, who answered by trembling a little more forcefully and hiding his face in Melody's arm.

Charlie's smile turned into a frown. "What's wrong with him? Is he cold? I can get a blanket."

"He's just nervous. If we sit down together on the sofa, I bet he'll settle down enough that you can make friends and then hold him in a few minutes, as long as you can be gentle."

"Okay. But I have to pee first. I was gonna do it outside but you got mad at me last time."

"Good call." Cooper barely had time to say the words to Charlie before he raced down the hall toward the bathroom at a pace that clearly indicated an emergency was imminent.

Man, he loved this kid. Charlie and his older brothers, Will and Ryan, were the most adorable boys. They were funny and sweet and openhearted. For the life of him, Cooper could not figure out what man in his right mind would walk away from the perfect family.

"So. This must be Olivia's dog."

Melody's eyes widened in shock. "How could you possibly know that?"

He had to smile. She had the same expression on her face that she used to get when he would pull a quarter out of her ear. For hours, he had practiced magic tricks he learned from a school library book, simply to earn that look of astonished glee from her.

"Seriously. Did Charlie tell you that?"

He shook his head, shifting his toolbox to the other hand.

"She was leaving as I was pulling in and told me she was leaving her dog here. From there, I could put the pieces together on my own. I didn't recognize her at first. It's been years."

"Neither of you has managed to make it back to town nearly enough over the years."

Was coming back to Cape Sanctuary as difficult for Olivia as it was for him? They shared some of the same ghosts. Her sister. Her father. He had loved them, too.

Guilt, his longtime companion, poked its ugly hand in the air for attention, but he had become an expert at ignoring it. For the most part, anyway.

"She was always a good friend to you."

Melody's features softened as she petted the trembling dog, who seemed to be settling down. "The best. I don't know how many nights I spent at Sea Glass Cottage with her family when I was growing up. Maybe more than at our own place."

He didn't blame her for that. The tiny two-bedroom on Harper Hill their mother had inherited from her grandmother when Cooper was ten had been cluttered, dilapidated, cold in the winter and sweltering in the summer. Melody had slept with their mother while he'd been in a tiny room of his own until he ended up carving another space for himself out of the attic by putting up his own drywall and laying down a floor he created out of secondhand boards so that Melody could take his old room.

At least it had been a roof over their head, which was more than they'd had at previous times in their childhood. The very best part about the house had been their neighbors, Steve and Juliet Harper and their daughters, similar in age to him and to Melody.

Steve and Juliet quickly had sized up the situation in their home. He didn't know how. Maybe they'd caught a glimpse of their garbage and had seen the outsize proportion of empty liquor bottles to food packaging. Or maybe they would have been just as kind anyway. Regardless, they had welcomed him and his sister into their home and into their lives.

He had been ten in years and about thirty in experience by then, wary, mistrustful, difficult. Because they had moved so much, all his previous close friendships had been painfully short-lived and he hadn't been looking for another, but for some bizarre reason he still didn't understand, Natalie Harper had decided they should be best friends.

Nat. His heart ached whenever he thought of her, yet one more woman in his life he couldn't protect.

"Is Olivia in town long?" he asked, hoping his voice sounded casual enough.

"I suppose that depends on what happens with her mom's surgery. I hope she can be here at least a few days so we have time to catch up."

"Her mom had a pretty bad fall. I don't think her recovery is going to be quick."

"Oh, poor Juliet. I should try to get to the hospital tonight, after she's out of surgery."

He loved that about his sister. Even after everything she had been through, after her world had basically imploded, she still was able to focus on others. She had always been that way. If they were down to their last can of tomato soup, she would find someone less fortunate to share it with them.

"I'm sure she would appreciate it," he said. "Now, which bathroom sink did you say was leaking?"

"The boys' bathroom upstairs. I wish you would let me call a plumber."

"You might still have to. I'm not an expert. But let me take a look at it first. I brought my tools and everything." He lifted his box.

"You're the best brother a girl could ask for. I would hug you, if I didn't think it would terrify poor Otis here," Melody said with a smile that didn't quite hide the shadows there.

"Save your hugs until we see if I can actually fix it. You might need to give them to a real plumber."

"That wouldn't exactly be a hardship, since my plumber is pretty cute."

"Send Charlie up when he gets out of the bathroom down here. I'll give him a quick lesson in how to use a pipe wrench."

"I'm not sure I want that one knowing how to take the pipes apart in this house. That's a skill that might come back to bite me."

He smiled. Charlie was a handful, which was one of the reasons he loved the kid. "Also, I'm here for at least a few hours. I can dogsit and kidsit for you, if you want to go to the store by yourself or even go sit by the beach with a book."

To his dismay, her eyes filled with tears and she hugged him. "You really are the best brother in the world. I have no idea what I would do without you. I would love to run to the garden center to pick up a few things for the yard without having to keep Charlie from jumping in all the decorative fountains."

"Have at it. Want me to take the dog?"

"I'll put him back into his crate for now. Liv said that's his happy place."

"Got it. I'll just carry the whole thing upstairs, where he can hang out with us. Send Charlie up before you leave."

As he headed up the stairs with his toolbox in one hand and the dog carrier in the other, he couldn't seem to stop thinking about Olivia and their intertwined lives.

Her dad had been a mentor to him, one of those genuinely good guys driven to try making a difference in the world. He might have done amazing things, if he had lived past his forties instead of dying in a fire where he never should have been in the first place.

His fault.

Cooper set the toolbox down a bit more heavily than he

should have, and Olivia's little dog whimpered at the sudden noise.

"Sorry, bud," he said, setting the carrier down more gently.

He still missed him. Olivia's father had been one of the most decent men Cooper had ever known. The fact that he went into that building because of Cooper's own stupidity still haunted him.

Join the club, Steve, Cooper wanted to say. The ghosts of all the people he couldn't save could probably fill the chapel of the local church.

His mother.

Natalie.

None of his efforts had been quite enough.

Yeah. All those ghosts were the reason he hadn't come back to town as often as he might have over the years. Cape Sanctuary didn't exactly live up to its name, in his case. For him, it was a place of sorrow and regret and inadequacy.

"Hey, Uncle Coop. I'm here to help."

As his nephew climbed the stairs in his oversize cowboy boots, Cooper pushed away the memories.

He couldn't fix the past, but he was here now for his sister. Melody was the entire reason he had decided to apply for the fire chief job in Cape Sanctuary.

She was stuck here alone with three boys, abandoned by her soon-to-be ex-husband. She tried to put on a good front, but he could see the baffled grief in her expression when she let down her guard.

He wanted everything to be perfect for his sister. That had been his goal since the day she was born. The fact that her life had come to this, that her bastard husband had destroyed their marriage and her self-confidence without a backward look, made Cooper want to punch his fist through a wall.

Okay, he would have preferred to punch his fist through Rich Baker's face. He couldn't do it, though. He didn't want to end up in jail, like his and Mel's father, who had spent most of their childhood as a guest of some correctional institution or other. Since he couldn't beat the living daylights out of the man who had broken his sister's heart, he would settle for stepping in and helping her out with the boys as much as he could.

If that meant coming home to Cape Sanctuary and taking the tame and rather staid job of fire chief in a small California tourist town, it was a sacrifice he was more than willing to make.

That was what he should focus on, Cooper told himself as he showed Charlie the water valve beneath the sink. These boys, his sister, his job. They were all that mattered. Not a certain lovely former neighbor or the shocking, unexpected awareness she sparked in him.

5

CAITLIN

She hated this so much. On a scale of one to ten, sitting in Mimi's hospital room and waiting for her to go into surgery ranked about a million times infinity.

Caitlin sat in the ugly, uncomfortable chair in her grandmother's room. Her head throbbed and her stomach felt a little sick, like that time she got food poisoning from eating bad potato salad at her friend Emma's house.

The hospital smelled. Mimi's room wasn't so bad. Her room smelled like all the flowers people had brought her, which Caitlin had arranged on a ledge beside the window, where her grandmother could see them.

The rest of the place reeked, though, of disinfectant and pee and despair.

Sitting here was so boring. She didn't have the focus right now to read anything and she was all caught up on her YouTube subscriptions. Sure, she could always play one of the games on her phone to pass the time, but it was hard to concentrate to beat another stupid level when she was so worried.

She looked over at her grandmother, whose eyes were closed. Every time she saw Mimi's bruises, Caitlin felt like she couldn't breathe.

What would happen to her if Mimi died?

She pressed a hand to her stomach, to the nerves there.

Mimi wasn't dying. She was only asleep, like she'd been most of the morning since Jake's dad dropped Caitlin off.

The nurses assured Caitlin that there was nothing to worry about—it was only reaction from the pain medicine Mimi was on and the residual shock from her injuries, especially the concussion. Caitlin hated it anyway. She was not used to her grandmother being like this, dozing like some old lady during the day.

Juliet wasn't old. She was only in her fifties. Caitlin had done the math once and knew her grandma had her mom when she was only nineteen and hadn't even been forty when Natalie had *Caitlin* when she was only eighteen.

Mimi would be fifty-three in a few days and usually seemed a lot younger than that. She worked hard all day long at the garden center and then came home and took care of Sea Glass Cottage. She came to every one of Caitlin's things, from soccer games to school plays to orchestra concerts.

She wasn't old. She was only injured.

On the other hand, at least when she was sleeping, Mimi couldn't nag at her to do her homework while she was sitting doing nothing or worry about the classes Caitlin had missed to be here.

Caitlin thought about taking a selfie in the dull hospital room and posting it with the hashtag #myglamorouslife, but she hadn't had time to do her makeup the way she liked it and didn't like being here anyway, so why take a pic to remember it?

"Cait?"

"I'm here, Mimi. Do you need something?"

"Water."

Caitlin rose from the chair, glad to give her muscles a break from it, and went to her grandmother's bedside. Mimi wasn't all the way awake. Her eyes were still mostly closed. They were swollen slightly, which the nurse had told Caitlin was from some of the medicine and also from her concussion.

"The nurses said no, remember?" she said softly, taking Mimi's outstretched hand in hers. "They don't want you to have anything in your stomach before surgery."

Mimi sighed and closed her eyes again, still holding Caitlin's hand. She stayed there for a long time, not wanting to move her fingers away and wake up her grandmother.

What would she have done without her grandmother all these years? Caitlin didn't even like thinking about it. Mimi had been more like her mother, really, since she was a baby. In fact, according to her grandmother, Caitlin had tried to call her Mama when she was first learning to talk because she spent so much time with Juliet. No matter how many times her grandmother tried to correct her, she still called her Mama. Somehow in those early years, that had morphed into Mimi. Apparently Grandma or Gamma or Gran had been too hard for her to manage when she was so little.

Caitlin was the only one who called Juliet that, which she had always kind of liked.

She knew that without her grandmother, she probably would have ended up in foster care. That might not have been so bad if somebody nice had adopted her, but she knew the odds of that weren't great. Juliet was on the board of directors for Stella Davenport's foster care organization and Caitlin knew the statistics. She knew a much higher percentage of girls in foster care ended up dropping out of high school, getting pregnant before age twenty and struggling with substance abuse issues.

Not every grandmother could step in to rescue a grandchild. She understood that and was deeply grateful that Juliet had been willing to raise her when Natalie's heroin addiction had landed her in and out of jail and then dead of an overdose a few days after she got out the last time.

She felt the familiar pang she usually did when she thought about her mother. By now, she knew it was more habit than actual grief. She hardly remembered Natalie except through pictures and the stories Juliet would tell her and a few fleeting images in her head she wasn't even sure were real or not.

Her mother seemed like some kind of exotic creature who didn't really exist, like something out of Harry Potter or Middle Earth.

She knew her mom was dead. She'd always known it, but when she was little, she used to like to pretend her real mother was the fairy princess in some kind of story, captured by an evil witch and forced to stay shut up in a castle somewhere until Caitlin performed some act of courage and daring to rescue her, like finishing all her times table flash cards the fastest in class or winning a race in PE.

Now that she was fifteen and almost an adult, she knew the truth was much less interesting and a whole hell of a lot more depressing. She knew Natalie had liked to party, that she had gotten pregnant with Caitlin when she was just a teenager. That she'd never told her family who the baby daddy was, which meant Caitlin had no idea, either.

Juliet had told her that Natalie was creative and funny, with a tender heart. That she loved art and cooking and working at the greenhouse with Steve, the grandpa who had died before Caitlin was born.

She'd come to know her mother much better since Christmas, after finding her diaries in the attic. She'd learned that Natalie had a sharp wit, was pretty observant and had terrible spelling. Mimi had told her Natalie had struggled in school. She wasn't stupid; she just couldn't seem to process math and science subjects well and she struggled to remember dates and names.

Her poor grades had put her in remedial classes and that had led her to hanging around with some kids who didn't always make good choices. Nat, in turn, had started making those bad choices along with her friends.

Caitlin turned back to her notebook, studying the three names there, unearthed after months of research, poring over her mom's journals and digging through any other information she could find.

One of these names was her dad. She was certain of it.

Jake thought she was wasting her time.

"You've got a wonderful grandmother in Mimi. Why do you have to keep digging into history? You know what happens when you start turning over rocks. You end up finding grubs and spiders and all kinds of distasteful things."

That was likely true but she had to know.

Anyway, she had a plan. A good one. Jake, who wanted to be a police detective when he grew up and was into all the true crime books and podcasts and YouTube videos, had given her the idea.

"If they can catch serial killers by connecting them to people who have sent in their DNA to be tested, certainly we can search the DNA database to find somebody who might be related to you."

"My dad is not a serial killer!" She refused to believe that.

"I never said he was," Jake had protested. "I'm just saying that the process to find your dad's identity would be the same. The DNA you inherit from both parents is called autosomal DNA. Once you take a DNA test at one of the genealogy websites, you can upload your genetic markers for free into several other sites. Then you sit back and wait to see if you come up with any close relationship matches."

Caitlin knew it was all a matter of luck that would depend on one of her relatives on her father's side taking a DNA test and being traceable. The odds weren't great but she had to try.

She had sent the test in three weeks ago, after saving her allowance for a month. According to the website, it generally took four to six weeks to get results. Any day now, she might know the truth about her dad.

She was looking at the list again, thinking about the sparse details she knew about the guys, when somebody knocked on the door.

"Come in," she called, assuming it was finally the anesthesiologist, coming to get Mimi to take her to surgery.

Instead, her aunt Olivia walked in, at least an hour earlier than Caitlin had expected her.

She must have broken some speed limits to get here so quickly.

A weird mix of conflicting emotions churned in her chest at the sight of her aunt. She hadn't seen her in person since she found Olivia's journals shortly after finding her mom's. She'd been dreading this moment, not sure what to say or how to act.

She had always admired Olivia. Her aunt always seemed so cool, so put together, as if she had everything figured out. She worked for some big health business in Seattle and also ran a start-up of her own. She traveled to exciting places; she had a great apartment and super nice friends.

All this time, she thought her aunt loved her. Olivia always sent fun gifts on birthdays and holidays, texted her funny memes she found, used to call her up sometimes, just because. Caitlin had even gone up to stay with her a few times and Olivia had taken her to cool restaurants and clothes stores that weren't like anything they had here in Cape Sanctuary.

She had loved her right back. In a way, they were more like sisters separated by about fourteen years, since Olivia's actual mother was Caitlin's mom, too, in every way that mattered.

Then Caitlin had read her aunt's diary and discovered everything was a lie. Her aunt didn't love her. She despised her.

Since then, Caitlin couldn't shake a terrible sense of betrayal, as if a best friend had humiliated her, stabbed her in the back in front of the entire school.

Olivia didn't look sharp or put together now, she thought with a small-minded sense of satisfaction she was immediately ashamed of. Right now, her aunt's eyes looked bloodshot and her hair was in a messy bun that looked more messy than bun. She wore yoga pants and an oversize sweater, and her face was pale and tired looking.

Olivia's eyes widened when she spotted her and Mimi inside the room. "Oh. You're still here," she whispered, with a careful look at the bed where Mimi was sleeping. "The nurse at information who gave me the room number thought Mom might be in surgery already. I'm glad I checked here first."

Hospital information ought to know where its patients were, Caitlin thought grumpily. She closed her notebook to hide the names there. Her quest to find her father was none of Olivia's business.

"We're still here. The anesthesiologist is on his way. You didn't have to come. I told you that on the phone. I can handle things."

She cringed inside as she heard her own tone. She sounded like a cranky three-year-old who insisted on crossing the street by herself, without holding a grown-up's hand.

All of her interactions with Olivia were like this lately. She wanted to sound cool and polite and detached. Instead, she suspected she usually came across petulant and childish.

The words she had read in her aunt's journal seemed burned into her brain, flashing there like glaring neon signs.

Whiny.

Brat.

Annoying.

Needy.

That had been hard enough. Who would possibly want to read that about themselves?

Worse, though, had been discovering Olivia's love-hate relationship with Natalie. Olivia's own sister and Caitlin's mother.

Her resentment had come across loud and clear on the pages of that journal. She had written about Natalie throwing her life away by having Caitlin, about the terrible choices she was making, about how she could never stay out of trouble.

Okay, Caitlin knew she should never have even looked at the pages of that diary. It had been a serious invasion of Olivia's privacy. How would she feel if somebody read her teenage diary sometime in the future and judged her for the things she'd written?

In her defense, Caitlin was on a quest to find her dad and had thought maybe her aunt's diary from that time when Natalie had still been alive might provide valuable information that might help her.

Instead, all she had discovered was exactly how much her aunt had resented her.

As if Caitlin could help the situation. She'd only been a little kid. It wasn't her fault her mom had been an addict who couldn't take care of herself or a kid, that she had been in and out of jail and Mimi had to take care of Caitlin or else let her go into foster care.

She wasn't a brat and she wanted to toss those words at her aunt right now like an ax at one of those throwing clubs.

Why did Olivia have to come back to Cape Sanctuary? They didn't need her. Mimi wouldn't want her here, either. Caitlin knew it.

As if Mimi sensed Olivia's presence, her eyes started to flutter open.

Right now her grandmother looked older than her years. She wasn't wearing makeup and the few wrinkles that fanned out from her eyes seemed more pronounced.

"Oh. You're here."

Mimi's voice was filled with so much relief and gratitude, Caitlin tried not to feel invisible.

"Hey, Mom." Olivia went to Mimi's bedside and stood kind of awkwardly, as if she wasn't sure whether to hug her or not.

While Caitlin and Olivia used to get along for the most part until she read that diary, she had always been aware that Olivia and Mimi's relationship was a little funky, as if both of them had a hundred things they wanted to say to each other but could never find the words.

Olivia was never mean to Juliet and vice versa, but they were always überpolite. Kind of like when Caitlin's friends Allie and Emma got in a huge fight then made up and were way too nice to each other for weeks.

Though she looked kind of out of it from the medication the nurse had given her, Juliet tried to sit up. "I told you not to come. Oh, honey. You must have driven all night."

"I'm glad I made it before they took you for surgery."

"I am, too. But you still didn't need to come."

Much to Caitlin's dismay, a tear leaked out of her grandmother's blue eyes. Juliet reached a trembling hand out, and after an awkward kind of moment, Olivia reached for it and squeezed.

"How are you feeling?"

How did Olivia *think* she was feeling? Jeez. Juliet had a grand total of four broken bones, including her hip and her ribs.

"I've been better," Juliet said, forcing a smile. "How are you? How was the drive?"

"Good. There's not a lot of traffic on the interstate at 3:00 a.m."

Before Juliet could answer, the door opened again. This time it really was the anesthesiologist, Dr. Zane, a really nice middle-aged man who had come in earlier to introduce himself to Mimi and Caitlin. She still wasn't sure if Zane was his first name or his last. Or maybe he was like Beyoncé or Drake and only needed one name.

"Are you ready for this?" he asked with a kindly smile.

Mimi suddenly looked nervous. "Do I have a choice?"

"Not if you want to heal properly. I'm sorry."

With a sigh, her grandmother nodded. "I guess I'm ready." She squeezed Olivia's hand again then released it, and Olivia stepped away.

"Bye, Mom. I…I love you."

Caitlin wanted to roll her eyes. It wasn't really that hard to tell someone going into surgery that you love them, was it?

"I love you, too, my dear."

"Everything will be fine," Caitlin said briskly, stepping forward to give Mimi a genuine hug. "You'll be back on your feet and getting things done at the garden center before you know it."

Her grandmother hugged her tightly. "You still should have been at school, but I'm glad you're here, too," she murmured.

Dr. Zane spent a moment unhooking the bed from the wall, set a chart at the foot of the bed and started wheeling the whole thing out of the room.

"You two can come as far as the door of the surgery unit, if you want," Dr. Zane said cheerfully. "We have a waiting area for family members that's closer. You're welcome to wait there or you can come back here and wait in the room. Either way is fine. The surgeon will find you after she's done and let you know how things went."

He pushed Mimi in her bed and they both followed after him like they were in one of those crazy New Orleans funeral processions she'd seen in a documentary once.

After a series of hallways, they reached an area of the hospital with a big sign hanging from the ceiling that said Surgical Suite.

"The waiting area is just through those doors," Dr. Zane said, pointing. "This shouldn't take long. Maybe two hours from start to finish. You've got plenty of time to go get something to eat, if you need to. We can page you overhead throughout the hospital if we need you."

They said their goodbyes to Mimi again and the look in her eyes made Caitlin's stomach hurt all over again.

Mimi looked scared. Really scared. And her grandmother *never* looked scared.

What if something happened to her during the surgery? She had heard about those things. Yeah, complications were rare, but they did happen.

Dr. Zane scanned his ID badge on a sensor on the wall and a door swung open.

Once he'd pushed Mimi through and the doors swung shut again, Caitlin felt like she was going to throw up.

"Don't worry," Olivia said gently. "Mom is tough. She'll be okay."

Caitlin was suddenly furious, all the hurt and betrayal and fear tumbling together in her chest into one thick, nasty ball. "What the hell do you know? You're never here. You don't even know her. Don't try to pretend you give a shit what happens to her."

She stalked off, needing desperately to be alone.

6

OLIVIA

What had she said?

Olivia stared after her niece as Caitlin stomped down the hall.

The girl was a mystery to her lately. She had no idea what was going on behind those hazel eyes. She *did* know Caitlin seemed to hate her these days. She obviously couldn't stand to be around Olivia.

That shouldn't surprise her. Caitlin's mother hadn't liked her much, either. After their father died, Natalie had largely ignored her. They had gone from being very close siblings to Natalie caring only about her friends, partying and the men in her life.

Caitlin was following the pattern, either distant and cool or straight-up rude to Olivia.

She didn't think it was just adolescence. A few months ago, she had asked her mom about Caitlin's attitude shift, trying to ascertain whether she was showing it to everyone or just to Olivia. Juliet seemed to think she was imagining things.

She took a chair in a corner of the half-full waiting room. The moment she stopped moving, all the nervous energy pushing her onward all night as she drove seemed to trickle away. Suddenly, she was completely exhausted, more tired than she ever remembered feeling.

She closed her eyes, thinking she would only rest them for a moment. The room was warm and soothing music played overhead.

She ought to take the anesthesiologist's advice and grab something to eat.

It was her last thought for a while.

She dreamed about the happy childhood family she remembered. Juliet, Natalie, Steve. They were having a picnic lunch on Driftwood Beach—Juliet's best fried chicken and the delicious potato salad she made where she used fresh herbs. It was the Fourth of July. Olivia could tell by the little kids running past with flags and the distant sound of a band playing patriotic music.

She was happy, her heart full as she savored this time with her family. Her dad, tall and handsome, pushed her and Nat on the swings, and they went higher and higher until her toes seemed to touch the clouds.

Then suddenly it was dark and the fireworks were starting. Only they weren't fireworks. Instead, with whistles and crashing booms, explosions started going off up and down the beach. Juliet screamed and grabbed Olivia, pushing her into the ocean, out of the way of the flames.

Natalie didn't want to go into the ocean. Her mom tried to call them both but Natalie wouldn't leave the swings. She kept wanting to go higher and higher, until she and Steve both disappeared into the smoke and fire.

Then, oddly, Olivia's little dog was somehow there, running

into the fire. She tried to go after Otis but she couldn't move, trapped in the water. Finally, out of nowhere, Cooper Vance appeared. He gave her a long, disappointed look, then took off into the flames after Otis.

Everything she loved. Gone, while she stood by, cowering in the water.

"Wake up. She's out of surgery."

Somehow the words pierced the tormented haze of sleep, yanking her out of that place of smoke and fear.

She blinked her eyes open for several seconds, disoriented. It took her several more seconds to register the bright glare of hospital lights and the muted chatter around her.

She found Caitlin standing a couple of feet away, scowling at her.

"What did I miss?"

"You slept like a baby through the whole surgery. Nearly two hours. I can tell you were really worried about your mom."

She scrubbed at her face and sat up, stung by Caitlin's sarcasm. Olivia wanted to remind her that she had just driven twelve hours across two states to get here before Juliet went under the knife but suspected it wouldn't make any difference to Caitlin.

Nothing she did would be right, as far as her niece was concerned.

She also didn't bother telling her about the week of sleepless nights she had endured since that attack that seemed a lifetime ago and how the cumulative effect of them must have caught up with her in this warm waiting room filled with low voices and calming music.

"Sorry. You said she's out of surgery?"

"Yes. They called from the operating room and said she would be going back to the same hospital room where she stayed the night for the rest of her recovery time. They said to wait here and the doctor would be out to talk to us, though."

Olivia still felt bleary-eyed and out of it. She wasn't at all competent for any discussion with a medical professional right now. She didn't have much choice, though. She needed to talk to the doctor and she wasn't about to reveal any sign of weakness to Caitlin, with her current attitude.

"Okay." She forced a smile. "Thanks."

She had barely formed the words when a woman approached them. She looked to be in her forties with close-cropped salt-and-pepper hair and kindly brown eyes. She was tall and appeared elegant, even in scrubs.

"Hi. Caitlin, right? I think we met yesterday."

"Yes. Hi, Dr. Adeno. How's my grandmother?"

The woman gave her a reassuring smile but turned to Olivia without answering directly. "Hello. I know I haven't met you. Are you a family member of Juliet Harper?"

"I'm her daughter. Olivia Harper."

"All right. Good. I have to check these days, with privacy laws. I'm Dr. Sylvia Adeno. I performed your mom's orthopedic surgery. Everything went great. As I spoke to your mother about before the surgery, we went ahead and did a total joint replacement because the blood supply to the ball joint was damaged in her fall. In that case, studies have shown that total replacement generally results in fewer complications in the long term. She's got some fun new hardware."

Just thinking about it made Olivia's hips ache in sympathy. Her mother would be miserable.

"How is she? Can we go see her yet?"

"They'll be taking her to her room shortly and you can join her there. I wanted to speak to you both first about her condition and what her recovery will require."

"Of course," Olivia answered. She still didn't feel quite on her game, but at least she was no longer groggy.

"Juliet has had a very bad fall. She's lucky to come out of it with only the injuries she had. The concussion is already healing nicely, though she may have lingering side effects for several weeks."

"We can watch her carefully."

The doctor paused. "I know your mother. She doesn't like to sit still for very long, but she's going to have to be realistic, and it is your job to reinforce that with her. Her recovery is going to take weeks, if not months."

Not the news Olivia wanted to hear but rather what she suspected, judging by the severity of her mother's injuries.

"Do you recommend she go to a rehab center during her initial recovery?"

"Can she get around the house in a wheelchair? Into the house and into the bathroom?"

"Some of it. Not all," Caitlin answered while Olivia was trying to picture her childhood home and envision the possibilities.

"You have to discuss that with her and consider your options, then. If Sea Glass Cottage can be made more accessible, she'll be able to recover at home."

"I have a feeling that's what she would prefer," Olivia said.

"Of course it is," Caitlin said. "She would hate having to go to a rehab center. They're like nursing homes, aren't they?"

The doctor shrugged. "Not exactly. But close enough that some people see them that way. You don't have to decide anything about this today. I want to keep her at least a couple of nights for observation. We'll make sure she has a safe place to go home to before we release her."

"What about the garden center?" Caitlin asked. "The first thing she's going to ask when she comes all the way out of anesthesia is when she can go back to work."

Caitlin apparently knew exactly the way Juliet's mind worked. Olivia could imagine her mother asking that very question.

"That's going to be a personal decision. You as her family will need to remind her that work-related stress impedes healing. I would recommend at least three or four weeks away from

71

the garden center and then she can slowly return for light office work only for another month."

"Two months?" Caitlin exclaimed. "That's the whole spring! She'll go crazy!"

"It's going to be difficult for her, certainly," Dr. Adeno said. "But if she wants to regain full mobility, she'll have to face the difficult and deal with it. She might need to find someone else to take over for her, at least for the first few weeks."

She eyed the two of them. "Perhaps a family member could step up."

"I can do it," Caitlin said immediately. "No problem."

Olivia did her best not to roll her eyes at her fifteen-year-old niece. "You're still in high school. You can't miss the last six weeks of school to run Harper Hill Home and Garden."

"Who else is there? The assistant manager quit a week ago and none of the other employees have been there long enough to know how things work."

Olivia was aware of the surgeon, watching the conversation with a polite but distracted expression.

"This isn't really your concern, is it, Dr. Adeno? You've done your part in performing the surgery. Thank you for that. It's up to us now to make sure Juliet gives herself all the time she needs to heal."

"Excellent. It's always so much easier for my patients when they have supportive family members. She should be coming out of recovery and heading to her room, if you want to head in that direction. Do you remember where to go?"

"I do," Caitlin said, looking sour, as usual.

"Thank you," Olivia said to the surgeon.

"You're welcome. Juliet is one of my favorite people and has been very kind to me since I moved to Cape Sanctuary. Also, my husband and I love to garden and count on Harper Hill to supply us with everything we need. We need her healthy and strong."

They all did, Olivia thought as she followed Caitlin along the hallways a few moments later.

The solution was clear. She was going to have to stay, at least through her mother's initial recovery. Caitlin certainly could not shoulder the burden of running the garden center and going to school at the same time. Knowing Juliet, her mother would hate being sidelined and would probably override any attempts by Caitlin or employees of the garden center to keep her away.

She had already been off since the attack in the coffee shop and would have to call human resources about arranging several more weeks of emergency family leave.

She was already edgy after being in town only a few hours and wasn't sure she could endure several more weeks.

But her mother needed her help. What choice did she have? She couldn't abandon Juliet or Caitlin. Olivia might not be able to tackle an armed gunman in a coffee shop. But she could surely manage to put her life on hold for a few weeks in order to help out in a crisis.

JULIET

She flashed in and out of awareness for what felt like a lifetime.

One moment she was with Steve again and they were walking the cliffs on a summer evening with his old dog on a leash.

Another, she was with Natalie in the delivery room, half of her heart aching for her child and the trials she would face as a single mother and the other half overwhelmed with the miracle of life and this tiny, crying little girl.

Then she was laughing with Olivia over a show they used to enjoy together, watching her younger daughter's face light up with glee as she understood some sophisticated, clever line of dialogue.

She hurt. Everywhere. She heard a whimper and realized it was coming from her.

"I think she might be coming out of it. She's been moaning in her sleep. Should she be doing that? Is there something else you could give her?"

That sounded like Caitlin's voice.

"Yes. We can give her more pain meds."

She didn't want to open her eyes to see who was speaking. It would hurt too much if she did.

Then a moment later, the tension and pain seemed to flow out of her like the tide receding, and she breathed out, her muscles relaxing.

It took her a long time to come back to full awareness. She didn't want to. The drugs were lovely. Why would she ever want to leave this place where she was free of pain and fear, heartache and regret?

Eventually, she knew she had to open her eyes, especially when she heard Caitlin and Olivia arguing.

"I'm staying here, Caitlin. I've been on the phone with my company and have already made all the arrangements to take leave. I can handle the garden center during the day and work long-distance in the evening for my employer and my own clients."

"Why? Don't you think I'm capable? I've been helping out at the garden center for years."

"It's not a matter of whether you're capable," Olivia began.

Juliet wanted to tell her not to bother. When Caitlin was in one of her stubborn moods, there was no debating her. The best thing was simply to move on to another topic and quietly do what you were planning anyway.

She closed her eyes. When she opened them again, the room was quiet and she felt a little more clearheaded.

Olivia was sitting beside her. So she hadn't conjured her in a dream, along with the husband and daughter she had lost.

"You're really here," she said, her voice croaking and her throat sore.

Olivia jumped up instantly. "Hi. You're awake. That's good. How are you feeling?"

"I've had better days." She cleared away the dryness of her throat. Had she swallowed an entire bag of potting soil?

"The nurse said you could have some ice water when you wake up."

Olivia retrieved a cup from beside the bed and the liquid trickling down her throat was the most delicious thing she'd ever tasted.

"Where's Caitlin? Did she go home?"

"I made her go grab some dinner in the cafeteria."

"She's a good girl."

"Yes."

She sipped more water as snippets she had heard while she was out of it filtered through her head. "Did you…? I thought I heard you tell Caitlin you're…staying."

"For now. A few weeks, anyway."

"You don't need to do that. I don't…want to be a burden."

She had dreaded that most of all after her initial diagnosis, that someday Olivia would hate her for this weakness.

"You're not a burden. I have everything arranged."

"What's…arranged?"

"I'm going to stay in town for now so I can take care of you and help out at the garden center until you're on your feet again."

"No."

The word came out sharp, gruff, and Olivia looked taken aback.

"You don't have a lot of choices here, Mom. Dr. Adeno says you need to take it easy for at least a month."

A month! That was impossible. "We'll be fine."

Olivia rolled her eyes. "Will you? Caitlin said there's no one to run the garden center right now. She, by the way, wants to drop out of tenth grade to take over."

"That's ridiculous. She can't do that. She's only fifteen."

"Exactly what I told her." Olivia studied her closely and Juliet was horribly aware that a tear might be dripping out of her eye. She pulled the scratchy hospital sheet up to wipe at it until Olivia handed her a tissue off the bedside table.

"I don't know what's wrong with me."

"It's the medication, I'm sure."

She nodded, though she knew it wasn't the medication. She was feeling sorry for herself. She couldn't really think straight, but she did know she didn't want to be in this hospital bed and didn't want to be dependent for help on a daughter who already seemed to resent her so much.

"You don't have to stay," she said again. "We can...figure something out."

"It's done. You don't have to figure anything out." Olivia's voice was gentle. "Your job right now is to focus on healing. Those are the orders from Dr. Adeno. She's quite fierce."

She closed her eyes as another tear dripped out. She wasn't even sad, really, just upset and emotional. "You hate the garden center."

Surprise widened Olivia's eyes. "What makes you say that? I don't hate it."

"You resent it, anyway. Or at least the time I spent there after your father died."

What a horrible time that had been. Another tear dripped out. She had loved the man with all her heart, had loved their life and their daughters and taking care of all of them.

Then Steve had run into a burning building and hadn't come out alive, and she had been left with all of it. The garden center, the house, two troubled girls, then Caitlin just a year later.

Their finances had been a mess. She'd only discovered it after Steve's death. The business had been deeply in debt, the house heavily mortgaged. She was afraid they would lose everything and she and the girls would be on the streets.

She had been wholly unprepared for the challenge of taking over the family business. Steve had run everything and she had been content to let him. They had divided their family responsibilities down traditional lines. He had been provider, protector, while she had been in charge of the home front, stepping in to help run the cash register during busy times of year, yes, and being involved in some garden design projects, but that was all.

She had loved their life. She had loved preparing healthy, nutritious meals for her family, creating a home they had all wanted to return to. She had taken every opportunity to volunteer in her daughters' classrooms, from home mother to field trip chaperone, even traveling with Natalie's choir group on a memorable visit to Washington, DC.

She wanted to think she'd been a good mother. At least a loving one.

Then Steve had died and 100 percent of the responsibilities had fallen on her. In the midst of that, just six months after Steve died, Natalie had come to tell her she was pregnant and keeping the baby.

It had taken everything she had to keep her sanity hanging by the tiniest thread. As a result, she had neglected her youngest child horribly.

She told herself it was all right. Olivia had been the strong one, the one whose report card was always perfect and who had friends around her and who seemed to make good choices all the time.

Juliet had failed her, maybe more than she had failed anyone else in her life. The worst part was, she didn't know how to fix it. Instead of healing the tiny cracks that had formed in their relationship, she had opted to ignore them, hoping they would fix themselves. Instead, they had grown into huge gaping fissures.

"I'm sorry," she said now, another tear dripping onto her pillow.

Olivia squeezed her fingers and Juliet wanted to hold on tight and not let go. "You have nothing to be sorry for. It was an accident. You don't need to worry about this right now. Just do your best to rest. Sleep while you can. Do you need more pain meds?"

"Maybe."

"I'll get the nurse."

"Thank you. I am glad you're here, Olivia. Thank you for taking care of Caitlin."

Her granddaughter came into the room just in time to hear that last comment. "I'm fifteen years old. I don't need a baby-sitter, Mimi."

The familiar nickname soothed her. "I know. You're right."

The nurse came in and bustled around, checking her IV and taking her vital signs.

"You're doing great. Everything looks normal," she said. Then she pushed a syringe full of medicine into the IV line. "This will help take the edge off. Don't hesitate to call during the night if you need more pain relief. Stay on top of the pain and your body will thank you, trust me."

Some pain was too big to climb, like trying to scale a steep mountain face alone in a blizzard.

She couldn't even take the first step right now and decided to sleep instead.

7

OLIVIA

She was so tired. That troubled, restless sleep at the hospital earlier had done nothing, really, to take the edge off her exhaustion.

She wanted to find the nearest flat surface and collapse for a few hours. First, she had to retrieve her dog.

"Why are we stopping here?" Caitlin asked as Olivia pulled up in front of Melody's house. Her voice had lost none of the attitude, despite the hours they had spent together in Juliet's hospital room.

If something didn't change soon, the next month would feel like an eternity.

"I left something here while I was at the hospital and I have to get it," she said. "I shouldn't be long."

Caitlin's sigh was heavy and put-upon. "Fine."

"Do you want to come in?"

She thought for sure Caitlin would refuse and was surprised

when her niece released her seat belt and opened her door in reply.

Melody's oldest boy, Will, eight years old with blue eyes and a widow's peak, answered the door. "Noooo," he exclaimed dramatically when he spied them. "Go away!"

Caitlin let out a gasp. "Will Baker. Is that any way to greet visitors? You don't have to be so rude!"

Oh, that was rich, coming from Caitlin, Olivia thought. The girl could give rude lessons.

"I'm sorry, but I know you're here to get your dog and I don't want him to go. He is so cute!"

Olivia managed a smile through her fatigue. "He is adorable. I must agree."

"You have a dog?" Caitlin's shock was clear. "How long have you had a dog?"

"Only a few months. We kind of adopted each other."

She hadn't been looking for a dog. Or any pet at all, really, given how chaotic her life was. But Otis had lived with a homeless veteran she passed on her way to the gym. She had always stopped to talk and had gotten in the habit of picking up dog treats or small bags of food for him and a breakfast sandwich and a banana or an apple for his owner, who called himself Beckett and introduced the dog as Otis.

She had been on her way to spin class when she spotted an ambulance and a couple of police officers near the spot where Beckett and Otis camped out.

"Overdose," one of the EMTs had said in a matter-of-fact voice.

Just then, Otis had jumped out of the arms of the police officer and rushed to her, trembling frantically and huddling at her feet.

"What will happen to him?" she had asked.

"He's headed to the animal shelter. Poor guy has fleas and

who knows what else. I imagine he'll be put down. Too bad. He's a cute little guy."

"I'll take him," she said instantly, scooping up the dog before she had a chance to think about all the ramifications.

The authorities at the scene had been only too happy to pass off responsibility for Otis.

It had been a crazy impulse, but she couldn't bear the thought of the forlorn and abandoned chi-poo being put down, simply because someone he loved had put their addiction first.

"Does Mimi know you have a dog?" Caitlin asked. "She would never let me get one. She'll be pissed that you have one in the house."

Of course, Steve Harper had always had dogs, including the ancient border collie who had died just a few months after Steve's death, possibly of a broken heart after losing her beloved master.

After Coco died, her mother had decided they would have no more dogs. They were too much work, she decreed, and she didn't want them in the house.

How would she feel about Olivia bringing Otis to the house? Probably not happy.

"She'll have to deal with it, won't she?"

"Or she might make you keep it here," Caitlin predicted darkly.

"Yay! We can totally keep him here!" Will exclaimed in an excited voice.

Olivia frowned at her niece. Great. Now they were giving ideas to Melody's boys that wouldn't end well.

Before she could break Will's heart by explaining that her dog would not be staying there, Melody came out of the kitchen, wiping her hands on a dish towel.

Her pretty but tired features brightened when she saw them. "Hey, Liv. Hi, Caitlin."

"Hi, Mrs. Baker." To Olivia's shock, Caitlin smiled at Melody. She had an even bigger smile for the two younger boys who followed their mother. "Hi, Ryan. Hi, Charlie. How are my two favorite Smash Bros. opponents?"

"Hi, Cait." Charlie beamed at her and gave her a fist bump.

She had known from Melody that her niece sometimes babysat for the boys, but Olivia hadn't realized how close Caitlin was with Melody's sons. They all looked at her with hero worship.

"How did things go with the surgery?" Melody asked, setting her dishcloth on a side table. "How's Juliet? I started to worry when we didn't hear from you."

Olivia winced. "I told you I would check in, didn't I? I'm sorry. It completely slipped my mind."

She wanted to blame her complete exhaustion, but that was no excuse for forgetting a promise.

"Don't worry. Your mind was on other things. How is she doing? Did the surgery go all right?"

She nodded. "The doctor seemed happy. She was all right when we left. I think she mostly needs uninterrupted sleep."

"Which she's not likely to find in the hospital, is she? Have you eaten? I was just heading into the kitchen to make spaghetti."

"We grabbed food at the cafeteria," she said. "But thank you."

Ryan, seven and small for his age with blond hair and thick glasses that magnified his impossibly blue eyes, beamed at her. "I sure like your dog. He sat on my lap and let me pet him for a whole half hour. Thor never lets me pet him that long."

"I hope he behaved for you," she said with a smile. These boys always tugged at her heart. Yes, Melody had a hard road right now, with a sleazeball husband willing to throw away their marriage of ten years for a hot young eighteen-year-old body. But at least Melody had these three adorable boys to help her through.

"Where is my little guy?" she asked.

"In there. He and Cooper both fell asleep."

She gestured from the entry into a small room with French

doors that Melody closed off so she could use the room as a formal living room and office and keep her boys' mess away.

Olivia hadn't even noticed them there, but now through the glass door, Olivia could see Cooper sprawled out on the sofa, eyes closed and his mouth slightly open. Curled up on his lap, looking perfectly content, was her little rescue dog.

Olivia told herself the sudden wobble in her knees and the soft warmth curling around inside her was simply a product of exhaustion. That was all. It had nothing to do with the sight of a gorgeous man cuddling her dog.

The last thing she wanted to do was open those French doors and face Cooper again, but she had no choice, unless she wanted to leave her dog here overnight.

The moment she slid the doors apart, Otis awoke. He lifted his head, wagged his tail and gave his Where-Have-You-Been little greeting.

It wasn't much of a bark. More like a squeak, really, but was enough for Cooper to open his eyes, still dazed with sleep.

What would it be like to wake up next to him and have him aim those vivid blue eyes in her direction, hungry and fierce?

Stop it, Olivia ordered herself sternly, appalled at herself for letting her mind wander in that direction when the man's sister was standing right beside her!

She didn't have time for this ridiculous attraction right now, with her mother in the hospital and the weight of responsibility resting on her shoulders like a steam train.

"Sorry to wake you but I need my dog. Come on, Otis. Let's go."

With surprising agility, the dog scrambled off Cooper's lap to the sofa, then hopped to the floor. He was at her side in an instant and she scooped up his warm weight, holding him close and trying not to think about where Otis had just been sitting.

She reached to close the door but Cooper's sleepy question stopped her.

"How's your mom?"

She paused, turning around with a sneaky suspicion that she would become very tired of that question during her time in Cape Sanctuary.

"The surgery went well, according to the doctor, but this was only the first step in a long journey to recovery."

"Juliet has always been one of the toughest ladies I know. She'll be okay."

Everyone loved her mom. It was hard to avoid that realization, now that she was back in town. Juliet was something of a heroine around town, a widow who had lost her husband to a tragic accident and a daughter to addiction but still managed to face her trials with a smile and a generous spirit.

Her mom was amazing. Olivia agreed. She wished she could be half the woman Juliet was. Her mother would never have let one traumatic incident in a coffee shop completely paralyze her. If her mother had been there and had seen that unprovoked attack, she wouldn't have cowered under a table. She would have been like the other customer who ultimately had come to the rescue. Resolute. Fearless. Powerful.

The complete opposite of her daughter.

"She is tough." Olivia forced a smile. "She'll need to be. I don't know how she's going to handle being sidelined for a month. That's how long the doctor says she should plan to be away from the garden center while she recovers."

"Oh. That will be harder on her than falling off a ladder," Melody exclaimed. "What will she do?"

"Good question. I guess I'll be sticking around for now, until we figure that out."

"Oh yay! That means you'll be here for longer than a few days."

Melody looked thrilled at the idea but Olivia couldn't read Cooper's expression.

Before she could respond, Caitlin came in with Charlie on

THE SEA GLASS COTTAGE

her back, which further confirmed Olivia's suspicion that her niece must babysit here often.

The teenager stopped in the doorway, stumbling a little before she caught hold of the wall to maintain her balance. Her gaze was locked with Cooper's.

"Oh. Hi, Chief Vance."

"Hi again, Caitlin."

He also had an odd look on his face and she wondered why for just an instant before she remembered. Caitlin was the spitting image of her mother. He had loved Natalie dearly, something Olivia had resented back in the day when she used to have a big crush on Cooper.

She was going on two hours of sleep over the last forty-eight hours and was afraid if she stopped moving, she would fall asleep. Once she had been able to recharge, she would be far more prepared to deal with this unexpected and unwanted resurgence of her childhood crush on Cooper Vance.

"Thanks again for watching Otis for me." She smiled at Mel.

"Anytime. I mean that. My boys love him. Otis provided the perfect distraction for today."

The slight note of determined cheerfulness in Melody's voice made Olivia's heart ache. She hugged her, aware Melody's journey to healing just might be harder than the one Juliet was facing, then led her niece out the door toward home.

COOPER

Once while fighting a wildlands blaze at a base he'd been working at in Texas, Cooper had been caught in a flashover, a wild and out-of-control blaze driven by wind and weather conditions that reacted unexpectedly. He had been forced to use his emergency shelter until it passed over, leaving scorched earth behind.

This day, seeing Olivia Harper again after all these years, bore some striking similarities to the way he remembered feeling as he climbed out of the shelter. Hot. Stunned. Shaken.

What was that about? He wondered as he watched from Melody's porch as she loaded her cute dog into her vehicle, then climbed in herself.

He had no idea what was happening to him. She was lovely, yes, with those hazel-green eyes and the soft smile for her dog that had made him wish she might aim it in his direction, even for a moment. He wasn't sure he'd ever had this kind of visceral reaction to a woman, this ache in his gut that left him slightly breathless.

Olivia Harper.

He could think of a dozen reasons he shouldn't be so drawn to her, all of them tangled in the past.

Guilt. Oh, he was tired of it.

Here was the problem with returning to his hometown, the main reason he had stayed away so long. When he had been busy with the military, it had been easier to block the guilt over the consequences of his own choices, the ghosts of regret and sadness that haunted him.

He had respected and admired her father more than just about any man he knew. Steve had been Cooper's mentor, a guy who saw potential even in *him*, who had encouraged him to take the military path and apply for the elite Air Force paratrooper rescue unit.

The man had loved his family, his community and his business, in that order. From Steve, Cooper had learned how to work hard and how important it was to give back.

The heavy burden of knowing the man had died because of Cooper's choices sometimes felt like more than he could bear.

Cooper wanted to think the way he had lived his life the past fifteen years had been an homage of sorts to a man who had set such a strong example to him, the one positive male role model of his childhood and youth.

He wasn't sure Olivia would agree. She had adored her father. He remembered the way she always used to follow Steve around, finding any excuse to spend a minute with him.

Because of Cooper, that had been taken away from her.

He hadn't meant for things to turn out the way they had, of course. He hadn't been trying to be a hero, the way people described him later. He had acted out of instinct the moment he had driven past the McComb building and had seen the flames.

He had run in after someone he thought was inside the building and Steve had come in after *him*.

Cooper had been lauded as a hero after he pulled Steve Harper out of the building, badly burned and unconscious from a beam falling on him, and tried to resuscitate him.

He knew it wasn't true. He was no hero. The man never would have gone in there if he hadn't glimpsed Cooper going in first. If he could relive that night again, he would have done it a thousand times over so he could make different choices. A man had died because of him. A good, honorable, decent man. It would have been far better if he had died in Steve's place. He suspected Olivia Harper must feel the same.

Wasn't it just like him to develop a completely inconvenient attraction to the one woman in Cape Sanctuary certain to want nothing to do with him?

"Wasn't that the cutest dog?" His youngest nephew, Charlie, sighed, looking after Olivia and Caitlin as they drove away toward Harper Hill.

"He really was."

"Weird looking, but cute," Will said.

Ryan snickered. "He was funny. We should get a little dog to be Thor's friend."

Melody shook her head. "One dog and two cats is enough for

our family right now. I still have to nag you boys all the time to feed them and check their water."

The bleak expression in her eyes made his heart ache. Cooper missed his smiling sister.

"What's up?" he asked quietly, after the boys ran off to return to the video game they'd been playing earlier.

"Bills and more bills. Rich is fighting the child support amount the attorneys agreed on. I thought it was all settled but he's now saying he can't afford that much. It was barely enough as it was to keep us going."

At least her house was paid off, a legacy from the aunt and uncle who had raised Melody after their mother died. "You know I can help."

She frowned. "I don't want your help. I almost didn't tell you about it because I knew you would offer and I would have to refuse. I need to figure out the rest of my life. I have to get a job. That's the only solution. I'll start looking next week."

Cooper wanted to punch something, preferably Melody's almost-ex-husband.

Rich Baker had turned Cooper's smart, beautiful sister into a pale imitation of herself. The man was living with his eighteen-year-old girlfriend, flaunting his affair while claiming the hot young thing was the true love of his life and he had never known the world could be so exciting.

"He and Sierra are getting married, apparently, as soon as the divorce goes through. He needs the money to set up their life together."

The bastard. The man had three amazing sons he had all but abandoned, sons who deserved a father in their lives.

The boys were struggling so much right now. Will was causing trouble in school, with frequent notes being sent home about his behavior. Ryan had developed anxiety issues and was afraid of everything from gym class to eating school lunch, retreating into a world of books to escape the stress of his family imploding. Charlie, the youngest and barely five, had become clingy and needy and never wanted to play with friends, only stay close to his mother.

"My attorney is going to fight his request to reduce the child support. She says I need to take Rich for everything he has."

"Sounds like good advice to me."

"I know. But I don't want to be the vindictive ex-wife. I hate what he's turning me into," Melody said, her voice troubled.

"He's not turning you into anything." Cooper hugged his baby sister, aching that he couldn't fix this for her. "You're amazing, still the sweetest, kindest woman I know. Nothing you do to retaliate against that bastard you married will ever change that."

She gave a rough-sounding laugh. "You're my brother. I know I can always count on you to back me up, no matter what."

"I mean it," he said gruffly, giving her another hug.

She hugged him back, and he couldn't help noticing she had lost weight even in the two months he had been back in Cape Sanctuary. Was she eating anything?

"This is so hard," she mumbled after a moment. "I really loved him, you know?"

"I know."

He hated this helpless feeling, one that seemed all too familiar. The grim knowledge that he couldn't fix everything wrong in his sister's life, any more than he could fix their alcoholic mother or breathe life back into Steve Harper's lungs.

"You're staying for spaghetti, right?" she said, pulling away after a minute.

"I've got a better idea," he said on impulse. "Let's go out to dinner. We can hit that new pizza place in town or go find burgers."

Melody gave a pained laugh. "I look horrible. I don't know if I want to be seen in public today."

"You look great, as always."

"That sounds like the perfect idea tonight," she said. "You're the best big brother on the planet. You know that, right?"

Both of them knew that was far from true, but he wasn't about to argue with her when she already had so much on her plate.

"Hey, guys. Grab your shoes. We're going out," Cooper called to his nephews.

He was still tired after working a double shift, but he would try to find enough energy for dinner, especially if it could make Melody smile.

8

OLIVIA

Walking into the main building at Harper Hill Home & Garden the next afternoon triggered hundreds of scent memories in Olivia, one after another. Loamy. Sharp. Sweet. Sawdust and flowers and dirt.

She had a million things to do. The list Juliet had texted her waited urgently on her phone. Olivia pushed everything away to focus on inhaling the scents of her childhood.

In many ways, she had grown up here at the garden center, even more than she had at Sea Glass Cottage. She had played dolls in the shade of the trees for sale, had engaged in hide-and-seek games with Natalie between the aisles, had gone for endless rides in the wheelbarrow, pushed by her father.

The family business was as much a part of her childhood as school, her friends and the recreational opportunities available along the coast.

The store had been started by ancestors on her father's side three generations back, first as an agricultural supply store frequented by all the farmers who had originally settled this area of California.

Around her grandfather's time, the focus of Harper Hill Home & Garden began to transition from working farmers to hobbyists, those who planted vegetable gardens in every available sun-facing patch and flowers in containers and baskets and patio strips.

Her father had enjoyed running a greenhouse and garden supply business, and was good at it, but he had loved helping others more. If Steve Harper could have made a living in Cape Sanctuary as a full-time firefighter and EMT, he would have jumped at the chance. During her childhood, though, the entire fire department had been volunteer except the chief.

Her dad had supported his family through the garden center instead, building it from a mom-and-pop store to one that drew gardeners from the entire region.

Some people loved nothing more than having their hands in the dirt and a flat full of flowers waiting to be transplanted. Though Olivia had spent so much of her childhood here, she had not picked up the gardening bug. She kept a few houseplants in her Seattle apartment, only one that had survived longer than a year or two.

Still, she loved the scent of the leather gloves hanging on a rack, the lemon smell of certain herbs, the rich, verdant scent of growing things.

She could think of worse ways to spend a workday. Like maybe staring at a screen for eighteen hours a day.

The traitorous thought popped into her head out of nowhere and Olivia frowned.

She didn't mind her job. She did important work, keeping her medical group's computers safe and up-to-date. She enjoyed the people she worked with and she especially loved her side hustle, helping her clients better convey their message to customers. She was good at it and had had more business than she could handle.

If she sometimes felt overwhelmed, as if the world was spinning so fast she was going to fall off the edge, that was all part of the price for success, right?

One of the garden center employees, a young college-age student with a goatee and a man bun, was watering the annuals from a coiled hose.

"Hi," he said rather laconically as their gazes met. "Welcome to Harper Hill Home and Garden. We have all your gardening needs. May I help you find something?"

How about a little enthusiasm? she thought, in response to the lackluster greeting.

"Hi. I'm Olivia Harper. Juliet's daughter."

This didn't earn her more than a blink of acknowledgment. "Oh. Then you probably don't need help. You probably already know where everything is."

"Not really. But I imagine I will figure things out over the next few weeks. I'm not here to buy anything. I'm going to be helping out, temporarily taking over for my mom while she recovers. Doug, is it?" she asked, reading his name tag.

"Yeah. Doug Carlson. How is your mom doing? It sucked, what happened to her. I had problems with that same ladder wobbling earlier in the day when I was pulling down a flower arrangement for a customer. Guess I should have said something."

You think? Olivia bit her lip to keep the sarcasm inside. She couldn't blame him. Her stubborn mother probably wouldn't have listened to him anyway. She never should have been up on a ladder in the first place, wobbly or not.

"She's all right. In a lot of pain, still."

"Oh man. I'm sorry to hear that. She's a nice lady. If you want, I've got some edibles that might take the edge off her pain."

She could just picture her mother zoned out on enhanced brownies.

"Right now, she's being followed pretty closely at the hospital. But who knows? She might take you up on that when she gets home."

At this point, Olivia wouldn't mind anything that might mellow her mother a little. Juliet still wasn't convinced that Olivia was the right person to take over her job here at Harper Hill for the next few weeks.

"You don't even like working at the garden center. You never have," Juliet had repeated, her hands curling around the lovely turquoise knit blanket one of her friends had brought her in the hospital.

"That doesn't matter," Olivia had said, doing her best not to be hurt at her mother's lack of confidence. "I'm only going to be there temporarily. I can handle it for a month."

Juliet had groaned, only partially in pain. "A month. I can't ask you to do that."

"First of all, you didn't ask. I'm insisting. Second of all, what's the alternative? Do you want to close the place during the busiest season of the year? What will you do with all your inventory? Think of the carnage. All those homeless plants, left to wither and die!"

Her mother had made a face and continued arguing, until Olivia was tempted to walk out of the hospital room right then, hop into her car, grab her dog and drive straight back to Seattle.

She wouldn't, though. She owed it to her father, if nothing else, to help keep alive the business he had loved during this temporary crisis.

"I'm going to be running things in name only. You'll be telling me what to do behind the scenes. Just think of me as your arms and legs. Your eyes and ears. As long as you give me a detailed to-do list every day, everything will work out."

Juliet hadn't looked convinced, but a nurse came in just then to change one of the medications going into her IV line and she had finally let the subject drop.

"When is your mom supposed to go home from the hospital?" Doug asked her now.

"A few more days. That's all I know right now. Her doctor wants to send her to a rehab facility for a week, but of course she's not happy about that. We'll see who wins."

"I'm betting on Juliet."

Maybe he'd been working here longer than Olivia thought. He certainly knew her mother well.

"I tend to agree, but we'll see. How have things been going without her these past few days?"

Before he could answer, a customer approached them, pulling one of the store wagons with tires big enough to handle the gravel and sawdust terrain.

"Hi. I've looked through three greenhouses and can't find what I need. Can you point me in the right direction? I'm looking for some ornamental grasses for my planters."

"Ornamental grasses are in Greenhouse Four," Doug offered.

"Can you show me?"

Olivia stepped toward Doug. "I can finish watering here, if you want to show our customer where to find the grass."

She really hoped he would stick to the ornamental kind.

"This way, ma'am," he said, leading the way through the door of the main greenhouse to the pathway leading to the others.

She didn't know how much water the plants needed but decided she would give them all a small soak and let one of the more knowledgeable employees fill in if some of the plants needed more.

Olivia had worked her way down one long row of annuals and was pulling the hose across the way to the other side, focused on the job at hand, when a voice spoke behind her.

"We keep running into each other."

She gasped in surprise and whirled around, completely forgetting momentarily that she still held a hose in her hand. Water splattered all over Cooper Vance. She froze for an instant, horrified, but finally managed to jerk the hose away from him and turn it back to the annuals.

"Oh. I'm so sorry!"

He looked down at the water splotched all over his navy fire department polo shirt and cargo pants. "It's fine. Don't worry about it."

"Look at you. You're soaked! Let me find some towels."

He shook his head. "Not necessary. It's a warm day and this will be dried before we know it. Trust me when I say this is nothing compared to being blasted with a fire hose by a rookie on his first day."

Not trusting herself to behave rationally when he was around, Olivia went to the wall, turned off the faucet and looped the hose against the wall holder to ensure no customers would trip over the line. He waited, wearing an expression of interest that left her feeling as if she had been the one doused in cold water.

"Can I help you with something?" she finally asked.

"I need to pick up a pruner. My sister has some shrubs and trees that need trimming, but her jackass soon-to-be ex-husband took all the lawn and garden tools with him, despite the fact that he currently lives in an apartment in Redding with no lawn whatsoever to speak of."

"I wish I could take a pruner to *him*," she muttered.

He raised an eyebrow and she thought she saw amusement flash in his eyes. "Agreed. I'm afraid that won't help clip back her honeysuckle, though."

She looked around the garden center. "I'm afraid I can't help you much. I don't know where anything is. I think I know where they used to be but I have no idea if my mom has moved things. If you want to wait a minute, I can find someone to help you."

"No problem. I can take a look around. I'll find what I need eventually."

The smartest thing would be to leave him to it. Hadn't she

told herself the day before to stay far away from Cooper Vance? But she needed to familiarize herself with the layout of the greenhouses anyway and it made sense for her to help out a client at the same time.

"When I was a kid, Dad kept the loppers and clippers and other gardening tools in here," she said, leading the way to a cavernous space next to the main greenhouse.

"Bingo," he said as soon as they walked through the doors. The room held shovels and spades, wheelbarrows, coiled hoses and a wall display of dangerous-looking pruning shears.

"I can help you find them but don't ask me which one is best for your job," she warned him.

"I can probably figure out that part," he answered.

"That makes one of us, then."

He grinned and went to the wall to better study the implements of destruction. After studying his options, he pulled down a long pair of shears with orange handles.

"I think these should do," he answered.

"For the honeysuckle or for Rich?"

"Both, if I'm lucky." Cooper grinned at her and Olivia felt hot and breathless suddenly.

Oh, cut it out, she snapped at herself.

"Excuse me," a voice cut in. "Do you work here? I have a question and can't find anyone else."

She cleared her throat and faced a man who looked to be in his sixties, wearing a Western-cut shirt, suspenders and Levi's rolled up at least twice. "Sort of, sir. I just started. How can I help you?"

"I need to buy a chain saw but you have so many. I have no idea what I'm doing."

She could totally relate. "Can you tell me how you expect to use it most?"

"Oh, you know. The usual thing. General use. Clearing away tree branches. Maybe cutting up firewood here and there."

Okay. That didn't help her at all. She had no idea how to guide the man to the right purchase. Fortunately, Cooper stepped in to her rescue.

"I don't work here, but I do know quite a bit about chain saws."

"You're the new fire chief, aren't you?"

He nodded and held out the hand not holding the pruning shears. "Cooper Vance."

"Walter. Walter Trevino. I knew your aunt and uncle some," the man said. "Good people."

Something sad flickered in Cooper's gaze. "They were great."

They were the ones who had taken in his sister after his and Melody's mother had died. Olivia remembered the uncle had died about ten years ago and his aunt Helen had remarried and moved to the San Diego area, leaving the house to Melody.

"I still miss seeing old Frank working in his yard. He loved that place. It's nice to have your sister and her little ones in the neighborhood. Shame about the divorce, isn't it?"

"Yeah," Cooper said, his voice clipped. "Let's see if we can find a good chain-saw fit for you."

For the next ten minutes, Cooper and Mr. Trevino—whom she recognized now as a man who once owned an insurance agency in town—looked through the available inventory until they settled on one that would meet his needs.

"Thanks for all your help, Chief," he said after loading down with chain oil and a gas can to fill it with.

"Glad to help." Cooper smiled and she felt slightly breathless again, trying hard not to notice how the sunlight filtering through the greenhouse room seemed to gleam in his hair.

"I can't ring you up since I don't have cashier credentials yet, but I'll see if I can find someone to help," Olivia said to both men.

She led the way back into the main greenhouse, where Doug

THE SEA GLASS COTTAGE

was working the cash register now, helping a young woman who looked to be buying only gardening gloves.

"You first." Cooper gestured to the other man, who got into line behind the young woman.

When the fire chief turned to face her, Olivia fought that stupid reaction again. "Thanks for your help," she said, hoping her voice didn't sound as breathless as she felt. "As you can tell, I'm a bit out of my comfort zone here."

"You're trying. That's the important thing."

She made a face. "I don't exactly have much choice. Juliet will be laid up for a while."

"Poor thing. She's not going to be happy on the sidelines."

"You don't have to tell me that. My mom thinks she has to do everything by herself and has a really hard time letting other people help her."

"Don't make the same mistake," Cooper suggested.

His words hit a little too close to home. She possibly might have inherited her mother's independent streak, at least in most areas of her life. "That shouldn't be a problem for me, at least while I'm working here."

She ought to have a better idea of how things worked at the garden center. At least where things were. She had worked here during high school, after all. Of course, that had been more than a decade ago, and even back then, she had been going through the motions, only doing what her mother told her to.

Juliet had never wanted to give her responsibility over anything, even the garden center's website.

"I don't want you working so hard. You have enough to do with schoolwork and your friends and extracurricular things. You should just enjoy your teen years, honey," Juliet had urged.

Right. *Enjoy* and *teen years* were not words she could easily put together. Her mother hadn't even been aware of how Olivia had struggled over losing her father and coping with the drama that always surrounded Natalie. The late-night calls from jail, the hospitalizations, the rehab that never stuck.

She knew everything her mother had been dealing with, especially after Caitlin came along. Her mother had been exhausted, overwhelmed. In response, Olivia had tried to be the perfect daughter, unwilling to add one more burden to her mother's shoulders.

She had felt a huge pressure not to rock their already wildly flailing boat. Her grades had been stellar; she had stayed out of trouble; she learned to cook and took over some of the housekeeping duties at Sea Glass Cottage to ease her mother's load.

Look at where it got her. She was now responsible for everything. The pot-smoking employees, the customers who didn't know what they wanted but expected you to find it for them, the payroll and the taxes and keeping the inventory alive.

This was going to be a disaster.

Olivia wanted to sink down next to the cash register and cry.

"You okay?"

She could feel the beginnings of a panic attack starting at the edge of her subconscious, the second one she had suffered in a week. She hadn't had one in ages, probably since college, when the pressure of trying to be the perfect daughter all the time had finally caught up with her.

She took a deep breath, willing herself to stay calm as she forced a smile for Cooper. "Fine," she lied. "Is that all you need?"

COOPER

He did not like the sudden pinched lines around her mouth or the way her high cheekbones had lost their color. She looked like she was going to pass out.

"I think I'm good for now," he said. "I was thinking about planting an herb garden at the fire station and might be back for some planning help with that. But for now, I only need the shears."

"Right. Okay. Good. I'll keep my fingers crossed that by the time you come back for that, things won't be so crazy around here. We're shorthanded. Apparently the assistant manager also quit this week."

He gave her a sympathetic look. "Rough timing."

"Tell me about it. The garden center does the bulk of its business in the spring and right now we're barely operational."

"I'm no expert, but it sounds like your first order of business is hiring a few more people to help you out."

"You're absolutely right. Well, maybe my second order of business. My first order of business is probably walking around to familiarize myself with the place so I don't sound like a total idiot to the next person who needs pruning shears."

He had to smile at that. Suddenly he had an idea, one that he was stunned he hadn't thought of before. "She'll probably kill me for mentioning it to you before talking to her, but have you thought about asking Melody to help you out?"

She stared, clearly shocked at the suggestion. "Melody? Is she looking for work?"

"She mentioned something last night about starting to look for a job. I think she's been so shell-shocked the last few months with the separation and everything that she has mostly been focused on survival and dealing with the boys."

"Do you think she'd do it?"

"You know how much she loves gardening. I think she'd much rather work here than stock shelves and bag groceries over at the supermarket."

"Melody. Oh, Cooper. I could kiss you."

As soon as she said the words, Olivia blushed. "I mean, that's an absolutely fantastic idea. Genius, even. I can't believe I didn't think of it first."

"I can't guarantee she'll do it. She still has her youngest at home and all three boys will be home for the summer once school gets out."

"All I can do is ask. And you can be sure I will. I'll call her this afternoon. Thank you, Cooper. I owe you a beer. Or a half dozen, if we want to be technical, from all the unpaid help you gave Mr. Trevino this afternoon."

"I would take you up on that offer but something tells me you're going to be too busy for a while to be buying me beer."

That was a pity, he wanted to add, but caution held his tongue. He couldn't flirt with Olivia Harper, as much as he might want to.

He was swiping his credit card to pay for his purchase when Olivia's niece walked in, tall and pretty and the spitting image of her mother.

Caitlin was a good reminder of another reason he couldn't pursue this attraction to Olivia. Natalie. Olivia's sister, who had once been closer to him than anyone else on earth.

Yet another person he couldn't save.

Caitlin looked startled to see him. "Oh. Hi, Chief Vance."

The girl always acted oddly around him and he couldn't seem to figure out why. She seemed like a nice kid, though. Melody certainly trusted her with her tribe of unruly boys.

"Hi, Caitlin. Hey, Jake."

"Hi, Chief Vance."

The teenager reached out to shake his hand and he was once more impressed by him. Jake was part of the youth EMT program in the community, the same program where Cooper had started. The boy demonstrated a calm leadership Cooper had to admire in one so young.

"What are you two up to today?"

"Uh. Not much." Caitlin didn't meet his gaze. He could never figure out what he had done to make her so nervous around him.

"We took a bike ride to the hospital to see Mrs. Harper and decided to stop here to grab a soda before we head home," Jake said.

"Mimi keeps them in a fridge in her office for me," Caitlin said, rather defiantly.

"She's really thoughtful about things like that," Jake added with a smile.

"Do you want one?" Caitlin asked Cooper, her expression oddly hopeful.

"Um, no. But thanks."

"I wouldn't mind a drink," Olivia said.

"I'll see if there are enough but I doubt there will be."

She headed through a door that had Head Gardener stenciled on the doorjamb but returned with only two sodas. "Sorry. This is all I could find," she said to Olivia, popping the top of one and handing the other to Jake.

"You can have mine," Jake said instantly, holding it out to Olivia, who shook her head.

"Thank you but I think I'm good. I can find some water."

Caitlin took a swig of her soda then turned to face Cooper, who should have left the moment he paid for his pruning shears but found himself strangely reluctant to leave, for reasons he wasn't sure he wanted to identify.

"You knew my mom, didn't you?" Caitlin said to him suddenly, the question coming out of the blue and just about knocking him over.

Olivia gave a sharp intake of breath, Jake looked startled and Cooper had no idea what to say.

"She was my best friend," he said, his heart aching at the thought of Olivia's sister.

"That's what my grandmother said. She said you guys were always together and you used to eat at Sea Glass Cottage a lot."

"Yes. Your grandparents were very kind to me."

"So, did my mom drink Coke?" she asked after a minute.

"Yeah. Diet Coke. She loved the stuff. Why do you ask?"

Caitlin shrugged, not meeting his gaze. "I just wondered. I don't remember her at all. I like talking to people who do, to kind of keep her memory alive. Mimi doesn't like to talk about her too much. It makes her sad."

It made him sad to remember, too. All that potential, wasted.

Every time he went out on an overdose call, he thought of Natalie and how she had thrown her life away.

"If you want to know about Natalie, you could always ask me," Olivia suddenly said briskly. "She was my sister. I lived in the bedroom next door at Sea Glass Cottage."

To Cooper's surprise, Caitlin flashed a look of deep loathing at her aunt. "I don't want to hear anything you have to say about my mother," she snapped, then turned and marched out of the store, leaving all of them staring after her.

Jake gave them both an apologetic look. "Sorry," he mumbled, as if her outburst was his fault, and hurried after her.

"See? We're a full-service nursery. Come for the pruning shears, stay for the drama," Olivia said.

He smiled at her attempt at a joke, though he could see she was still hurt by Caitlin's sudden attack.

"Anyway, thanks for your help. When you're ready to plant the garden at the fire station, let me know. We would love to help."

"I'll do that," he said, then waved and headed away, aware as he did that anticipation curled through him, knowing he would have an excuse to see her again.

9

CAITLIN

"Wow. That was unnecessarily harsh."

Caitlin, in the middle of trying to get her bike out of the rack in front of the store, glared at Jake, mostly to keep from bursting into tears.

She couldn't believe she had gone off on Olivia like that, in front of Cooper Vance. Her mother's best friend.

She was such a child.

"I know. I shouldn't have said that. I swore to myself I would be polite to her the next time I saw her. But then we walked in and she was laughing with him and hanging out at the cash register like she worked there and I just got so…pissed, you know?"

Jake raised an eyebrow and Caitlin fought the urge to kick him.

"You wouldn't understand."

"I'm sorry, but I really don't. Olivia's always been cool to me. Remember that time in eighth grade when I had to do a report for computer tech about someone who worked in the industry and she let me interview her for like an hour and sent me all that swag from her start-up? She didn't need to do that but she went out of her way to help me."

She didn't want to answer. All she could think about was the hurt she hadn't been able to shake, even though weeks had passed since she found out how her aunt really felt about her.

"Big deal," she muttered.

"I don't get all this antagonism. You used to think Olivia was totally chill. Now you can't stand to be in the same room with her."

"You wouldn't understand," she snapped again. Somehow it made everything worse that Jake wasn't on her side on this.

"You're still going on about the journal, aren't you?"

"Maybe," she admitted, hating that he made her feel like she was six years old, crying on the playground because another girl called her a name.

This was so much more than a playground squabble. She had always adored Olivia. For most of her life, she thought her aunt loved her, too. To read the truth felt like someone had tossed her over the cliffs above town, into the cold waters of the Pacific.

Worse had been reading Olivia's feelings about Natalie. Her own sister. It had been more than clear that Olivia had despised her.

"You need to let that go," Jake said, for about the hundredth time. "It's totally unfair to blame Olivia for things she wrote years ago."

"That's easy for you to say. If somebody had called you an annoying, bawling little brat who was ruining your life, you might not be so quick to forgive."

Okay, yeah. She shouldn't have read the journal. Duh. Those had been Olivia's private words, written when she was around Caitlin's age.

She got that. She wasn't stupid. She totally understood that

Olivia hadn't written those things to be hurtful and mean but to vent about her feelings, about her dad's death and her sister's drug addiction and the void her mother had left in her life by focusing so much time and attention on Natalie's bratty daughter. The bratty daughter who should have been given up for adoption to a loving family so she could have a chance at a normal life instead of growing up with a junkie for a mom.

Those words Olivia had written seemed scarred on her subconscious.

It seemed so stupid to focus on them, to let them haunt and torment her, especially with all the other things she had to worry about.

She couldn't seem to help it. Every time she looked at Olivia or saw Mimi talking to her on the phone or heard her grandmother mention her name, those words seemed to echo in her head like a fire alarm.

"You know you're going to have to let it go, at least if you want to have a relationship with your aunt," Jake said, his brown eyes soft and compassionate.

She frowned and tossed her soda in the recycling bin outside the greenhouse. "That's kind of the point. I don't *want* to have a relationship with her. I don't want her anywhere around. She doesn't belong here anymore. We're doing fine without her. As far as I'm concerned, it would be better for me and Mimi and the garden center if Olivia would just pack up her weird dog and head back to Seattle, where she belongs."

"Wow. Don't hold back, Cait."

At the words behind her, Caitlin's insides seemed to shrivel. She turned around and found Olivia standing in the doorway to the main building, studying them both with an impassive expression.

How much had she heard? Did she know Caitlin had read her journal? Judging by the confused hurt in her aunt's eyes, Caitlin doubted it. Instinctively, she wanted to apologize, to assure Olivia she was talking smack and didn't mean anything by it.

That would be lying, though. On some level, she was kind of relieved her feelings were out in the open. Not that she'd really made a secret of them, but at least Olivia now knew where they stood.

"That's how I feel," she said defiantly. "Mimi says you can't argue with someone else's feelings. They are what they are."

"True enough. But I'm sure Mimi has also told you that whatever your feelings about them, you should not go out of your way to hurt people deliberately."

Oh, like writing down those horrible things about Caitlin and her mother hadn't been hurtful?

"I didn't know you were there," she said stiffly.

"I came out to see if you were still here. I was going to see if you happen to know my mom's computer password. I can always call her and ask her but didn't want to bother her while she's resting. Unfortunately, my weird dog and I are here to stay, at least for a few weeks, and I have work to do."

The dog wasn't weird. He was odd looking, yeah, but in an adorable way. She shouldn't have said that part. Still, she bit her lip to keep from apologizing.

At her stubborn silence, Jake gave her an exasperated look. "I can tell you the password, unless Mrs. Harper changed it recently. I helped her update some software recently. The password is *flowers*. Lowercase."

Olivia smiled at Jake and the traitor seemed to glow under her approval.

Seriously?

Sure, Olivia was pretty. She had that boho style thing down, with her wavy blond hair and hazel eyes and cool clothes. That didn't mean Jake should just roll over like his dog Rosie, looking to have his belly scratched.

"*Flowers*. Got it. Thank you."

"You're welcome. Glad to help."

"And I don't have to bother my mom," she said. "The sooner she heals from this accident, the quicker she can return here to work and I can go back to Seattle, where I belong."

She gave them both a cool smile and headed back inside the garden center.

Jake drained his soda and tossed the can into the recycling bin. "I know you don't want to hear it, but you have to let go of your anger or you'll be in for a miserable month while your aunt is here."

A month. How would she endure it?

"Maybe I'll just move to your house," she said. "Or better yet, I'll find my dad and go live with him while Olivia's here."

Jake rolled his eyes, but to her relief, he didn't nag her as they grabbed their bikes and started up the hill.

10

JULIET

On her fifty-third birthday, Juliet woke up in a hospital bed, wondering how she had become so ancient.

Until four days earlier, she had felt young for her age, healthier and more active than she'd been in years.

She went to the gym three times a week; she walked; she had a physically demanding job that kept her moving all day long. When she looked at her smartwatch every night at the end of a long day, she was thrilled at the step count on her tracker.

She ate better than she had as a young mother; she cooked healthy meals; she meditated most mornings before she went to work.

She had lost forty pounds over the past four years and she did everything she could to stay healthy and fight back the inevitable progression of age and disease.

Now, because of one stupid decision, one ridiculous moment

in time, she felt as if all her progress toward becoming a healthier version of herself was for nothing.

She had stopped wearing her watch because the step count for each of the past four days was laughably small. She had hardly gotten out of this hospital bed. When she did, each of those trips had been assisted by someone else.

She sighed, telling herself not to be too depressed. Today was her birthday, not her death day. She was still strong, still vibrant, still committed to being her healthiest self.

Yes, she was injured, but she wasn't out of the game yet.

She was still trying to give herself a pep talk when her orthopedic surgeon came in for morning hospital rounds.

"Everything looks good," Dr. Adeno said after going over her chart, then giving her a quick physical exam. "I think you should be able to go home today, as long as we have all the home care elements in place to make sure it's a safe place for you."

Home.

An image of Sea Glass Cottage formed in her mind, warm and welcoming. Her refuge and her retreat.

"That would be wonderful," she said. Could Dr. Adeno hear the longing in her words?

"You obviously can't be there on your own, at least at first. I need to ask, will you have someone there who can help you for the first few weeks, until you're a little more independent? After that, you shouldn't need as much care."

"My daughter and my granddaughter."

"Perfect. Now let's talk logistics. Tell me some particulars about your house. Is your bedroom on the main floor?"

"Yes. And I have an en suite bathroom as well."

"Good. Good. What about getting into the home? Do you have stairs?"

"Yes. Four up to the porch. I've been worried about that."

"That will present a problem," Dr. Adeno said.

"No. It won't." At the new voice, she looked up, beyond Dr.

Adeno. Henry Cragun stood framed in the doorway, looking big and tough and wonderful.

"Why is that?" Dr. Adeno asked him.

"She has a ramp now."

"Since when?" Juliet exclaimed.

"Since Jake, Caitlin and I built one last night. It's only temporary, from the sidewalk out front up to the porch, but it should work while you need some extra help. When you no longer need it, we can take it down and you'll never know it was even there. We didn't trample so much as a flower while building it."

His thoughtfulness made her want to cry, though she told herself it was simply a side effect of the pain medication. "Thank you!" she breathed, her heart warming.

"You're welcome. Like I said, Jake and Caitlin helped. It was really a team effort."

Maybe, but she was fairly confident she knew who provided the brains and the brawn and the pocketbook behind it.

"Happy birthday." Henry came closer and her heart danced a little, as it had been doing for weeks whenever he was near.

"Thanks," she said, hoping he didn't notice the heat she could feel rising on her cheekbones.

"You didn't tell me today was your birthday," Dr. Adeno chided. "I should have noticed that on your chart. What are you now? Thirty-nine?"

Juliet rolled her eyes. "Considering I have a granddaughter who is a sophomore in high school, thirty-nine would certainly make me precocious."

Today in this hospital bed, she felt every one of her fifty-three years, but she chose to focus on the positive. "I can't believe you built a ramp."

He shrugged. "Like I said, it's temporary. Totally removable. I just figured you won't be able to get around at all if it's impossible for you to easily get in and out of your own house. This should help."

Drat the man. Why did he have to be so… Wonderful?

It was a question she had been asking herself for months.

Juliet couldn't escape the grim realization that her birthday marked yet one more milestone, another year between them. He was forty-five, which meant she was officially eight years older than he was now. A lifetime, it seemed, though she knew his birthday in September would shorten that age gap.

She managed a smile. "Thank you. I don't know what to say."

"You don't have to say anything. It was nothing, I promise. I had extra wood from a job I did up the coast. Caitlin and Jake were happy to help. Olivia pitched in, too, but she was busy at the garden center until we were almost done."

Dr. Adeno smiled. "What wonderful neighbors you have, Juliet. People told me I could expect this kind of thing in Cape Sanctuary. It's nice to see the town lives up to the hype."

"It's wonderful but I hope you never find yourself in a position to need help."

"I have to say, having your home more accessible does set my mind at ease about releasing you from here, especially since you're determined not to go to a rehab facility."

"I want to go home," Juliet said. She would much rather recover at Sea Glass Cottage than in a rehab facility with strangers taking care of her.

She wanted to be home, so desperately. She missed her cats; she missed the view of endless sea; she missed Caitlin running in after school, slamming her backpack onto the kitchen table.

"I don't blame you. I think most of my patients who can manage it do better in their own spaces, in their own beds."

"So you think she can go home today?" Henry asked.

"We'll have to work on arranging physical therapy and possibly home care to come in and help you at first, but if all goes well, then yes. I don't see any reason Juliet can't sleep in her own room tonight."

She closed her eyes, appalled at the tears that burned there.

Henry rested a comforting hand on her shoulder and she had to fight the urge to lean into him.

When she opened her eyes, she saw the doctor taking in the gesture with one slightly raised eyebrow. Juliet could see her leaping to entirely the wrong conclusion.

She and Henry were *not* a thing. He was her dear friend. That was all. Even if her pulse did race whenever he was nearby and she always felt a little breathless and off balance these days.

She had to cut this out. For heaven's sake, she had been lying in a hospital bed for four days. She was only wearing mascara and lipstick that Caitlin had brought her and her hair was a rumpled mess, though she'd tried to style it as best she could.

She probably looked every single one of her fifty-three years, but she supposed he needed to see her at her worst.

Something seemed to have changed between them in the past few months. From a few things he had said and hints he had scattered in conversation, she had begun to wonder if it was possible Henry might want more from her than friendship.

She thought she might have been imagining things until three weeks earlier, when he had come in after hours at the garden center so she could help fill an order for a job he was doing and he had asked her to dinner that weekend.

At the time, in the moment, she hadn't been exactly sure what was going on. Surely he was not asking her on a date. Was he?

They had been friends for years. She had been best friends with his wife and had grieved with Henry when Lilianne lost her long and difficult battle against cancer three years earlier.

When he asked her to dinner, she had been caught so off guard that for a horrifying moment, she hadn't said anything. And then she had managed to turn the whole thing into an outing with Caitlin and Jake, which she knew wasn't what he meant.

He hadn't mentioned going out again. She had to hope time and a little reflection had shown him how ridiculous the idea of them dating was.

Age was only part of it. She couldn't tell him the much greater reason why he should look elsewhere, if he was lonely and in need of some female companionship.

"What else can I do to help you get ready to go home?" he asked now.

"You've done more than enough, Henry. Really. I'm grateful, believe me, but I don't want you to feel obligated to babysit me."

"You need to call Olivia and tell her, don't you?"

"Yes. I suppose. I'll need a ride home from the hospital."

"I would offer my pickup but I'm afraid that might be a little tough for you to climb into just a few days after hip replacement surgery."

"You're probably right."

"I'm available all day, though. If you want, I can stick around long enough to help you into whatever vehicle you take home."

"There are orderlies and staff who could do that."

"And friends," he pointed out with that smile she adored.

She sighed, not knowing how to refuse. She was so weak where Henry was concerned.

"Tell you what. It likely will take some time for them to work through your discharge orders. I'll keep you company until then. If you don't need my help leaving this place, I'll at least head to Sea Glass Cottage so I can be there to help you into the house and to your room."

She was fully of the opinion it was better to give than receive, but in this case she had to learn to accept help more gracefully. Especially now that she couldn't avoid taking help from others over the next few months. If he wanted to help her, it seemed churlish and small to refuse.

"Thank you. I would appreciate that," she said.

"While you wait for all your discharge orders to go through, want to watch another episode of *Doctor Who*?"

"Sure. I would love that."

They had been slowly working their way through the seasons over the past few months, usually watching at her house while Caitlin and Jake did homework or watched a movie in the other room.

She wondered if he had any idea how much she treasured those quiet moments with him.

The hospital was set up for streaming services and Henry quickly found the next episode.

He sat beside her bed and she thought this was the perfect way to spend her birthday, though she had to admit to herself that she spent more time watching Henry out of the corner of her gaze than the show.

She had missed this quiet time with him. She smiled a little, settling back into her pillows, at peace for what felt like the first time in days. Henry was here and she could finally relax her guard, content with the sweet, comforting feeling that he was watching over her.

11

OLIVIA

She stood in her mother's hospital room, struck by the sight in front of her. Juliet was asleep, her features free for the moment of the pain that had furrowed her brow and added extra lines around her mouth the evening before when Olivia had last visited her room.

Right now, her mother looked…comfortable.

In the visitor chair beside her, Henry Cragun was asleep as well, his head back against the headrest and his hand on the bed, almost—but not quite—touching Juliet's fingers.

The tender scene somehow rocked her to the core.

Her mother and Henry? Was something going on between them?

Henry had been a neighbor and friend for years, since before Olivia had left for college. She used to babysit Jake when he was little.

Henry was younger than Juliet, probably in his mid to late

forties. He was good-looking, in a rugged, outdoorsy kind of way, with dark wavy hair threaded with a bit of distinguishing gray, and a tan that came from working outside all day.

He stirred a little in his sleep and his hand curled, his fingers coming closer to Juliet's, and Olivia felt as if she were watching something intimately personal.

Were the two of them involved? She had always assumed theirs was simply a friendship based mostly on Juliet's granddaughter and Henry's son being inseparable friends.

For some strange reason, she had never contemplated the idea of her mom being with anyone else. How stupid of her. She could see that now. Her father had been gone for years. While it sometimes seemed like he had died only yesterday, it had been more than sixteen years.

Juliet was still a vibrant, healthy woman. Why wouldn't she want to have a man in her life?

But Juliet and Henry? Olivia couldn't quite make the pieces fit together and felt as if her entire worldview had been shaken.

She hated to wake them. Should she slip out again? As she was trying to decide, Henry opened his eyes. He looked briefly confused, his warm eyes blurry with sleep. Then he looked down at his hand, only a few inches away from Juliet's, and she watched as a rather adorable blush climbed his cheeks.

He slid his hand from the bed. "Olivia. Hi."

Her mother stirred but didn't awaken.

"Hi, Mr. Cragun."

He looked pained. "Please. You should call me Henry, don't you think?"

I don't know. Are you angling to become my new stepfather?

She couldn't ask that question, of course.

"How are things going here?"

With a careful look at a still-sleeping Juliet, he stood, gesturing to the door.

She walked out of the hospital room into the hallway. After

one more careful glance toward the bed, Henry closed the door behind them.

"I think things are good," he said in a more normal voice. "The doc was here when I showed up about, oh, an hour ago. She's talking about sending your mom home and is in the process of writing up the discharge orders."

Home. Juliet could return to Sea Glass Cottage.

Panic flared. She wasn't at all ready! At least while her mother had been in the hospital these past few days, Olivia could focus on the garden center. Now she would have to split her time between caregiving and trying to figure out what she was doing at Harper Hill, as well as juggling her own clients and the long-distance work she was doing for her day job.

"Terrific news," she managed, forcing a smile.

"Isn't it?" He looked relieved. "She'll heal faster once she's in her own space."

Was it difficult for Henry to spend so much time visiting someone in the hospital? His wife's cancer fight had been long and painful. This must bring up all kinds of memories.

"Thank you so much for all you've done," she said. Okay, maybe she wasn't yet comfortable with the possibility that he and Juliet might be a thing. She could still be grateful for his help. "I don't know how we would have managed her coming home without that ramp you and the kids built last night."

"I can't do much to help her heal. That's a battle she'll have to fight on her own. But at least I can make it easier for her to be in her own home, where she feels best."

"It's brilliant. I never even thought about the logistics of helping her up and down the steps."

In truth, she hadn't really given much thought to Juliet's return, other than clearing a few pieces of furniture out of her bedroom so the wheelchair could move more easily.

"She should be set now. But if you think of anything else I can do, you know where to find me."

"Thank you."

Henry and Juliet.

The idea still boggled the mind. She knew his late wife had been one of Juliet's dearest friends and that her mother had grieved deeply when cancer had taken Lilianne three or four years earlier.

Should she say something? No. She had to wait for Juliet or Henry to broach the subject.

She couldn't stop thinking about his hand just inches from Juliet's in sleep and how he had colored so tellingly when she had caught him.

Did Caitlin know?

"What other help will you need to care for her at home?"

All the help. She had no idea where to start.

She forced a smile. "I think Cait and I can handle most things. It will mostly be getting Mom up and down, making sure she does her physical therapy exercises, taking her to doctor appointments. We will probably have to figure out most things as we go along."

A hint of a dimple appeared in Henry's cheek. "That seems to be a common trait in the Harper family."

"More like our family motto. Jump and the net will appear, grasshopper."

He smiled but Olivia didn't feel much like smiling back.

She was terrified at the idea of caring for Juliet. Her mother had a broken hip and broken ribs and would be able to do very little for herself.

What if Olivia made everything worse? If she messed up her mother's medication or stumbled when she was trying to help Juliet transfer positions or mismanaged the garden center into the ground?

She could feel a panic attack starting and tried to breathe through it until it faded. One stress at a time. Right now, she had to focus on helping her mother go home from the hospital. She could panic about the rest later.

"It's so good that you were able to come home, Olivia. I know it couldn't have been an easy decision to pick up and leave, even for the few weeks that you'll be here, but I hope you know how lost your mom would have been without you. I know she's hurting, but she still seems happier now that you're home."

She seriously doubted that. And now she was doubting her own suspicions about what she had seen. Maybe she had misunderstood that moment of tenderness she had witnessed. Henry and her mother couldn't be together if he was that clueless about the tangled, difficult relationship she so carefully navigated with Juliet.

While she was busy trying to do everything else to keep the family business running and take care of Juliet, why couldn't she try to heal the subtle rift in the relationship with her mother?

The seductive question made something ache in her chest. How could she do that when she still wasn't sure why it felt so broken? Every time she tried to analyze it, she felt as if she were chasing ghosts.

She loved her mother and admired her. On the one hand, she wanted to be close to Juliet, to feel as if she could confide her troubles and weaknesses. On the other, Olivia couldn't seem to shake the habits developed after her father died and Natalie began getting into trouble.

During those difficult years, her mother had too much to handle with the struggling business, the house, Natalie's wild behavior. Olivia hadn't wanted to give her mother one more thing to worry about. She had developed strange, magical thinking, afraid that if she wasn't the perfect daughter, her mother would crack apart and the entire fragile family structure they were both clinging to would collapse.

Could she be vulnerable enough to admit to Juliet that everything wasn't ideal in her life? She had fears and weaknesses, worries and stresses.

She would try, she told herself. She had to. She was trying to find more courage, to become not perfect but someone she could admire.

Sometimes being brave wasn't about confronting an armed man in a coffee shop as much as finding the strength to be vulnerable and open about her weaknesses with someone she loved and admired.

Like her own mother.

"Since you're here to be with your mom," Henry said, "I should go somewhere quiet and return some calls."

"You don't have to leave."

"I could use some air. Not a big fan of hospitals, you know? I mean, they're great to have around when you need them, but they're still not my favorite place."

"I totally get it," she answered, touched again that he was willing to step up and visit her mother even when he didn't want to be there. "Thank you."

Courage came in many forms, some quiet and all but unnoticed.

"I won't be long, in case you need help transferring Juli into your vehicle. Then I'll follow you to the cottage to help get her into the house."

"You've been so kind, Mr. Cragun. Henry," she corrected. "Thank you. I know my mother appreciates it."

"I'm more than happy to help. Your mom is always helping everyone else in Cape Sanctuary. I'm grateful for a small chance to help her in return."

He left soon to make his phone calls and Olivia pushed open the door. Juliet's eyes opened as she walked inside and she looked around the room, her features confused.

"Was... Wasn't Henry here?"

"He left to make some phone calls. He'll be back soon, I'm sure."

Her mother looked to the door then back at Olivia with a lost sort of look. "Oh. All right."

She stepped closer to the bed and leaned down to kiss Juliet on the cheek. "Happy birthday, Mom."

"Oh. Thank you. It's a strange sort of day, really."

"I know it probably doesn't seem like much of a birthday."

"I might be going home. That's all the present I need."

She thought of her mother's searching look and the tone of her voice when she had asked about Henry. She had bought some slippers and a new bathrobe for her mother, but perhaps Olivia ought to try her hand at matchmaking for her mother's birthday gift. Henry really was a sweet man and he seemed to have genuine feelings for her mother.

How best to push the two together? She mulled the question, then caught herself. Managing her mother's love life wasn't in her job description. Didn't she have enough to do right now?

Anyway, what did she know about romance? She could hear her mother. If she told Juliet she wanted to help with her love life, her mother would tell her to mind her own business and focus on her own.

Probably good advice.

"Do you have anything to wear home? I should have thought to bring you something from your closet."

"I have clothes. When Caitlin brought me my own pajamas to wear here in the hospital, I had her toss in a dress for the trip home."

"Smart. Much more convenient."

"I thought so." Juliet seemed to become more awake from her nap. "You look tired. Are you sleeping all right?"

Her mother was the one lying in a hospital bed with a broken hip and she was worried about how *Olivia* slept?

"I'm fine," she answered. "I was at the garden center late."

"Oh, right. Yesterday was Thursday. That must mean you had a new shipment from the wholesaler."

"That's right. It took us past ten to unload the truck and organize everything."

"I never thought I could say I'm sorry I missed a Thursday-night delivery but I do. I wish I could have been there to help you."

"If you had been able to be there, you wouldn't have needed my help," Olivia pointed out.

"True enough." Juliet grimaced in pain but covered it with a little cough. "Besides the delivery, how are things going at Harper Hill?"

"So far so good. We haven't gone out of business yet, but then, it's only been a few days."

She had been looking for a chance to broach the idea Cooper had suggested. It made all the sense in the world to hire Melody, but she didn't feel right about making major personnel decisions without input from Juliet.

"Mom, how would you feel about hiring Melody Baker to help out while you're recuperating?"

"Melody? Oh! That's a brilliant idea. Do you think she might be interested?"

"It was Cooper's idea, actually." He deserved credit where credit was due. "I wanted to talk to you first before I asked her."

"Yes. Absolutely. She has a beautiful garden and knows more than I do about some of the plant species. Oh, well done. I love it. She'll be a wonderful addition."

Juliet simply glowed when talking about the garden center, likely the way Olivia did when proposing a social media campaign to a new client, she admitted.

"I'll give her a call, then."

"I always liked her. That poor girl. She deserves better than that fool she married."

"We definitely agree on that."

Though she didn't want to bother her mother with more questions about the garden center, Olivia needed information. She and her mother talked details about inventory and staffing for a few more moments. She thought she knew exactly why her mother's gaze kept drifting to the door.

"So," Olivia finally said. "Henry Cragun. What's going on there?"

Color climbed her mother's cheeks. "Nothing! Henry is a good friend," she said, rather primly.

"A very good friend, apparently. He was at the cottage past one in the morning working on a ramp for you."

"Along with Caitlin and Jake."

"Right. But Henry was the one who instigated it. And he's also the one who insisted on hanging around to make sure you can get home safely from the hospital."

"Don't go getting any ridiculous ideas," Juliet said, her voice stern. "Henry Cragun and I are friends and that's all we'll ever be. Is that clear?"

"Perfectly," a deep voice answered. With a sinking feeling in her stomach, Olivia looked to the doorway to find Henry framed there, his features impassive.

Oh darn. This was her fault. She should never have teased her mother about him. Apparently Juliet didn't have a sense of humor when it came to Henry.

Olivia waited for her mother to apologize or say she didn't mean her words, but Juliet only lifted her chin. "I cherish our friendship," she said, stressing the last word.

Henry didn't look offended at all, which made Olivia wonder if she was imagining the entire thing.

The nurse pushed her way into the room amid the awkwardness. "Sorry to interrupt," she said. "I wanted to let you know the doctor has put in all the discharge orders and I've got a few things to go over with you about what you can expect after your release."

"Perfect," Juliet said brightly, obviously eager to change the subject.

The nurse pulled up a chair next to Juliet's bedside and Olivia grabbed her phone so she could make notes about what might be required.

Henry stood for a moment, then appeared to think his presence was superfluous.

"I've got more phone calls to make," he said.

"You don't have to hang around all day waiting on me."

"I'm here," he answered, his voice just as firm. Without waiting for her to argue, he headed out the door.

The nurse, going through papers in her hand and apparently oblivious to the subtle tension in the room, stood back up. "I forgot to add a couple of important contact numbers. Sorry. Give me a minute."

As soon as she left the room, Juliet turned on Olivia. "You don't have to say anything." Her mother looked rueful. "I know. I was rude."

Olivia raised an eyebrow. "I didn't say a word."

"You were thinking it, weren't you?"

Olivia had no answer and after a moment her mother sighed. "He doesn't mean it. Henry understands there will never be anything between us but friendship."

She wasn't sure she wanted to have this conversation with her mother. She still couldn't wrap her head around the idea of her mother in a relationship with *anyone*. If her goal was to improve her relationship with Juliet, though, she would have to be more open to the possibility.

"Why, though? Henry is a terrific man. He's good-looking. He's hardworking. He's a great father. He's always been a good friend to you. What better basis can you ask for a relationship?"

Her words seemed to distress Juliet further. "I can't and that's all I'm going to say about it."

Olivia blinked at her mother's vehement tone. "Okay. Sorry. Forget I said anything."

The nurse came in right after that, holding out the papers. "All right. I think I've got everything now."

"No problem," Juliet said with a smile that betrayed none of her earlier frustrated tone.

While the nurse began going through the information they would need for Juliet's care, Olivia listened with half of her attention, the rest of it focused on her mother's love life. Or lack thereof.

Her father had been gone a long time. A lifetime, it sometimes felt. Steve Harper's death had devastated all the women in his family.

His wife and his two daughters reacted so very differently to his death. Juliet became focused on saving the family business.

Already hanging with a wild crowd before Steve died in that building fire, Natalie seemed to have lost all restraint afterward, burying her deep unhappiness beneath a crackly veneer of exuberance. She started staying out all night, partying hard with her friends, smoking, skipping school. Juliet and Nat would have big fights, which would usually end with Natalie slamming a door and leaving the house for a night or two or twenty.

Six months after Steve died, Natalie announced she was pregnant and didn't know who the father might be.

Juliet had been devastated at her daughter's choices but she had opened her heart to Natalie, who wouldn't consider giving up her baby. Nat had sworn off drugs and partying and had focused on her pregnancy. The baby had at least given them all something else to think about during that painful, difficult time.

"I'm just waiting for one more prescription to come up from the pharmacy and then we can get you out of here." The nurse interrupted her thoughts. "Meanwhile, you can change into your own clothes. Unless you want to go home in our fashionable hospital gowns."

"I'm good. Thank you," Juliet said with a grimace.

"Great. You can go ahead and have your daughter help you change. I'll let you know when the prescription arrives. It might be an hour or so."

After the nurse left, closing the door behind her, Juliet gave Olivia a rueful look. "You don't have to help me, whatever she said. I'm still capable of dressing myself."

"I'll be here if you need a hand with anything." She sat down and opened her phone to catch up on business. She was scrolling through her clients' Instagram feeds, lost in business, when a knock sounded at the door.

"I'm decent," Juliet said, and Olivia saw she had finished putting on a loose flowered sundress with cap sleeves in a sunny apricot. Olivia helped her up so Juliet could pull it down behind her.

"There. Now you're decent," she said, not quite sure how Juliet still managed to look fresh and composed after four days in the hospital.

The door opened and Caitlin burst through, all long limbs and energy.

"What are you doing here?" Juliet frowned.

"Early release Friday and I skipped my last hour. Don't worry—I talked to Coach Landry and he was cool about it."

Olivia knew Coach Landry was Shane Landry, a former professional football player who lived in Cape Sanctuary. Last she heard, he was engaged to marry Beatriz Romero, ex-wife of Cruz Romero, the local celebrity.

"You're all dressed. Is it true? You're going home today? I heard the nurses out there talking about discharging you."

"Yes. We're waiting on some prescriptions," Olivia said. She and her niece had achieved a détente of sorts while Juliet was in the hospital, mostly staying out of each other's way.

"Oh yay."

For the first time since Olivia had arrived, Caitlin lost her sullen, resentful look. If Olivia didn't know better, she would almost have said Caitlin looked happy.

"How soon can we leave?"

"I'm sure it won't be long now," Juliet said.

The words were no sooner out than the nurse knocked on the door, then pushed it open a moment later. Olivia could tell instantly by her expression that they were facing another delay.

"I just heard from Dr. Hall. Your neurologist. Dr. Adeno wanted him to take one more look at you before we send you home, while you're still an inpatient. He's with another patient but said he would be in shortly."

"Why do you need to see a neurologist?" Caitlin asked with a worried look.

"I had a concussion, remember?" Juliet said in a distracted tone, though Olivia was certain her mother had looked slightly panicked. "I'm sure Dr. Hall wants to be sure my head is all right after the fall. But it might take a while before he gets here. You don't need to stick around. Why don't you two go grab a coffee or something in the cafeteria while it's still open?"

Olivia had the distinct impression her mother was trying to get rid of them.

"I don't mind staying."

"Who knows how long he'll be. You don't want to be stuck here for an hour. Did you have lunch at school?" she demanded of Caitlin, who looked away.

"I wasn't hungry at lunchtime."

"You're probably hungry now, though."

"Not too bad."

Olivia didn't really want to go get coffee but she could tell Caitlin was hungry, despite her protests. She didn't want hungry to turn into hangry.

"I can wait," Caitlin said.

"Go on," Juliet said. "Both of you. The cafeteria here in the hospital isn't bad. I'll be fine. I'll text you when we're finished."

"Okay," Caitlin said, giving Juliet a quick hug and heading for the door. Her willingness to go after she had only just arrived seemed proof that she really was hungry. Stubborn girl.

As soon as they walked into the cafeteria, Olivia knew she had made a mistake.

The cheerful space decorated in brick and exposed walls wasn't at all like the café where she had witnessed the attack, but it smelled the same, of coffee and pastries and, somehow, chicken soup, and was filled with the low clatter of dishes and conversation.

Olivia froze in the doorway, suddenly shaky as a panic attack nudged at her.

"Are you getting something?" Caitlin asked, looking back at her.

She jerked her mind away, pressing it down. It wasn't that café in Seattle. This was a cafeteria in a well-secured hospital. Nothing would happen to her or anyone else here.

"Um. Yes. I could use some coffee." And she would sit inside this cafeteria and drink it, if it was the last thing she did.

"I don't have any money on me," Caitlin said.

"I can pay."

"Thanks."

Caitlin hurried off to fill a tray while Olivia gave her order to the barista inside the cafeteria. As she stepped away, she had to fight the urge to rush back out the door again.

"What's wrong?"

She had stopped stock-still inside the cafeteria, her mind awash in memories. The taste of fear was metallic, like blood.

"Nothing," she lied to her niece. How could she ever admit she was still fighting down panic from something that had happened days ago?

"I'm starving. Right now, I could eat a whole pizza by myself."

"Get what you want. I don't know what dinner will be tonight, especially since I don't know when we'll be able to make it out of here. We will have to figure out meals moving forward for the next few weeks."

"I wouldn't worry about it. When word gets out that Mimi is home from the hospital, we'll be deluged with neighbors bearing casseroles. You won't have to cook anything for a while."

Olivia had missed that about Cape Sanctuary, the kind, generous nature of the people who lived here year-round. After her coffee was ready and Caitlin filled her tray with food, Olivia paid. Then they went into the dining area for a table. The cafeteria was busy with nurses, physicians and family members of those receiving care.

She sat with her back against the wall, where she could see any potential threats. She had a feeling this would be her new normal. Caitlin ate in silence, most likely determined not to bend an inch and engage in anything that might resemble a polite conversation.

A couple of newcomers entered the cafeteria and Olivia tensed, uneasy, braced for danger. The feeling did not abate when she recognized one of the newcomers as fire chief Cooper Vance, wearing a paramedic uniform and looking big and tough.

He was holding a tray that held the special of the day, a smothered chicken burrito. The only empty table was, naturally, next to theirs. His gaze met hers, and with a rueful kind of look, he came closer.

"Hey, Olivia. Hey, Caitlin."

"Hi, Chief Vance," her niece answered, but Olivia merely nodded.

"You must be visiting Juliet. How is she?"

"Pretty good," Caitlin answered. "She's going home today."

"Great news." He looked genuinely pleased.

"That's the plan, anyway," Olivia was compelled to say. "I'm sure you know how long and complicated it can be to spring someone from one of these places."

131

"Yeah. It's a process."

Another firefighter joined them, sliding into the chair across from Cooper.

"I should have ordered the burrito like you did," the guy complained. "That burger took forever and I'm still not sure it's cooked through."

"Take it back," Cooper advised. "Olivia, this is a new guy in the department. Mike Walker. Today was his first day. He's transferring from the Bay Area. Mike, this is my friend Olivia Harper and her niece, Caitlin."

"Pleasure to meet you," she said. "What brings you to Cape Sanctuary?"

The man smiled at her and she didn't miss the way his gaze flicked to her ring finger then back to her eyes.

"I needed a change." He had a deep, pleasing voice, and while his expression was light, almost flirty, she caught shadows of something darker there.

"It's a nice town," she answered.

"I've only been here a few days but I like what I see so far. I sure can't complain about the view."

"Olivia's mother had a bad fall a few days ago," Cooper explained. "That's why they're here."

"Oh, too bad," Mike said with a sympathetic look.

"She broke her hip and some ribs and is recovering from surgery," Cooper said. "I'm surprised to hear she's going home instead of to a rehab center."

"Doctors would have preferred that, I think, but Juliet is determined to go home," Olivia said.

"Of course she wouldn't go to a rehab center." Caitlin sounded as if no other option should have even been considered. "Sea Glass Cottage is her home. She loves it there."

"Unless things have changed since I was there, which was years ago, the house isn't very accessible. Won't she need a wheelchair for a while?"

"She can get inside, at least," Olivia said. "The house has a new ramp. Henry Cragun and his son and Caitlin worked on it last night."

"It's awesome. You should see it." Caitlin's voice filled with pride.

"I saw lights and activity at the end of my shift last night. Now I wish I'd stopped to check it out. I could have helped."

"We were fine," Caitlin said with that nervous laugh she did around him. "Thanks, though."

Olivia was grateful he hadn't stopped, she told herself. She had already seen him at least once every day since she'd been back in town.

"Is there anything else I can help do with your mom?"

"I don't know yet. Henry Cragun is going to come over once we leave the hospital to see if we need assistance getting her inside and settled into her bed."

"That's nice of him. He's a good man, Henry. If he's not around and you ever need an extra pair of hands to help her transfer or anything, give me a call."

His words warmed her, helping to ease some of her panic.

For a crazy moment, she wanted to lean into those wide shoulders and let him take some of her burden. No. She was a strong woman. She could handle it.

"Thanks, but I'm sure we'll be fine. Caitlin and I can handle anything that comes along."

Her niece looked surprised at the vote of confidence but, she thought, pleased.

They spoke for a few more moments to Mike about his background and learned he and Cooper had been pararescue troopers together. Caitlin seemed fascinated, asking him questions about the job, the training required and some of the exotic and remote places where he had performed rescues. She seemed to have no problem talking to Mike but grew tongue-tied when it came to Cooper. Olivia couldn't really blame her.

She felt much the same, though she had calmed considerably from when she first walked into the cafeteria. It was hard to feel threatened when they were at a table next to a couple of big, strapping firefighters.

Mike was telling them about the apartment he was renting on the other side of town when Olivia heard a loud, sharp crashing noise coming from the other side of the cafeteria and all her thoughts of calm left her in a wild rush.

Gunshot!

She wasn't aware of sliding under the table, but the next thing she knew, she was crouched there, heart pounding and hands shaking. She couldn't catch a breath, waiting for screams and yells and panic.

Caitlin. She needed to save Caitlin. She was grabbing at the girl to pull her down, too, but she wouldn't budge. Why wasn't anybody else panicking?

"Easy, ma'am. Somebody just broke some dishes. That's all." Mike Walker gazed down at her with calm, kind, warm dark eyes.

Dishes. Of course. That was what it had been. No one was screaming in terror or shouting out in unrestrained fury.

"Oh. It sounded like…" *Gunshots.* She couldn't say the word, mortified that she had completely overreacted.

Cooper, who was closest to her, stuck a hand out to help her. "It's okay. Come out. Nobody's going to hurt you."

"Unless you happened to cut yourself on the broken plates, anyway," Caitlin pointed out, looking baffled at Olivia's reaction.

More embarrassed than she remembered feeling in her entire life, Olivia ignored Cooper's hand and climbed out on her own, sitting again at the table. She couldn't meet any of their gazes and certainly couldn't have explained to them all why she had completely lost it at such an innocuous sound.

She lifted her coffee to her mouth with a hand that shook and drained it in one swallow.

"I should…check on my mom. She's probably ready to go by now."

"I'm done, too," Caitlin said, rising from the table.

"Are you sure you're all right?" Cooper asked.

No. She hadn't been all right in a week. When would the nightmares and flashbacks leave her alone?

"Fine. Just embarrassed at overreacting."

"No need to be embarrassed," Mike said softly. "We all have things that make us jump."

They were firefighters who ran into burning buildings, she thought as she headed back to her mother's room. They faced danger constantly.

They couldn't know how it felt to receive undeniable proof that you were a coward.

CAITLIN

She didn't want to feel sympathy for Olivia. Caitlin wanted to nurture her anger and hurt against her aunt, this deep sense of betrayal that had been building inside her for months. As they walked back to Mimi's hospital room, all of that seemed to fade, replaced with curiosity and something that felt like pity.

"What was that about? You sliding under the table like it was an active shooter drill at school or something?"

Olivia didn't meet her gaze. "I was startled. That's all. Can we just forget it happened? It was an embarrassing overreaction. I didn't ask—how was your pizza?"

Huh. Did her aunt really think she was that stupid? But if Olivia didn't want to talk about it, Caitlin wasn't going to push.

"Fine."

She had more important things to worry about than Olivia's

weird freak-out, anyway. For one thing, she couldn't believe that she had just sat next to Cooper Vance for fifteen minutes and hadn't been able to find the nerve to ask him more questions about her mother. What was *wrong* with her?

Just the day before, Jake had been bugging her to bring up Natalie with him.

"Everybody says they were best friends. Don't you think he might have known who your dad was?"

"I can't ask," she had protested. "I don't even know him!"

"Chief Vance is a great guy. Not scary at all. He'll answer your questions. If he knows anything, I'm sure he would tell you."

How could she possibly simply blurt out the question? *"Look, I know you were my mom's best friend for years. Do you have any idea who her baby daddy might have been? Any idea at all? I would kind of like to know."*

It should be easy to do but she could never seem to find the words around him. She would stick to the DNA test. That would give her answers and then she would know.

Another week or two. Excitement shivered through her. Soon enough, she would know who her father was. She was close; she sensed it. Soon she would have answers about who she was and where she came from.

Then what?

The question had bothered her since she started looking for her birth father. What if she found the man and discovered he had known all along about her, he just hadn't given a shit?

As always, that thought made her feel a little sick to her stomach. No. She wouldn't believe that. She couldn't.

Instead, she focused on her aunt, who still looked red in the face as they reached Juliet's room.

What the hell had happened back there? Why had Olivia freaked like that?

While she did feel sorry for her, Caitlin also couldn't deny she kind of liked finding out Olivia wasn't perfect.

Her aunt might be successful and cool and always put together. But she could still shriek like a little kid scared by a monster when she heard a loud noise.

Why, though? She wanted to ask again but knew it was a waste of breath.

12

OLIVIA

"Are you good? Can I bring you anything before dinner?"
From the recliner in the whitewashed and timbered front room of Sea Glass Cottage that had become her favorite spot in the week she had been home from the hospital, Juliet gave Olivia a small smile.

"I'm perfectly fine," her mother insisted. "Why wouldn't I be? I have a good book, a glass of water and a view of the ocean. I've told you before. You don't have to hover over me all the time."

What her mother called hovering, Olivia preferred to think of as concern. Juliet wasn't doing as well as Olivia had hoped. A week out of the hospital, she was still in a great deal of pain and struggled to get around, yet she never complained. The ribs seemed almost more painful than the hip, yet she took as few of the prescribed painkillers as she could get away with.

She slept restlessly and had difficulty even with the simplest movements.

She seemed oddly fragile.

Olivia had started sleeping on the sofa outside her mother's room so she could hear Juliet stir and help her to the bathroom if she needed it. Because she was splitting her time between here and the garden center, Olivia had enlisted a willing army of Juliet's friends to sit with her for a few hours in the morning so she could work. They were managing, though Olivia couldn't remember when she had been so tired. It was all she could do to stay awake on these evenings when she worked at her laptop, trying to keep up with Harper Media content for her clients.

The doorbell rang out suddenly, startling both of them. Otis hopped up from the rug and danced to the doorway, then planted his haunches expectantly.

"Are you expecting someone?" she asked her mother. Olivia kept a detailed schedule of when the physical therapist and home care nurses were to come in and out but wondered if she'd missed something.

"I don't think so." She set aside her book as Olivia went to the front door and opened it.

"Oh, Jacob. How are you?" Juliet called to Caitlin's friend, who stood on the doorstep holding a colorful bouquet of flowers.

"Good. Thanks." His smile was sweet and conveyed a maturity that never failed to impress Olivia. She wished she had been half as composed as the young man. "Hi, Mrs. Harper. How are you feeling?"

"Fine. Thank you for asking."

He suddenly seemed to remember the flowers in his hand. "Oh. These are for you, from my dad. He's at a job site today but wanted me to bring over a bouquet from our garden. He said you are particularly fond of the peonies."

"Your father knows me so well, doesn't he?"

Juliet looked more annoyed than pleased by this.

Jake only smiled. "He was sorry he couldn't stop this afternoon but said he will see you when he comes over tomorrow."

"Tomorrow?" Her mother looked slightly alarmed. "What's tomorrow?"

"It's Melody's birthday dinner at The Sea Shanty. Remember?" Olivia said. "We talked about it a few days ago."

"Oh. Right. I forgot which day it was today. They all seem to run together."

"I don't have to go, if you would rather I didn't."

"No. You don't need to miss her birthday on my account. Melody should be out there socializing with her friends. It's part of the healing process. I had just forgotten Henry was coming over, probably because it's completely unnecessary."

"It's not. Caitlin's babysitting for Melody's boys and you can't be alone that long. Henry offered to hang out with you. Problem solved."

"So Henry is *my* babysitter," Juliet said grumpily.

"You can look at it that way. Or you can focus on how nice it will be to spend time with your friend."

"Is Caitlin in her room?" Jake asked, obviously uncomfortable with the conversation. "I'm helping her study for a Spanish test."

"She is," Olivia answered. "You can go up."

The boy bounded out of the living room and up the stairs with all the enthusiasm and grace of his father's Labrador retriever.

"He's a good boy," Juliet said, admiring the flowers Olivia was arranging into a vase. "Always so kind and considerate."

"Like his father," Olivia said, earning a pointed look from her mother.

"I can cancel," she finally said, when Juliet continued to look obstinate. "Mel has other friends who will be there to celebrate her birthday. I can take her out another night, just the two of us, when Caitlin can be available to stay with you."

Juliet sighed. "No. Henry and I will be fine. We can watch a few more episodes of *Doctor Who*. We're almost done with the season we've been watching and will be moving on to the next Doctor."

Her mother and Henry were perfect together. Why couldn't Juliet see what everyone else did?

CAITLIN

Jake looked over the list of names he and Caitlin had examined endlessly. She was sprawled out in the window seat overlooking the ocean while Jake was sitting in the hammock chair Juliet had let her hang from a support beam in her bedroom, the one where she did most of her studying.

"What are you going to do if your father turns out to be none of these guys?"

She wouldn't even consider that possibility. "He has to be. I have scoured through every page of both my mom's and Olivia's journals. My mom mentions three names around the time I'm sure she got pregnant with me. One of them has to be my dad."

Jake didn't roll his eyes at her, but Caitlin could tell he wanted to. "I have to say this again. You're being shortsighted. You can't know that for sure. It's always possible Natalie didn't write down his name. And it's more than possible that Olivia didn't know everyone your mom was hanging around with. She was only thirteen or fourteen, right? I would guess there are plenty of things your mom never told her younger sister."

This was the same argument he had been giving since she started out on this quest, that she might be going through all this effort and still have nothing to show for it.

"I know. But I have to start somewhere, don't I? The diaries are all I have."

He gave her a careful look. "I just don't want you to be disappointed. What's going to happen when your DNA tests come back without any connection to another soul in Cape Sanctuary."

"It's possible," she said. Even probable, though she wouldn't admit that to Jake. "I'll just have to assume that none of my dad's relatives took the same test."

"You're prepared for that?"

"Yeah. Of course I am," she lied. She was pinning all her hopes on the test and would be devastated if she couldn't find any results, but she wasn't about to tell Jake that.

"Even though it might not be any of them, you still want to check them out?"

She shrugged. "I just want to get to know them more. See if there's any kind of instant bond between us, you know. I thought maybe I might be able to get them to talk about my mom."

"How, exactly, do you intend to do that?"

She loved Jake but he was always such a doubter.

"I'll wing it. So let's go through the names again."

"Coach Hardcastle, Paul Reyes, Jeff Seeger," Jake recited from memory.

"Right. Coach Hardcastle is a strong contender. He dated my mom a few times in high school. He's mentioned in the journal and she liked him a lot."

"Paul Reyes, who used to party with your mom and whose youngest daughter, Melissa, goes to school with us."

"Exactly. I know they had an affair, even though he was married at the time and already had a couple of kids. Melissa's older siblings."

That was the creepiest of the possibilities and she couldn't imagine why her mom even used to hang around with him when he already had a wife and kids. It was another mystery into Natalie and one she knew she'd never solve.

"And Jeff Seeger," Caitlin said.

"Pastor at the church on Shell Street."

"That's right. Pastor Seeger, who used to be my mom's pot dealer."

"It could be any of them. Or none. How do you expect to talk to them without revealing your suspicions?"

"Well, I've signed up to take German instead of Spanish next year, which Coach Hardcastle teaches. And I've already been to Melissa Reyes's house once to hang out, but her dad wasn't there. I thought maybe I'd see if I could talk her into inviting me over again somehow."

"And Pastor Seeger?"

She gave her partner in crime a long look. "How do you feel about checking out a new church youth group with me this week?"

Jake sighed, showing no sign of surprise. "Do we have to?"

"You don't, but I'm planning to go. He's a really promising possibility. My mom mentioned meeting up with him a lot in her journal. A girl who sits next to me in social studies goes there, so I asked her about it. She was excited to tell me all about it. She says Pastor Jeff is cool."

"I still can't believe your mom's dealer is now a pastor. Maybe it's a completely different Jeff Seeger."

"I won't know unless I ask him. I'm going Thursday. They only meet once a month and that's the next time."

"You've been thinking about this awhile, haven't you?"

All the time. Somehow reading those journals had made her feel closer than she ever had before to her mother, which led her, naturally, to want to find out more about her father.

"I just really want to know. If you were in my shoes, you would, too."

"First, I would be happy that I have a loving grandma and aunt who have taken care of me all these years," he said. "But, yeah. I would probably want to know."

"So will you come with me?"

He shrugged, swinging the hammock with his foot. "Sure. I've got nothing else to do. Only mountains of homework to wrap up the school year."

She smiled and touched his hand. "You're the best, Jake. I mean it. I don't know what I would do without you."

He gave her a long look, one she couldn't quite figure out. Whenever he looked at her like that, she felt like she'd just dived from the cliffs into the Pacific.

She had to stop being stupid about that. Jake wasn't interested in her romantically. He was her best friend but that was all and she wasn't about to ruin what they had by twisting his reaction into something it wasn't.

She had too many things going on right now. Her life was so stressful, with Mimi's injury and Olivia's return. Jake was like a steady lighthouse on a stormy day, reaching out to find her and bring her home safely, no matter what else was going on in her world.

"When do you think the results will come back from the DNA test?"

"It has to be soon," she answered. "The website said four to six weeks and it's been almost four."

"Again, you know you might be right where you started, with no more information about your father than you have now."

"I know. But I might find him, too. I had to take the chance."

If she ended up disappointed, at least she would know that she tried, and she would never forget that Jake had been willing to help her every step of the way.

1 3

JULIET

Sometimes her daughter left her so exasperated, she wanted to scream. Not loudly. Just enough to get her attention and make her see how silly she was being. Instead, Juliet petted Olivia's cute little chi-poo, Otis, and tried not to show her annoyance.

"I thought we settled this already. You're going out tonight and Henry's coming over to watch *Doctor Who* with me."

Olivia sighed. "We did. Or I thought we did. But you've had such a difficult day and I have so much work to do, catching up with payroll and orders from the garden center and also trying to work on this big campaign one of my clients is doing to push their new line of services. I don't feel good about leaving you and everything on my to-do list so I can go socialize."

"Stop that right now. Your to-do list can wait until morning, can't it?"

Olivia didn't answer, only looked overwhelmed, which made

Juliet feel guilty and worthless. Right now, her own to-do list was ridiculously empty, consisting of only *finish a chapter* and *take your medicine on schedule.*

"Melody needs you more than I do tonight," she went on. "That girl has had a terrible year, filled with disappointment and betrayal. For once, she's being kind to herself by letting some of her friends celebrate her birthday with her. A good friend would do everything she could to support that, not look for excuses to wriggle out."

Oh, the classic guilt trip. Juliet experienced a qualm at employing it but only for a minute. She felt worse at the idea of Olivia sacrificing the opportunity to lift a friend who needed her because she felt she had to stay here at Sea Glass Cottage with Juliet.

Even if that meant spending the evening with Henry.

The doorbell rang through the house before Olivia had a moment to reply and Otis jumped off Juliet's lap with his surprising agility.

"That will be Henry," Olivia said with a sigh. "I suppose it won't hurt to leave you in his capable hands for one night."

The pain medication was sending her imagination into overdrive. That was all. She did *not* need to think about Henry Cragun's capable hands right now. Still, the image was in her head now. Her face felt hot suddenly, her breathing shallow.

"Go celebrate with Melody. We will be fine," she insisted. "I would be perfectly fine on my own, which I've told you again and again, but of course nobody around here listens to me."

Olivia ignored her, which didn't surprise Juliet at all, and opened the door.

"Hi, Henry."

He was carrying two reusable grocery bags and wore a smile that made Juliet's skin feel prickly and hot.

"Hi, Olivia. You look lovely tonight. I hope somebody has

warned the men of Cape Sanctuary to leave their hearts at home tonight unless they want them broken."

"Yes. That was exactly the message I Tweeted a few minutes ago." Olivia gave a rueful shake of her head but couldn't quite hide her smile.

As Henry and Olivia smiled at each other, Juliet was aware of a stupid, wholly unreasonable quiver of jealousy.

The two of them were only about fifteen years apart, not an unreasonable span when the man was older than the woman. Yes, that was a traditional, patriarchal idea but unavoidable.

In the eyes of many, that fifteen-year gap was virtually insignificant, as long as Olivia was the younger of them. How unfair that Juliet's eight years of seniority should loom so largely between them.

Of course, it seemed to bother *her* more than anyone else. Was she the misogynist?

"Thanks for being available tonight," Olivia said. "I still don't feel good about Mom being alone right now, in case she falls or needs something she can't reach. I think another few days and she'll be fine on her own for brief periods of time."

"I'm so glad you called. I would have been sitting at home watching a baseball game anyway. This is much more fun."

"You have a strange idea of fun, if you think hanging around babysitting an invalid will be at all entertaining," Juliet snapped, then felt crusty and cranky, like a sour old lady in need of a nap.

He ignored her, just like everyone else did, and held up his bags. "I brought things to make dinner. I hope you haven't eaten. I thought I would make linguine and clams, since I know how much you like it."

Juliet's appetite seemed to have disappeared since her accident, thanks mostly to the painkillers she hated, but her mouth watered suddenly. She really did love his linguine with white clam sauce, which he made with fresh butter and Italian parsley.

"That sounds delicious," Olivia said.

"I would offer to save you some leftovers but we usually don't have any," Henry said.

Still looking reluctant, she picked up a large purse from the entry table. "I shouldn't be too late."

"Take your time. We'll be fine," Henry assured her.

Juliet wasn't so certain. She wasn't sure it was a good idea to be alone with him right now, when she was feeling so weak and vulnerable.

"Don't forget to take a jacket," she said as her daughter was leaving. "Evenings are still cool here."

Okay, her daughter was thirty. But Juliet would always be her mother and would always worry about her, whether Olivia liked it or not.

Her daughter lifted her bag. "Got one in here. Along with an umbrella, pepper spray, a flashlight and an extra phone charger."

"Sounds like you're covered," Henry said.

"You can't be too careful," Juliet said, feeling even more like an old lady with every passing moment.

"You two have fun. Thanks again, Henry."

The house, her refuge and her sanctuary, seemed to echo with emptiness after Olivia left. Otis stood at the door for a moment, as if making sure his owner wasn't coming right back. Eventually he wandered back over to Juliet, who ignored the pain and scooped down to lift him into her lap.

"You could let me do that for you."

"He only weighs five or six pounds. I should be good." She paused. "I know you told Olivia you would stay here the whole time but you really don't have to."

"I'm staying. I'm looking forward to it. Why wouldn't I be? It's a lovely spring evening in Cape Sanctuary. You've got the windows open. I can smell the flowers and the sea and I can hear the sound of the waves. What's not to love?"

Juliet sighed. Why did he have to be so blasted cheerful all the time? She hurt and wanted to wallow in her misery. That was extremely hard to manage around Henry Cragun.

"I'm going to start dinner."

"I can help."

"Not necessary. You stay right there and let me wait on you for once, unless you'd rather go outside."

"I would enjoy that," she admitted. She felt as if she had been cooped up inside for months. This was a horrible time of year to be down with an injury. Spring was the most glorious season here in Cape Sanctuary and she was missing it because of a single act of stupidity. "I would love to go out to the back terrace but I don't think we can manage. You could just wheel me out to the porch."

"Why can't we go out back?" he asked, with the air of a man who had just been issued a challenge.

"Because you built the ramp out front. To use the terrace, you would have to wheel me around on the grass. It will be too hard."

It sounded ridiculous when she said it aloud. Why would he have trouble, for heaven's sake? The man worked outside all day digging holes for plants, carting around hundred-pound bags full of mulch.

"We should absolutely eat out there. Do you want to go out now or when dinner is ready? The pasta is quick. It should only take me about twenty minutes."

"I'm good here for now." He was right. Why wouldn't she be good? She had the dog, the breeze, her book and the added advantage of being able to enjoy the guilty pleasure of watching him cook.

She settled in her recliner while he went to work, grateful for the open floor plan on this level of the cottage that allowed her a clear view into the kitchen.

Through the windows, she could hear the sound of the sea below, merging in a pleasant symphony with the sound of Otis snoring, the clatter of pans in the kitchen and one of her cats purring from the back of the sofa.

Eventually she gave up reading her book and just watched him work.

"That smells so good," she said sometime later.

"It's almost done. While the pasta cooks and the sauce simmers, let's get you outside. How can I help you transfer?"

This was the humiliating part, but she would simply have to endure it. "I need the walker to help me stand and then the wheelchair."

He brought both things over to her and stood at her side while she went through the difficult and onerous task of transferring from the recliner to the wheelchair.

"I wish you would just let me lift you."

She shivered at the thought of being in his arms and had to hope he didn't notice. "That would be easier right now, but you're not always here and Olivia can't lift me. It's good for me to practice transferring myself."

The doctor had told her to expect things to be hard like this for the first month. Then she would gain a little more mobility. After a week, she was already better at it.

Once she was settled in the chair, with Olivia's dog on her lap, he pushed her outside into the soft perfection of a coastal evening.

Years ago, she had landscaped a hard-packed gravel walkway from the front yard to the back garden. The wheelchair's big wheels still seemed to catch on the gravel, but Henry was able to power through and push her without too much bumping to the wide back flagstone patio overlooking the Pacific.

"I do love the view you have here."

"You have virtually the same view down the hill," she had to point out.

"Maybe. But there's something magical about this particular spot."

She couldn't argue. When Steve had inherited the house from his parents, it had been ramshackle, worn down by years of neglect. They had worked hard to make it shine, inside and out.

Right now the garden felt ramshackle and overgrown to her. Even on a good year when she was capable of working in it, she didn't feel like she had things under control until June or July. She was always too busy at the garden center, helping other people create perfection in their outer space, and couldn't focus here on her own garden until things slowed down.

This year would be worse. She couldn't ask Olivia to take care of the flower gardens at the cottage in addition to everything else she was doing, but maybe she could hire a yard service to at least maintain it.

Even with that wild, slightly unkempt air, it was still undeniably beautiful, colorful and bright against the deep, dark ocean background.

"Is this good?" Henry asked as he rolled her chair to the wrought iron table.

"Perfect."

"Give me a moment to finish up in the kitchen. Then I'll bring you out a plate."

She wasn't used to being waited on. It went against every instinct she had. She was usually the one helping others. This past week, she had tried, but it never seemed to get easier.

A few moments later, Henry walked out the back door and down the steps carrying two plates of pasta.

"I forgot to ask if I can get you something to drink."

"I had better stick to water. Painkillers, remember."

"Of course." After setting down the plates, he returned to the house then brought out a couple of glasses of water and silverware.

"Wow. This looks terrific."

"You're the one who told me everybody needs one show-off dish. This is mine."

She wanted to tell him he didn't have to show off for her. They were longtime friends, with no need for pretense or grandstanding, but she was too busy enjoying the clams and the lemon butter sauce.

The evening was beautiful, the scent of the sea mingling with the flowers in her wild mess of a garden. Except for the pain, her constant companion, it was the most perfect evening she'd known in a long time.

"Tell me what's going on in your world these days," Juliet said. She was tired of how self-absorbed she had become because of her accident. Every conversation seemed to revolve around her, much to her chagrin. She hadn't realized until now how exhausting it all was.

He expertly twisted pasta onto his fork before answering. "Busy. This time of year is always frenetic."

"I get it. Everybody thinks their project is the most important thing on the planet and every single element has to be finished right this minute."

"Exactly. I've told you about that resort I'm working on down the coast."

"Hidden Creek. Do you finally have approval for your plan?"

"Yeah. This week. I got a call a few days ago saying they love it and want everything done so that they can open June 1."

She shook her head in dismay as she scooped a little neck clam from the shell. "That's hardly a month. Do they think they're your only client?"

"Apparently."

"I knew you had more urgent things to do than babysit me. You probably have a million things to take care of right now."

"Things are progressing," he said. "But I've hit one roadblock on the job and was actually hoping to get your input on it."

"Of course!"

They often discussed his landscaping projects. She was always flattered that he seemed to value her opinion.

152

"I've got one section that's giving me problems. It's south-facing but fairly acidic soil, and the project manager wants a garden that will have visual interest through all four seasons."

"Tricky."

"Right? I came up with a plan for it, but I'm not sure it's going to work, given all the site parameters. I'd love you to look it over and offer any suggestions."

"Of course! If you want to bring me over the plan and maybe some photographs of the site, I can take a look. If you have drone shots, that would be especially helpful."

"I do have all that." He gave her an appraising look. "It would be better if you could make a quick visit out there with me. Do you think you might be up for that, maybe next week or the week after? I think being able to see the actual site would be helpful."

A road trip. Could she do it? Her pain had begun to recede more every day, but how would she do on a road trip for at least an hour or more?

"I don't want to push you, though," Henry said quickly. "I can work on everything else and this section can wait until you're feeling better."

"Next week might work. I would just be riding in the car, right?"

"Yes. I hate to ask. Normally, I know you would never have time, especially this time of year."

"Right now I have nothing but time," she said, trying not to sound too glum.

"You would be helping me out so much. But I don't want to push you, if you don't think you'd be up for it. The drive to the resort takes about an hour. Then I figured we would spend another half hour to an hour looking around, then another hour home. Is that feasible?"

Two and a half hours, roughly. She could make it that long, couldn't she? "I think so. But I should probably wait until next week to be sure. I wouldn't want to promise something I can't deliver. I do feel better every day. Maybe toward the end of next week, I'll be ready for a road trip."

"Fair enough."

"Meanwhile, it would help if I could look over the plans."

"Excellent. I'll drop them off later this week."

They talked about other projects he was working on as they finished the meal while the sun began to slowly dip into the ocean.

A cool wind blew through the trees, making the flowers dance and sway. She shivered a little, which Henry didn't miss.

"You're cold. Let's get you back. Then I'll clear these dishes."

She only really needed a sweater or a throw, and she was enjoying the garden so much, she didn't want to go inside. Still, it was nearly dark and she knew it would only get colder.

He took as much care as before wheeling her back across the packed gravel walkway and into the house.

"Thank you again for the ramp," she said as he opened the front door for her. "I really would have been lost without it. I certainly wouldn't have been able to come home. I suppose I would have tolerated a rehab center. They're all very nice. But this is much better."

"You belong here at Sea Glass Cottage," he said gruffly, which she found quite the sweetest thing he could possibly have said.

"Now, I can help you into bed if you're tired or we can watch the Doctor. Up to you."

It wasn't yet 8:00 p.m. Even if she was exhausted, she wasn't about to go to bed this early.

"Doctor," she answered promptly.

He smiled. "I was hoping you'd say that. I've been dying to find out what happened but didn't want to cheat and watch ahead without you."

"I almost streamed an episode in the hospital, but at the last moment I chose something else instead."

"Excellent." He smiled and she tried not to stare. "Where's the most comfortable spot for you? I'll get you settled, then go clear up the dishes."

"Not this wheelchair, that's for sure. How about back into the recliner?"

"You got it."

Before she realized what he intended, and before she could tell him again that she was perfectly capable of transferring, he scooped her out of the wheelchair, taking care with her hip.

His body was warm, his muscles hard against her, and he smelled delicious. He always did. He must use some secret kind of fabric softener. She wanted to lean into him, throw her arms around his neck and stay right here all evening, nestled against him.

Too soon, he carefully lowered her to the recliner.

"How's that?"

So good. She fought the urge to ask him if he would mind terribly just holding her again.

"I'm great, for now. Thank you. You do know I can transfer myself, right? You saw me do it earlier. I'm not completely helpless."

"Maybe I just like taking care of you."

A lump rose in her throat at his words and she wanted to burrow into him all over again. Since Steve died, she had fought every battle by herself. Losing Natalie, raising Caitlin, running the garden center.

Wouldn't it be heavenly to have someone by her side, someone willing to walk beside her and let her lean against for support when she needed it?

Juliet swallowed a sigh. Henry was her dear friend and she cared about him too much to add another burden to his life.

"I need to clean up my mess in the kitchen. Are you good?"

"I have my book. I'm fine. Thanks."

After he walked back outside for their dishes, her older cat,

Felicity, came over and rubbed against her leg. She didn't know where Felix was. Probably under the sofa being his usual obstinate self.

Before she could pick up Felicity, Otis trotted over and scrambled up into her lap, the little rascal. Felicity gave her a disgruntled look and wandered into the kitchen for water.

The cats had come to tolerate the little dog and she thought perhaps they secretly enjoyed having someone new in the house. She certainly did, far more than she'd expected. Maybe she wasn't as set in her ways as she thought.

She petted him absently, her mind still on Henry and all the things that could never be between them.

14

OLIVIA

She stood outside the faded turquoise door of The Sea Shanty with her stomach in knots and her palms sweating.

Music thrummed into the night and she could hear the clink of glasses, the thud of billiards, the hum of conversation. It all sounded perfectly harmless, the kind of scene playing out at bars all over the world.

The chance of anything dangerous happening inside the tavern was as remote as it would have been the other day at the hospital cafeteria or the day she had stood outside the Kozy Kitchen near her apartment in Seattle.

She knew she would be perfectly safe. She wanted to celebrate Melody's birthday with her. To do that, she would have to override her brain's annoying, panicky new wiring in order to push open the door and go inside.

She could tell herself that a thousand times but she still couldn't bring herself to do it.

This was getting ridiculous. In the nearly three weeks since the attack she'd witnessed, she seemed to be becoming more anxious, not less, about going into public areas.

Was she really going to let her cowardice control the rest of her life?

"What are you doing out here? Trying to decide whether to go in?"

She tensed at the familiar voice and turned around to find Cooper Vance walking up to The Shanty, wearing a curious expression.

"Something like that."

"We can't offer the kind of entertainment you're probably used to in Seattle, but the cover band is a local favorite. They're not bad, which I think is why Melody wanted to come here for her birthday celebration instead of going to The Lookout."

"I'm sure they're great."

"Then why are you out here instead of in there?"

She couldn't tell him what a coward she was. Cooper would never understand. The man risked his life on a daily basis to help others.

"It's been a long few days. I'm worried about my mom and not really in the greatest mood to party. I guess I was trying to gear up for it. But I'll do my best, for Mel's sake."

He gave her a long look. "You're a good friend to my sister. I appreciate that."

She hadn't been but she didn't want to argue with him.

"Do you need a few more minutes out here?"

She mustered a smile. "I think I'm ready."

When he opened the door, the noise blasted through, a bluegrass band that wasn't half-bad. She followed him inside, wondering if she was betraying the sisterhood by finding so much comfort and security in the presence of the big, tough fire chief. She couldn't help thinking that any threat would have to go through Cooper first and nobody in their right mind would want to tangle with him.

Of course, he had been right next to her that day in the hospital cafeteria and she had still panicked. But she would try to do better.

They found Melody and a group of about six others at a table in the back. Cooper's sister looked happier than Olivia had seen her since returning to town.

"There you both are," she exclaimed. "I was afraid you wouldn't make it."

"Sorry, sis. We had a call just as I was walking out the door." Cooper kissed his sister and waved to everyone at the table before taking a seat across from Melody.

I was here ten minutes ago but was busy trying to get up my nerve to walk inside.

Olivia didn't want to admit that, so she smiled instead. "Happy birthday, darling. I'm so happy I can be here to celebrate with you."

"So am I." Melody beamed. "Everybody, you all know Olivia Harper. Juliet's daughter."

"Oh, how is your mother?" someone she didn't know asked.

Olivia forced a smile at the question that was becoming entirely too familiar. "She's fine. I think she's feeling better every day."

"I was so sorry to hear about her accident," another woman said.

"I didn't know until yesterday and felt awful that I haven't been by yet," the first one said. "Is she home now? Is she up for visitors?"

"Yes. She's been home about a week. And she's had a nonstop stream of them since the accident. She would love to see you, I'm sure. If you don't have her contact info, let me know and I can put you in touch with her."

"Sit," Bea Romero urged. The only empty seat at the big

table was next to Cooper. After an awkward little moment of hesitation, she sat down.

Now that they were inside The Sea Shanty, she wasn't eager to be this close to him for the entire evening when she was fighting this ridiculous attraction. She couldn't see a choice, though, unless she asked someone else to trade places with her.

A server she thought she recognized as a previous neighbor came over and set down cocktail napkins in front of them. "What are we drinking?"

She gave her order and Cooper did the same.

"I haven't been here in forever," she commented after the woman walked away. "Oddly, I don't think it's changed at all. I think they even have some of the same posters on the walls they had when I was in college."

It wasn't exactly a dive. In fact, The Sea Shanty gave off a distinctly retro vibe that would have made it a hit among Seattle hipsters. She settled in to enjoy the band and being with friends, though she kept one eye on the door the whole time.

"How's your social media business going?" Beatriz asked. "Your mom has nothing but good things to say about you whenever I ask. According to Juliet, you're becoming the go-to social media marketing maven in the Pacific Northwest."

Her mom had said *that*? She blinked, not sure how to respond. "I wouldn't go that far. But things have been good. I stay busy."

She actually had far more work than she could handle, though she was very selective about her client list. She was going to have to either add more consultants or start contracting out some of it.

"You were a great help spreading the word about our Arts and Hearts on the Cape project last year," Bea went on. "Our likes and shares went up like crazy on social media after you stepped in to handle it. Aunt Stella was thrilled!"

Bea's aunt ran a nonprofit aimed at helping encourage and support foster families. Each year the organization hosted an arts festival in Cape Sanctuary that drew in tens of thousands of people.

"I was happy to help, especially for a good cause."

Rosemary Duncan, a friend of Juliet's who had been mayor of Cape Sanctuary for a decade or more, was sitting across from Bea. She seemed to sit up straighter during their conversation.

"That's right! I had forgotten you have a social media marketing start-up. You might be just the person we need!"

Olivia tried not to flinch. She was used to this kind of thing at social occasions. When people found out what she did on the side, they often asked her to help them get the word out about their own start-up or their brother's new indie record album or the lemonade stand their kid was running.

"Do you remember Pete Gallegos?" Rosemary asked.

Now, *that* was a name that dredged up memories. "Of course. He was a good friend of my father's and worked with him in the fire department. We always used to go camping with him and Sheila and their kids."

She hadn't thought about the Gallegos family in years, though she knew her mother remained close with both of them.

Pete had been there the night her father died. He had responded quickly and had been on the scene shortly after Cooper. He had been the one to pull Cooper away from his frantic efforts to do CPR.

He had been so very kind to her and Nat and Juliet at the funeral and after, she remembered.

"Maybe you don't know," the mayor went on, "but he was diagnosed with Parkinson's disease a couple years ago."

"Oh. That's too bad! I hadn't heard."

"It is a shame. That's why he had to step down as fire chief."

He had always been vigorous and healthy, she remembered, always in competition with her father to see who was stronger in fitness tests for the department.

"We've been sorry to lose him but were so glad we could

bring in Cooper, here, to fill his shoes and helm the department. He's done an excellent job."

"Try to fill his shoes, anyway," Cooper said with a rueful expression. "Pete is a tough act to follow."

"You're doing a great job," Rosemary assured him. "Everybody is happy. You know I just have one complaint. We've talked about it before."

That he was too gorgeous? That she wouldn't be surprised if women were calling in fake 911 calls, just to have him come to the door in his EMT uniform?

"Cooper Vance has a flaw?" Bea Romero asked with a teasing look. "I can't believe it."

"Would you like the list in alphabetical order?" his sister asked, making everyone laugh.

Rosemary chuckled, too. "It's not a huge flaw, all things considered, but a problem right now nonetheless. He refuses to use social media to spread the word in the community about what his department is doing."

Cooper sipped at his beer. "I'm here to help people, not post Instagram pictures of what we're having for dinner every night at the firehouse."

Rosemary made a face. "I don't want you to do that, although there are plenty of people who would be all over that kind of thing."

A woman Olivia didn't know raised her hand at the end of the table, earning another round of laughs.

"As much as you might dislike it, we do have to get the word out about special activities, like the fund-raiser you're doing for Pete and Sheila."

She turned to Olivia. "Unfortunately, Pete has started having to use a wheelchair recently and we were hoping we could raise enough for modifications to their house and also a van with a ramp to help Sheila get him to doctor's appointments."

"Sounds like a worthwhile project." Exactly the sort of thing the people of Cape Sanctuary tended to rally around.

"Where do I come in?" she asked, though she thought she knew the answer. She'd been down this road before.

"Any chance you might be able to help us out like you did the Open Hearts Foundation? Stella couldn't stop raving about all the interactions they had as a direct result of your efforts."

"What kind of fund-raiser?" she asked warily.

"A pancake breakfast at the fire station, two weeks from today. It was Cooper's idea, actually."

"Pete is a great guy who dedicated his whole life to helping his community," Cooper said, his voice gruff. "We're just trying to give back a little."

"It would be great if we could give back a *lot* and make a real difference in their lives," the mayor said.

Olivia wanted to refuse. Between overseeing the garden center, taking care of her mom, corralling Caitlin and trying to work on projects for her employer *and* her Harper Media clients, she didn't have a clue how she could take on one more thing.

How could she say no, though? Pete had always been good to her family. If she could help in some small way with the trials he was facing now, she didn't see how she could refuse.

"Sure. I could do something."

Rosemary's lined features lit up. "Excellent. That's wonderful news. Where should we start?"

"I'll take a look at what you've already done and see where we can give a few nudges. We can talk about a budget for running carefully targeted ads to select populations, both in the area and slightly beyond, and make sure we're smart with the timing of the posts for best coverage."

"All of that sounds excellent." Rosemary beamed. "Thank you so much."

"You're welcome," she said, already trying to figure out where in her crowded schedule she might find room.

"I would love to engage more people in the community with what our public safety departments are doing. You would truly convince me you're a miracle worker if you can give Chief Vance here some media training. He hardly even checks his text messages."

"I check my messages," Cooper replied. "But I have a rule that any conversation requiring more than five back-and-forth texts should be handled by a phone call."

"Not everybody loves technology. I get that," the mayor said with a fond smile.

"I don't mind technology," he protested. "You make me seem like some kind of a Luddite. I'm not. We lose sight that sometimes the old-fashioned way can still be better. I can communicate more in a five-minute phone call than I can by having a text conversation that takes all afternoon."

"Agreed," Rosemary said. "But you can't have a phone call with everyone in town whenever there's an incident that needs to be reported, for the public interest. Maybe Olivia could help you kick things up a notch on the social media front. That's all I'm asking. She's an expert, with clients around the world. We're lucky to have her here in our little corner of it."

At his pained look, Olivia had to smile. "I can try to make it as painless as possible. With a few tweaks, such as post scheduling, we can make a big difference. Maybe you can designate someone else in your department to handle that."

She really didn't need another excuse to spend more time with Cooper when she was already having a tough time getting him out of her head.

"I'll think about it," he answered.

To her relief and his, the band started up again, making conversation difficult.

She sipped her drink, listening to the animated conversation at the table and wondering how early she could safely leave

164

without offending Melody. She was just about to make some kind of excuse when Cooper turned to her. "Want to dance?"

She gaped, completely not expecting the invitation. The music was slow and sultry now, heavy on the saxophone. She could feel it vibrate through her. A dozen other couples had taken to the small dance floor in the bar, including two couples from Melody's birthday celebration.

If she were smart, she would try to come up with some excuse, but she couldn't come up with anything on the fly.

"Um. Sure," she answered. "This is a great song. Plus, I could spend the whole time introducing you to the joys of algorithms and analytics."

"Great. Can't wait."

He rose and held a hand out to her. With a deep breath, she slipped her hand into his and let him lead her out to the dance floor.

COOPER

Why had he asked Olivia to dance?

Halfway through the song, he still didn't have a good answer. The invitation had rolled out of him, impulsive and ill-considered. He should be doing his best to keep her at arm's length. Instead, he was looking for any excuse to hold her.

It was heavenly, he had to admit. He wasn't a dancing kind of guy, usually preferring to sit on the sidelines and enjoy the music in these kinds of situations. This dance with Olivia just might change his mind about that. Holding her was as perfect as he might have imagined. She was warm and soft, and she smelled delicious, like apples and vanilla.

When was the last time he had danced with a beautiful woman?

Cooper scanned through recent memories and came up blank

except for the wedding of some friends the summer before, when he had danced with the bride.

Apparently it had been too long. He had forgotten the delicious lethargy that seeped through his bones, how he wanted to close his eyes and sway to the music, enjoying every moment of having her in his arms.

Who would have guessed that the somewhat abrasive, nose-in-book Olivia would have such an effect on him, all these years later?

She hummed to the song, seeming much more relaxed than the anxious, nervous woman he had encountered outside the bar.

He was glad. While he wanted to take credit, he knew that would be typical male arrogance. He sensed it had more to do with being in comfortable, familiar surroundings along with friends and neighbors in an easygoing celebration.

What had made her so jumpy? He thought of her fear the other day at the hospital cafeteria, how she had looked around the place like she expected an imminent attack. He didn't like thinking about it, or the protectiveness that made him want to tuck her close and keep her safe all night.

"So what happened to you?"

She stiffened slightly, but she quickly recovered, arching an eyebrow and meeting his gaze. "That's a blunt question. And also rather vague. Would you like to be more specific?"

"I'm a blunt guy. And you know what I mean. The other day at the hospital cafeteria and then tonight, outside the bar. You seemed a little…nervous."

He didn't think she would appreciate it if he told her she had seemed jumpier than a bag full of frogs.

Her mouth tightened. "Maybe I'm just not a fan of crowded bars. Or crowded cafeterias, either."

She obviously didn't want to tell him. Why should she? They didn't have that kind of relationship, really. He was just a guy who had once been friends with her sister.

"I'm not crazy about this bar, anyway. I was shocked when Melody said this was where she wanted to celebrate her birthday."

"The band is good," she pointed out. "And I can't blame her for wanting to enjoy a little nightlife. She hardly ever gets the chance to go out."

"Agreed. But The Sea Shanty? Really? I just wish Cape Sanctuary had a little wider selection of nightlife."

They danced for a moment in silence, the music weaving a spell around them that Cooper found as seductive as it was troublesome.

"Why did you come back?" she asked after a moment. "I always thought you hated it here and couldn't wait to leave Cape Sanctuary."

Surprise made him stumble but quickly catch the beat of the music again.

He hadn't hated it here. Not really. The town had a gorgeous setting beside the sea and plenty of kind people. Still, Cooper had never been able to see a future for himself here. He had too many difficult memories of his childhood, being the son of the town screwup. He was tired of being an object of pity and scorn, of hearing the whispers. After his mother died and their aunt and uncle offered to take Melody in for her remaining high school years, he had jumped at the chance to sign up for the Air Force and let the military give him a second chance.

"I never hated it," he protested. "I left for the military."

"And didn't look back."

"I'm here now."

"Because of Melody."

How had she guessed that? He shifted, uncomfortable with her scrutiny. "Yeah. Because of Melody. She doesn't have any other family here now that Aunt Helen is in San Diego, and her boys take a lot of energy. They're too much for her to handle on her own."

"So once more, Cooper steps in to save the day."

"That's what families do. Aren't you back in town only because your mom needs your help?"

"Point taken." She smiled, her features soft and lovely, and he wanted to brush a thumb over that tiny dimple in her cheek. More than that, he had a sudden fierce urge to press his mouth to the corner of her smile.

"Mel starts next week at the garden center. She probably told you."

He glanced over at his sister, sitting among her friends and trying to hide her pain and loss with forced animation. "Yeah. She's excited about it. The job will be terrific for her. She needs to get out and she has always loved gardening. You won't be sorry you hired her."

"It was a brilliant idea. I can't believe I didn't think of it myself. I owe you one."

He hadn't really done anything, but that didn't stop him from coming up with a dozen ways he would like to have her repay him. He could share none of them with her, of course.

The song segued to another slow song. He really ought to leave the dance floor but he found himself strangely hesitant. One more song, he told himself. Then he would lead her back to the group and do his best to put this inconvenient attraction out of his mind.

15

OLIVIA

As the band led into another song, Olivia waited for Cooper to stop dancing and return them to his sister and her friends. When he continued swaying with the slow, sultry song, she decided she was enjoying herself too much to say anything.

Other than a few nightclubs in college and a tango class she took when she first moved to Seattle, she hadn't danced with someone in a very long time.

That was a true shame. There was something so sensual about it.

She closed her eyes, inhaling the scent of him, masculine, clean, some sort of woodsy soap with a hint of aftershave. The muscles beneath her hands were strong, taut, and she couldn't help thinking that these muscles saved lives and helped people protect their property.

Again, it seemed a betrayal of the girl power movement she so strongly believed in, but everything inside her wanted to nestle against him, safe in his arms.

She fought the urge to rest her cheek against his chest and listen to his heartbeat. *Let's not get carried away or anything.*

She could easily see herself making a fool of herself if she wasn't careful. There could never be anything between them and she needed to remember that. This was Cooper Vance. Her best friend's brother. Her sister's best friend. Her childhood crush.

The man who had tried and failed to save her father.

Their history was entirely too tangled and complicated for her to unravel during the short time she would be in Cape Sanctuary.

The song was almost over when a shriek rang out from the corner of the tavern.

A few other people cried out and Olivia almost dived for cover until she heard the follow-up cry.

"Help! My sister! Someone help her!"

If she had any doubt that Cooper Vance was a first responder to the bone, that was eradicated in one single instant. He whirled on the spot, dropping his arms from her and rushing to a nearby table.

She stood on the dance floor, not sure what to do. He might need help. She couldn't do much but she could at least call 911.

She hurried to join him in time to watch Cooper lower a woman about her own age to the floor.

"Does your sister have any allergies or any history of heart or lung problems?" he asked, his voice as calm as a summer breeze.

Another woman stood nearby, expression frantic and her hands shaking.

"She's allergic to shellfish. But we didn't order shellfish or anything with shellfish in it! I've never seen her have this reaction. She said she was having trouble breathing and then she just passed out."

"Does she have an EpiPen?"

"She always carries one, but I couldn't find it on her. She switched purses at the last minute. I…I wonder if she forgot to put it in her bag."

He adjusted the woman's head, which looked swollen and

blotchy, and felt for a pulse. The band had stopped playing and a crowd had gathered.

"Anybody have an EpiPen?" he called out.

"I do. Here."

A man thrust one at Cooper, who shoved it into the woman's upper thigh and held it there for ten seconds or so.

"What can I do?" Olivia asked quietly as he massaged the spot where he had injected her with epinephrine.

"Call 911. Tell Dispatch we have a possible allergic reaction and the female patient is having trouble breathing."

Even as he spoke, the woman gave a ragged breath and her eyes fluttered open.

"There you go," Cooper said in a soothing voice.

"Come on, Carla," her sister said. "Wake up."

Olivia spoke quickly into the phone, relaying to the dispatcher the information Cooper told her. It took about seven minutes for paramedics to arrive, and by that time, Carla, a tourist from Iowa on a bucket list trip with her sister, was sitting up and answering his questions.

"Do I have to go to the hospital? I'm feeling much better."

"You do. Sorry," he said. "You know how serious anaphylactic shock can be. You need to be checked out in the ER."

She sighed. "I'm sorry, Terri. I shouldn't have had the fish tacos."

"We asked if there was shrimp in it and the server said no."

"Maybe she didn't know. Or maybe I had a reaction to something else. I don't know. Either way, coming with me to the ER is a sucky way to celebrate your divorce."

COOPER

"You're not coming with us to the hospital?"

Cooper shook his head at one of his best paramedics, Lindy Melendez, as he watched them load the patient onto the ambulance for the short ride to the local ER. "It's my sister's birthday and I don't want to ditch her. You all look like you have it covered."

"Good thing for her you were here."

"Right place, right time. I'm glad it worked out for the best."

The patient would be fine. Already, she was almost back to normal, though it had taken a second epinephrine injection. It had been determined that a new cook in The Sea Shanty's kitchen had added some shrimp when he started running low on halibut for the fish tacos, without informing the servers. It was a rookie mistake that might have been disastrous.

He headed over to Melody's table to find his sister opening presents.

"You all didn't have to get me anything," she said to her friends. "I told you I only wanted to spend time with you all."

"Shush," said Bea Romero with a stern look. "You're always the first one to give a gift to someone else. This is our chance to do something for you."

As he sat back down beside Olivia, Cooper was awash in gratitude for all of Melody's friends. His sister had been through hell since her husband walked out. It warmed his heart to see her friends rally around her to support her.

After she opened all her presents and they all raised their glasses to toast her and all the wonderful things in store for her, the party began to break up as Rosemary Duncan got a phone call from her husband and then said she had to leave to deal with an issue with one of their kids. Shortly after she left, Olivia rose, too.

"I'm so happy I could be here to celebrate with you but I should probably go. I don't feel great about leaving my mom this long, even though Henry is with her."

"I completely understand. Thank you so much for coming. Give Juliet my love. Drive carefully."

"I would, except I walked," Olivia said with a smile. "But I won't jaywalk and I'll be sure to stay on the sidewalk."

With a general wave to everyone gathered to celebrate with Melody, she headed toward the door.

She had walked to the tavern and was now walking home, alone? Not on his watch. It was only a few blocks but he still didn't feel good about it.

Cooper glanced at his sister. "I think I'll take off, too, if you don't mind. I'm on duty early."

She looked between him and the doorway where Olivia had just left, a wrinkle between her brow as if trying to locate a frustrating puzzle piece.

"No," she said slowly. "I don't mind. I'll be leaving soon, anyway. I told Caitlin I would be home around eleven. That's only twenty more minutes."

Was it that late already? He hugged her. "Happy birthday, kiddo. You've got a lifetime of happier ones ahead."

She smiled, though it didn't hide the lingering shadows in her eyes.

He headed out into the night, one of those perfect, cool, sea-scented evenings along the coast. It didn't take long for him to catch up with Olivia.

She looked surprised and not precisely pleased to see him. "What are you doing? You don't have to leave the party."

"Things are wrapping up. The guest of honor is leaving soon."

"I don't need an escort, Cooper. I'll be fine. I like to walk."

"I like to walk, too. But then, I'm not a lone woman wandering around after dark."

She looked exasperated but didn't argue, and they set off toward Harper Hill.

It wouldn't have mattered if she *had* argued. He wouldn't back down. He had seen too much bad stuff happen to people who weren't quite careful enough.

Yes, he could be overprotective. Melody called him a fussy mother hen. Cooper knew his instinctive need to protect others was rooted in his childhood, when he had carried far too much responsibility for someone so young.

Classic consequence of growing up a child with an alcoholic mother. Because of those scars from watching his mother relapse, fight her way back and relapse again, he had an inherent need to watch over those he cared about.

He was being a polite neighbor, he told himself. Only making sure she made it back to Sea Glass Cottage safely.

"That was something tonight," she said as they headed through the mostly darkened downtown. "Saving that woman's life. How did you know she needed an EpiPen?"

"The hives. They were a dead giveaway. She didn't appear to be choking and had airflow when I checked. So I had to assume something more systemic was to blame for her reaction. If her sister hadn't said she had allergies, I would have had to figure something else out."

"How does it feel? Saving a life, I mean."

"I don't spend a lot of time thinking about it, if you want the truth. Because then I would have to think about the plenty of people I haven't been able to save."

"Like my dad."

The words sliced at him. "Yeah. Like your father."

"But you keep trying, even though you know you won't save everyone. You're willing to risk your life sometimes in the attempt."

He didn't ever think about it that way. In the moment, he did what was necessary. While there was sometimes an element of risk involved, especially when he had been part of the Air Force's elite special forces pararescue unit, his attention was always focused on trying to help.

"I would make a trite comment about how I'm just doing my job, but I know it's more than that. What I do is important."

"You're a hero, Cooper. You do what you have to without

even thinking about it. While I can't even walk into a bar without a panic attack."

There was a quiet intimacy here as they headed up the road toward her mother's house, as if the two of them were alone here in the night except for the constant murmur of the sea, the occasional owl swooping overhead and wispy clouds drifting across the moon.

"What happened to make you afraid?" he asked again, sensing it would be easier for her to share here in the dark than it might have been inside the bar.

She looked over at him, moonlight turning her features silvery. "You don't want to know."

"I wouldn't have asked if I didn't. Were you attacked?"

After a long moment, she finally sighed and answered him. "Not me. That's the stupid part. I was perfectly safe the entire time, but I…I was a witness to someone else's attack."

They had reached one of his favorite parts on this walk, a spot not far from her house overlooking the cliffs, where the city had installed benches at intervals for those who wanted to stop and savor the scenery.

Olivia seemed to notice the nearest bench. She moved to it and sat down, hands folded on her lap. He joined her, not sure he wanted to hear her story.

"I was working from home that day, something I'm lucky enough to do a few times a month. I had taken my laptop in a favorite coffee shop late one morning, since I'm often more productive there."

She gazed out to sea, where up the coast a lighthouse revolved slowly, steadily. "I had been there only twenty minutes or so when a man came in, dirty and unshaven, a meth head, if I had to guess. He had a…a gun and a knife and was waving them around, demanding money. The barista didn't move quickly enough, so he…he started attacking her. He didn't shoot her, but he stabbed her then started beating her with the gun and anything else he could find."

"How scary."

"It was terrible. She was screaming and trying to fight back, but he was crazy-strong. I didn't know what to do. He was huge and I didn't have any kind of weapon, so I hid under the booth and called 911."

Her voice quivered and he thought he heard shame in it. Unable to help himself, he reached for her trembling fingers. Her hand stiffened in his and he thought she would pull away, but finally her fingers curled around his and he held his breath, as touched as if he had been able to coax a hummingbird to land on his palm.

"What a terrifying situation. Sounds like you did the smartest thing possible."

"Smart, maybe. But not what my father would have done. Not what you would have done. You jumped out of airplanes to help people. I couldn't even cross a coffee shop."

He resisted pointing out that her father had died because he ran into a burning building without adequate protection. Cooper hadn't been able to save him, or countless others.

"What finally happened?"

"Another customer stepped in. Someone my mom's age. While the rest of us cowered, she took on this man who was out of his head with drugs and adrenaline. She was able to distract him from the injured barista long enough for her to scramble for a weapon. The two of them held him off until the police came."

He couldn't imagine what Olivia had endured in those terrifying few moments while waiting for law enforcement to arrive.

"I'm sorry." It seemed wholly inadequate.

"It's been nearly three weeks and I've had a hard time with crowds ever since," she admitted. "I keep feeling like I'm back there in that coffee shop, only the junkie is coming after me.

The day my mom was hurt, I tried to force myself to go into another coffee shop in my neighborhood and I couldn't do it. I honestly felt like I was on the brink of agoraphobia. I was coming up with a plan to work from home all the time, just stay in my apartment and order all my groceries online."

"Instead, you drove six hundred miles in the middle of the night to her rescue," he pointed out.

"That's different. I was helping family and I didn't have a choice. You said it earlier. Families help families. My mom needed me."

"Plenty of others wouldn't have been so quick to drop everything and step up."

She slipped her hand away, not looking convinced. "I may have come back to help my mom, but that doesn't change the fact that I did nothing to help another person in jeopardy in that coffee shop."

"You called 911. That helped. And I'm guessing you stuck around afterward to give police your statement, right?"

"Yes."

"Sounds like you did exactly the right thing. We all respond to danger differently, Olivia. There was nothing wrong with how you reacted to the situation."

"Dad would have stepped in and tried to stop the attack," she said stubbornly. "He would have been ashamed of me."

"Your dad weighed two hundred pounds and was one of the strongest men I've ever known. If any of us tries to compare ourselves to Steve Harper, we would all fall short."

She sighed. "I miss him. Coming back to Cape Sanctuary has made me realize all over again what a hole he left in our lives. None of us was ever the same."

"I know I haven't been," Cooper said quietly.

To his eternal amazement, she reached for his hand and they sat that way for a long time, listening to the ocean and the night. Cooper couldn't remember when he had felt more at peace, sitting on a garden bench on Harper Hill, watching a falling meteor shoot across the sky, listening to her quiet breathing, savoring the quiet Cape Sanctuary night.

Sitting here alone in the dark with Olivia Harper was one of the most profoundly perfect moments of his life, something he knew he would remember forever.

"Thanks," she finally said, turning to him with her face in shadows. "I feel better. I haven't told anybody what happened. It helped."

"You're welcome," he murmured. He hadn't meant to do it. The kiss came out of nowhere. But the moonlight was so enticing, the night its own kind of miracle, and she looked lovely in it, soft and warm and delicious.

She made a surprised kind of sound at first, and then she wrapped her arms tightly around him and kissed him back with a heat that stole his breath. He had guessed correctly. Her mouth was sweet, warm, and tasted like strawberry margaritas.

He groaned and kissed her more deeply, hunger flaring instantly.

On some level, he was aware of a voice telling him he shouldn't be doing this. This was Olivia Harper, whom he had known since she was a cute kid with freckles and pigtails, always walking around with her nose in a book.

He heard that voice but chose to ignore it, entranced by how perfectly she fit in his arms and how tightly she held on to him, as if they were jumping together at forty-five thousand feet with only one parachute between them.

He wanted the kiss to go on and on. He wanted to stay here until morning, lost in the magic of a heated kiss on a soft spring night with a woman who took his breath away.

He wasn't a guy to lose his head over a woman, but Olivia Harper affected him like no other woman ever had. She was smart, funny, compassionate. And she kissed him like she couldn't get enough. How was he supposed to resist that?

He needed to be careful, his conscious whispered loudly. He knew secrets that would hurt her. Under normal circumstances, he wouldn't be concerned about revealing those. He was good at keeping things to himself, but he had a feeling Olivia Harper was the sort of woman who could make a man spill every secret he ever had.

OLIVIA

Heaven.

Olivia wrapped her arms around his neck, eyes closed, relishing the wonder of being in his arms. This didn't seem real. Was she really here, in the soft perfection of a Northern California spring evening, kissing Cooper Vance?

Oh, her younger self would be freaking out right now. Back then, she had been kind of obsessed with Cooper and had written page after page in her diary, fantasizing about exactly this. Kissing Cooper Vance.

Her crush on him had been huge and overwhelming. She used to write his name in her diary, linked to hers with hearts and swirls and flourishes.

Cooper had been everything she wanted in a guy back then. Older, a little bit dangerous, already determined to become a firefighter. He had been a loving and protective older brother. He didn't go overboard but he made sure Melody knew he would do everything possible to take care of her. And he always had been kind to Olivia, though she knew he considered her only his sister's pesky friend and Natalie's younger sister.

He had tried to save her father, had run in after Steve and dragged him out into the night. Though it had been clear to everyone that Steve wouldn't make it, Cooper refused to stop CPR even after other first responders arrived.

How could she help but fall a little in love with him after that?

Her younger self would have been over the moon to know she would one day be here in his arms, with heat simmering between them and his mouth firm and determined on hers.

No.

She couldn't do this. What would ever come of it? Nothing but trouble.

Olivia wasn't in a good place for a fling, emotionally or mentally. She was a mess, completely overwhelmed with caring for Juliet and the garden center and her own business.

The last thing she needed right now was to become tangled up with a man who would end up breaking her heart.

With great effort, she slid her mouth away and stood up abruptly from the bench, breathing hard and trying to gather her wildly careening thoughts.

What had she been thinking? Anyone could have seen them here. Her mom. Caitlin. A passing car.

She let out a shaky breath, not sure what to say or how to act.

"I should…go." She gestured weakly toward Sea Glass Cottage, which she could see at the top of the hill. "I have to open the garden center early in the morning."

He looked as if he wanted to say something but appeared to change his mind at the last minute. "All right," he said, his voice low and a bit raspy. Then he rose and started walking in the direction of her mother's house.

"The house is only a hundred yards away. I'll be fine. You don't have to walk me the rest of the way."

"I don't mind," he answered, without breaking stride.

What if *she* minded? Now that she was no longer in his arms, now that all her doubts and insecurities came crashing back, she felt extremely awkward, as if she were still that teenage girl with a terrible crush on him.

She didn't know how to get out of the situation gracefully, so she continued walking toward home.

Streetlamps and moonlight illuminated the path, and the air

was sweet with the scent of flowers and the cypress and pine that grew in abundance along the coast.

They walked in silence, not touching but their shoulders brushing every once in a while. She was intensely aware of him, big and gorgeous and completely out of her league.

Had he really kissed her? If she couldn't still taste his mouth against hers, she might have thought she had imagined the whole thing.

She couldn't let this awkwardness grow or she wouldn't be able to face him again. While she might have preferred that option, she couldn't avoid him in a small town like Cape Sanctuary. His sister was her best friend. Not only that, but she had just agreed to help him promote an upcoming event. They would have to clear the air.

"Look," she began, "that kiss was amazing. I'm not going to lie."

"Um. Thanks?"

She sighed. "I wish I were in a better place to...to start something with you while I'm in town, but I'm not. I'm sorry. I've got way too much on my plate. I'm trying to work long-distance *and* run my business from here, which has been a nightmare, as well as manage the garden center, where I'm completely out of my depth. In between, I am caring for my mom, who constantly tries to assure me she doesn't need any help, plus keeping an eye on Caitlin, who hates me and doesn't want me around at all."

She clamped her mouth shut, horribly aware she was rambling, spilling out way too much information.

"Okay," he finally answered.

She stared at him. "That's all you have to say? *Okay?*"

"What else do you want me to say? We shouldn't have kissed. I get it. And you're right. This...attraction between us is pretty inconvenient, all the way around. We can go back to being friends, if that's what you want."

"Okay. Great. I guess that's settled. No more moonlit walks for us, then."

"Too bad."

She wasn't sure if she'd really heard him say the low words or if it had just been the wind blowing in from the ocean.

"Good night. Thanks for walking me home safely."

"You're welcome." He leaned in and kissed the corner of her mouth, a gentle kiss that friends would give. Though she was wildly tempted to wrap her arms around him again and shift her head, she forced herself to give a polite smile instead.

"I'll be in touch about the social media campaign for the pancake breakfast."

He groaned softly, which made her smile, then gave a wave and headed back down the hill.

16

JULIET

Henry fell asleep about fifteen minutes into the program they were watching together, which she didn't find surprising. He put in long days and worked hard to make his landscaping business a success, often on a job site from before dawn, when it was cooler and the winds weren't as bad, until after dark.

His work ethic and dedication to his clients were some of the things she admired most about him.

She paused the show and let him sleep, enjoying the quiet peace she found in his presence. Otis went to his crate to sleep and Felicity took his place on her lap. She petted the cat, watching Henry and wishing desperately that things between them could be different.

If only she had never been diagnosed, would she let the age difference between them bother her so much? Probably not.

She was unlikely to age as gracefully as other women. While she considered herself extraordinarily lucky that her multiple sclerosis was mild, the symptoms under control, she knew she couldn't continue to roll the dice successfully forever. The odds were good—or bad, as the case may be—that she would eventually start showing more effects. She would likely begin to have balance issues, vision problems, tremors. Eventually she might lose the ability to walk.

How could she burden him with that? Who knew? In five years, she could be using a wheelchair all the time.

Henry released a heavy breath in his sleep, his features twitching. What did he dream about? she wondered. Something wonderful, she hoped.

She pressed a hand to her chest, to the ache there. Okay. She loved him. Here, alone in the darkness, she could admit it to herself. Somehow over the past few years as their friendship had deepened, her feelings had begun to grow. He was her best friend and so very much more.

As if sensing the distress she could not show, Felicity licked her hand with a little meow that made her want to cry all over again, her green eyes sympathetic.

Unfortunately, the tiny sound from her cat was enough to wake up Henry. His eyes flickered, then opened. He looked confused, as if he didn't quite know where he was. Then his gaze landed on her and she saw awareness come back.

He scrubbed at his face, his cheeks turning slightly pink. "I think I fell asleep."

She mustered a smile, hoping he didn't see any evidence of her emotions on her features. "Only for a moment. You looked as if you needed it. I didn't have the heart to wake you."

"I'm supposed to be keeping an eye on you. Not the other way around."

"I was perfectly fine. The animals kept me company. I did turn off the show, so we can save it to watch another day."

"Thanks for that, anyway." He rose. "It's late. I was supposed to be helping you to bed."

Juliet tried to ignore the heat that flared through her at his words and the image they conjured. For heaven's sake. She had a broken hip. The last thing she should be thinking about was Henry Cragun taking her to bed in the non-sleeping kind of way, something that would never happen.

"You don't need to do that. The girls will be home soon and they can help me. I've actually become pretty good at doing it myself, too."

He looked mutinous. "I said I would help."

"Henry. Go home. It's hard enough having you see me like this. Having anyone see me," she quickly corrected, hoping he didn't notice. "I don't need you to put me into my bed like I'm an ancient old woman in a nursing home. Olivia and Caitlin will be here soon and one of them can help me."

He still looked as if he wanted to argue but he finally sighed. "Fine. But I'm not leaving until one of them returns. I'll try not to fall asleep this time."

He had that stubborn set to his jaw that told her nothing she said would change his mind. Up from his own nap, Otis wandered out of his crate across the room to stand by the door. "I think Otis needs to go out. Can you help him?"

"Sure. Come on, bud."

The dog padded after Henry to the back door off the kitchen. Henry opened the door for Otis and stood while the little dog hurried outside to do his business.

He was still standing there waiting for Otis when the front door opened and Olivia walked inside. She paused, looking startled to find Juliet still in her recliner.

"Oh. You're not in bed."

Henry and Otis both came back at that moment, the dog dancing with joy to see Olivia. She picked him up and held him close, her cheek resting on his head as if she needed to find comfort there.

What had happened?

185

"I did try to help her settle for the night, but she is being her stubborn self," Henry said.

"I feel like I have done nothing but sleep all day. I really wasn't tired." She wouldn't admit that she was actually quite tired now. Instead, she mustered a smile. "How was the birthday party?"

"Good. I'm glad I went. I think it gave Mel a nice lift to know her friends love her so much. Everyone asked about you. Oh, and Cooper saved a woman's life who went into anaphylactic shock from shellfish."

"Did he?"

Something else had gone on. She didn't know exactly what, but her mother instincts were humming. Little subtle clues in her body language hinted that Olivia's emotions were in turmoil.

"Sounds like we missed an exciting night."

What had happened to upset her daughter? If Henry weren't there, would Olivia tell her? Probably not, she thought sadly. She and her daughter didn't have that kind of relationship, much to her regret.

"It was." Olivia smiled at Henry. "Thank you so much for hanging out with Mom and keeping an eye on things."

"My pleasure. Really. I'm happy to hang out anytime. You know where to find me. And, Juliet, I'll be in touch next week about that field trip."

"Okay."

He leaned in to kiss her on the cheek, as he had done dozens of times before. For one crazy moment as the clean, masculine scent of him teased her, Juliet wanted desperately to shift and brush her mouth against his. At the last instant before she could do something stupid, sanity returned and she sat back in the recliner, trying to ignore the pounding of her heart.

He waved to both of them and headed out the door.

"What field trip?" Olivia asked.

"If I'm up for it, he wants me to go down the coast with him next week to check out a job site. I'm not sure I can sit in the car that long but I'll have to see."

"Who knows? You might be more than ready to get out of here for a few hours."

"I already am," Juliet admitted.

When Olivia didn't answer, Juliet turned and found her daughter gazing out the window at the dark night, her features distracted.

Henry's departure had almost pushed her concern to the back burner but it instantly reignited.

"What's wrong? You're upset."

Olivia frowned, looking flustered. "I'm not. Everything is fine. Why wouldn't it be?"

They might not be as close as she would like, but she could still sense Olivia's moods. "I'm your mother," she reminded her. "I know when something is bothering you."

Olivia gave a smile that seemed forced. "Nothing's wrong, Mom. I'm tired. That's all. And you should be, too. Let's get you settled into bed."

OLIVIA

Her mother didn't let up. Even as she helped transfer her to her wheelchair and pushed her into her bedroom, Juliet continued to dig.

"Did one of the tourists say something to you? Sometimes they can be pushy, especially at a place like The Sea Shanty."

She certainly wasn't about to tell her mother about that stunning kiss she and Cooper had shared.

"Mom. Nothing happened, okay? Give it a rest."

She hadn't meant to speak so sharply. The words slipped out and she could instantly see her tone had hurt her mother.

Juliet seemed to shrink back against the pillows, her features closing up.

"I'm sorry," her mother said stiffly.

Oh, parental guilt. Juliet was a professional at it, laying on a heavy layer without even trying hard.

Olivia sighed. "I'm the one who's sorry. I'm tired and feeling a little overwhelmed right now. If I seem distracted, that's the reason. That's all."

"I hate being such a burden."

Her mother's voice wobbled on the last word. Then she looked appalled at herself.

"You're not a burden. None of this is your fault, Mom. You didn't get hurt on purpose. It was an accident. It happened and now we are dealing with it."

"But it's so much trouble for you."

"If anything, you're going out of your way to prove how much you don't need my help. I know you would much rather be running the garden center yourself."

"I hate being out of commission."

"You'll be back at work before you know it." Was her mother crying? Her eyes seemed shadowed and sad, her lashes damp.

"What's going on?" She looked up at the words to find Caitlin standing in the doorway. Apparently they had both missed her coming home.

She gestured to the bed and her mother, in her nightgown. "I'm helping Mom to bed." What did Caitlin think? That they were playing Monopoly?

Caitlin glowered at her. "She looks upset. What did you do to make her cry?"

"She didn't do anything, Caity," Juliet said quickly. "I wasn't crying."

Caitlin still looked suspiciously between the two of them. Olivia refrained from rolling her eyes but it wasn't easy. Did she think Olivia was beating Juliet?

"Are you hurting?" Olivia asked her mother. "I can check your med schedule to see when you can take another pain pill."

"I hurt, but I really don't want to take another pain pill. They make me feel so strange. I'll be honest—I would rather be in pain than feel out of it for hours."

"If there is a good time you should take it, right before bed has my vote so you can get a better night's sleep."

"Don't forget what Dr. Adeno said," Caitlin said, unexpectedly on her side for once. "You should listen to your pain cues and stay on top of it in order for your body to heal. That's the only way you're truly going to be able to heal."

"Dr. Adeno is a wonderful doctor and I trust her, but I also know my body. I don't need a pain pill right now."

Olivia sighed, not wanting to fight this battle right now. "I'll go fill your water bottle and then leave a pill here beside the bed. Don't suffer unnecessarily, Mom. You're only going to stress your body more."

After she filled the insulated bottle with ice and water, she returned to her mother's bedside. "Here you go," she said, setting it on the nearby table along with the little medicine cup holding the pain pills.

"Thank you, dear."

"Good night, Mimi," Caitlin said, kissing Juliet on the top of her head. "Love you."

"I love you, too, dear."

Caitlin rose from the bed and headed out of the room.

"Good night," Olivia called after her. As she expected, her niece didn't turn around or acknowledge her. She thought things had been slightly better, but apparently common courtesy was too much to ask for tonight.

She wasn't in the mood to try unraveling Caitlin's attitude right now, especially not when she was still trying to process that stunning kiss.

"Call me if you need anything in the night."

"I will," Juliet said, though both of them knew it was a lie. Her mother went out of her way not to ask for help.

Could one person in her life not fill her with frustration right now, please?

Juliet looked toward the door where Caitlin had exited. "I wish that girl wouldn't shut me out. Do you have any idea what's bothering Caitlin?"

Besides Olivia's very existence? She didn't have a clue. "First me and now your granddaughter? I think you need to stop worrying about everyone else and focus on yourself right now, Mom."

Juliet made a face. "I'm being a pain. I know. I'm sorry. But I worry about her."

"Caitlin will be fine. She's stressed about your injury and doesn't like seeing you this way. You're the only parent she's ever known, really. It's only natural for your injury to hit her hard. No doubt, it's a reminder to her of how important you are to her."

Though spontaneous physical affection did not come easily between the two of them, Olivia ran a hand over her mom's hair. "You're important to both of us."

Juliet again looked as if she wanted to cry. "You are a wonderful daughter, if I forget to tell you that often enough."

"Thanks, Mom." She kissed her mother's cheek as well. "Have a good night."

She left the room thinking that at least her relationship with her mother, while not exactly ideal, seemed to be improving. She would be here for several more weeks. Maybe by the time she returned to Seattle, she would be able to have a conversation with Juliet without wanting to tear out three or four hanks of hair.

17

JULIET

"I am tired of having this argument with you, young lady You're going to school today. I will be just fine."

Juliet gazed firmly at Caitlin, who seemed to grow more obstinate by the moment. Every day she asked if she could stay home with Juliet. Again and again, Juliet had to tell her no.

"I just worry about you being here by yourself."

"I'm not by myself. Your aunt stops and checks on me throughout the day and so do some of the other employees at the garden center. I have friends popping in at all hours of the day and night. I'm hardly ever alone, and when I am, I keep my phone on me so I could call if I needed help. I know you worry about me, sweetheart, but you need to focus on school. And if you don't hurry, you're going to be late for the bus."

Caitlin sighed, obviously defeated. "Fine. I'm going."

With the morning sunlight hitting her just so, she reminded

Juliet forcibly of Natalie. Her heart ached, the constant small hole there that would never heal, missing the child she couldn't save.

She forced a smile. "Before you know it, the school day will be over. Maybe the two of us can watch a movie or something after you get your homework done."

"Um, I have plans tonight," Caitlin said, looking vaguely guilty. "I guess I forgot to tell you."

"What kind of plans?" She had tried to tell her granddaughter that all social activities on a school night had to be cleared with her first, but Caitlin had a bad habit of forgetting that particular house rule.

"Jake and I are going to that youth group at the church down on Shell Street."

Juliet blinked, taken completely by surprise at that one. "Are you?"

Caitlin's features took on a secretive look, one that made Juliet highly suspicious again that she wasn't being completely truthful. "What? I can't explore different ideas and theologies?"

"Of course you can. You know my philosophy has always been that everyone walks his or her own spiritual journey. I have always encouraged you to have questions and seek answers."

She had always taken Caitlin to her own church but had tried to expose her to other faiths as well. "I just wondered what prompted this interest now."

"Nothing." Caitlin did not meet her gaze, giving Juliet the distinct impression she was hiding something. "I just know a girl who goes and she likes it. She said they were doing some community service tonight for that group home where people with disabilities live and it sounded fun. But I won't go if you don't want me to."

"I never said I didn't want you to," Juliet said mildly. "I'm sure you will enjoy it."

"I'll come home first and check on you. And I'll keep my

phone on while I'm at school. I told my teachers I need you to be able to stay in touch with me right now and they were all cool with it. So call or text me if you need me to come home."

Juliet would never do that and both of them knew it. She would call anyone else in town before she dragged her granddaughter out of school.

Caitlin finally grabbed her backpack and headed out the door. A moment later, Olivia hurried out of her bedroom, wearing one of the garden center polo shirts and typing something into her phone. Everyone else had somewhere to go except her and her stupid broken hip.

"I guess you're off," Juliet said, trying to ignore the wave of fierce longing that washed over her like heavy surf in an autumn storm.

She missed her job. She never would have imagined she could miss it so very much. She missed the employees; she missed the dirt under her hands as she potted plants; she missed the customers, even the clueless ones who came in not knowing a pansy from a petunia.

"I'm training Melody today," Olivia said. "It's her first day."

"That's exciting."

"It should be interesting, anyway, since I still have no idea what I'm doing."

"You're doing fine. Everyone says so."

"You know my goal is only to keep the place going until you get back."

"Hopefully that will only be a few more weeks," Juliet said, though she wasn't entirely certain that was true. She was still so weak, something she would not admit to anyone.

She was desperately worried it was her multiple sclerosis that left her feeling exhausted and wrung out, but of course she couldn't tell that to Caitlin or Olivia.

"I'll have someone swing by this morning and I'll try to check on you at lunchtime."

"You don't have to worry about me. I'm fine. I have my cell phone and can call for help if I need it."

"I'm just worried about you."

"Otis and the cats will keep me company."

Olivia gave her a funny look and Juliet could guess what she was thinking. After Steve died, she had been determined never to have another dog in the house. They were so much bother, always needing to be walked and fed and entertained, and she didn't have the time or energy when their lives were so stressful.

Okay, she'd been wrong. She loved her cats for their easy natures and occasional affection, but she had forgotten how a dog's energy and enthusiasm could be contagious. She and Olivia's dog had bonded since she had been home from the hospital. He had become her constant companion and her nap buddy. Juliet had to admit, she was going to miss him dearly when the two of them returned to Seattle.

After Olivia left, Sea Glass Cottage seemed silent and still except for the dog's quiet snores.

The house wasn't particularly large, though it was bigger than the usual definition of cottage, with five bedrooms and three bathrooms spread across two floors.

She adored this place, had loved it from the time she was a newlywed, when she and Steve had moved in. It had been too big for only the two of them, but she became pregnant with Natalie right away, and they had dreamed of filling it with a half-dozen children.

But they had struggled with fertility issues between Natalie and Olivia and then she'd had to have a hysterectomy because of pregnancy complications after her younger daughter. She thought they would only have two. Then she'd been blessed with her granddaughter at a time in her life when she thought she was done with children. She had adored mothering her granddaughter. It had probably been the best thing that could have happened to her at that stage in her life. Caitlin, like the little dog, had reminded her that life couldn't always be like a formal garden, structured and neat. It was more like an English cottage garden, messy and busy and chaotic but still full of light and color, blossoms and beauty.

The doorbell rang, distracting her from her thoughts. Otis jumped off her lap and hurried to the door, but it took Juliet a few more moments to wheel herself closer to it. As she had told Caitlin, she was rarely alone. She needed a revolving door for all the friends and neighbors who insisted on stopping by.

It was one of the things she loved most about living in Cape Sanctuary—at least when that neighborliness wasn't driving her crazy.

"I'm coming," she called out. She had to reach up to unlock the door. When she did, she was somehow not surprised to find Henry there, wearing one of his cotton work shirts and a baseball cap.

Rats. She wished she had at least gone to the trouble of putting some makeup on that morning. At least lipstick. The man had a knack for finding her at her very worst.

"Morning," he said cheerfully.

"Hi."

"Are you up for visitors?"

The easy but cowardly thing would be to tell him no and shut the door in his face. She couldn't do that, though.

"Come in," she said instead, wheeling her chair backward a few feet to make room for him.

"How are you feeling?" he asked.

She was becoming very tired of answering that particular question. "Better," she said. It wasn't precisely a lie. Her pain had begun to ease and she felt as if she was getting around better, or at least figuring out how to maneuver with the wheelchair and walker.

"I'm heading down the coast to check out the resort property we talked about the other night and I wanted to know if you are up to going with me yet. I don't want to push you. Tell me if it's too early in the game."

Given the tenderness of her feelings for him, the smartest thing would be to decline his invitation. Spending more time with Henry when she knew they could never have anything but friendship was guaranteed to end in heartbreak.

But she wanted to go. Oh, how she wanted to go.

She was tired of being here. She craved a change of scenery, another view of sea and sunshine and growing things. More than that, she couldn't deny she was flattered that he wanted her opinion.

She might come to regret it, but she decided to worry about that later.

"Do you mind taking Otis? I don't want to leave him here alone."

"Of course not. I have Rosie with me, too. They can be traveling companions."

"I'm going to need some pillows."

His grin of delight completely stole her breath.

"I can take care of that."

Making sure she had everything she needed for a half-day journey took some logistical planning, and she also had to text both Caitlin and Olivia to let them know she was leaving with Henry for a few hours.

Wish I could go with you, Caitlin had texted.

Have fun. Don't overdo, was Olivia's response.

Finally she was ready, filled with a sense of anticipation she hadn't known since before her accident.

Part of that stemmed from the unexpected chance to see something outside of Sea Glass Cottage for a few hours, part was her eagerness to have something worthwhile to occupy her time, helping him with his project. She had to admit that a big measure of her anticipation came from knowing she was about to spend the next few hours in his company.

Henry was her friend, she reminded herself. That was all. A good friend, who understood her restlessness and knew she would be eager for something constructive to do.

Only after he had wheeled her out of the house to the driveway, where his large blue pickup truck waited, did she begin to think through exactly what she had signed up to do.

Disappointment crashed over her, sharp and intense. She couldn't go. She could conceive of no possible way she would be able to get herself into his high cab.

"I didn't think about your truck," she admitted, hoping her voice didn't betray her sudden devastation.

"I did. I was planning for it. I can lift you in, as long as we're careful and keep your hip stabilized and don't hurt your ribs."

"You can't lift me that high."

Henry laughed. "A little thing like you? I spend all day tossing hundred-pound bags of fertilizer into the back."

True to his word, he seemed to effortlessly scoop her up out of the wheelchair and into the passenger seat.

She didn't want him to let her go. She wanted to stay here cradled in his arms.

No. What she really wanted to do was throw her arms around his neck and kiss him fiercely.

Oh, she was so very stupid. Juliet shoved aside the inappropriate thoughts like so much fertilizer and resolved to simply enjoy the gorgeous April day, sunny and bright with promise.

After helping her inside, Henry lifted Otis to the back seat of the crew cab, where his old dog Rosie immediately licked the smaller dog, who wagged his tail and vibrated with happiness.

"See? I knew they would be friends," Henry said. With the dogs settled, Henry turned his attention back to her and took inordinate care arranging the myriad pillows he brought out of the house to cushion her hip and her ribs, until he was ultimately satisfied she would be protected from every bump and jostle as he drove.

"Are you sure you're up for this?" he asked once he had climbed into the cab.

"Are you kidding? After all the work you just did, there's no way I could say no. I'm fine. Really. I'm looking forward to it."

"So am I." He backed out of her driveway, driving slowly and carefully to avoid unnecessary movements.

"I'm really okay," she said. "Don't feel you have to drive any differently than normal."

He seemed to relax with every passing mile. Juliet felt some of her own tension trickle away. This was the most gorgeous time of year here, when everything was green and lush and brightly colored wildflowers took over the hillsides climbing down to the sea.

"So, Jake tells me he's going to a church youth group meeting tonight with Caitlin. Did you know about that?"

"She told me they were going this morning. It's a little out of the blue, don't you think?"

Henry shrugged. "Doesn't bother me at all. I've always encouraged Jake to explore different beliefs and philosophies."

He was an excellent father, though she knew from bitter experience how difficult it could be to raise a teenager as a single parent.

"He's a good boy, your Jake."

Henry smiled across the length of the cab. "No arguments here."

"A lot of kids might have become bitter and angry, losing a parent at that age."

That was what had happened to Natalie, anyway. In her grief and sorrow over Steve's death, she seemed to have gone wild, drinking and using drugs, staying out all night. Juliet had been lost in her own grief and struggling to keep the business afloat and had been completely powerless to control her at all.

"I think losing his mom has made Jake more compassionate and understanding," Henry said.

"Agreed. He's been a wonderful friend to Caitlin."

Henry appeared lost in thought and Juliet looked out the window as the road took them in view of the ocean far below, where the morning sun gleamed on the water.

"Have you noticed anything odd about the way they've been acting? Jake and Caitlin?" he asked.

She frowned. "Odd?"

"Not odd, I guess, as much as…secretive. Like they might be cooking something up between them?"

She frowned again, reviewing her interactions with her grand-daughter over the past few weeks. She had said much the same thing to Olivia the other day. Caitlin seemed to be waiting for something, but Juliet had no idea what that might be.

Now she remembered that for some weeks and even months before her accident, Caitlin had been asking strange questions about her mother. Did her behavior have anything to do with that?

"They're both good kids. I guess we have to hang on to that. I can't see anything wrong with them going to a church youth group, but if you notice anything else unusual or different in their behavior, I know you'll keep me posted."

"This parenting thing is not for the faint of heart," Henry said with another smile.

Juliet told herself it was only the over-the-counter pain medicine that made her insides feel so fluttery and weak.

"How's everything with Olivia?" he asked. "Is she settling in okay?"

"It's fine. She runs in and out, trying to juggle everything. I worry she's working too hard. Plus, she seems really jumpy these days. I'm not sure what that's about."

"Maybe you need to stop worrying about everyone else and focus on yourself and your own healing right now."

Juliet made a face. "That, my friend, is easier said than done. I can't help worrying about my girls."

They drove in a comfortable silence for several minutes. Juliet could feel herself relax, lulled by the rhythm of the vehicle, the dogs sleeping in the back seat, the sense of security she always felt in his presence.

She could feel her eyes drift shut a few times and did her best to jerk them open again. Henry, glancing over, smiled softly. "Feel free to sleep, if you want."

She didn't want to sleep. She wanted to enjoy every moment of this magical escape.

"Tell me more about this job site before we get there. I looked over the plans you sent me and think I have a pretty good idea of the geography. What do you feel is your biggest challenge?"

"Right now, it's the owner. I think we're close to a plan he agrees on. Most of the work is done—it's one section we seem to be struggling with."

For the rest of the drive, they talked about landscape and his master plan for the other areas of the property. She was so engrossed in the conversation, she hardly noticed when he began to slow and finally pulled over.

"Here we are," Henry said.

Juliet rolled her window down, completely entranced. Even studying photographs and drone footage and plat maps had not prepared her for the stunning beauty of the place.

"Oh," she whispered, completely speechless.

"Right? It takes my breath away every time I come here."

The area was lush and green here, with thick forests that rose up the mountainside on one side of the road and groomed gardens that sloped down to the sea on the other. The inn itself was almost concealed by trees, an architectural masterpiece of glass and stone that seemed to merge with the landscape.

"This is stunning," she murmured.

"It will be when it's finished."

He punched in a code and a wrought iron gate slid effortlessly open.

"We have the place to ourselves right now, from what I understand, and we can drive right to the spot where I'm having trouble so you can take a better look."

Up close, the structure seemed even more impressive, with massive sliding glass walls leading out to multilevel terraces overlooking the ocean. Already the gardens he had created seemed to flow right into the house.

"I can't imagine you need any help from me," she said after she looked around. "Everything looks perfect."

"You'll see it in a minute."

He drove a little farther from the house, to the end of the driveway. Finally she saw a spectacular infinity pool surrounded by several gardens that held only bare dirt.

"Still plenty to do back here," he said.

"I'd love to take a closer look."

"All right. I should let the dogs out anyway."

He pulled the folding wheelchair out of the back of his pickup truck, set it up, then reached in to lift her down. After she was settled, he hooked leashes on the dogs and let them out as well. The dogs stuck close, sniffing at the dirt of the empty gardens, as Henry wheeled her down the long sidewalk.

Henry paused every once in a while for her to look more closely at an area and offer suggestions of shrubs and perennials she thought might grow well there.

"Wow. That's perfect," he exclaimed after she told him her ideas. "I knew you were the right person to help me out."

He didn't really need her help. Both of them knew that. He was an accomplished landscape designer, while her expertise was only plant selection and a wide background in knowing which flowers and shrubs grew best in this area. Still, she appreciated him giving her a distraction for the day.

Not that her contribution was meaningless. She was good at her job and loved running the garden center. It still sometimes shocked her, how far she had come from those early days after

Steve died, when she had been completely clueless, a frightened, grieving widow with no experience at all.

"You'll have to bring me back after everything is in the ground," she said.

"Absolutely. It would be my pleasure," he answered with so much sincerity that she couldn't doubt him. "I'm hoping to finish everything within the next week or two."

"I would love to see it finished."

"Done," he said with a smile. "Now, I brought a picnic lunch, if you're interested."

"You didn't have to do that."

"It's not much, only a couple of box lunches I picked up at Ed's deli. There's a nice little spot overlooking the water where most of the workers eat."

"That sounds great."

He pushed her to a paved area that would be perfect for a couple of lounging chairs when the project was done, then returned to his pickup for the meal, taking the dogs on their leashes with him.

Juliet closed her eyes, enjoying the sunshine on her face and the sound of the water below, ignoring the throb from her leg and the fatigue she could feel weighing down her shoulders.

She had not overdone it. This was just the usual midday wall she tended to smack into.

They ate with the dogs sitting at their feet while birds chirped in the trees and the waves crashed below them.

Despite her less-than-ideal physical condition, it was a perfect afternoon and one she knew she wouldn't soon forget.

She sighed, setting the rest of her sandwich aside. She didn't want reality to press in again.

"Are you all right?"

"Fine. Just fine," she lied. She didn't want to say she had overdone it, but she was feeling achy and tired.

He seemed to see through her protestations. "We had better get you home now. I promised I wouldn't keep you out long."

She wanted to argue but knew he was right. On the drive home, he put on soft jazz music. This time, she was unable to stay awake, no matter how hard she tried. She didn't awaken until he was pulling into the driveway of Sea Glass Cottage.

Oh. She had missed the whole ride.

"You shouldn't have let me sleep so long."

He shrugged. "You seemed comfortable. I didn't want to disturb you."

"I'm so sorry I was terrible company."

"You might be surprised," he answered obscurely.

Henry again set up her wheelchair before opening the passenger door.

"Thank you for a wonderful day," she said before he could lift her out. "I had a great time. Hidden Creek is a beautiful spot and I know whatever you do with the rest of the landscaping will be perfect."

"Thank you for your help," he answered. He reached to scoop her out, but instead of lowering her to the wheelchair, he held her in his arms, her weight still on the passenger seat. He studied her for a moment. Then before she realized what he intended, he lowered his mouth to hers.

She gasped a little, unable to process that Henry was really kissing her in her driveway. And then she stopped thinking altogether when he moaned low in his throat and deepened the kiss.

Oh. She had ached for so very long to experience this heady, wild, completely impossible magic of being in his arms. She wanted to stay right here forever, cradled in the arms of the man she loved.

It had been so very long for her. Around the time Caitlin started kindergarten, her friends had pushed her to get out there and start dating again. Reluctantly she had agreed to go out with a few perfectly nice guys they set her up with, but nothing had ever clicked. Finally she had gently told her friends to stop, that she wasn't ready and wasn't sure if she ever would be.

Oh, but she had missed a man holding her, touching her, making her feel like the most important thing in his world. That the man in question was Henry Cragun only made everything more intense and she didn't want the moment to end.

Several things happened at once to yank her back to reality. A car drove by, the dogs barked, she jerked instinctively and her ribs gave a spasm of pain.

Oh heavens. Was she really kissing Henry in her *driveway*?

She met his gaze, then had to catch her breath at the look in his eyes.

"I have been wanting to do that all day," he murmured.

The words thrilled her and broke her heart all at once. She was going to have to ruin their friendship. She didn't know any other way to convince him they could never be romantically involved.

"Now you've done it. You've gone and ruined a perfectly lovely morning."

He laughed, apparently unoffended by her cranky tone. "If that's what you think just happened, you and I have very different definitions of the word *ruin*."

Why did he have to be so very wonderful and so very impossible at the same time?

She was going to have to be harsh and she didn't want to. "Can you help me down?" she said abruptly.

His smile slid away and a muscle worked in his jaw, but he said nothing as he lowered her to the wheelchair, then let Otis out of the car. The dog trotted up the walk as if he had lived there forever. Henry pushed Juliet more slowly. By the time he pushed her up the ramp and opened the door to wheel her inside, her heart was aching at the impossible situation.

"Look, Henry. Our friendship is important to me. *You* are

important to me. But I have explained before that I don't want any other kind of relationship with you. You're my dear friend. Why can't you accept that's all we can ever be?"

"I'm not some sixteen-year-old kid, Juliet, with no concept about what a woman is thinking or feeling. There's more between us than friendship."

"There's not," she started, but he cut her off.

"Explain to me, then, why you can say one thing but kiss me like we're far more than just friends."

"You're imagining things." Even as she said the words, Juliet could feel her face heat. If he were to touch her again, kiss her again, both of them would know she was lying.

"Why are you fighting so hard? You are the most important woman in my life. The only woman I'm interested in. I have feelings for you. You have to know that."

She wanted to argue with him, to tell him there were a hundred reasons why he couldn't have feelings for her. Why, oh, why couldn't things be different between them?

"Maybe it has nothing to do with you," she said quietly, trying to keep emotion out of her voice. She was going to have to implode their friendship. She couldn't see any other way through this. He was persistent and would keep trying to wear her down. Eventually she would give in.

She knew herself well enough, knew her own weaknesses. She did not have the strength to continue fighting him. Eventually, he would win and both of them would end up miserable.

Not yet, though, she told herself. She didn't have to end it yet. It was only a kiss, not a marriage proposal or anything.

"Thanks again for a great day," she said quickly, hoping she could change the subject and hold off saying things she would . never be able to take back. "I loved seeing the project but I think I may have overdone things. I really need to lie down now."

He opened his mouth as if he wanted to argue, then closed

it again. To her vast relief, he seemed willing to let the matter drop for now.

Maybe if they both pretended hard enough, they could go back to the way things were, when he was her dearest friend and she could keep her feelings to herself.

18

CAITLIN

Was there really a chance this dude was her father?

Caitlin stood just inside the door to the Fellowship Hall of the church where Jeff Seeger was the pastor. He looked like an aging surfer, with a receding hairline and blond hair that he kept long and tied back in a man bun. He wore a bushy blondish beard and had brown eyes that seemed warm and friendly.

Just your friendly neighborhood serial killer, she thought, then immediately felt guilty about it. Apparently she and Jake listened to too many true crime podcasts.

"Hi. Welcome. Looks like we have a couple of new faces. We're thrilled to have you join us."

He had a nice, comfortable voice and seemed genuine. But what did she know? Caitlin couldn't think of anything to say. Finally, much to her relief, Jake stepped in.

"I'm Jake Cragun and this is my friend Caitlin Harper."

"Welcome, Jake and Caitlin. What brings you here tonight?"

Caitlin looked around, registering there were about twenty other teenagers there, most she recognized from school. A couple of cheerleaders, a student body officer, even a football player or two. Who would have guessed that so many of the cool kids would come hang out at a church thing?

"Um, we've just heard kids at school talking about, um, how much fun they have here at youth group and, um, we wanted to check it out. I guess you could say we are kind of on a spiritual quest."

She should have stopped before that last bit. Beside her, Jake didn't say anything. He didn't even call her out for her bald-faced lie.

That was one of the things she loved best about him. He always had her back, no matter how awkward she made things for them.

Pastor Jeff beamed at both of them, buying up her story like discount Bibles at a yard sale. "Excellent. We welcome all searchers into our midst. You picked a good day to visit. We've got a fun activity tonight. We're making fleece blankets from material that has been donated by members of the community. I don't expect that will take us long. Then we're all going to take them up the street to some of our friends who live in a residential home for adults with disabilities."

She supposed it could be much worse. At least they were doing something nice for someone, a service project, not holding hands and singing hymns or something. She wasn't sure how far she could take this whole spiritual quest thing.

Some of the students took charge of the activity, which surprised her. They were all separated into four groups, charged with making two blankets each. To her relief, she and Jake ended up in the same group. Maybe they wanted to keep the newcomers together.

Unfortunately, she didn't have a chance to talk to her prospective father, as Pastor Jeff was busy moving between the groups and helping them with the blankets. They didn't really take much effort. All the groups did was go to work with scissors and cut strips around two pieces of fleece that were the same size, lay them back-to-back and tie the strips together. Since there were five of them working together, it only took about fifteen minutes to finish both of their blankets.

They made a brown-and-blue one with circles on it that would work for a guy and a cute pink one with splotchy purple flowers.

Everybody was nice to her and Jake, not making them feel weird or out of place at all. Caitlin didn't consider herself one of the popular kids. She had plenty of friends in the band, where she played the clarinet and Jake was on percussion, but she didn't usually hang out with jocks or student body officers.

It was kind of nice, actually, though the whole time she was aware of Pastor Jeff talking to the other kids and moving between the groups.

It might have been her imagination, but a few times she thought she caught him giving her a weird look, as if he knew her but couldn't figure out how.

"Okay, everybody. It looks like all the groups are done. Now it's time to visit our old friends at Sunshine House and deliver them."

Everybody seemed actually excited about the errand as they moved outside and started walking as a group up the hill, away from the coast.

"You guys do this kind of thing often?" she asked Andrew Allen, one of the football players who was in her Spanish class.

"Not super often but we stop by maybe every three months or so. We did some yard work there in the fall, and then at Christmas we hosted all the residents at the church for a little party to bake cookies and gave them gifts. They're all cool."

She wasn't sure what to expect as they arrived at the building she had noticed before, a few blocks away from the church.

It was larger than a regular house with a ramp out front and a couple of big wheelchair vans in the driveway.

The residents of the house were gathered in a large room just inside the facility, some watching television and others doing what looked like a puzzle in the corner. They all got really excited when the youth group showed up.

"Hey, everyone," said a woman who appeared to be a worker there to the residents. "Pause the show and come over. Our friends have come for a visit again."

It really did feel like that, just a group of friends hanging out with other friends. The residents were delighted at the blankets and Caitlin even got a hug from a man who looked like he had Down syndrome.

They didn't just drop off the blankets and leave, as she had expected might happen. The other youth seemed familiar enough with the residents of the group home that soon they were laughing and talking together. Caitlin made friends with a woman in a wheelchair, whose speech she didn't quite understand but who beamed and cuddled the flower blanket. Jake, she noticed, was soon deep in conversation with the man who had Down syndrome.

All in all, Caitlin enjoyed herself far more than she had expected. Mimi was always doing nice things for other people and enlisting Caitlin's help, and this gave her the same kind of warm glow.

If all their activities were like this one, she might even consider coming again, even if the DNA test wasn't a match to Pastor Jeff.

After about forty-five minutes, Pastor Jeff started gesturing to the door to let the youth group know it was time to go. After goodbyes and more hugs, they all started walking back toward the church.

"So. What did you think of your first meeting?" Pastor Jeff joined up to walk beside her.

She couldn't pass up the opportunity to talk to him, though she wished Jake were closer to be her backup. He had struck up a conversation with another guy who had band with them and they had fallen slightly behind.

"It was fun. Thanks for letting us come along."

"You're welcome anytime. We meet twice a month, the first and third Thursday nights."

"Thanks." She paused, then knew she had to take a chance. She might not get a better opportunity. "So, Pastor Jeff. I think you knew my mom when you were younger."

In the fading light, she thought she saw a wary expression in his eyes. He looked a little trapped, kind of like Jake did whenever she asked him who his latest crush was.

"I might have. I knew a lot of people back then. It's no secret among the youth I work with that I was in and out of trouble a lot when I was your age and into my early twenties. I guess you could say I had kind of a misspent youth. But we're all works in progress, right? God loves us, no matter what we've done."

She agreed about the works in progress, at least.

"I guess."

"Who is your mom?"

"Was. Natalie Harper."

They passed under a bright streetlight and she thought she saw sadness and something else, something like guilt, in his expression. "I thought so, when I saw you walk in. You are the spitting image."

"That's what people tell me."

He shook his head, giving her a closer look. "I saw you a time or two when you were just a baby. I can't believe so much time has passed."

He knew her when she was a baby. Her heartbeat accelerated. Did that mean he was her father?

But wouldn't someone who professed to be a man of God have stepped up to take care of his personal responsibilities, if he knew he had a child? Yeah, she'd only spent a few hours in his presence, but it was clear everyone in the youth group adored him. Would that kind of guy really have walked away from his daughter?

"Do you…remember much about my mom?"

They were almost back at the youth center and she was wishing she had waited until after everyone else left to ask questions about Natalie, especially when she saw sadness cross his features again.

"Your mom. She was a bright star. Sweet. Too sweet for the road she chose to walk, you know?"

Why had she? What had made a young woman from a loving home start using drugs and eventually throw everything away for them? That was the mystery that haunted her.

"I grieved when she died," Pastor Jeff said quietly. "I grieved hard. But in the end, her death saved me, I guess you could say. It made me see that I was headed for the same fate if I didn't do something fast."

"You were her pot dealer."

He made a small sound, like an animal caught in a corner. "How do you know that?"

"She left a diary," Caitlin confessed.

He was quiet for a long time. By now, they had reached the church and Pastor Jeff stood by the door while the other young people went inside. "I can't deny it. I told you I had a misspent youth. I hurt people. People I cared about. You should know, I was your mother's friend, too. I could justify and say it was only pot and I never supplied the hard stuff she eventually started using. I could also tell you I stopped dealing to her the first time she went into rehab, but by then she had found another source. She tried to get clean so many times. She wanted that for her and for you. You should know that."

Caitlin felt the familiar knot in her stomach whenever she thought about her mom, who had given up custody of her to

Mimi and had died of an overdose just hours after being released from jail, which Caitlin had learned wasn't uncommon for addicts who had been clean for a while, then abruptly returned to their old ways.

"You were her pot dealer. Any chance you're also my dad?"

"What? No!" Pastor Jeff looked shocked and so completely horrified at the possibility, she wished she had never said anything.

It was too late to back down now, though. "My mom left no information about my father and she never told anyone who he was, either. I've gone through her journals and other information I can find from that time and I've been trying to track down all the men she mentioned. That's the real reason I came tonight."

"Ah." He didn't seem offended by her honesty.

"You're sure there's no chance?"

He shook his head. "I'm sorry, Caitlin. There was never anything like that between your mom and me. We had a friendship and, for want of a better word, for a time we had a business relationship. That was all."

She was more disappointed than she had expected to be by this development. "All right. Thanks for answering my questions and for letting my friend and I tag along tonight."

"You are still welcome anytime you want to come back. We would love to have you." He was quiet and then gave her a piercing look that seemed to see deep inside her. "For the record, I would have been delighted to find out I was your father."

His voice was so kind and honest that she couldn't help smiling back, even though her heart ached a little.

He pointed to his collar. "And forgive me for being a little preachy for a minute. Even if you never find out who your earthly father is, don't forget that you have Someone else who loves you and will never let you down."

"You have to say that. You're a pastor."

"As a man who received a second chance I still don't feel like

I deserve, I would say it anyway," he said quietly, then headed inside, where the rest of the youth group was probably wondering what was taking them so long.

Caitlin lingered outside, listening to the sound of the sea and looking at the few stars she could see peppering the sky and, okay, feeling a little sad, until Jake came out.

"No luck?" Jake asked as they both unlocked their bikes from the rack and started walking them back toward Harper Hill.

"No. He seems like a really nice guy, but he said there's no chance at all he's my dad. Just like you suspected."

Jake wasn't enthusiastic about any of the names on her potential dad list, but he must have heard the disappointment in her voice. "I'm sorry."

For some silly reason, she suddenly felt like crying. Instead, she shrugged. "At least it narrows the field a little."

"True. One more down. And tonight was actually pretty fun."

"Thanks for coming with me," she said. "You're the best BFF a girl could ever want."

Jake looked as if he wanted to say something, but she tripped over a bump in the sidewalk and stumbled. He reached to steady her, and by the time she found her balance again, the moment was gone.

1 9

OLIVIA

She was so exhausted, she just wanted to put her head down on the kitchen table and take a nap before finishing her work with Harper Media.

Just a few hours. Was that too much to ask?

Olivia sighed. She didn't have tons to do. She only had to power through for another hour or so. Then she could finally sleep.

Running the garden center during the busy springtime and juggling responsibilities she couldn't hand off to others for her own business, plus managing Juliet's care, was turning her narcoleptic. She found herself falling asleep at odd moments of the day—including at 9:00 p.m., when she ought to have at least a few more good hours in her.

She didn't dare take any more caffeine or else she wouldn't be able to fall asleep, once she eventually found her way there. Using a trick she had stumbled onto in college, she stood up, set a timer on her phone for two minutes, and started doing jumping jacks to get her circulation flowing and wake up her brain.

She had just started up when the back door opened and Caitlin walked inside.

Her niece stopped and stared at Olivia, midjack, with her arms above her head.

"Obviously I'm interrupting something."

Olivia lowered her arms. "No. I'm trying to stay awake so I can finish some work."

"Okay." Caitlin looked at her like she was a few cans shy of a six-pack.

Olivia sighed. Her niece's attitude was really beginning to wear thin.

"How was your evening?" she asked, her voice determinedly cheerful. "Did you enjoy the youth group?"

"It was fine." Caitlin walked across to the refrigerator and reached inside for a yogurt.

She grabbed one of the spendy French kind in the cute jar that Olivia had bought for her own breakfast the next day, but she decided not to quibble.

"Were a lot of your friends there?"

"A few."

"And Jake Cragun went with you, right?"

"Yeah."

"He seems like a nice kid," Olivia said, undeterred by the monosyllables. "Are you two friends or are you a thing?"

"First of all, I don't know what being a *thing* means. We're friends. That's all. Second of all, mind your own freaking business."

Serves her right for trying to make conversation. "You're right. It's not my business. But you don't have to snap at me. It was a simple question. That's what humans do with each other. They interact. They ask questions. They show they care about each other's lives."

Caitlin scoffed. "Except you don't care. You don't have to pretend with me."

"You know that's not true," she said, fighting for calm. "Until a few months ago, everything was fine between us. I have no idea what I did to piss you off, but here's another little communication tip. I can't fix it if you won't tell me."

She thought Caitlin might finally break her silence and reveal just why she seemed so filled with resentment, but she turned away.

"Just because we're related by blood doesn't mean we have to be best friends."

Olivia frowned as the words struck a chord deep in her memory. She remembered Natalie saying something very much like that to her after their dad died, when Olivia had tried to reach out to her sister.

She desperately had wanted to turn to Nat, the only one who might be able to truly understand the pain in her heart. Natalie had not been at all interested. She had addressed her own pain by spending more time with her friends, by staying out late, by drowning her sadness with first booze and then pot and then harder drugs.

The memory hurt, especially knowing she would never be able to heal that rift with her sister that had grown between them before Nat died.

Was she subconsciously trying to do that through Caitlin? Were her efforts to make everything right between her and her niece another way to keep a piece of her sister close?

She was way too tired to figure this out tonight.

"Is Mimi sleeping?" Caitlin asked stiffly. "I told her I would let her know how youth group went, but I don't want to bug her if she's already down for the night."

"I think so. Her light has been out for a few hours. She went for a drive today with Jake's dad. I think it kind of wore her out."

She decided to try one more time to find common ground

with Caitlin, or at least a topic they could discuss without sniping at each other.

"While we're talking about people who may or may not be a thing, do you think there's any chance Juliet and Henry might be...involved?"

Caitlin stared at her as if she had just pulled a chipmunk out of her ear. "Involved how?"

"Are they dating?"

"Ew! No!"

"Why does that warrant an *ew*? Juliet is not exactly an old lady. She's only in her fifties, which is the new thirty these days."

"Hate to break it to you, but thirty is old, too."

Olivia, who would be thirty in only a few months, decided not to be offended. She did feel old sometimes, as if life were passing her by.

"Why do you care whether people are seeing each other? Maybe you need to focus on your own love life and stop worrying about everyone else."

"I don't have a love life. Why else would I be so interested?" Sadly, there was more truth to that than she wanted to admit. That kiss she had shared with Cooper, the one she couldn't get out of her head, was the most excitement she'd had in months. Much longer, actually, which was one of the main reasons she had broken off her engagement to Grant.

"Mimi and Henry are not dating. I'm sure of it. Lilianne, that's Jake's mom and Henry's wife, was one of Mimi's best friends."

Olivia did not see that Lilianne had anything to do with the situation, considering the other woman had been gone for years, but since Caitlin was talking to her without yelling, she decided not to argue with her.

"I knew her. Henry's wife, I mean. I always liked her."

A massage therapist, Lilianne had been one of those New Age, bean sprout types who would have fit in well in Seattle, she remembered. She had always been kind to Olivia when she would babysit for Jake.

"She was super nice. Everyone was really sad when she died. Jake still misses her a lot, though he doesn't talk about it much."

"It's tough to lose a parent at his age," she said. "I still miss my dad, your grandpa Steve, all the time and he died right before my thirteenth birthday."

"I don't miss my mom," Caitlin said, her voice hardening. "I barely even remember her."

Before Olivia could confess she missed Natalie as much as she missed Steve, Caitlin stood up abruptly. "I'm going to bed," she said, tossing the yogurt container in the bin.

She turned to go, but as she did, her backpack fell on the floor and the contents spilled out.

Caitlin swore an oath that Olivia had a feeling she would never have said if Juliet were there, then bent down to pick them up. Olivia knelt to help. They appeared to be schoolbooks and folders, except for one pink-covered book with a gold spine.

"What's this?"

"Nothing. It doesn't matter."

But it was too late. Olivia recognized it. Every year for Christmas, Juliet would give both her and Natalie identical new journals for the year. She remembered this one from the year her father died, when she had poured out all her sadness and grief, her feelings of being abandoned by Juliet, too.

"Is this my journal?"

"It's my mom's," Caitlin said, snatching it away from her.

"Where did you get it? Did my mom give it to you?"

Caitlin said nothing, which made Olivia suspect the girl had found it on her own. She wasn't sure Juliet would have wanted Caitlin reading her mother's thoughts and emotions around that time. Natalie had been wild before Steve's death, but she seemed to have lost all restraint afterward, staying out for days at a time and coming home drunk or stoned.

She'd become pregnant with Caitlin sometime in the next five or six months and had given birth the following year.

Would Nat have written any of that in her journal? If so, Olivia wasn't sure it was appropriate reading material for a fifteen-year-old girl. She didn't quite know how to navigate these treacherous waters. Not when she and Caitlin were barely on speaking terms.

"You know," she said carefully, "if you want to know about your mother, you can ask me or Mimi. I said that before to you and I meant it. We could tell you more than you will read in her journal. Those are her thoughts, maybe. Her perspective. And that's great. But you could also ask others who loved her."

"You didn't love her," Caitlin snapped. "You hated her. That's what she said in her journal. You told her you didn't want to be her sister anymore."

The accusation sliced through her, sharp and vicious. She could remember that very conversation, right here in this kitchen, those ugly words spilling out between them.

She closed her eyes, guilt and sorrow a tangled mess in her heart. "I did say that. I said a lot of things in anger that year. I would say I had reasons but none of that matters now. For what it's worth, it wasn't true when I said it and it's not true now. I adored Natalie. She was my only sister, and for a long time, I wanted to be just like her."

"Too bad you couldn't have bothered to tell her that when she was alive. When it might have made a difference," Caitlin snapped, then scooped up her bag along with the journal and rushed out of the kitchen.

As soon as she left, Olivia closed her laptop, knowing she wouldn't get any work done now, when her heart was aching with memories of the sister she had loved and how everything had changed after their father died.

2 0

OLIVIA

She was a freaking genius.

To be fair, Cooper had actually been the one to suggest she hire his sister to help out at the garden center, but Olivia had been the one who had instantly known it would be a fantastic idea.

She had only been on the job a few days, but it was already clear Melody was a natural and Juliet should have hired her years ago.

She knew where to find everything in the garden center before she even started, she was fantastic with the customers and she had more gardening knowledge than most of the part-time staff combined.

With her help, there was a chance Olivia might be able to keep the garden center afloat long enough for Juliet to return to work.

"Thank you for stepping in and helping Mrs. Palmer," she said after Melody returned from helping a customer load new plants into her vehicle. "I didn't have the first idea how to help her pick out those irises she wanted. You are straight-up amazing at this."

Melody's features already seemed brighter, her eyes happier than they had been since Olivia had returned to Cape Sanctuary.

"I have to tell you, I am loving this job. I had no idea how much I was missing adult interaction. I love my boys. Don't get me wrong. But some days I'm afraid that if I have to pretend I give a darn about the *Star Wars* universe one more minute, my head is going to turn into the Death Star."

Olivia had to smile. "I'm so happy you're enjoying it so far."

"What's not to love? There's nothing better than talking to other people with a passion for flowers."

Okay, she got the whole *Star Wars* thing, but had to admit that Melody lost her at flowers. She loved them, of course. They were gorgeous. Who didn't? But she much preferred them arranged in a lovely vase than growing in a garden.

In her perfect world, flowers grew abundantly without any care needed. Of course, then her mother's garden center would probably be out of business.

"How is Charlie doing with day care?"

"It's only a few days a week. My friend Penny, whose son is Charlie's best friend, offered to take him when she can."

"Is that where he is today?"

"Actually, Cooper had the day off today and offered to hang out with him."

She had not seen Cooper since the night of Melody's birthday party. She had been doing her best to put him out of her mind, which was proving much more difficult than she had expected.

"Is that right?"

Did Mel hear how breathless her voice sounded, suddenly? Oh, she hoped not. This was ridiculous. She and Cooper had shared one silly kiss in the moonlight. There was absolutely no reason for her to obsess about it.

Melody apparently did not notice her sudden distraction, much to Olivia's relief. "He offered to pick up the other boys after school and then bring them here to go home with me when my shift is over."

"If you ever run into trouble with caregivers, we can certainly adapt around the boys' schedule. I'm so happy to have you working here that I want to be as flexible as possible with your needs."

Melody flashed her a smile as she started rearranging some potted vegetables that had been moved to the wrong spot. "I so appreciate that, but so far things are working out. I'm struggling with the same issues every mom who works outside the home has to manage. How do I split myself into five different people so I can take care of everything?"

She didn't have children, but Olivia could certainly relate to that right now. This time in Cape Sanctuary was giving her an entirely different perspective.

Since that conversation with Caitlin in the kitchen the other night, she had also begun viewing history through a new lens.

She wasn't sure she had ever fully acknowledged how angry and resentful she had been as a teenager at Natalie for the choices she had made and at Juliet for focusing all her attention on the garden center and Caitlin.

She had swallowed everything in her quest to be the perfect daughter. But talking to Caitlin the other day and remembering that time had brought back all those feelings of abandonment. Juliet had worked from sunrise to past Olivia's bedtime here at the garden center. There were days she didn't even see her mother; they only communicated through notes and text messages.

She had been a teenage girl, grieving the loss of her father and feeling as if she had lost her mother at the same time.

From her point of view, any emotional reserves Juliet had left after pouring her heart and soul into Harper Hill Home

& Garden by necessity had gone to Natalie, who had been so very troubled.

Juliet had little left to give to Olivia—and even less after Natalie announced she was pregnant and keeping her baby.

Now, after she had spent three weeks stepping into her mother's shoes, Olivia was beginning to see things differently.

Juliet had been doing the best she could under the circumstances.

They had all been in crisis mode and Juliet had chosen the more urgent things to focus on, but that didn't mean other things or people weren't as important.

Her mother loved her. Had always loved her. She had never doubted that, even then. No, Juliet had not been able to be the most attentive mother during Olivia's high school years and had left her mostly to her own devices. But she had survived and had gone on to have a pretty good life, even if she was only now coming to acknowledge that she had always chosen the safer course.

It was unfair of her to blame Juliet for leaving her rudderless in a stormy sea when her mother had been doing her best to keep her own head above water.

She hadn't realized how much resentment she had been clinging to all these years. Now that she did, Olivia knew she needed to work toward forgiving her mother.

"So far, you're doing great," she said to Mel. "But if you're ever scheduled for a time that doesn't work, don't hesitate to let me know. We can adjust."

"I hope you don't think I expect or need special treatment because I happen to be the boss's best friend," Melody said.

"That's not special treatment," Olivia protested. "That's just good business sense. I don't want to lose you and want to do everything I can to make sure the job works for you."

Melody smiled, but before she could answer, a customer came

in asking about the best organic pest removal techniques and Olivia gratefully let her new hire handle the question.

The rest of the afternoon was so busy, with a constant flow of customers, that she didn't have a chance to talk to Mel again.

Their conversation completely slipped her mind until she was busy restocking their fairy garden supplies and heard a sweet voice call out, "Mom! Where are you?"

She instantly recognized Charlie's lisp and turned to smile at him when suddenly her breath tangled as she spotted Cooper walking in, surrounded by his nephews.

Oh. Right. He had the boys.

"Hey, guys," she said, hoping Cooper couldn't hear the sudden pounding of her heartbeat.

He was looking at her with an unreadable expression, making her wonder if he was also remembering that kiss along a moonlit path.

"Hi, Livie," the adorable Charlie said, pronouncing her name Wivvie.

"Hello, Sir Charles. How are you this fine evening?"

"Good. Hey, where's your dog? Can I play with him?"

"Oh, he would love to play with you, but I'm afraid he's home babysitting my mom right now."

Charlie giggled. "A dog can't babysit a lady."

"My amazing wonder dog can."

"Uncle Cooper has a dog, too," Ryan, the middle boy, chimed in.

"His name is Jock. He's old and sleeps a lot." Charlie said "sweeps" but she interpreted that to mean "sleeps"—unless the dog was some kind of neat freak, which would be odd but undeniably handy.

"He's earned a rest," Cooper said. She still couldn't get a read on the way he was looking at her. He seemed a little uncomfortable, but she couldn't tell whether he was regretting that they had kissed or wishing they could do it again.

"Why is that?" she asked, then cringed at the unnaturally high tone of her voice.

"He is almost fourteen. That is pretty old in dog years."

"Jock used to be a fire dog," Will informed her. "He would ride in the fire truck and everything."

"I didn't realize fire departments still had dogs."

"A few still do. He was kind of the mascot with the fire department at my last base in Texas. Then he got too old and had bad hips and couldn't climb into the fire truck anymore, so I took him home so he could live the good life and take it easy. So far, he's enjoying his retirement here, though he still perks up anytime we hear a siren."

Oh, the man was making it tough for her to remember all the reasons she couldn't fall for him.

First, he came in being so sweet with his three adorable nephews. Then she learned he had taken in an aging fire dog. How on earth could any woman resist him?

"Do you know where my mom is?" Charlie asked.

"I think I saw her in the next greenhouse over. Should we go take a look?"

"You look like you're busy here," Cooper said, gesturing to the miniature toadstools, arbors and bridges on the cart next to her. "We can find her."

"This can wait," she assured him, and led the way into the next greenhouse, where she found Mel deep in conversation with Henry Cragun.

The two of them were filling a huge cart, loaded with shrubs and perennials.

Henry must be working on a job and Melody was helping him fill the order.

"Looks like she's busy for a few minutes," she said. "You guys are welcome to wait in my office, if you want. Or you can hang out at the sandpile."

In a strategy move Olivia thought was genius, between greenhouses her mom had constructed a sandpile filled with trucks and shovels, where kids could hang out and play while their parents shopped.

"Maybe you could help us," Cooper said.

"Um. Sure," she said, trying to keep the wariness out of her voice.

"We're on a quest," Melody's oldest son, Will, declared.

"An important one," his brother Ryan added.

"Wow. Sounds serious. How can I help?"

"We need to find some plants for Uncle Cooper to grow at the firehouse."

"He says this is the best place in town to buy plants," Ryan said.

"I can't argue with you there," Olivia said with a smile. "What kind of plants did you want?"

To her surprise, Cooper looked uncomfortable, as if suddenly wishing he hadn't said anything. "There's a small plot of land along one side of the fire station. It's south-facing and gets sun most of the day. Right now it's kind of an eyesore, choked with weeds. I need to clear them away, and I thought instead of just filling that space with rocks or some other kind of ground cover to keep the weeds out, maybe we could plant some vegetables and herbs there that we could then use to fancy up some of the food in the station kitchen."

"That sounds like a great idea," she said with a smile. "My mom always had an herb garden off the kitchen. You would be amazed at how a little snip of tarragon can enhance a chicken marinade. And pizza just isn't the same without a few fresh basil leaves."

"That's what I thought. Usually the food we get is pretty basic. It's okay but nothing fancy. I figured a few herbs would be a good way to dress it up. Plus, it would turn an eyesore into something a little more attractive."

As he spoke, Olivia suddenly had a great idea. Here was Cooper, looking buff and gorgeous, and his adorable nephews. She could only imagine that people in Cape Sanctuary would love to see their new fire chief trying to beautify his space while providing some color and flavor to his firefighters' meals.

The mayor had asked her to highlight the fire department before the breakfast in a few weeks. The planting of an herb garden at the fire department seemed the perfect place to start.

"I love this idea," she said. "And I think members of the community who are on social media will love it even more. What if I take some pictures while you're picking herbs and post them to the fire department page? I can even mention that some of the herbs might be used at the firefighter breakfast that you're doing to benefit Chief Gallegos."

As she might have expected, Cooper looked vaguely horrified at the idea. "Who in their right mind would want to see photographs of me digging in the dirt to plant some herbs?"

Only every female in town. And possibly in all the neighboring towns, too. And maybe across the entire state of California.

"Think of the positive PR for the fire department, with very little effort on your part. And not much on mine, either, only a few photographs. I even have my good digital camera in my mom's office, since I was shooting some of our new plant arrivals this morning for the Harper Hill website and social media properties."

He had an obstinate set to his jaw that told her he still wasn't very enthusiastic.

"This is a great idea. Trust me. Who knows? You might even get more donations for your fund-raiser. Plus, maybe some of the decent cooks in town will provide a few meals for your firefighters so you don't have to take turns cooking."

"I'll be in your pictures, Livie," Charlie offered.

"Me too!" his older brothers both said at the same time.

She smiled down at all of them. "That would be terrific. I have to talk to your mom first to make sure it's okay, though."

"Can we, Uncle Coop?"

He still looked trapped, but as he looked down at the trio of eager faces, he sighed.

"I still think no one's going to care. But you're the expert."

People would care. She would make sure of it.

"What do I have to do?"

"Nothing at all except what you came to do. Let me run and grab my camera and talk to Mel. Then I'll take care of the rest."

Only after she hurried to her mom's office in a small building her father had constructed between the buildings and over-looking the water did she realize this maybe wasn't the smartest idea she'd ever had.

It was hard enough hiding her growing feelings for Cooper. How would she conceal them when she had to stare at him for the next twenty minutes or so through her camera's viewfinder?

21

COOPER

This might be the most uncomfortable thing he had ever done.

He wouldn't want *anyone* taking pictures of him. He especially didn't enjoy that it was Olivia, the woman he hadn't been able to get out of his head since the night he had made the colossal mistake of kissing her after Melody's party.

It didn't help that he drove past Sea Glass Cottage every day on his way to the fire station. Each time, he couldn't help longing for a glimpse of her, wondering what she was doing, what she might be thinking about.

Seeing her now, her hair pulled up into a messy bun and wearing a purple Harper Hill Home & Garden polo shirt, all he could think about was pulling her hair down, removing that expensive-looking camera hanging from a strap around her neck and devouring that delicious mouth again.

He didn't want to say he was the kind of man who could

ever kiss a woman and then forget about it, but he couldn't remember another kiss that had rocked him to the core like the one they had shared.

Now he had to act like nothing had happened, like he was completely blasé about the whole situation, while she walked around him holding a camera and studying him from different angles.

Right.

She had quickly asked Melody's permission to photograph the boys and use the images on the fire department's posts. He heard her promise she wouldn't identify them and would shoot the backs of their heads for privacy.

"That's great," Melody had said, then had turned back to helping Henry Cragun, a neighbor and local landscape designer.

He liked seeing his sister working so hard. She seemed to be enjoying her new job. She was obviously in her element, happier than he had seen her since coming back to Cape Sanctuary.

Olivia moved around him, the camera up to her eye.

"I'm not sure what you want me to do," he finally said, feeling stupid.

She fiddled with some adjustments on her camera. "Exactly what you came to Harper Hill to do. That's all. Shop for plants. Compare different ones. Maybe discuss with the boys which varieties you ought to select. Really, I want you to simply pretend I'm not even here."

He couldn't quite stretch his brain that far. Olivia was unavoidable, the kind of woman who commanded attention, who wormed her way into a guy's mind and stayed there.

Not his, of course, barring the past few days. That was completely a fluke. He was working on it and expected to have a handle on this sudden fascination any minute now.

"This is so boring. We're just standing here," Ryan complained.

Yeah, he needed to focus on the situation here and bring his

A game or he was about to have three little boys ready to go on a rampage through the garden center.

"Okay, guys, we have a job to do. We need to find a plant called rosemary."

"Hey," Will exclaimed, "our mom has a friend named Rosemary."

He knew, entirely too well. Mayor Rosemary Duncan was to blame for this whole fiasco. She was the one who set Olivia loose on the city social media properties. "In this case, we are looking for the herb called rosemary. It has pointy little leaves, kind of like a mini Christmas tree. Can you see if you can find that?"

All the time the boys looked, he was aware of Olivia taking pictures, studying them like they were zoo exhibits. Every once in a while, she would have the boys turn a different way, probably so she could avoid taking pictures of their faces.

Fifteen minutes later, their wagon was filled with a couple of tomato plants, some cucumber starts and some four-inch pots containing several different herbs that would likely never be used in the fire station kitchen except by him.

"That was perfect. Better than I ever imagined," Olivia exclaimed, her eyes bright and happy. "Everyone is going to love these pictures. Cape Sanctuary's sexy new fire chief picking out plants with his cute nephews. Are you kidding me? It's pure social media gold."

He didn't hear much after the word *sexy* as heat seemed to crawl up his skin.

"Can we see the pictures?" Will asked.

"Sure. I've already picked a couple of my favorites."

She sank onto one of the benches set out around the garden center and his nephews clustered around her, Charlie on her lap and the other two peering over each shoulder as she showed them pictures on the camera's screen.

Cooper couldn't look away from the picture she made, tanned, glowing, happy.

"That's a good one of Uncle Coop," Ryan said with a grin. "He looks like Captain America with dark hair in that one. Show him."

Olivia dutifully held up the camera. Unfortunately, he couldn't see from his angle, so he had to move until he was standing right behind her, close enough to smell that apple shampoo.

He never should have danced with her, damn it. What had he been thinking? He would have been fine, if he had never made the mistake of holding her in his arms.

Right now, he wanted to reach under that messy bun and kiss the back of her neck.

He stepped away quickly, before he could do something absolutely stupid.

"Looks like a regular guy buying plants to me."

"I think they're perfect. I have a feeling Rosemary will love them, too. I'm sending them to my phone now so I can edit and upload them."

"So we're done here?"

"I think so."

"Right on time," he said as he spotted Melody approaching them.

"Hi, Mom!" Charlie said, beaming at her from Olivia's lap. And why wouldn't he be?

"Sorry about that, guys. I was helping Mr. Cragun with his order. His huge, five-figure, more-than-I-make-in-six-months order." She looked exuberant, as if she wanted to start dancing among the aisles of flowers.

Olivia fist-bumped her, which resulted in all the boys holding up their fists, too. "Good job, Mel! You win the sales associate of the day."

"Is that really a thing?" Melody asked. "Because if it's not, it should be. And I should definitely win it."

"It is today. Way to go."

Olivia's enthusiasm was genuine. She was a good friend to

Melody and sincerely seemed to want to help her regain some of the confidence that had been gutted by that bastard Rich Baker.

"Way to go, Mom," Charlie said, clearly not knowing what they were talking about but not wanting to be left out.

"Thanks, kiddo. It was pretty cool. I can't wait to see the landscaping job he's doing down the coast. It sounds spectacular."

She looked over the wagonful of plants. "Wow. You obviously found some good things for the firehouse garden."

"Yeah. I think we're all set."

"For your information, you've already got twenty likes in about thirty seconds," Olivia informed him. She had uploaded something already? Apparently. Her smile of delight left him more than a little uncomfortable.

"Well, people obviously are bored tonight."

"Either that or I take really great pictures and know what human interest angles people will love."

"That's so cool," Melody exclaimed.

"We're going to be celebrities," Will said, puffing out his chest.

Olivia laughed and it was like the sun bursting through dark clouds after a rainy day, full of light and joy and hope. Something stirred in his chest and he wanted to stare at her all day.

"You're already celebrities, as far as I'm concerned," she said. "But now the rest of the town can see how awesome you guys are."

"Now the only thing left to do is plant them," Melody said. "I'm working in the morning, but maybe I can come over when I'm done and help you put them in the ground."

"We can help, too," Charlie offered.

"As long as you think that will get us more likes," Ryan said, with a worried look.

"Here's a little free advice, kid," Cooper said. "You should never be worried about how many likes you're getting but on the life you're creating."

"You should put that on a T-shirt," Olivia said.

"Yeah," Will said with a mischievous grin. "Then we can put it up online and I bet you would get a million likes."

Cooper laughed and tugged down Will's baseball cap so it covered his eyes. One of the best things about coming back to help Melody had been getting to know these boys as individuals. He had always stayed in touch with emails, text messages and video calls, but interacting with them every day brought an entirely new dimension to their relationship. He loved Will's boldness and his funny sense of humor, Ryan's overriding sense of concern for his mother and brothers, Charlie's infectious joy in life.

"Maybe I will make T-shirts. And you can be the first one to wear one."

"Okay," Will said. "As long as Olivia takes my picture and puts it online."

"You got it," she said with a smile that again made Cooper want to kiss her.

"Come on," he said instead to the boys. "Let's go pay for these before the place closes or we might have to spend the night sleeping in the rows between the plants."

"I happen to know the family who runs the place," Olivia said. "I bet somebody would at least cover you with dirt to keep you warm."

All the boys giggled at that and even Cooper couldn't hide his smile. It slipped away when he caught Melody gazing between him and Olivia with growing speculation in her eyes that sent sudden panic flaring through.

Oh no. If Mel had any idea that he was interested in Olivia, that they had shared a heated kiss after her birthday party, she would be thrilled and would do her best to throw them together at every opportunity.

He had to figure out a way to head her off. While he wanted his sister to focus her attention on something besides her divorce and her sleazy ex-husband, he did *not* need Melody to decide to meddle and matchmake between her brother and her best friend.

"I would love to put up some follow-up photos of you guys actually planting the garden," Olivia said. "That will definitely keep people engaged, especially everybody who is liking today's posts, and remind them again of the fund-raiser. When do you think you'll put in the plants?"

He sighed. "A day or two. I'm not sure."

"Well, keep me updated so we can do another push for the fund-raiser before Saturday. Then maybe in a week or so we can put up a photo of something you or one of the other firefighters has cooked using some of the herbs you planted."

"Sure. You can follow us all summer as we pull weeds and water and pick the tomatoes."

"I might do that," she said, undeterred by his sarcasm. "For now, I'll stick with taking pictures of you planting the garden. Later, we can come up with a strategy for the rest of the year."

He wasn't sure if she was joking or serious. He supposed it didn't really matter. Right now, he couldn't seem to think beyond the fact that he would at least get to see her again in a few days.

22

JULIET

She was a lousy patient.

That was a rather humbling realization for a woman in her fifties to discover about herself but was nevertheless the absolute truth.

Juliet shifted position on the recliner where the physical therapist had returned her when he left an hour earlier.

She hadn't been very nice to the poor man. The memory made her cringe. She should have been more cooperative. He was only trying to help her heal. Instead, she had been sarcastic and sharp, especially after he had suggested she was perhaps not giving her all to her recovery.

Something about his patronizing tone had made her want to yank his ID badge off and shove it into his flapping cake hole.

The man was two decades younger than she was and obviously fit. He probably subsisted on only tofu and kale. He had no idea how hard these exercises were for her. She *was* trying her best but everything was harder. In addition to multiple broken bones, she had a serious neurological disease.

Her multiple sclerosis complicated everything, especially her confidence in herself. She hated that part, the little creeping doubts that had begun to take over.

She had always told herself she could learn to live with her diagnosis and handle her disease with grace and dignity. She had met others online who were dealing with their symptoms superbly. Many of them had been in remission for years and were using a combination of diet and exercise to stay as healthy as possible for as long as possible.

She wanted to be among that group. Many, like her, had chosen not to reveal the diagnosis, at least to coworkers and associates. Most had valid reasons. Inevitably, when someone announced they had a serious condition, the ripple effect included workplace discrimination, relationship problems, social stigma.

She still wasn't sure if her decision not to tell Caitlin and Olivia about her condition had been correct. When she had been diagnosed four years earlier, after suspecting something was wrong for several months before that, she had been shell-shocked and told herself she needed time to come to terms with it herself before she told them. And then Olivia had been at a transitional time in her life, dating the man she would later become engaged to and starting a new job with a new apartment, and that hadn't seemed right, either.

How could Juliet mar her daughter's newfound happiness by telling her she had been diagnosed with MS, especially when she had still been adjusting herself?

Because she didn't want Olivia to know, she hadn't felt right about telling Caitlin, either. Her granddaughter had enough worries in her life and she knew Caitlin well enough to be certain her granddaughter would turn clingy and overprotective.

In her heart, Juliet knew those were simply excuses. She hadn't wanted people to know about her multiple sclerosis because she didn't want them feeling sorry for her.

She had found it unbearably difficult to be branded the sad young widow in town after Steve's untimely death. She had hated the pitying looks she would see in other people's faces, the awkward, uncomfortable gaps in conversation in social situations, the way some of her friends had dropped away because they hadn't known what to say to her.

That pity was only magnified after Natalie's overdose.

She could have told Olivia and Caitlin about her MS at any time in the past four years. She still wasn't sure why she had been so fiercely determined to keep it to herself. Pride, maybe? Or was it simply habit?

Olivia didn't need another burden to carry. Juliet knew it was hard enough for her to leave her job in Seattle to come back and help her recovery. She absolutely didn't want her to feel obligated to move home permanently.

Guilt twisted through her. She should just tell everyone and be done with things. She wouldn't be able to keep her MS a secret forever anyway.

If nothing else, she would at least have to tell Henry, especially if he persisted in thinking they could have some kind of relationship.

She was going to miss his friendship so dearly.

She didn't want to think about the Henry-shaped hole that would be left in her life without him in it. He had brought so much laughter and joy these past few years.

She loved being with him, no matter what they did. Taking a walk on the beach with his dog leading the way. Working in her garden together. The quiet, simple winter evenings when she would pop a batch of popcorn and they would watch a movie with the kids.

Otis scampered over and put his front legs up on the recliner, holding his furry little face close to her. He was so very gentle around her, careful not to nudge her or wander across her path when she was using the walker or the crutches, as if he knew she was fragile right now and needed only love and support from him.

Why couldn't Henry take a lesson from the dog? She sighed. "Do you need to go out?"

Otis gave her a look she clearly interpreted as an affirmative answer. Taking him out had become her biggest exercise during the day, the one time she made a concerted effort to use the crutches. He was trained to use a puppy pad but seemed to like a certain patch of grass in one corner of her yard.

It was good for her to have to move, even when it was hard. All the literature Dr. Adeno gave her said she should change positions at least every forty-five minutes.

She carefully went through the ordeal of standing up with the walker, then laboriously headed through the kitchen to the back door. As slowly as she moved, it was a good thing the dog seemed to have a patient bladder or there would be accidents throughout the house.

The pain had eased over the past week. It was always there but more like a dull throb than the piercing agony of the previous week.

She had become good at ignoring it and she was more grateful than she could say that she had spent the past four years since her diagnosis building muscle tone. If not for that, she feared she would have suffered a far more debilitating injury.

Otis was eager to go out, dancing around in front of the door.

"Give me a minute," she told him. With the crutches under her arms, she reached to open the door and he was out into the fenced backyard in a flash.

The words of the PT seemed to ring in her ear, that the harder she pushed herself, the sooner she would be able to return to her life.

She wanted to be back at work. She missed the garden center

so much, she ached. The doctor had said maybe if she felt strong enough, she could return to part-time work after another week or so. With that in mind, she pushed herself to walk back from the kitchen at the rear of the cottage all the way to the front door. Still feeling good, she opened the front door, thinking she would sit out on the porch to rest for a moment before she had to go let the dog back in.

Outside, the afternoon was glorious, with high puffy clouds in an otherwise spectacularly blue sky. She breathed in the sea air and listened to the gulls wheeling and diving, then began to make her way to one of the porch chairs.

She made it to the chair, then started to shift her weight so she could back down into it. She knew in an instant something was wrong. One of the crutches caught on an all-weather area rug she had put out here and started to slide in the wrong direction.

Her balance was off. She didn't know if it was the MS or the crutches or the hip injury. She only knew she was going down and wasn't going to hit the chair.

She shifted at the last minute so her other hip took the brunt of the fall to the porch floor. Pain still smacked her hard, stealing her breath and bringing tears to her eyes. Shocked and dazed, she gave in to the tears and the pain as bruises that had begun to fade from her original fall off the ladder reminded her they were very much still there and still sore.

Gradually, she knew she was going to have to get up. She couldn't lie here on the porch in a crumpled heap all afternoon. Especially not when Otis was beginning to bark in the backyard to come in and would be wondering why she was leaving him out there.

She shifted positions and only then did she realize what a fix she was in.

She couldn't possibly lift herself from the ground in her current state—not when she couldn't put her full weight on her left hip.

Shoot. What was she going to do? She didn't want to call Olivia. Her daughter still seemed convinced Juliet needed someone here all day with her and this would provide fuel to her argument. Caitlin was in school. She couldn't call her. Maybe one of Juliet's friends could come by. Or she could call Cooper and have him send one of his cute firefighter friends over.

She reached inside the pocket of her sweater for her phone and had the horrifying, sickening realization that she must have left it beside the recliner earlier, when she got up to put the dog out. Now what? If she couldn't call for help, she simply would have to get up on her own. She could not spend the afternoon here, with pain still throbbing through her.

She was trying to twist herself into a position so that she could use the chair behind her for leverage when she heard a vehicle pull up. An instant later, Henry was racing toward the porch, a horrible look of fear on his features.

"Juliet! Good Lord. What are you doing? What happened?"

Though it had only been maybe five minutes since she fell, it felt like forever. She sighed, mortified that, of all the people in town who might have driven by and seen her predicament, Henry had to be the one who came to her rescue.

"Don't make any jokes, but I really did fall and couldn't get back up."

"I'm afraid to move you. Should I call the paramedics? Did you hurt anything?"

"Only my pride. Who knew I had any left? I didn't have my phone to call for help and was just trying to figure out how to get back up on my own when you pulled up. I just need a helping hand."

In answer, he reached down and lifted her effortlessly, pushed open the door and carried her inside.

"Bed or chair?"

"Wheelchair. It's in the kitchen. Thank you. But you don't have to carry me. I can walk."

Kind of.

"Be quiet," he ordered, and carried her through the house to the wheelchair, where he lowered her down with a tenderness that made her throat ache.

"How long were you on the floor?"

"Not long. Maybe five minutes. I got yelled at by the physical therapist today for not pushing myself hard enough, so I decided to go a little farther on the crutches."

"Why isn't someone here with you?"

"I don't need a babysitter. For the most part, I'm able to get around. I can get in and out of my chair, the bed, the bathroom and can go into the kitchen for something to eat. Olivia checks on me during the day and usually sends someone from the garden center over, too. I knew if I waited out there long enough, someone would come."

She just hadn't expected it to be Henry.

What would she do if her condition worsened and she needed more consistent care? It was a worry that kept her up at night. This hip injury had only reinforced it.

She was a lousy patient and had a feeling she would only get worse.

"You don't have to tell me. I should be more careful about keeping my cell phone on me at all times so I can call the garden center if something happens."

"Good thing I was passing by and happened to see you up there—though I think I lost ten years of my life."

Too bad he hadn't. Then he would be two years older than she was and one more obstacle between them would be gone.

"Thank you."

"You're welcome," he said gruffly.

"Would you mind letting the dog back in?"

"Sure."

He went to the back door and opened it for Otis, who rushed

inside and immediately jumped into her lap, as if to reassure himself that she was all right.

Henry followed more slowly. "Since I'm here, I've got a truck full of shrubs and plants ready to go in at Hidden Creek. I bought them yesterday and I'm heading down today. Do you want to see what we're planting?"

"Yes!" she exclaimed. "I would love to. I think I'll have to use the wheelchair, though."

She started to wheel through the house, but Henry quickly took over, helping her out onto the porch and down the ramp to his vehicle.

She couldn't see everything from her vantage point in the chair, but what she did see was beautiful. "Love your choices," she said. "Did Olivia help you pick them out?"

"No. Melody Baker, actually. She's very knowledgeable and actually directed me away from a couple of things, toward some choices I think actually will work better."

"Oh, I'm so glad she's working out. I hope she'll stay on after I'm back. If I ever get back."

Suddenly, without warning, she could feel tears burning again in her throat. She was so tired of the pain and the uncertainty and, yes, the fear. She had been afraid when she was stranded there on the ground earlier. Only now did she realize how much. It had been a terrifying thing when she couldn't make her body cooperate, something she worried was only a precursor of things to come.

"You'll get there," he said softly. "I know it's hard to be patient but right now your body just needs time to heal."

"I know." To her mortification, she felt a tear slide down. Henry reached a thumb out and wiped it away, which only made more tears trickle down after the first one.

"I'm sorry. I don't know why I'm crying."

The lie tangled in her throat. She knew why. She was crying because her heart ached at the idea that soon she would have to push this wonderful man out of her life and she was crying because she selfishly wanted to hold on to him as long as she could.

"I've got a crew meeting me down the coast to help me plant these tomorrow. Want to come along?"

"I shouldn't." She wasn't sure she could afford to spend more time with him.

"But you want to."

So desperately.

"It will take you the better part of the day to plant everything. I don't think I'm up to that," she said honestly. "I would hate for you to have to cut away early to bring me back."

"Understood." He sounded as disappointed as she felt. "Maybe we could take a drive down later to see it, though."

She should not be encouraging him to spend more time with her. She knew it would not end well. But she was weak and stupid and hopelessly in love with him.

"I would love that," she murmured.

He pushed her back into the house, Otis trotting after them.

"Where do you want to settle while you wait for Olivia and Caitlin to get back?"

"The wheelchair is fine for now. By the window, where I can enjoy the view."

He situated her just so, then stepped back. "Anything else I can get you before I leave?"

"I'm fine," she said.

He leaned in to kiss her cheek. The feel of his mouth against her skin sent shivers down her spine.

One kiss.

What would be the harm in sharing another one?

She turned her head, her gaze locked with his, but before their mouths could meet, she heard someone at the front door and quickly leaned her head away just as Caitlin rushed inside.

"Hi, Mr. Cragun." She sounded slightly breathless, as if she had run up Harper Hill.

"What are you doing home so early?" Juliet demanded, grateful beyond words that Caitlin hadn't caught her kissing Henry.

"It's not that early. I just skipped my last hour, which is PE. I had a stomachache. I talked to Coach Landry and told him I would go for an extra run this weekend to make up for it."

She didn't appear to have a stomachache. She seemed fine, if a little on edge. Juliet frowned but didn't want to reprimand her in front of Henry for skipping her last class again.

"Well, I need to take off. I feel better now that you're here," he said to Caitlin. "Take care of your grandmother. Make sure she takes her pain medicine, since she fell a little while ago."

Caitlin's distracted expression shifted to concern as she focused on her grandmother. "Wait—what? Are you okay? Did you reinjure your hip or your ribs?"

"I'm totally fine. Don't worry about me, darling." Juliet glared at Henry. He should never have even mentioned that to Caitlin. The girl had enough worries on her mind.

"I'll see you later," he said. "Be careful."

She nodded, though she knew it was far too late for that.

23

CAITLIN

She was about to go out of her freaking mind.

Caitlin carefully set her backpack on one of the kitchen chairs, her attention completely focused on the laptop and the email that had come in just as she was shutting down in the school library at the end of fifth hour.

Her DNA results were in.

She had wanted to stay in the library and explore everything contained in that email but she had been terrified at the same time. What if she lost it? This wasn't something she wanted to read in a public place, where anyone could see her if she broke down.

She was about to find answers. She knew she was. She simply had to pore over the information until she found them.

Where was Jake? She needed him! He was so much better than she was at sifting through this kind of information to make the connections.

She had texted him again, asking him to come over as soon as he was done with his orthodontist appointment, but she had yet to hear back.

Could she wait long enough for him to come over? Or should she open the email and start looking herself?

She gazed at her laptop like it was a coiled snake, about to hiss at her.

"What's on your mind, honey?"

Mimi had wheeled into the kitchen behind her, her expression concerned. Caitlin shifted, embarrassed at her self-absorption. Mimi had fallen, Mr. Cragun had said, and had been hurt. Instead of worrying about her grandmother, she was sitting here glaring at her laptop.

"Nothing," she lied. "Just schoolwork."

"Anything I can help you with?"

"I think I'm good," she mumbled. "Thanks, though."

For a moment, she was tempted to confide in her grandmother. This news seemed too huge to hold inside and she would die if she couldn't tell someone. Since Jake wasn't here, who else could she tell?

No. She couldn't tell Mimi. Her greatest fear was that Mimi might think she had embarked on this quest to find her father because she felt like her grandmother wasn't enough for her.

That wasn't the truth at all. Mimi was the most amazing grandparent anyone could ask for and Caitlin loved her with all her heart.

"Are you sure? What course are you having trouble with?"

"Uh…" Her mind went blank. "Biology," she finally said quickly.

"Really? You usually do well in the class."

"We're studying DNA and it's kind of confusing but I'm sure I'll be fine. Jake's really good at this stuff, though. I'm sure he can help me as soon as he gets here."

"All right. Well, if you change your mind about me helping you, I won't be far. I'm going to move to the recliner for a while."

"I'll help you transfer," Caitlin said.

"Not necessary," Mimi said. "Stay here and have a snack or something."

She didn't want a snack. She wanted to go on her laptop and read that blasted email. Instead, she went with her grandmother and, despite Mimi's protests, helped stabilize the walker so she could transfer out of the wheelchair.

"Thank you," Mimi said. "Now don't worry about me. I'm fine. Go focus on your homework."

Homework. She couldn't even think about homework right now. She wanted to run to Jake's house with her laptop. She would have, except she didn't feel good about leaving Mimi after her fall.

To keep herself from opening the email, she sat on the sofa, not far from Mimi, and texted Jake again.

To her vast relief, he texted her back immediately.

Just got this. Sorry. On my way. Be there shortly.

"Is that Jake?" Mimi asked.

"Yes. He's on his way. Whew."

"That's a relief." Mimi smiled. "You might as well invite him for dinner, if he's interested. Olivia put something in the slow cooker this morning. It smells like sweet-and-sour chicken."

Her stomach growled, reminding her she hadn't eaten much lunch.

She should get a snack now but she was way too excited to wait.

To her relief, Jake showed up at the door just a few moments later.

"Hey," he said, with a worried look. "What's up? You said it was urgent."

"Um, yes. You said you would help me with my biology homework."

When he looked confused she gave a pointed look at her computer. "You know. We're studying DNA and stuff."

He stared at her for a second, then shook his head. "I'll help you. But you know how I feel. DNA can only take you so far. The choices we make and the people we surround ourselves with are more important than our DNA."

She frowned, not in the mood for a lecture. Jake knew how important this was to her. She didn't want to hear how she should focus on being grateful she had a loving grandmother.

"Before you start on homework, maybe you could help out with dinner," Juliet suggested.

Ugh. Caitlin wanted to bang her head against the door. She couldn't wait another minute.

"Sure. No problem. What can we do to help?" Jake asked.

Some days, Caitlin really wished her best friend wasn't such a nice person.

"Not much. I think we only have to throw some rice into the rice cooker."

Caitlin ground her back teeth. Dinner was the last thing on her mind right now, when the answers to her quest might be only a few clicks away. But how long did it really take to start a rice cooker? It was so brainless, even she could do it, and she didn't like to cook.

She and Jake worked together measuring out brown rice then adding the water and a smidge of coconut oil, Mimi's special twist.

Once they hit the right button on the cooker, Caitlin scooped up her laptop.

"Okay. Rice is cooking. It will take about fifteen or twenty minutes, which will probably be enough time for us to make a good start on my homework. Are you okay if we go up to my room?"

"Sure," Mimi said. "I have a feeling whatever you're burning to talk about has nothing to do with homework, but go ahead."

It was very hard to get anything past Mimi. Caitlin leaned down and kissed her grandmother on the cheek. "Thanks. Love you. Be back in fifteen."

She raced up the stairs to her bedroom that overlooked the ocean. She sat in one corner of the window seat and Jake sat in the other one.

He had grown so tall over the past few years that it was hard for both of them to fit here anymore.

He would be going to college in another year.

What would she do without him?

She wasn't going to worry about that right now.

"My results came in, if you couldn't figure that out by all the hints I dropped on your head."

"Yeah. I got that," Jake said. "What do they say?"

"I don't know. I haven't had time to look. And anyway, I feel better about waiting until you are here with me to help me interpret them."

She opened her laptop and quickly hit the link in her email that took her to the genealogy website.

"I'm so nervous," she whispered.

He reached a hand out and squeezed her knee. "You won't know until you look. But just remember, even if you don't find any connections, you still have a family and friends who love you."

"I know that."

"I just don't want you to be too disappointed if you end up not knowing anything new."

She drew in a deep breath and looked over the chart showing her results.

"I have some Native American in me. That's cool. That's got to be from my dad, since I don't think Mimi has any on her side.

And I have some from Eastern Europe. Russia or the Ukraine. That could be from my grandpa Steve's side."

Jake looked over her shoulder. "Look. You're 20 percent Irish. My mom's mom came over from County Clare."

What if Jake was related to her? She'd never thought about that. Wouldn't that be weird?

And more than a little horrible.

"That's interesting info. I have a lot of Western European ancestry, too."

"Where's the part that shows who you might be related to?"

She looked around. "I don't see anything like that." Had this all been for nothing, as he had warned her?

"Can I take a look?"

Jake was tons better at computer stuff. Caitlin handed over her laptop, and after a few clicks around the website, Jake paused and gave her a funny look.

"What?" she finally asked when he said nothing.

"There's a link. Someone else related to you has entered their DNA into the database."

She wanted to snatch the laptop back from him. "Is it my dad?"

He shook his head. "It says first cousin. But according to the info, that could also be an aunt or a grandma or grandpa. It just means one step removed from a sibling or a parent."

"It's probably Mimi or Olivia," she said, kind of afraid to think anything else.

"It's not. There's a username. Do you want to see it?"

Suddenly, she wasn't sure. Fear seemed to hit her in the gut like one of those giant inflatable balls from PE class.

Why had she ever started this? What a stupid idea. Jake should have talked her out of it.

She didn't want to know. Her mom hadn't loved her enough to stay off drugs. What made her think her dad would want anything to do with her? He had walked away and had never looked back, as far as she knew.

"No," she whispered, closing the lid of her laptop. "We should forget this whole thing."

"Really? After you've gone to this much work to find answers? I mean, we went to the church youth group the other night and everything. This is a big clue, Cait. Everything you wanted to know."

She had dragged him along with her, every step of the way. From the moment she put the dream of finding her dad into words, Jake had supported her. She couldn't chicken out now. He was right. She was so close.

She opened the laptop, still facing the screen away from her. "Is there an email address we can look up?"

"It's a username. And it's someone you know. We both know."

"Who?"

He met her gaze. "It says Melody Baker is a close relative of yours. You share a significant portion of DNA with her."

Melody Baker.

Holy shit. She hadn't seen that coming.

"Mel is related to me?"

"Looks like it. It says first cousin, aunt or grandparent."

Melody Baker. Melody Vance Baker, whose brother, Cooper Vance, had been her mother's best friend. The implication left her light-headed.

"She's my aunt." She drew in a breath then another one, feeling like someone had just thrown another of those balls at her. "Mel is my aunt. She has to be. It's the only explanation that makes sense. Will, Ryan and Charlie are my cousins."

"You can't know that for sure."

"I do. I absolutely know it for sure."

She should have seen it before. How could she have been so stupid? Her mother only mentioned him every other page in the journal.

"So that means…" His voice trailed off.

"That means Chief Vance is my father. That's the only possibility."

"We can't know that for sure. Maybe there's another brother. Maybe there's a dad somehow in the picture."

"First of all, *ew*. My mom would never sleep with her best friend's dad."

She didn't know how she could be so sure of that but she was, 100 percent.

"Second of all, Melody told me once that her dad was not in the picture from the time she was little. Third, I know there's not another brother. Melody and Cooper were the only two kids. Their aunt and uncle lived here, but she told me he was an uncle to her by marriage, so he can't be my dad. And they didn't have kids. No. It has to be Cooper."

All this time, the answer had been right in front of her. She had wondered if he might be one of the candidates, but her mother's diary only mentioned him as a friend. Never anything romantic.

Olivia's diary, on the other hand, had overflowed with gushy stuff about Cooper Vance. When her aunt had been Caitlin's age, she had definitely been thirsty for Cooper. She had written *Mrs. Cooper Vance* about a hundred times inside her journal.

She looked at the information, everything inside her reeling.

She knew her dad.

Chief Vance was her dad!

Her first instinct was to hurry downstairs and tell Mimi. Did she know? Somehow Caitlin doubted it. Whenever she had brought up her father with Mimi, her grandmother had seemed genuinely baffled about his identity.

"Do you think he knows?" Jake asked.

She thought of the few interactions she'd had with Cooper and the times she had brought up her mom with him. He had seemed genuinely sad about Natalie. She had seen no trace of guilt or weirdness in him.

"Maybe. I don't know. He doesn't really seem like the kind of guy who would just walk away."

"So that means your mom never told him."

She couldn't know for sure, but that was what she suspected, too. Why hadn't she told him? "I guess not."

"What now? Will you tell him?"

She had to, didn't she? But how exactly did someone go about blurting out the news to a guy she barely knew that he had a fifteen-year-old daughter?

"What do you think I should do?"

Jake slid from the window seat to the floor, where he could stretch out his long legs. "It's a can of worms, Cait. There had to be a reason your mom never told him she was pregnant with his baby."

What could that be? She couldn't for the life of her think of a reason. Why had Natalie been so careful to keep the identity of her baby's father a secret? Had she not wanted Cooper to know he had a child? Or had she been with more than one guy and genuinely hadn't known who, exactly, had fathered the baby?

"I don't know what to do. I almost wish I hadn't done the DNA test now."

"At least you know now. The big mystery has been solved."

Funny, she didn't feel that way. She almost felt like she had more questions now than she'd ever had.

The timer on her phone suddenly went off, and she jumped in shock for a minute before she remembered why she had set it. The rice for dinner was done, which meant Olivia would be home soon.

How was she going to face Mimi and Olivia without revealing everything she had just found out?

Forget Mimi and Olivia. How was she ever going to face Melody and her boys?

And, more significantly, how was she going to tell Chief Vance that she was his long-lost daughter and wanted more than anything to have a relationship with him?

Or at least she thought she did.

24

OLIVIA

After several sixteen-hour days in a row, Olivia wanted a long bubble bath, a glass of wine if she could find it and a good book that would help her escape to another world.

More likely, she would be lucky to grab a quick shower and maybe have time for dinner before helping Juliet with her nightly routine then collapsing on her bed.

She walked in and was pleasantly surprised to hear the rice cooker going off and see Caitlin stirring the stuff she had thrown into the slow cooker that morning, while Jake and Juliet set the table.

"Hi," she said with a smile that Jake and her mother returned.

"Dinner's almost ready. Go ahead and wash up while we finish setting everything out," Juliet said.

Apparently, her mom had had a good day. Juliet's voice sounded strong and almost cheerful.

Wouldn't it be a dream if she could come home to a cooked

meal every day? As unlikely as that might be, she could at least enjoy it tonight.

"Thanks for cooking the rice," she said to Caitlin after she had washed up and changed out of her work clothes and they were sitting down to eat.

"It was nothing. All I had to do was measure stuff into the cooker and turn it on. A trained monkey could have done it. Even an untrained one."

"Too bad we don't have a trained monkey."

"Or an untrained one," her mother chimed in.

"Nope. Only me." Caitlin looked down at her food, pushing it around her plate with her fork. Why wasn't she eating?

Olivia glanced at Jake and found him watching her niece with a concerned expression. When he sensed her attention fixed on him, he gave an obviously fake smile and returned to his meal, with twice Caitlin's enthusiasm.

What was wrong? She hated all the secrets in her family. Why couldn't people just say what was going on with them?

"How did Melody do today?"

Caitlin looked up sharply at Juliet's question, then returned to staring at her food.

"Good. She only worked part of the day. One of the boys had something at school today."

"She sure has her hands full with those boys," Juliet said.

"She does. Did I tell you about the fun impromptu photo shoot I did with them last night at the garden center?"

By the time she had returned home the night before, Juliet had been tired and they hadn't had a chance to talk.

"I told you the mayor asked me to help spread the word about the fund-raiser they're doing this weekend for Chief Gallegos by increasing engagement with the fire department's social media sites, right?"

"How is that going?" Juliet asked.

"So far, I have to say the campaign is a huge success. It's been a slow and steady build, but the fire department account picked up four hundred new likes overnight."

"All because of you? That's amazing," Juliet said.

"Not me. Not really." She knew just where to give the credit. The city's hunky new fire chief. "I had a good subject. Cooper came in last night with Melody's kids to buy some plants he could put in around the fire station. Herbs and some vegetables to brighten up the meals served to the firefighters and EMTs."

Oddly, for reasons she didn't quite understand, this seemed to grab Caitlin's attention. She lifted her gaze from her plate to stare at Olivia, eyes wide.

Jake, on the other hand, hardly seemed to be paying any attention to Olivia. His attention was now completely focused on Caitlin, with more of that worry in his eyes.

"Oh, good for Cooper," Juliet said. "What a good idea. Steve used to complain about the bland food at the station."

The reminder of her father, as usual, made her heart hurt for a minute before she pushed it away.

"I took some pictures of Cooper and his nephews picking out all the plants for the garden. You know how adorable they are."

"Cooper has turned into a good-looking man, too. He was always cute, but he's definitely grown into his looks."

Her mother. A genius at understatement.

"Yes. Yes, he has. As a result of all the cuteness, I added hundreds of people who are now following the fire department."

"Good job, honey," Juliet said.

"And of course I tagged the garden center to make sure everybody knows they should come to Harper Hill Home and Garden for all the best gardening supplies."

"Smart," Jake said with a smile.

Caitlin, Olivia noticed, hadn't said anything. She seemed to be growing more and more tense.

"Cooper didn't love being the center of attention but too bad. I'm going to do it all over again tomorrow."

"Is he coming back for more plants?" Juliet asked.

"No. He and the boys are going to be planting what they bought and I plan to be there to capture it all."

"How fun," Juliet said. "I may have to go into my sadly neglected profile so I can see them."

"Chief Vance has been a friend of your family for a long time, hasn't he?" Jake asked in a nonchalant sort of voice that Olivia found highly suspicious—especially when she caught Caitlin elbowing him.

"Oh my, yes." Juliet smiled, apparently not noticing anything out of the ordinary. "He and Natalie were the best of friends. A lot like you and Caitlin, Jake. He came for dinner all the time, didn't he, Olivia?"

Yes. And she had been gawky and tongue-tied around him from the age of about eleven. "Yes. He and Mel would both eat here at least once a week. Maybe more."

"And he and Caitlin's mom were never anything more than friends?"

Again, Caitlin seemed to elbow him.

Olivia wanted to elbow him also, especially since she couldn't seem to stop thinking about the kiss she and Cooper had shared.

Okay, she could admit it. She had always been more than a little jealous of his friendship with Natalie. They had been so close and had shared everything.

When she was younger, she had resented him because she missed her big sister and knew Natalie shared things with him she never shared with Olivia. As she got older, she had come to resent Natalie more, because she was able to spend so much time with Cooper when Olivia had been the one with the fierce crush on him.

"They were good friends. That's all," Juliet said. "I always hoped their friendship could have turned into something more. Cooper was always a great kid, so much better than some of the other guys she dated."

Natalie hadn't always gone for the wild, party type. After she turned about sixteen, she had started hanging with a different crowd at school and started wearing edgier clothes, wearing way more makeup, dyeing her hair. She had also started staying out late.

It was around that time she stopped bringing Cooper around as much, which had broken Olivia's heart.

"Anyway, that was a long time ago," Juliet said, giving a smile that only looked slightly forced.

"Do you need any help with your photo shoot tomorrow?" Jake asked. "Somebody to hold the flash or something? Maybe Caitlin and I can help you. I would be interested to see what you do."

She blinked, surprised at the offer. "You're welcome to come if you want, but it's not really an official photo shoot in the traditional sense of the word, just a casual, fun thing."

"I don't know. We might be busy," Caitlin said, with a meaningful look at Jake that Olivia couldn't interpret.

"Well, if you're in the neighborhood of the fire station, come by. We're meeting up about five."

"Maybe we will," Jake said. "Thanks."

He was a good kid, too. If her niece had any sense, she would grab hold of a good guy like Jake Cragun and not let go.

Olivia finished her meal, trying not to think too hard about the next day and the anticipation zinging through her at knowing she would see Cooper again.

He might not be that tough-looking teenager and she might not be twelve and gawky with braces and pigtails, but she was still entirely too obsessed with Cooper Vance.

COOPER

Today was the kind of day that made him question all of his life choices.

Reports of a brush fire had dragged him out of bed at 3:00 a.m.

By the time they had fought it to containment, the fire had burned one house and threatened several dozen more.

The worst of it was, he knew this had been a human-caused fire. Some idiot teenagers decided to light a campfire at their backyard keg party using gasoline, right in the middle of an area with plenty of dry scrub.

Where the hell the parents had been, he didn't know.

At least no lives had been lost, unlike some other nasty fires he had battled—including the one that killed Steve Harper.

He didn't like thinking about that night, about his own choices and their terrible consequences. He had not exactly blocked it out over the years, but he didn't spend a lot of time obsessing about what had happened.

Somehow the memories seemed sharper and more intense over the past few weeks—probably because Olivia was in town and he couldn't seem to stop thinking about *her*, which inevitably led him to thinking about her father.

Not that he had a lot of time to dwell on the past. After the brush fire was out, the morning had been one call after another, most of them sad and difficult. He had responded to a heart attack that Cooper was quite sure the man would not recover from, a car accident with injuries where they had to extract the driver with the Jaws of Life, and a drowning by an inexperienced diver who shouldn't have been anywhere near the cliffs.

He loved what he did. He loved being able to help people, especially when the outcome was better than it could have been.

He loved putting out fires with minimal damage, suppressed by a fast-acting, well-trained fire response team. He loved responding to a call he thought would be a bad one, only to find injuries were less severe than feared. He loved helping kids get their heads unstuck from banisters, rescuing kittens out of trees, delivering babies, which he'd done four times now.

He loved helping people. That was the basic truth. Yeah, he knew the desire had deep roots in his psyche. He hadn't needed the military shrink he'd gone to early in his service to tell him his need to help others stemmed from a childhood of trying and failing to fix his mother, with all her mental and emotional problems and the substance abuse she couldn't seem to beat.

Most days on the job were a mix of good and bad, which he had a much easier time processing. Today had been relentlessly bad. He was tired, sweaty, mentally and emotionally drained.

He wanted to grab a pizza and a six-pack, go down to the beach and just sit on a blanket while he let the waves soothe his battered spirit.

That plan would have to wait. First, he had to plant some herbs as part of this stupid public relations promotion cooked up by the mayor and Olivia Harper. On the positive side, at least he could work out some of his tangled emotions by digging in the dirt, which had its own rewards.

While he waited for Olivia and his nephews to arrive, Cooper picked up one of the fire department shovels he had used on that brush fire earlier to turn the dirt so he could mix in some of the soil prep he had bought.

He was almost done when he heard a car pull up and turned around to find Olivia climbing out of her hybrid, along with her funny-looking dog.

Late-afternoon sunlight glinted in her hair and seemed to make her features glow.

"Hi," she said, a little breathless. "Sorry I'm late. Everyone and their aunt Gladys came into the garden center today. I've been running all day and still haven't caught up."

He wanted to just stand here in the sunlight and stare at her as he felt a funny kind of peace trickle through him. How did she manage to push away all the dark sadness of the day, just by existing?

"I didn't even realize the time," he said. "I was busy trying to prepare the dirt."

"I can help you with that."

"You've been working in dirt all day. You're probably tired of gardening right about now. I know the garden center was never your favorite thing."

"How did you…?" She blinked, obviously taken off guard that he knew that about her. "I never really hated it. I guess I just…resented it. Does that sound stupid?"

"No. I get it."

"It was all-consuming for my family, you know? That first year or so after my dad died, my mom threw herself into the garden center. She was busy with it from first thing in the morning to long after I went to bed at night. She didn't have a lot of room left for anything else."

Yeah, he got that. Only his mom hadn't been interested in anything but booze and pills and men.

"And then Natalie got pregnant with Caitlin and Juliet *really* didn't have time for a needy adolescent. I guess you were gone by then."

Yeah. His mom had finally died of alcohol poisoning only a few months after Steve's death. After making sure Melody had a good home with their aunt and uncle, Cooper had enlisted as soon as he could and left for basic training.

"Anyway, the point is I don't really hate the garden center. In fact—" she looked around as if preparing to reveal a big secret "—don't tell my mom, but these last few weeks have taught me a new appreciation for it. I never realized how satisfying it can be to help someone find exactly the right plant they need for a certain spot in their garden."

She smiled. "Don't get me wrong. It will never be my first love. But if my mom ever falls off a ladder again and I have to come back to town to help her, I won't be completely miserable."

"Let's hope that doesn't happen," he said.

When she looked disconcerted, he realized what he had said. "That your mom falls off a ladder, I mean. Not you coming back. You can come back whenever you want."

"Um. Thanks," she said, leaving him feeling like a fumbling idiot.

"We should probably get the garden prepped before the boys get here," she said after he couldn't think of anything to say for several long seconds.

While Otis stretched out in a patch of sunlight, she went to work with a second shovel he'd brought out to the project. As they worked together, he could feel more of his tension trickle away.

The patch of ground wasn't particularly large, only about two feet wide by six feet long, so it didn't take them long to work in the bag of soil prep.

When they finished, she stepped away, setting the shovel against the wall of the building. "There you go. Ready to plant."

"Now if only the boys would get here. I guess everybody's running late tonight."

As soon as they said those words, they heard children's footsteps and the boys raced around the corner of the building. Otis jumped to his feet, wagging his little tail.

"Hey, Uncle Cooper. Hi, Olivia," his oldest nephew, Will, said, gasping to catch his breath. "We ran all the way down the hill to here."

"Where's your mom? I thought she was bringing you down," Cooper said, frowning.

"She said she has a migraine, so she called Caitlin and asked if she would come down with us."

Cooper smiled at the girl, struck again by how much she looked like her mother.

Someone else he couldn't save.

"Thanks, Caitlin. Nice of you to help out."

"You're welcome," she said without meeting his gaze.

Odd. Her face was pink and she looked like she wanted to be anywhere else in town. To be fair, if he had just run down the hill after three little boys, he might feel the same.

"This shouldn't take long," Olivia said. "We only have about a dozen plants to put in the ground."

"Do we have to pull any weeds? I hate pulling weeds," Charlie said.

"That part, lucky for you, is done. You only have to do the fun part now—planting the garden, while I take pictures of you."

He wasn't dreading that as much as he had expected, Cooper realized, surprised to discover more of his dark mood lifting. His day had been hard, but there was undeniable peace in being here with the boys and Olivia and her niece, planting something in anticipation of a big reward at some future time, even if he had to have his picture taken.

25

CAITLIN

She was being so stupid.

Caitlin wanted to dig a deep hole in the corner of his garden and bury her head in it.

What was *wrong* with her? She couldn't seem to put two words together. Everything she *did* say came out sounding backward and ridiculous.

Cooper Vance would never want to even speak to her again, let alone have a father-daughter relationship with her.

After a full day of trying to process the DNA results, she still couldn't accept the idea that she had found her dad. None of it seemed real, like it was something she was reading about in a book, happening to someone else.

She had a father. And she couldn't even say two words to him without fumbling and stuttering over her words.

She almost passed out when Melody called her, explaining that she had a migraine and asking if Caitlin would mind walking the boys down to the fire station so they could do the photo shoot with Olivia and Cooper. Her dad.

She had almost said no. She wasn't ready to see him again. It felt as if a bomb had exploded in her life and she needed like a week or two or twenty to process everything she had figured out the night before.

DNA didn't lie. That was what she kept saying to herself over and over again. If Melody was a close relative of hers, that had to mean Melody's brother was Caitlin's father. She couldn't come up with any other explanation.

Why hadn't the genealogy website explained to her how she was supposed to have a conversation with someone who didn't have any idea they were connected to her?

"Want to help plant a couple?" Chief Vance asked her now.

"Great idea," Olivia said, gesturing with her camera at Caitlin. "You're so photogenic. You would be great in the shots. We can show it's a real community effort. Kids, teens, everyone."

She did *not* want to plant some stupid vegetables, but she couldn't think of any way to get out of it. "Okay," she said, looking down at the dirt. Anywhere but at Cooper or Olivia.

"Here's a shovel," her aunt said. "Just make enough room for the start."

Caitlin had spent her entire childhood at the garden center. Jeez. She kind of knew by now how to put a plant in the ground, but she didn't want to sound like too much of a brat in front of the fire chief, so she obediently followed directions.

"Now a little water," Chief Vance said.

"Can we use the fire hose?" Ryan asked eagerly, which made Cooper smile.

Did they have the same smile? She kind of thought so. Their mouths were shaped the same and she had that same little dent in her chin. Her butt chin, Jake called it.

"I'm afraid the pressure of the fire hose would kill the plants,"

Cooper said. "How about we just fill a bucket from the faucet there?"

"What's the fun in that?"

He smiled and rubbed Ryan's head in a kind of cute, sweet way. Caitlin couldn't seem to look away from the sight of that big hand on the little kid's head, a deep ache in her chest.

Suddenly, she was aware of something else churning inside her. Something she completely hadn't expected.

She was angry. Full-on pissed. And she hadn't realized it until right this instant.

Why hadn't he been around to rub *her* head or smile like that at her? She'd never had a dad to teach her how to ride a bike or take her fishing or take her to daddy-daughter dances.

Where the hell had he been all her life?

He had slept with her mom. He must have. While that made her feel weird to think about, she had to face facts. He had slept with her mom, at least once. When Natalie showed up pregnant, why hadn't he stepped up to take responsibility?

She was finding it more and more difficult to believe he hadn't known. He had been in the military but he hadn't been on another freaking planet.

Okay. She was willing to give him a little latitude. He must have been, what, nineteen when she was born? He was the same age as her mother, so that would have been about right. Maybe he had been too immature and hadn't wanted to step up and be a father. That sucked, but she could understand it.

What about now, though? He wasn't a nineteen-year-old kid now. He was a man. Her dad, who had made zero effort to reach out to her.

She couldn't do this anymore.

"You should at least smile and pretend you're enjoying yourself," Olivia said.

Why would she do that?

"Are we done here?"

"I think so."

"Good. Can you make sure the boys get back home? I have homework to do. I can't spend all night here."

Otis whined and Cooper seemed a little taken aback by her sharp words, but Olivia didn't react. Her aunt was probably used to her by now, which made Caitlin feel like the biggest beyotch on the planet.

"I think so," Olivia said. "Thanks for helping."

"Definitely," Chief Vance said, giving her another smile that made her chest ache. "I'm sure Melody really appreciates you giving her a break, too."

Maybe if she'd had more time to prepare, she wouldn't be such a mess about being with him right now.

"Do you want me to take Otis with me?"

"No," Olivia said. "He's fine to hang out here."

"And don't worry about the boys. I can drop them off on my way home."

"All right."

She turned to go, suddenly afraid she would do something completely ridiculous like burst into tears, for no reason at all.

"If you wait a couple of minutes, I can give you a ride back to Sea Glass Cottage," Olivia offered.

"I prefer to walk," she snapped, then turned away feeling horrible and cranky.

She was an awful person, she thought. Since Olivia had been back in Cape Sanctuary, she had been nothing but kind to her, but Caitlin couldn't get past words her aunt had written years and years ago. She was a big baby. It was no wonder her dad didn't want anything to do with her.

She walked back up Harper Hill, her eyes burning. Tears began to drip down before she even made it to the house.

She thought she would be so happy once she found her father.

Taking that DNA test was supposed to be the answer to everything, all the questions that had haunted her throughout her life.

Now that she knew the truth, why did she feel worse than
ever?

OLIVIA

Olivia watched Caitlin stalk away, all too familiar with the
frustrated feeling.

What had she said this time? She went over the interaction
of the past fifteen minutes and couldn't figure out any triggers
that might have set Caitlin off.

Everything was going fine. Then suddenly Caitlin's mood
had changed abruptly, as if somebody had made the mistake of
flipping her angry switch.

Olivia was beginning to think just her very existence was
enough to annoy her niece. Stubborn girl. She sighed. It was
at least half a mile back to the house from the fire station. She
wanted to call her back and insist Caitlin allow her to give her a
ride, but held her tongue. If Caitlin wanted to work off some of
her pubescent angst by walking, Olivia wasn't about to stop her.

"What was that all about?"

She glanced at Cooper, trying not to notice how gorgeous
he looked in jeans and a fire department T-shirt that clung to
his muscles.

Who was she fooling? The man was so hot, she could barely
keep her hands off him.

"Who knows? Welcome to my life. Caitlin is always mad at
me for something."

He looked after her niece, frowning. "Funny. I got the distinct impression she was mad at *me*."

"Why would she be mad at you? She barely knows you."

"I don't know. Maybe she has a thing against herb gardens."

"I doubt that. She couldn't be a Harper, Juliet's granddaughter, and be opposed to any kind of garden. I can tell you that trying to figure out what goes on in that girl's head is guaranteed to give anyone a migraine. Your garden is lovely. I hope you can harvest some fresh herbs for years to come and make delicious meals for the fire department."

"Thanks for your help."

"And look! We've already got twenty comments on the post."

"Yippee," he said, his tone and expression conveying exactly the opposite of the enthusiastic word.

"You've been a good sport. The mayor will be happy and hopefully it will bring more people to the fund-raiser. That's the important thing."

"You're right. Thanks for the reminder."

He looked so tired suddenly, his features tight and tiny lines spanning out from his eyes. Since the moment she arrived at the fire station, she had sensed something was wrong, something she suspected had nothing to do with her or this photo shoot.

She thought he had perked up after the boys arrived, but now she could see traces of that discouragement return.

Caitlin was heading home. And Juliet wasn't there, which meant Olivia had an hour or two free.

She suddenly had an idea that might lift his spirits while also giving his sister a break from having to fix dinner. It meant she would have to spend more time with him than she knew was good for her, but she would somehow manage.

"Hey, it's such a pretty evening, I was thinking about grabbing a pizza from DiPalma's and eating at the park. Are you guys interested? It would be my treat, my way to pay you back for helping me out."

"Yay!" Charlie exclaimed.

"We love pizza," Will informed her.

"I want to go to the park!" Ryan added, as if the food was incidental.

They all turned their attention to Cooper. He hesitated, then gave a smile that seemed mostly genuine.

"Sure. Pizza is always good."

"Great. It will take me a few to check in with Melody and give her the new plan, then order the pizza. I just hope she hasn't planned something for dinner."

"I think she was making a casserole," Will said. "But she could always eat it herself and give us leftovers tomorrow."

She smiled at his logic. "That's true. Okay. I'll call her to make sure she doesn't mind. If it's okay with your mom, then I'll order the pizza. You guys have to promise you won't complain if your mom wants you home. We can do the park another time."

"We won't," they all promised. She wasn't sure she believed them but the point was moot anyway, since Melody was thrilled to have an evening to herself.

"Are you sure it's not too much trouble?"

"Not at all," Olivia said, glad she could give her friend a break.

Once that was settled, she called to order the pizza, instructing the delivery driver to meet them at the park, then grabbed a blanket out of the back of her SUV.

"Everybody ready?" she asked when Cooper and the boys rejoined her after putting away the tools.

"Ready!" all three boys called at once.

They headed off for the two blocks from the fire station to the largest city park, Driftwood Park, which led down to an easily accessible beach.

The boys fought over who could hold Otis's leash, so she came up with the idea of setting a timer on her phone and having them trade off every three minutes.

"You're full of surprises," Cooper said as they walked. "I know you're putting in long days at Harper Hill and also running your own business. Keeping track of three active boys is probably the last thing you must feel like doing."

"I don't mind," she answered honestly. "I didn't have anything else going on tonight."

"Where's your mom?"

"If you can believe it, Henry Cragun took her down the coast to look at a job site. This is their second trip down there in a week."

"That's nice."

"Especially because that gives me my first evening free since I've been back. I would love to spend it watching the sunset over the water and Driftwood Park has a great view."

"That does sound nice."

"If Melody has a migraine, she could probably use a rest, too. Or if she's feeling better, she could go to the grocery store on her own or sit in her beautiful garden and read a book."

She was painfully aware of him walking beside her, tall and tough, his features unreadable.

"You are a good person, Olivia Harper," he said gruffly after a moment.

She basked in the warmth of his words, though she knew they weren't precisely true. She was still haunted by the events in that coffee shop. If she were truly a good person, she wouldn't have cowered under that booth. She would have stood up to protect the barista the moment the attack started.

If she were a good person, her relationship with Juliet wouldn't feel so strained and difficult and maybe she could have a conversation with Caitlin without wanting to bang her head against the wall.

"I'm not as good as I should be," she admitted. "But I'm working on it."

"That's what life is about, isn't it? We're all works in progress, aren't we, just trying to become a little better every day?"

Yes. He was exactly right. She was taking small steps, but at least she wanted to think she was heading in the right direction.

They reached the park soon and headed for the grassy play

area overlooking the beach, where she had told the pizza delivery service to find them.

The sunset looked as if it would be spectacular, with puffy clouds on the horizon that would add depth and interest to the sky. She wished she had brought her good camera instead of leaving it locked back in her car but figured if the sunset was truly wonderful, she could at least capture it with her phone.

The boys immediately hurried to the play area, soon swinging and going down the slide. They hadn't been there long before the pizza driver showed up.

"I got this," Cooper said, pulling out his wallet.

"Forget that! It was my idea," she protested.

They bickered for a moment, but then Cooper ended the argument by handing money to the driver, who closed his hand around the bills.

"Keep the change," Cooper said. The driver grinned at the big tip and hurried back to his truck before Olivia could stop him.

The boys were instantly drawn to the food and hurried back to the blanket for a slice of pizza. Olivia had ordered root beer as well as a couple of water bottles. She wasn't at all surprised when each of the boys went for the soda.

They ate on the blanket, laughing while the boys told knock-knock jokes and tried to do tongue twisters.

She was glad she had a jacket as the evening air began to cool. It didn't seem to bother the boys, who ate quickly and then hurried back to the playground.

After they were gone, Cooper stretched out beside her on the blanket. "This was a good idea," he said.

"Thanks. I do have them once in a while."

"I think you have them more than once in a while," he said, his eyes closed behind his sunglasses.

Unable to resist, she snapped a couple of pictures of the boys playing together with her phone, lit by the fading light, to send to their mother. By the time she turned back to Cooper, his breathing was steady and she realized he had fallen asleep.

He seemed relaxed and comfortable, with his ankles crossed and one hand above his head.

Under other circumstances, she would have been tempted to take a picture of him for the fire department's social media site, labeling it The Chief At Rest. It would definitely go viral, but she knew he would hate that. Anyway, it would be a gross invasion of his privacy.

Instead, she watched him sleeping, noticing how the tension seemed to seep out of him as he truly relaxed his guard.

She was failing miserably at protecting her heart around him. Every time she thought she was safe, that she couldn't possibly fall for him, he did something sweet like help Charlie with his *R*s in one of the tongue twisters or catch Ryan at the bottom of the slide or check in with his sister to see how she was feeling.

Or trust her enough to fall asleep next to her.

Yeah, she was falling hard.

She watched the boys, trying not to give in to the panic suddenly kicking through her like Will beating against the air on the swings.

She couldn't. She had her life figured out. She was going back to Seattle as soon as it was safe for her mom to return to the garden center. She had an apartment there, a job, her company, a life.

She couldn't risk everything she had worked for by doing something completely stupid like opening herself up to having her heart broken—especially not by a man like Cooper. If she wasn't brave enough to climb out from beneath that table at the coffeehouse, she certainly didn't have the strength to take on a man like Cooper, who risked his life on a daily basis.

She had seen firsthand how losing someone you loved so deeply could devastate an entire family.

What if she was too late to protect her heart?

The thought haunted her as she sat in the park beside him, watching the boys play and the sun slide lower into the ocean. She had dated Grant for two years and been engaged for two more. Theirs had been a comfortable, quiet, easy relationship. She had cared about him and wouldn't have agreed to marry him if she hadn't thought she loved him, but in all that time, she had never known this wild tangle of tenderness and heat and aching need for Cooper.

No. Coming home to Cape Sanctuary had simply messed with her psyche. Dealing with her mother's care, the constant tension with Caitlin, her stress over the garden center. Her emotions were on edge right now, everything close to the surface. Once she returned to Seattle and the life she had created there, she would regain perspective and be able to see the difference between physical attraction and deep, meaningful love.

She was still trying to convince herself of that when Cooper woke up.

The sun had only just finished sliding below the horizon in a blaze of orange, lavender and peach. Will and Ryan were still on the swings, but Charlie had come to the blanket and was now sitting on her lap, with Otis on *his* lap.

She watched as the sleep faded from his eyes.

"Hey. You weren't supposed to let me sleep."

"I didn't know those were my orders."

He sat up, scrubbing his face. "Sorry. It's been a really long day, starting with a fire in the early hours."

Thank you for another reminder of why I can't fall for you, she thought. "We should probably get these guys home. The older two still have school tomorrow."

"I don't. I could stay here all night," Charlie declared.

"You could, but I'm afraid Otis and I need to go to bed."

Charlie sighed. "Can we come back tomorrow? This was the best night."

She smiled and hugged him. "It really was," she said. For all her angst, she didn't want the magical evening to end, either.

"We still have to walk back to the fire station and then I'll give you a ride home," Cooper said. He stood and his nephew did the same. Then Cooper reached a hand down to help her stand. His hand was warm and she thought for a moment he would pull her into his arms. To her relief, he must have remembered his nephews were there because he released her hand.

"Thanks for the pizza," he said.

"You paid for it. Next time it's my treat."

"I'll hold you to that," he said with a smile. He scooped Charlie up onto his shoulders and reached for Ryan's hand.

"I think it's your turn to hold Otis's leash," she told Will.

"Yay!" he exclaimed, reaching for it, then completely stole her heart by slipping his other hand in hers, and together they walked through the quiet streets, with Olivia wondering how she was going to say goodbye in a few weeks.

2 6

JULIET

The gorgeous California coast rolled past her window as she and Henry drove south toward the Hidden Creek Resort again.

With each mile, Juliet could feel more of her tension disappear.

She knew she shouldn't be here with him. For all her determination that she would be strong and protect him, even if it meant sacrificing what she wanted, she had folded completely when he had texted an hour ago, asking if she wanted to take a trip down and see what his crew had been doing all day.

"It's a gorgeous afternoon, isn't it?"

"Stunning."

She wanted to open the windows of his pickup truck and let the wind ripple through her hair. Even with her hip and her ribs aching, she felt alive and vibrant.

"I feel so fortunate that I've been able to get out twice in one week. I'm glad you called. Thank you. We live in one of the most beautiful places on the planet and I don't take the opportunity often enough to simply enjoy my surroundings," she said.

"We are lucky to live here, aren't we?"

"Yes. I sometimes forget just how gorgeous it is, until we have a clear afternoon like this one to remind me."

"Maybe your accident is turning into one of those blessings in disguise."

"I wouldn't go that far," she said with a smile. "I don't think I can ever say I'm grateful that I fell. But at least being sidelined has reminded me how important it is to stop and look around once in a while. It's a lesson I won't soon forget."

At least she hoped not, anyway. Once she returned to work, would she jump right into the busy whirl of activity, running the garden center, helping Caitlin with homework, volunteering in the community?

"What's the latest from the doctor?"

"At my last appointment, she said things are healing nicely. She said I could go back to work next week part-time, if I feel like I'm up to it."

"Great news."

Strangely, the prospect did not fill her with as much excitement as she might have expected. "I suppose. I'm not sure I've been missed all that much, to tell you the truth."

He gave her a long look. "You're not happy things have gone smoothly with Olivia at the helm?"

She gazed out the window at the passing shoreline, wishing she hadn't brought this up, especially since she didn't know exactly how to articulate what she meant. "Harper Hill Home and Garden is my livelihood. Of course I'm happy things have gone smoothly. I certainly didn't want Olivia to fail."

"What's the issue, then?"

"I guess I hoped she might turn to me for a little more help. My pride hurts to realize I'm not completely indispensable."

Henry was the only person on earth with whom she felt free enough to express those feelings because she knew he would never judge her harshly. Who would she possibly tell these things to when she didn't have him anymore?

"Olivia seems to be doing a very competent job. But you know her heart isn't in it, like yours is. You love running the garden center, which is one of the reasons people from across the region come to you for their gardening needs. Your enthusiasm, your passion and your knowledge are at least as important as your high-quality inventory, if not more so."

His words comforted the sting she hadn't fully realized had been there under her skin. "Thank you."

"I'm sure Olivia has had plenty of problems, too. She probably just doesn't ask you questions because she didn't want to burden you right now while you're busy healing."

"You could be right."

He gave her a careful look across the pickup cab. "What other reason could there be?"

Some of her delight in the afternoon's beauty seemed to seep away like sand washing out to sea. As much as she trusted Henry, she had never spoken to him about her secret sorrow, about how Olivia had become so adept at shutting her out over the years.

"My daughter is fiercely independent. She has been most of her adult life, basically because I gave her no choice."

"There you go, being too hard on yourself again."

"Not hard enough," she admitted. "We don't have a perfect mother-daughter relationship and I know it's entirely my fault."

"Is there such a thing as a perfect mother-daughter relationship?" Henry asked. "I know Lilianne struggled with her own mother, even as she was dying. She couldn't let go of some of her past hurt, as much as she wanted to. I think toward the end, she was at least able to find peace with it."

As he spoke of his late wife, she missed her dear friend with a fierce, visceral ache.

"I wasn't a very good mother to Olivia after Steve died. I was terrible, actually."

"I don't believe that."

"I was, Henry. Ask her. I wasn't a good mother to either of my girls. I was too wrapped up in my own pain and in over my head trying to run the business. I see you with Jake and I'm filled with shame and guilt."

"You shouldn't be!"

"The two of you are so close. You've handled single parenthood wonderfully. I didn't. Far from it. I didn't enforce any rules with Natalie, and as a result, she ran wild for that first year and ended up pregnant with Caitlin."

"Don't blame yourself for that. Your daughter made her own choices."

"I can't help asking myself if she might have made different choices if I'd been more present in her life during that time."

She had spent many sleepless nights wondering how she could have been stronger, if Steve's influence while he was alive might have tempered some of Nat's wildness.

"And poor Olivia. I was running in a hundred different directions during her teenage years. It was completely unfair to her. I neglected her, first because of my grief, then because of Natalie's and Caitlin's needs being so overwhelming. I can't blame her for being angry about that. I wasn't there for Olivia when she needed me. I can never fix that."

"Don't say never," he said gruffly. "It might be too late to change anything for Natalie, but Olivia is still here and she still needs her mother. Have you talked to her about this?"

It was the huge unspoken elephant in the room every time she was with her daughter. "No. Not in so many words."

"Maybe it's time to do that. Maybe Olivia never saw things that way. Or maybe she's just waiting for you to acknowledge what happened. You won't know until you have a discussion."

The idea terrified her, even as she knew she had to do it. "You're right. I know you are."

"You can't change what happened after Steve died, Juliet. All you can do now is move forward and forge the kind of relationship she needs now, as a strong and successful adult woman."

His words resounded deep in her heart. That was where she had been going wrong. She had been trying to mother Olivia the same way she did Caitlin. That probably wasn't what Olivia needed right now. She didn't need to be nagged about remembering to wear a sweater; she needed to be supported and encouraged for the choices she was making in her life and perhaps guided toward different ones.

"How do you always find exactly the right thing to say?"

Henry smiled. "All the years of watching you, the smartest woman I know."

She scoffed but didn't have a chance to answer because they had reached the sign for Hidden Creek Resort. The site was even more lovely than she remembered, now that the empty places in the landscaping had been filled in with verdant new plants.

"Oh," she breathed, struck almost speechless with delight. "It's absolutely gorgeous."

"Thank you. I'm thrilled with the way it turned out. How would you like to be the first one to have an official tour?"

"I would be honored," she said.

He climbed out of the pickup truck and went around for her wheelchair, then rolled it to her side of the vehicle.

Again, he had to lift her out and into the chair. Was it her imagination or did he hold her a little longer than strictly necessary before lowering her to the chair?

"Ready?" he asked.

"Yes. I can't wait," she said, even as she wished he could hold her just a bit longer.

Again, they were the only ones around as he wheeled her to the garden so she could see the finished product—though she

certainly knew well enough that no garden was ever truly finished.

The shadows were long as the sun began to set. In the sweet
light of dusk, the colors of the flowers were intense and vivid.
Breathtaking. Everywhere she turned, they provided a feast for
the eyes.

"I love it," she said, when he wheeled her to the terrace overlooking the ocean, where containers of flowers spilled over with
color. "I'm going to save every penny I have so that I can stay
here someday."

He watched her. "What would you do if you stayed here?"

"Absolutely nothing." She laughed. "That probably sounds
silly when I've been complaining about how doing nothing has
been making me crazy since my accident, but this seems different somehow. I would love to sit right here with a book and a
glass of something cold. How heavenly, to sit and watch the sunset, looking out over the beautiful gardens leading to the sea."

"We don't have the book or the beverages, but it still feels
pretty heavenly to me."

"Same," she admitted with a smile.

They sat there, her in the wheelchair and Henry on the bench
beside her, and watched in a perfect, almost reverential silence
as the sun slipped into the ocean in one last vibrant orange-and-
lavender blast across the sky.

Juliet released a deep sigh she had not realized she had been
holding in. "Wow. That was stunning. I'm not sure we could
have asked for a more beautiful evening."

"Agreed," Henry said quietly. "Thank you for sharing it with
me."

She wanted to weep, suddenly, for reasons she could not have
explained. With all her heart, she suddenly wished for more
peaceful evenings with him like this.

A lifetime of them.

She tried so hard not to be bitter about her diagnosis. Everyone had some trial or heartache to deal with. It was part of the miracle and challenge of being alive.

Yes, having multiple sclerosis had complicated her life, with the pills and the worry and the things she could no longer do. But it wasn't the end of the world. In the online support group she followed, she had met others who had lived for many years with MS. The progression of her disease had been relatively slow and the symptoms mild so far. She knew she was lucky.

But as she sat beside the man she loved, sorrow and anger spiraled inside her, both equally powerful.

"Are you all right?" he asked.

No. Far from it. My heart is breaking.

Of course she couldn't tell him that.

"Sunsets sometimes make me a little melancholy. I'm not sure why."

"Maybe because this day, this moment, won't come again. It's fleeting and precious. We want the sun to stay right on the horizon but it never will."

Yes. One of the few constants in life was that no one could stand still. "Yes. Something like that."

"Don't let it ruin what's been a really wonderful evening."

"It has been perfect. Exactly what I needed."

He looked over at her and she almost wept again at the tenderness in his gaze.

"Juli."

Only her name. That's all he said. And then he kissed her with a soft tenderness that left her helplessly entangled.

The moment was perfect, there in the dusky purple light after sunset, when colors were muted and the night was quiet around them.

She didn't want it to end, even as she knew it had to. "I wish we could stay like this forever," she murmured after several long, delicious moments.

He was silent, his forehead pressed to hers. "I do, too. Sooner or later, I'm afraid it will get dark and cool and we'll have to head back to real life."

She didn't want to. She knew what waited back in real life. Loneliness. Emptiness.

"Just because we can't stay here forever doesn't mean we can't have other kisses and other sunsets, Juli."

His words doused her like a bucketful of seawater in the face.

She wasn't being fair to him. This game she was playing, this back-and-forth, this yes-then-no was wrong, bordering on cruel.

"We have to go." She rolled the cursed wheelchair away from him, just far enough that he couldn't miss the message.

He looked as if he wanted to say something but finally gave a nod and pushed her silently back to his pickup truck. He didn't say anything when he lifted her in again and made sure the seat belt was fastened or after loading her wheelchair into the back of the pickup truck and climbing in himself.

The distance between them seemed vast and unbreachable, as far as it would take her to reach Hawaii by canoe, the drive to Cape Sanctuary far less comfortable than the one they had taken on their way down the coast. Tension filled the cab of his pickup truck. She could feel it rolling off him in waves. He played the stereo, one of those adult contemporary rock stations where she knew the words to every song, but she had no desire to sing anything.

The coward in her wanted to curl up in the corner pretending to sleep, but she forced herself to stay awake mile after painful mile as the tension between them ratcheted up.

When he finally pulled up to Sea Glass Cottage, she saw lights on in the upstairs rooms, both Caitlin's and Olivia's. Good. Her girls were home safely.

"Thank you for a lovely day," she said with the politeness of someone expressing appreciation to a cashier at the grocery store.

He uttered an epithet, an ugly, raw word she'd never heard him say.

286

"You're doing it again."

"What?" she asked, though she knew perfectly well what he was talking about.

"Pushing me away. You let me inside one minute, then close yourself up completely the next. You do it again and again. And I just let you."

She heard the pain in his voice and closed her eyes, hating herself. She had created this situation, had hurt him, because she was too weak to make the necessary break between them. She cherished their friendship so much. Losing it was going to devastate her, but she didn't see any other choice.

Anything she could think to say sounded horrible, so she finally just spilled the words that came to her.

"I told you we could never have a relationship. I don't know why you're making this so ugly."

"You did. You absolutely did. You told me we couldn't have a relationship."

"I'm sorry," she said, curling her hands in her lap and hating herself and this entire situation.

"I love you, Juli. You have to know that."

His words were raw with emotion and she stared at him, shocked to her core. She hadn't. She knew he cared about her as a friend and that he was attracted to her, but somehow she had convinced herself things hadn't progressed as far as love.

How stupid of her. She had been shortsighted and selfish and cruel.

Henry Cragun was not the sort of man who would kiss a woman he didn't care for deeply.

"You...don't," she said feebly.

"Stop. I've been trying to tell you for months. Every time you let me close enough that I think you might be ready to hear it, a moment later, you shut me down. Why do you push me away, again and again?"

Because I'm broken.

She couldn't tell him. The words clogged in her throat. She had to get out of here. Instead she was literally trapped in this truck with him.

"I can't have this conversation with you right now. Not here. I need to get out."

"Why? So you can run away again?"

"I wish I could run away."

He stared at her, the truth of her words stark and unadorned between them. He drew in a sharp breath, then let it out slowly.

"Why? Just tell me that. Why are you running so hard? Obviously not literally right now, but you have been running figuratively from me for weeks."

When she didn't answer, when she *couldn't* answer, he sighed heavily and climbed out of the vehicle to get her wheelchair.

He hardly touched her this time as he lowered her to the chair, then pushed her to the porch. She wanted to tell him she could do it herself but didn't trust herself to speak without bursting into tears.

Sea Glass Cottage was usually her haven, the place to which she had escaped after Steve died, where she had begun to heal. Right now, it didn't feel like a sanctuary as he pushed her up the ramp he had built to the porch.

Finally, she knew she had to say something. She owed him that, at least. "I'm sorry, Henry."

"For what?" He looked stony, his expression harsh and distant.

"That we can't be...more than friends. I've been trying to tell you. I value your friendship. So much. I don't want to hurt you, but I don't know how else to get it through your head that I...I can't have a relationship with you."

"Why? You still have not answered that."

"I...I'm just not interested," she lied. "Why can't you just accept that?"

"Maybe because I don't believe you. How can I, when you send out conflicting signals every time we're together?"

He was right. How could she blame him for not knowing what she really wanted?

"I'm attracted to you. Any woman would be. But a purely physical relationship wouldn't be enough for me. I don't think it would be for you, either. There are a hundred women in town who would love to date you. If you want, I can set you up with some of my friends."

It was exactly the wrong thing to say and she knew it before the words were even out. He glared at her, his expression finally revealing frustration and anger and hurt.

"You want to set me up with your friends."

"I just don't want you to be lonely, Henry."

He shook his head. "I think you're full of more chickenshit than your best fertilizer."

She stared at him, shocked again that he would swear at her twice in a matter of moments when she had heard expletives from him so rarely over the years.

"Believe what you want. It doesn't change the fact that my mind is made up."

Here was the hard part, the bitter words she didn't want to say but knew she must.

"I don't want to hurt you, but I...I need to ask you to give me some space. I hoped we could stay friends, but we obviously can't manage that between us now, without all this awkwardness and the...the expectations I can't meet."

In the darkness, she couldn't completely see the expression in his eyes, but she could feel the shock and pain that seemed to radiate from him.

"Message received," he finally said abruptly and started down the ramp. "I won't bother you again."

She couldn't bear this. "Henry."

He turned back and somehow the moonlight caught his features, stark and angry and sad.

She had destroyed her closest friendship. How would she ever go on without him?

What else could she have done? She couldn't inflict her condition on him. Not when he had already been through so much.

"Goodbye, Juliet."

He walked the rest of the way down the ramp, climbed into his pickup and drove away without another word, leaving devastation behind.

She didn't know how long she sat there feeling numb with pain. It could have been a few moments or a few days before Olivia pushed open the front door and looked around.

"I thought I heard a vehicle out here. Was that Henry? Did he really just leave you here on the porch like an Amazon delivery? That's not like him."

"Maybe I wanted him to," she snapped, but the words seemed to implode the dam that had been holding back all her feelings. They smashed through in a mad, terrible rush and she burst into raw, agonized tears.

2 7

OLIVIA

At first, Olivia was so shocked by her mother's sobs that she did not know how to respond.

Juliet was not a crier. Oh, there may have been times over the years when her mother had lost control of her emotions, but Olivia could probably count the times she had seen her really weep on one hand, most of those after her father died and then again after Natalie's death.

"Mom. What's going on? What happened?"

Juliet looked up, her fine-boned features haunted. "Nothing. I'm fine."

Really? Her mom was really going to play the *I'm-fine* card?

"You're obviously not. You're sitting on the porch and weeping. I can't believe Henry would leave you out here and not take you into the house."

"It doesn't matter." Juliet's voice was listless, defeated. She sounded so unlike herself that Olivia began to worry even more.

"What happened? Did you and Henry have a fight?"

Juliet gave a humorless laugh. "A fight. I guess you could say that."

She looked so very bleak, a few more tears trickling down her cheeks. For one cowardly moment, Olivia wanted to ignore the whole situation, to wheel her mother inside the house and help her transfer to bed. She did not want to know about her mother's relationship with Henry. With any man.

The easier choice would be to simply leave Juliet to handle things in her own way.

She couldn't do that. Her mother was obviously hurting. Olivia had to try to comfort her, if possible. Hadn't she vowed to stop being a coward all the time?

She swallowed and uttered a silent prayer for courage. "Mom. Talk to me. What's going on?"

Juliet made a hysterical-sounding sound. "Oh, nothing. I just completely ruined my friendship with Henry. That's all."

At that, her mother broke out into renewed sobs.

"I'm sure it's not as bad as you fear," she said, though of course she couldn't be sure of any such thing. "You used to tell me there was nothing the Harper family couldn't fix."

Of course, that had been before her father died, before Natalie gave in to her drug addictions, before they both realized some wounds would never completely heal.

"I said a lot of stupid things to you, didn't I?"

"I don't remember those. Only the smart things," she said gently.

"You wouldn't say that if you could have heard me tonight."

"What happened?" she asked. "Do you want to talk about it?"

Her mother buried her face in her hands. "I did what I had to do," she said, her words muffled. "I broke things off with him. I...I ended our friendship."

She wasn't crying about a friendship. Or at least not *only* a friendship. This went much deeper than that.

"Why would you do that? Henry's been a dear friend and support to you over the years. He and Lilianne both."

"The man isn't thinking straight. He gave me no choice."

Olivia didn't say anything, sensing her mother would tell her in her own way and her own time.

"He wants a relationship," Juliet finally whispered. "He says he's in love with me."

Yeah. She really didn't want to have this conversation with her mother. She knew her mother was a young and vibrant fifty-three, but she was still Olivia's *mom*, and thinking of her having relationship troubles was just weird.

But Juliet was confiding in her, needing someone to turn to. Olivia couldn't walk away from that.

"Why is that so terrible, Mom?" she began, choosing her words carefully. "It seems perfect to me. You and Henry have so much in common. You have both lost someone you love. You're both in similar businesses. Caitlin and Jake are best friends. I'll be honest—I don't understand why this is stressing you so much."

"Because it's completely impossible! It's ridiculous to even consider it. Look at the age difference between us!"

Olivia stared at her mother. "It can't be more than a few years. Maybe five."

"It's eight!"

"Eight is nothing, especially at this stage of your life. No one will even notice."

"*I'll* notice. If he was eight years older than me, it wouldn't matter. Nobody would say a thing. But in another dozen years, I'll be an old woman while he's still healthy and strong and energetic. I have a broken hip, for heaven's sake!"

"That came as a result of you climbing a ladder at the business you own and operate. Very successfully, I might add. You're not exactly a doddering old lady in a rocking chair."

She had to be missing something here. Juliet seemed the last person who would be bothered by a few years' difference in age.

"Is that the only reason you don't want a relationship with Henry?" she asked carefully.

Juliet didn't say anything, her breathing measured as she appeared to be trying to contain her emotions. Something told Olivia there was more to the story.

"Is this about Dad?" she guessed.

Juliet wiped her eyes. "I loved your dad with all my heart. He was a wonderful man. My first love."

Olivia's throat felt thick as she pictured her father and the adoring way he always treated Juliet, as if he was the luckiest man in the world to have her by his side.

"Yes. He was a wonderful man who wouldn't want the woman he loved to spend her life unhappy and alone. You grieved a long time for him. Dad would be the first in line to tell you that you deserve a little happiness now."

"I have been happy over the years, running the business, raising Cait, watching you grow into a strong, capable woman."

Olivia didn't feel very strong or capable at the moment, but she appreciated the sentiment coming from her mother.

"I don't need a man in my life to make me happy," Juliet went on firmly.

"I would agree with you in general terms. But when the idea of not having one particular man in your life, even as a friend, makes you this *unhappy*, maybe life is trying to send you a message."

Juliet gazed at her, eyes stark and filled with pain.

"It's impossible," she whispered. "That's all. I can't go into all the reasons, but you just have to trust me."

"I don't think I'm the one you have to convince," Olivia said.

Juliet let out another sob, then seemed to square her shoulders. "I told Henry we need to take a break from each other. He didn't like it but he will honor my wishes. That's the kind of man he is."

While she might have wanted to argue with her mother, Olivia also knew Juliet could be stubborn.

She must have her reasons. Nothing she had said seemed compelling, but Olivia sensed there were things her mother wasn't saying.

"Let's get you inside. It's chilly out here and you should be in bed. You'll feel better after you've washed your face and changed into your pajamas," she said, as gently as if Juliet were a child.

"I won't be able to sleep."

She had a feeling Juliet was far more exhausted than she wanted to admit. She opened the door and pushed the wheelchair over the threshold and into the house.

"Is Caitlin home? I don't want her to see me like this. I'm such a mess."

From Olivia's perspective, Juliet looked as she always did, elegant, lovely, ageless, if a little red-eyed right now.

"She was in her room when I got home about an hour ago and hasn't come out. She did her typical grunt when I knocked on the door and said she was fine."

Now wasn't the time to mention to Juliet her worry about her niece. Caitlin seemed troubled, but Juliet didn't need another burden right now while she was dealing with her own problems.

28

OLIVIA

Over the years, she had become used to thinking of Cape Sanctuary as the place she couldn't wait to leave, a place filled with sad memories of her father and of Natalie. Heartbreak, loss, resentment. All the tangled emotions of her youth.

Somehow, she hadn't left enough room in her memories for the things she had loved about her hometown.

The things she *still* loved.

As Olivia walked into the fire station early the following Saturday, she couldn't help but remember. This was a town where people cared about each other. The firefighters had removed all but one of their trucks from inside the station in preparation for the fund-raiser for Chief Gallegos. Instead of trucks, the fire station was now filled with row after row of long white tables and chairs.

An hour from now, those tables would be filled with families. Judging from the social media posts filling up the city's feed, the entire town was planning to come out to support one of their own.

Cape Sanctuary was a tourist town. During some busy summer weekends, tourists could outnumber locals three to one. But when one of the locals needed help, everyone rallied around.

After her father died, people had been so kind and supportive. She could remember now how meals had filled their freezer, how neighbors would stop often to check on them, how they hadn't had to mow the lawn at Sea Glass Cottage for at least a year because random neighborhood youths had stepped up to take care of it without being asked.

The town wasn't perfect. It had its share of problems. Suicide, drugs, alcohol, divorce, domestic abuse. Any social problem could be found here. But there was goodness, too. In Cape Sanctuary, people came together to lift and help each other, regardless of demographics, religion, social status.

While she enjoyed the unique flavor and vibrancy of her neighborhood in Seattle and had made good friends there, Cape Sanctuary was home. It always would be.

Inside the modern-looking fire station, new since her father had been a volunteer here, Cooper seemed to be directing traffic. He appeared to be setting up a camp grill in the middle of a group of people in fire department T-shirts.

He appeared completely at home, a true leader in the middle of the craziness.

Was he as comfortable here as he appeared? Olivia had thought he would never come home again. His reasons to stay away were far stronger than her own. While Olivia's family had always been beloved, supported by the community, Cooper's home life had been very different. His mother, like Natalie, had been an addict. Olivia didn't think she'd ever held down a job.

The family hadn't been destitute. Cooper's mother had family who helped them, including the aunt and uncle who had taken in Melody for her last few years of high school.

Life could not have been easy for them. Had it been difficult for Cooper to come back to town? It must have been, yet he had done it for Melody and her boys.

As she watched him interact with his firefighters, warmth washed through her, sweet and healing.

It would be so easy to fall in love with him.

Olivia caught the direction of her thoughts and quickly pushed them away. She wasn't going to think about that right now. She had a job to do and wasn't here to gawk at the city's sexy fire chief. She picked up her camera and started snapping pictures of the fire department setting up for the breakfast, of the big sign overhead that read WE LOVE YOU, GALLEGOS FAMILY, of the bags full of pancake mix, the bottles of syrup, the stacks and stacks of paper products.

While she was photographing the scene for social media, Rosemary Duncan spotted her and hurried over. "Isn't this wonderful?" the mayor gushed. "I hope we knock it out of the park with the crowd."

"I'm sure you will. It's the perfect day for a pancake breakfast."

After a week of steady rain following the night she and Cooper had taken the boys for pizza at the park, the sun had finally come out. The day promised to be bright and beautiful. At least the morning, anyway. The forecast called for more storms, but she had to hope they would hold off until later.

On a nice day like this, the garden center would be hopping with customers, but she knew the other employees could handle things in her absence.

Rosemary looked around. "I just have to tell you what an amazing job you've done helping us spread the word. I have been astonished over the past week how our traffic has increased across the board."

"It helps that we have a good cause, one people want to get behind."

"Don't underestimate yourself. You seem to know exactly

what to post and when. I've been so impressed. In fact, I've spoken with the city council about seeing if we can contract with you even after you return to Seattle."

"I'm glad you're happy. That's what we like to hear at Harper Media."

"Of course, I would be even happier if you decided to stick around. It has been wonderful having you back. I'm sure Juliet agrees."

She wasn't sure of anything in regard to Juliet right now.

"Is your mother coming?" Rosemary asked.

"She'll be here later. A friend is bringing her. I had to come early so I can post a few more times, just to remind people. We might be able to bring in a few people from out of town, too, since it's for a good cause."

"That's terrific. You've thought of everything." Rosemary beamed. "I don't know what we would have done without you."

Olivia smiled back, but was relieved when someone else came over to the mayor, needing her attention.

As the mayor left with an apologetic backward glance, Olivia's gaze unerringly seemed to find Cooper. He was looking at her, she realized. Their gazes met, and for an instant, she was back in his arms that night outside Sea Glass Cottage.

He smiled and gave a small wave, then turned his attention back to someone who was talking to him.

Oh, she had it bad. The man only had to look at her and she forgot everything she was doing. With great effort, she drew herself back to the task, and for the next hour as people started to show up and the tables began to fill, she wandered around the fire station, snapping pictures here and there and interviewing people in short snippets of video she posted on social media.

She was so busy, she forgot to be nervous about the crowd filling up the fire station until a door suddenly slammed shut somewhere in the building. She froze for just an instant, panic spurting through her, then took a deep breath, shoved it back down and returned to her interview with a couple of school-children, who were talking about how the pancakes might be the best they'd ever had.

After she was done talking to them and the kids returned for another helping of pancakes, Olivia took a moment to reflect. Was it possible she was getting over her anxiety about crowds? It had been at least two weeks since her last panic attack. She wanted to think so but was afraid to hope.

Finally, as she worked her way through the crowd, she knew she couldn't avoid the cook stations, where crews were flipping pancakes, stirring hash browns, turning bacon.

Camera in hand, she finally walked in that direction. As she did, she noticed Caitlin chatting with a group of other teenagers in a corner. She scanned the room but didn't see Juliet yet. She might have worried but she knew her mother's friend Stella would be driving her to the breakfast.

Caitlin laughed at something her friends said. It sounded forced, which didn't really surprise Olivia. The mood around Sea Glass Cottage had been so strange all week. Caitlin seemed subdued. She had refrained from sniping at Olivia like usual and she stayed mostly in her room. Olivia and Juliet both had tried to talk to her about what might be bothering her, but she had simply said she was busy with homework.

Juliet, on the other hand, seemed determined to show she hadn't been affected by the rift between her and Henry. She was over-the-top cheerful, working hard on her exercises, practicing her knitting, writing thank-you notes to everyone who had helped out after her accident.

Olivia wasn't fooled. She had come across Juliet more than once looking tearful. Her mother would quickly wipe at her eyes and put on a bright smile, as if she really thought she was fooling anyone.

Henry was here but she hadn't had the chance to talk to him yet. It would be interesting to see how they reacted to being in the same room together, once Juliet arrived. As far as she knew, this would be the first time they had seen each other since that night he had brought her home.

She glanced at Caitlin again, tempted to approach her niece and her friends and ask to take their picture for the social media campaign, but she still wasn't quite sure where she stood with Caitlin and didn't want to risk an explosion of snark.

Her mom finally arrived a short time later. Olivia couldn't resist finding Henry, just in time to see his expression turn even more stoic, if possible, as he nodded at something his friend said.

What was the real reason her mother didn't want a romantic relationship with Henry? Olivia was convinced the conflict couldn't simply be about the age difference. Her mother wasn't that vain and shallow that she cared what others thought at the expense of her own happiness, was she?

She had a job to do here, Olivia reminded herself. One that didn't involve meddling in her mother's love life.

Still, when Henry passed her on the way back from throwing away his plate a short time later, she couldn't resist stopping his progress. "Hi, Henry."

If Juliet acted almost maniacally happy right now, Henry Cragun seemed the opposite. He had deep circles under his eyes and more lines around his mouth. He looked as if he hadn't slept in days.

Impulsively, she reached out to give him a quick hug. "How are you? I've been meaning to ask how the landscaping project went at Hidden Creek."

"Good. It turned out better than I'd hoped. You ought to drive down the coast to take a look for yourself."

"I really should take Melody for an outing, since she did all the hard work of helping you find the right plants. I'm sure she would love to see them in the ground."

"Definitely."

Maybe she could get away on Monday, since business at the

garden center was slower that day. It would be good to take pictures of the landscaping work for the Harper Hill social media properties.

"The hotel doesn't officially open for another two weeks but there are people coming and going all the time. You should be able to get through the gates, but if you have trouble, send me a text and I can give you the access code."

"Thank you. I'll do that." She looked around to make sure no one else was within earshot. Then she touched his arm. "How are *you*?"

He looked startled. Then his mouth tightened. "I suppose you've been speaking with your mother."

"A little. She hasn't told me anything, really, only that the two of you are taking a break from your friendship because you want different things."

"That's one way of putting it."

Olivia knew she should probably mind her own business. Okay, there was no *probably* about it. Both of them were hurting, though, and from the outside, the whole thing seemed so pointless.

"I'm sure it's no consolation, but she seems pretty miserable right now."

Henry glanced over to where Juliet was sitting in her wheelchair, surrounded by friends. She was laughing at something one of them said, her face bright and cheery.

"I can see that," he said dryly.

"Give it a few days. Maybe a week. She'll come around."

His sigh seemed to come from deep inside. "You are far more optimistic than I am."

"Juliet can be stubborn but she's not stupid. Eventually she'll have to see how perfect you are for each other."

His mouth twisted into a caricature of a smile. "I guess the two of us see things that way, but our opinions don't really matter here, do they? Your mom has made her position clear and I won't push her."

From Olivia's perspective, Juliet needed just that—a big, hefty shove in the right direction. Too bad Olivia didn't know how to do that.

"I think she's afraid," she said softly.

"We're all afraid, Olivia," Henry answered, his voice quiet. "You can't make it through life without it. The trick is figuring out that the thing you need is just on the other side of that fear. The only way you can reach it is by going right through the center of it."

"For what it's worth, I'm rooting for you."

His smile was filled with an ocean of sadness and very little hope. "Thanks," he said, then waved and headed back to his friends.

As she found a corner where she could log in to the fire department's account and upload some of the pictures, Henry's words seemed to echo in her head.

We're all afraid. The trick is figuring out that the thing you need is just on the other side of that fear. The only way you can reach it is by going right through the center of it.

She was doing that. Letting fear stand between her and the life she wanted. It was controlling so many aspects of her life, from the restaurants where she ate to the relationships she created.

She was living in fear.

Right now, she seemed to be handling her anxiety about crowds. She no longer jumped and wanted to hide in the corner if she heard a loud noise. But she was still running away emotionally, afraid to trust. She had been running a long time, long before that attack. Throwing herself into her business so she didn't have to think about how alone she felt.

She was tired of running. She wanted a deep, loving relationship like her parents had shared, like her mother could have with Henry Cragun.

Look at Pete Gallegos and his wife. The previous fire chief had Parkinson's disease and couldn't even shake hands at the event without severe trembling, yet his wife, Sheila, stood at his side, her hand on his shoulder, looking at him with so much love, everyone around was touched by it.

Olivia wanted that. She wanted a relationship with someone she knew would be in her corner, no matter what.

She spotted Cooper, who had stepped away from the grills and was talking to an older couple she didn't know.

Was it possible Cooper was the person she had been waiting for all this time? Did she have the strength to find out?

If she didn't, if she continued to hide rather than plow through the middle of her fear, as Henry had said, was she really in a place to lecture her mother about taking a chance at love?

JULIET

This had been a mistake.

She should have stayed home, where she could continue to smile and pretend everything was okay. She could manage that for a small audience. Caitlin. Olivia. Her physical therapist.

Now that she was here among hundreds of her closest friends, keeping up the facade was proving to be more exhausting than she could handle.

"This is a great crowd, isn't it? How wonderful, that everyone is coming together to help Pete and Sheila." Stella Davenport Clayton sipped at her orange juice.

Juliet forced a smile, wondering how long it would take before her cheerful front would crack apart like a fragile robin's egg. "It's terrific. I always love when we rally around a common cause."

"Yes. Like our Arts and Hearts on the Cape event."

Stella organized an arts festival each year, which benefited a charity intended to encourage and help foster families in the area.

"Pete and Sheila are a big part of the community. Everyone loves them and wants to help them," Juliet said.

It was hard for her to see Pete struggle with his disease. He was using a wheelchair more these days, likely because he didn't have the strength to stand for long periods of time.

Parkinson's and multiple sclerosis weren't the same. While both affected the central nervous system and some of the symptoms could be similar, she knew MS impacted the myelin sheaths of the nerves, while with Parkinson's, cells in part of the brain died off.

She understood hers was an autoimmune disorder and that, unlike Parkinson's, people could be in remission for years, as she had been. She still found it painfully difficult to watch the rapid progression of Pete's disease over the past three or four years.

"You said you weren't hungry when we first came in, but I think you need to eat something," Stella declared. "You stay here. I'll go get your food and bring it back to you."

"You don't have to do that. You should be the one sitting while you have the chance."

Stella had two very active twin babies who were currently home with her husband, who was a doctor in town.

"Caitlin's over there. I can have her grab a plate for me," she protested.

"She looks busy talking to her friends. I don't mind, honey. It's my pleasure."

Oh, it was so hard to let people do things for her. She hated being dependent on others.

What would she do when her MS flared and her condition regressed? She would have to start researching care facilities in the area. She refused to let Olivia or Caitlin care for her.

Her gaze unerringly went to Henry, sitting with a couple of

friends, as it had done the moment she walked into the fire station and a hundred times since.

Oh, how she missed him. She had almost texted or called him a dozen times a day, until she remembered she couldn't anymore, that she had pushed him away.

He shifted his gaze from his conversation to meet hers and she caught her breath at the pain there.

She had done the right thing, she thought, looking away quickly. The only possible thing. Yes, it hurt. She wasn't sure how she could endure the pain of not having him in her life. But she couldn't be selfish. She loved him. More than anything, she wanted him to be happy.

She had to think about what was best for him, even when she knew that could never be her.

29

COOPER

Why, again, had he dreaded moving back to Cape Sanctuary?

As Cooper moved through the crowd inside the fire station, greeting old friends as well as people he didn't know, he was aware of a strange, unfamiliar feeling.

He struggled to place it, until it finally hit him in a rush. He felt like he belonged here.

How had that happened?

He had struggled hard with the decision to return to Cape Sanctuary. This was the place where he had never really fit in, where he had always been aware that people saw his mother and her problems when they looked at him. He had suffered great loss here and had never quite understood Melody's desire to stay and raise her family in their hometown.

He would come back to visit his sister, but whenever he did, he would be haunted by memories of his mother and the stigma he had felt as a child of the town drunk.

When he made the decision to come back, Cooper had expected to be unhappy but had told himself he could stand it for the sake of Melody and his nephews.

How funny, that he had been so very wrong. He was discovering he was happier here than he had been in a long time.

He had come to appreciate the people here. He enjoyed the casual, relaxed beach vibe. The work was challenging and fulfilling, with something different happening all the time. He hadn't found it at all staid and boring, as he feared he would after leaving the higher-risk world of military rescues.

Most of all, he absolutely enjoyed the crews he worked with, both the paid paramedics and the volunteer firefighters who filled in the gaps. They had all embraced and accepted him warmly.

He had to wonder if his recollections were completely accurate. Had his filter been skewed? Maybe people hadn't looked down their noses at him and Melody because their mother was a drunk who couldn't keep a job. Was it possible that all the actions he had perceived as disdain or unwanted charity had actually been driven by compassion and concern?

He only had to look at how the community had rallied around Pete. The line for people wanting breakfast went out the door and through the parking lot, though it was a half hour past the time they were supposed to be serving, heading into lunchtime.

At this rate, they would run out of food before they ran out of the people wanting to donate to the cause.

"This is amazing." Mike Walker looked astonished at the crowds.

"It's Cape Sanctuary," Roy Little, an old-timer, said simply.

"All the people aren't from the Cape," Cooper said. "I've

talked to people from as far as Santa Rosa who drove up to support the cause."

Olivia's social media blitz had done its job. Several of her posts about the breakfast had gone viral, including some older pictures she must have found in archives of Chief Gallegos as a young firefighter in action.

She was everywhere during the breakfast. Each time he looked up, he seemed to find her somewhere in the firehouse talking to someone else, looking as pretty as a summer's day.

"Good job with the breakfast, Chief."

And now she was right in front of him and he had been too busy thinking about her to notice. His heart gave a little kick in his chest, and he managed, barely, to fumble a pancake back to the grill before it could fall to the floor.

"Hi there."

He wanted to kiss her. It was rapidly becoming an obsession. Every time he saw her, he wanted to grab her close and hold her in his arms again. "Thank you for getting the word out. We wouldn't have had nearly this crowd without your efforts to publicize it for us."

"I'm glad to do my part. It's for a wonderful cause. Hi, Mike. Good to see you again," she said, smiling at his new hire, whom she had met that day at the hospital.

"Hi there, Olivia. Good to see you again."

"Hey, Roy. How've you been?"

The older man beamed at her and left his bacon station to wrap her into the hug Cooper wanted to be giving. "There's my little Olivia. My wife said she saw you at the garden center this week. I've been meaning to come in and say hello. How long are you in town?"

"I don't know," she said. "I need to get back to work, but they've been good about giving me the time off I need to help my mom."

"Your mom." Roy shook his head. "Sure was scary when we rolled up and found her on the ground like that. I thought Cooper here was like to pass out."

He refrained from rolling his eyes as he flipped another pancake. Cooper had been upset to find Juliet injured, but Roy had been the one who had been nearly in tears about it. *Nice lady like that. Sure hope it's not serious*, he had said more than once.

"How is she doing now?" he asked.

"Good. She's here, sitting at the table next to the fire truck."

Roy looked over and beamed. "I should go say hello. What a relief to see her looking so good."

He headed in that direction, leaving one of the backup guys to take over handing out strips of bacon.

"It's a great turnout, isn't it?" she said to him.

"Yes. Amazing. Mostly because of you."

She shrugged off the compliment. "People love when you give them a call to action. I'm of the opinion that most people are good—they only need an excuse to show it. Do you have anything you would like to say to the fire department followers on social media?"

"On record?"

She held up her camera. "Sure. I can do video. Let me set it up. Just a moment."

She fiddled with the settings, then smiled and gestured at him. "Okay. Go ahead."

He didn't love media interviews but this one was for a good cause. He could handle that, couldn't he? He made a brief statement expressing his gratitude to everyone for their support. She asked a couple of questions about how much longer they would be open and where people could donate, even if they hadn't been able to make it to the breakfast. They had just wrapped things up and she had put down her camera when Sheila Gallegos approached them.

"Chief Vance. How can we ever thank you for everything?"

"It was our pleasure," Cooper said. "You know this was completely a team effort."

"Please be sure to let everyone know how much we appreciate them. I've tried to get around to everyone, but I don't know if I've been able to hit them all. But now I think we need to go. Pete is getting tired. He would like to say a few words before we leave. Would that be okay?"

"Of course," he said. "We already have a microphone set up. I just need to grab it."

He found the cordless mic they had been using for announcements and carried it over to Pete in his wheelchair. He was aware as he walked that Olivia was following behind, her camera ready again.

Even though Pete Gallegos's voice was weak and his hand holding the mic trembled, his words were heartfelt as he talked about how difficult it was for a proud man to accept help, but how very grateful he was for everyone's efforts.

When he finished thanking everyone and the crowd responded with huge applause and a standing ovation from those who were seated at the long tables, Pete handed the microphone back to Cooper.

"We have loved doing it. From what I understand, we've raised more than enough to modify the bathroom of your house, with several thousand dollars left over for other modifications."

Pete beamed, his smile somewhat lopsided now.

Daisy Davenport, an accountant and artist in town who had volunteered to handle the financial details of the fund-raiser, took the microphone. "We have one more announcement. Because of the generosity of the people of Cape Sanctuary, a couple of last-minute large donations and in cooperation with a dealership in Redding, we now can tell you that there are enough funds to purchase a ramp-equipped van for you."

Pete and Sheila began to cry and hugged each other. Cooper felt suspicious emotion in his chest, too, but managed to stay in control while they expressed their gratitude once more before handing back the microphone.

Cooper loved seeing people come together. Like Olivia had said, people were mostly good. They just needed an excuse to show it.

"Thank you again." Sheila Gallegos hugged him.

"You know I didn't do much. It was a whole community effort."

"Not just the fund-raiser. Everything. You have no idea what you've done. It's a great comfort to Pete to know you're here."

"That's right," the former chief said. "I can't do the job anymore, but at least I know it's in good hands."

"It's my honor and challenge to try filling your shoes," he said, taking the man's outstretched and trembling hand in his once more.

"I knew you had the makings of a fine firefighter from the time you were seventeen years old, when you risked your life and tried to save Steve Harper."

Cooper saw Olivia pale at the mention of her father.

"I'll never forget the sight when we rolled up on scene after you called in the report of the fire. I don't know how you did it, a skinny seventeen-year-old kid, pulling out a man who probably weighed fifty pounds more than you did. By the time we got there, you had started CPR and wouldn't stop, even after we tried to take over. I'll never forget the sight of you, your face black and your hands burned, tears rolling down your face from the pain, but you still didn't stop."

Cooper didn't want to talk about this. Not ever, but especially not right now in front of Olivia. It had been the single defining moment of his life and he hadn't discussed it with anyone, not even the woman he was coming to care for so deeply.

"He was a man I admired and respected."

"Darkest day in the history of this department," Pete said.

"Your father was a hero, Olivia. Not a day goes by that I don't think of him."

"Thank you," she mumbled, not looking at Cooper.

"We should get you home," Sheila said to her husband, giving Cooper an apologetic look.

"Thank you again," she said, then pushed her husband through the crowd toward the door.

"I'm sorry," he said to Olivia.

"You called in the report of the fire. I never knew that."

"Yes. I was, uh, driving past and saw smoke, so I called it in."

Her gaze narrowed. "You're lying," she said flatly.

His mother used to tell him he was a lousy liar. Apparently, age and maturity hadn't improved that.

"I don't know what you mean."

"I've always wondered why my dad went into that burning building without gear or without waiting for the rest of the department to come. It didn't make any sense. Now it does. He didn't just randomly run in. All this time, everyone said you ran in after him, but that's not what happened, is it? He ran in after you."

Cooper felt sick, the smell of syrup and bacon congealing in his stomach. He couldn't have this conversation with her here, in a crowded fire station.

"It wasn't like that, Olivia," he said.

He was going to have to tell her. He didn't want to but Cooper could see no way to avoid it. He should have told her a long time ago. She had lost her father and deserved to know the truth about why, no matter how painful.

He would have chosen a hundred different places or times to do this. He *should* have done it somewhere else when he had the chance. Since he hadn't, he could only think of one private spot where they might have a few undisturbed moments—his office.

He gestured to the front of the fire station, with a small reception area and his office leading off it.

She followed him as if in a daze. Cooper felt a tight pressure in his chest, as if he were inside his mask without the oxygen hooked up.

She pushed the door closed behind her. "Tell me what happened that night," she demanded. "What *really* happened."

He leaned against the desk, wishing he could take her in his arms, more for his sake than hers.

"Tell me the truth."

He was silent, the words catching in his throat like creosote. "I was looking for a…friend that night. This friend was going through a hard time. I was worried she was…suicidal because of something that had happened to her a few weeks earlier. When she didn't answer my text that night, I went looking for her. I knew she and some friends had broken into the house a few times to party, so I thought that's where she might have gone. Turns out she did, but she had someone with her. A guy I didn't know. A tourist, I think. She wasn't suicidal. They were smoking weed and fooling around. I…tried to get her to leave but she wouldn't. Since she didn't seem in imminent danger, I left, feeling stupid for trying to help."

"Sounds to me like you weren't stupid. You were worried about a friend."

She was trying to comfort him, despite everything. That was simply the woman she was. How the hell was he supposed to resist her?

"I left and went to the grocery store. On my way back home, I saw smoke and flames pouring out of the upper windows, where they had been. I called in for help, reporting there might be people inside. The dispatcher told me it would be at least eight minutes before the first engine could reach the scene and I was afraid that would be too late. I knew I had to go look. If she…if they were both stoned, they might not wake up. I should have waited for the engine, but I couldn't stand by."

He could so vividly remember the heat and the flames and the fear as he had tried to explain to the dispatcher that he thought people might have been in there earlier.

After waiting a few minutes, he couldn't stand by another second. He had hung up, had poured water on his T-shirt and had rushed inside, using all the training he'd picked up along the way as a junior EMT and first responder, which hadn't been nearly enough.

He had made his way upstairs through the heat, calling out without an answer. In a very short time, he knew the house was empty and that he'd risked his life for nothing. Then he heard Steve Harper call his name.

"I was sick that Steve had come in after me. I yelled at him that I couldn't see or hear anyone else, that I thought the building was clear. We were both on our way out when...when it happened."

He still had nightmares about it, still sometimes cried out in his sleep until he was hoarse, begging Steve to go back.

She looked pale and he could see her knuckles were white where she clutched them together. He didn't want to tell her but she deserved to know the truth. It seemed wrong to keep it from her, especially with these growing feelings between them.

"By then the stairs were on fire. He yelled at me to go down first, probably worried it wouldn't hold both of us. I made it, barely. As soon as I reached the bottom, he started down, but he only took a few steps before..."

"Before the stairs collapsed."

She said the words flatly, without emotion, though he could see the stark grief in her eyes and had to grip his hands tightly at his sides to keep from reaching for her. Not yet, until he finished.

"The ceiling above gave way first and the weight of that collapsed the stairs. Your dad... I saw the beam hit him as he went down."

"You pulled him out."

"I couldn't leave him there. He shouldn't have been inside in the first place. That's on me and I've had to live with it all these years. He would never have gone inside without gear, if he hadn't seen me run in or heard the report there might be people inside. And it was all for nothing. She...my friend wasn't even there anymore."

"You didn't know that at the time."

"If I hadn't called it in, he wouldn't have responded. And he would still be here."

"Someone else would have," she said.

Yes. Someone else might have reported it, but maybe they wouldn't have been foolish enough to say they thought someone might be inside.

His office was quiet. He knew the fund-raiser would be wrapping up soon, that he should be out in the bay talking to people and thanking them for coming. Right now, that seemed a world away. He was back in the past, trying to resuscitate a man he respected and admired.

"Your friend. The one you tried to save."

He braced himself, knowing somehow what was coming next.

"It was Natalie, wasn't it?"

Of course she would guess. What other conclusion would she arrive at?

He wanted to lie but, again, he was lousy at it. Yet how could he give her one more reason to resent Nat and her terrible, pain-fueled choices?

"Does it matter? It was a long time ago."

"Yes, it matters. It was Natalie. Oh, Cooper. You were trying to save my sister."

She wept then, as he had feared she would. Now he couldn't help but reach for her, though he was half-afraid she would push him away. She should despise him for what he had done. She should not want anything more to do with him. Instead, she burrowed into him, sobbing quietly, her shoulders shaking, and he could do nothing but hold her.

3 0

OLIVIA

She couldn't seem to breathe as emotions tumbled through her. Anger, hurt, horror. Grief.

"Did she...set the fire?"

"Not on purpose. I don't think she even realized until after the fire that she had left a candle burning, one that ended up finding fuel in old newspapers others had left behind."

"She never said a word."

"The guilt and the pain chewed her up inside. She hated herself even more after that. So she self-medicated with more booze, more drugs, more men. Anything to help her forget."

So many things about her sister began to make sense, finally, after all this time. Natalie had gone crazy after Steve died, not following any of Juliet's feeble rules. She had stopped going to school her senior year, had spent her days sleeping and her nights partying.

THE SEA GLASS COTTAGE

"Why didn't she tell Mom? She would have put her in counseling to help her see it was…was an accident."

"I don't have a good answer to that. I think she was afraid of facing you and your mom with what she had done. So she ended up making everything worse."

His words came back to her, about looking for a friend who had been suicidal. That had been *Nat*? "Wait. You said she was depressed and even suicidal *before* the fire. Why? What happened?"

He eased away from her, sitting on the edge of the desk, his features dark and troubled.

"Earlier that summer, Nat had sneaked out of the house to go to a beach party with some tourists, including a college kid she really liked. She drank more than she should have and… she was sexually assaulted by this guy she liked and one of his friends. It was her first time."

She was going to throw up. She couldn't bear it, thinking of her sister feeling helpless and afraid. "Oh, Nat," she whispered.

"I figured out pretty quickly that something was wrong and pushed and pushed until she finally told me what had happened. I tried like hell to convince her to press charges but she couldn't accept that it wasn't her fault. She said she shouldn't have been there that night and it had been her choice to drink too much. She thought your mom and dad would hate her when they found out."

She closed her eyes, unable to imagine the pain her sister must have carried by herself.

Not by herself, she corrected. Cooper had been there for her. She held on tightly to him, feeling the tension in his muscles. He had carried Natalie's pain, too, all this time.

"I should have been a better sister," she said. "I should have seen she was hurting."

"Hey, you can't blame yourself. You were just a kid. You

319

couldn't have known what was in her head. What were you, thirteen when your dad died?"

"Almost. He died the night before my thirteenth birthday."

He looked at her, shock and dismay in his eyes. "I never realized that. Oh, babe. I'm so sorry."

"We were at dinner, just the two of us, when he got the call. Dad always liked to take us out on our birthday eve. Just us. We would all do something together as a family on our actual birthday, but Dad would say it was his last chance to hang out with us before we turned a year older. He could be such a dork."

She rested her cheek against his chest, listening to his heartbeat and remembering. "He got the call in the middle of dinner about a fire with possible juveniles inside. We were right there, just down the street. I begged him not to go, but he said he had to and he would be right back."

A sob welled up at the memories flooding back. "I yelled at him as he was leaving and told him I hated that I never came first. He kissed the top of my head and said I always came first, that he loved me to the stars and back, but someone needed help, so he had to go. I wouldn't say 'I love you' back. I was so mad at him for leaving. I didn't tell him I loved him."

She was unable to hold back the sob now or the one after it. Cooper's arms tightened around her. "He knew, Liv. I never knew a man who loved his family as much as Steve Harper did."

She knew it was true. He loved her. No matter what. He would have loved Natalie, too, and would have grieved if she had told him what had happened to her. He and Juliet would have told her over and over it wasn't her fault and would have tried to persuade her to file charges against the boy who had attacked her.

Her father would never have been ashamed of Natalie. Neither would Juliet. They would have loved and supported her and tried to get her help. If only she had turned to them, instead of traveling through her pain alone. So much heartache could have been avoided.

Cooper held her for a long time, until all the tears were gone and she was left feeling an odd sense of relief. She had known there were things yet to learn about her father's death. Discovering the truth didn't ease the pain, but it did give her a new perspective, as well as compassion for Cooper, who had carried this alone all these years.

"Thank you for telling me the truth. I know you didn't want to."

"I didn't want to cause you more pain. And, I guess selfishly, I didn't want you to hate me for the part I played."

"It wasn't your fault, Cooper. None of it. You were trying to protect Natalie when you ran into that building, and you have been trying to protect her all these years by keeping the truth about her involvement to yourself."

"I wish I could have helped her."

"We all do."

They stood wrapped together for a long time. She didn't want to move because she knew that when she did, she was going to have to face the difficult truth that she was in love with Cooper and that she had been forever.

Sometime later, the mood between them shifted as the pain and sorrow began to recede, and she became aware of the heat of him against her, of his heart beating in time with hers.

She wasn't sure if he moved first or if she did or if they moved at the same time so that his mouth slid over hers. This kiss was slow, sweet, filled with a tenderness that made her ache. She wrapped her arms around him, lost in the peace.

31

CAITLIN

"Are you sure you don't want a ride home with us?" Ms. Clayton smiled. "I've got plenty of room for one more."

Caitlin shook her head, as always, a little freaked out by the idea of Mimi being close friends with one of her teachers. Ms. Clayton taught her fourth-hour sophomore English. Her classes were fun and she somehow managed to make dry, dusty highbrow books interesting, but that didn't mean Caitlin wanted her to be besties with her grandma.

"I'm good. I rode my bike down, so it's easy enough for me to ride home."

She looked around the rapidly emptying fire station. Where had Chief Vance gone? He had been there one minute; the next he had disappeared. Oddly, Olivia had disappeared as well.

"Anyway, I think I'll stick around and help clean up a bit."

"That is so sweet of you." Mimi smiled at her from her wheelchair. "I am sure the firefighters will appreciate your help."

She didn't care about the rest of the firefighters. She only wanted to spend more time getting to know her father.

"It shouldn't take too long. Looks like they're nearly done."

"All right. I'll see you at home."

Ms. Clayton wheeled Mimi out of the fire station and Caitlin headed to where some of the firefighters were taking down the tables and chairs.

"Can I help with anything?" she asked Roy Little, a neighbor of theirs who was always nice to her and her friends.

"We're just tearing stuff down now but we won't say no to help."

Chief Vance hadn't appeared again by the time all the tables were down. She should probably just go home.

"Can I do anything else?" she asked.

"You mind taking these extra paper plates and cutlery into the mess hall? It's just through there," Roy said, pointing to the front area of the fire station.

"No problem." She loaded her arms full with as much as she could carry and headed down the hall where he had indicated. The room was empty. Since she wasn't sure where to put anything, she ended up just stacking it neatly on the counter.

She headed back out toward the large area where the breakfast had been and had made it a few steps down the hall when she heard voices. She recognized one of them. It was her father. Curious, she turned toward a half-open doorway she hadn't seen before. That was when she found her father. He was inside, leaning against the desk.

And he wasn't alone.

He was kissing Olivia.

She stared in shock, a sick feeling spreading in her stomach.

This couldn't be happening. Her aunt and Chief Vance?

She didn't think she made a sound but she must have gasped or squeaked or something. They both turned around and spotted her looking in through the slim crack in the door like some kind of weird pervert Peeping Tom.

"Caitlin! Oh. I… This isn't… We were just…"

All her anger at her aunt, the hurt and betrayal she had nursed for months, seemed to come spilling through her, thick and fast.

Her aunt hated her and had hated her mother. She couldn't seem to wrap her head around the fact that Chief Vance would be kissing her. It hadn't seemed like a sexy rom-com kind of kiss, she realized, but something softer. More gentle. Somehow that seemed to make everything worse. Did they have *feelings* for each other?

"It's fairly obvious what the two of you are doing."

Horribly, stupidly, she wanted to cry. He was her dad and she hadn't even had the chance to get to know him and now Olivia was going to ruin *everything*.

"Are you two having sex?"

Olivia's jaw dropped at the question that Caitlin couldn't believe had even come out of her mouth.

"None of your business," she exclaimed. "What kind of question is that? You're fifteen, not eight!"

She drew in a sharp breath, feeling exactly like she *was* eight again, like a child all by herself in a corner, watching all the other girls have Doughnuts with Dad at some stupid school thing and wondering why she didn't have a dad to share her doughnut.

"You're right," she snapped, not thinking through the words at all, driven only by years of pain and loss and lack. "It's none of my business. You're an adult. You can sleep with my father if you want to."

Again, she couldn't believe the words had come out of her. This didn't seem real. It was as if somebody else was here, spewing all this ugliness.

Chief Vance had recoiled at her words as if she'd slapped him with them, while Olivia just stared at her.

This wasn't the way she wanted this to go. She had imagined

it a hundred times since finding out those DNA results and never had she imagined Olivia there at all.

"With your *what*?" Chief Vance exclaimed.

"Nothing. Never mind." She turned to go, needing only to get away from the shock and disbelief and, yeah, horror in his eyes. Those tears burned again, stupid and immature, and she could feel them spilling over down her cheeks.

"Hold on. What did you say?" Cooper demanded.

She drew in a breath and swiped at her eyes. At least she knew one thing now. Nobody could act that well.

"You didn't know," she stated. "I wondered if you didn't or if you knew and just didn't care."

"It's not true," he said sharply. "It can't be true. I'm not your father. Why would you even say such a thing?"

She wiped at her cheeks. Damn it. Why wouldn't the stupid tears stop? They were angry tears, she told herself. She wasn't hurt at all by his reaction.

"DNA doesn't lie. I took a test at one of the genealogy sites. It sent me the names of people who are closely related to me and, guess what, your sister came up as linked to my DNA profile. Since she is closely related to me, that means you have to be my father."

Chief Vance sank down onto his desk. Olivia just stared at both of them.

"There must be a mistake. She told me I wasn't the father. She swore up and down. She swore on her dad's memory."

"You slept with Natalie." Olivia looked like somebody had just punched her in the gut, like that time Caitlin had fallen climbing the ropes in PE class and had the wind knocked out of her and had gasped on the ground for like five minutes.

Chief Vance—her *father*—looked about the same.

"Once. The night before I left for basic training."

He scrubbed a hand over his face. "Only that one time. I don't think either one of us meant for it to happen. It was just…one of those things. She was upset about me leaving. I'd had more to drink than I should have. It was… It shouldn't have happened. We used protection but…"

"But it doesn't always work," Olivia said, her voice sounding strange and distant.

He gazed at Caitlin, his eyes still stunned. "When I found out from Melody that Nat was pregnant, I came home as soon as I could get leave to ask her if you were…if you were mine. She said no. She swore it. She had a boyfriend but she wouldn't give me his name. She…she claimed he was married and that she didn't want to ruin his life."

"I know his name. Paul Reyes."

Olivia looked astonished. "You can't know that. How could you possibly know that?"

Caitlin shrugged. "She wrote a lot of stuff down. Not everything, apparently, since I didn't know about you until after the DNA test."

"That's why you read her diaries," Olivia exclaimed. "You were looking for your father."

She shrugged, which wasn't really an answer.

"I've been curious for…for a while about my dad. Mimi wouldn't tell me anything. She said she didn't know. One day after Christmas when I was carrying decorations up to the attic for her, I found a bunch of my mom's stuff. I went through and found her diaries. So, yeah. I read them looking for answers. She didn't leave me much else."

If she sounded bitter, too bad. Her mom had chosen drugs over being a parent to her. How could that not leave scars on her heart?

For all her hurt, Caitlin knew she was one of the lucky ones in the opioid epidemic. She might not have a mom and dad but at least she always had her beloved Mimi to take care of her. It was important to focus on the positive in the situation, on what she had and not what she had missed out on all these years.

"Mimi has told me stuff about my mom over the years when I've asked, but I think she only tells me the good things. Not necessarily the truth. I wanted to know who she was."

"You could have asked me."

"What would you have told me? You would have just told me the whitewashed stuff, too. Anyway, you weren't around. You couldn't wait to leave your mom and Nat's Brat. That's what you called me in your diary."

Olivia looked stricken. "You read mine, too."

Caitlin shrugged again. "Okay, I was wrong to do it. I guess maybe I thought you might know who my dad was."

"I obviously had no idea who your father was," she said stiffly, not looking at Cooper. "I had a few suspicions but apparently all of them were wrong. Cooper would never have been on my list because Nat always said he was like her brother."

Chief Vance looked like he wanted to throw up. "I didn't know, Caitlin. I swear it. I asked and Natalie told me I wasn't. I suppose I...should have insisted on a paternity test."

She faced him, her chin up. "So why didn't you?"

COOPER

He didn't know how to answer her. How could he come up with something coherent when he could barely put two thoughts together?

He felt as if a flashover had just destroyed everything he thought he knew about his life, his past.

This couldn't be true. He didn't want to believe it. Even as he instinctively fought against it, something inside him knew she was telling the truth. Caitlin would never lie about something as important as this.

He had a daughter.

He didn't know how to react. He wanted to hug her at the same time he felt physically ill.

A daughter.

Caitlin Harper was his child.

He was numb. How did a guy react to suddenly discovering he had a teenage daughter?

Olivia looked as shell-shocked as he was. Her features were pale again and she was gripping the edge of the desk as if afraid she would fall over if she let go.

How could it be true? Why had Natalie lied to him? She had been so convincing, had looked him straight in the eyes and promised him on Steve's grave that he wasn't her baby's father.

All through basic training, he had felt so guilty about sleeping with her. She had been the one pushing it, had told him she felt dirty and she wanted to be with someone she knew loved her as a person, just once, so she could know what it felt like.

He'd been eighteen, drunk, horny, scared about going into the military in the first place and more than a little terrified the other soldiers would find out he was a virgin.

None of those reasons justified sleeping with his best friend, someone he had never had romantic feelings for in his life.

Still, when he found out she was pregnant, he had finagled leave and had rushed back to talk to her. Even after she swore he wasn't the father, he had asked her to marry him. He had told her he didn't care whether the baby was his or not; he would help raise it.

Nat had laughed, told him she would never do that to him. They would make each other miserable. Anyway, she said, she had started dating someone right after he left and she had fallen hard for him. He promised he was going to leave his wife, and as soon as he did, they would get married and he would help her raise their baby.

And if that never happened, Nat had said with a cheerful smile, she was perfectly happy to raise her baby herself.

Had she lied to him on purpose? He couldn't imagine why she would.

Was it possible Natalie hadn't known herself who had fathered her baby? That she had wanted to believe it wasn't him?

"I have no good answer for that," he finally said to Caitlin. "She was convincing. I didn't really see a need to push it, assuming we were still close enough that she would tell me if she suspected I was your father. I was wrong. To be honest, maybe I...didn't want to know the truth. I'm ashamed to admit that. For that I'm so, so sorry."

She swallowed and he saw another tear trickle down. He should hug her but he had no idea what to do in this situation.

"For the record," she said, lifting her chin just like Natalie would have done, "I'm not looking for a relationship, if you don't want one. I just wanted to know who you were. I always felt there was something missing in my life, something other girls had. Mimi is wonderful and I love her with all my heart. But she was my grandma. I would see my friends with their parents at school things and always felt a little...empty."

How could he be what she wanted? Hell, he was barely managing the uncle thing to Melody's boys. Before he could answer, Olivia stepped forward.

"Oh, honey. I wish you'd said something."

She wrapped her arms around Caitlin, as he should have done. The girl—his daughter—bristled for a moment, then seemed to relax into the hug.

"What would you have done? You couldn't be my mom or my dad. Anyway, I was just Nat's Brat to you."

Olivia winced. "I can't believe I wrote that in my diary. I was the bratty teenager. Completely self-involved and grieving for my dad. I wanted some of my mom's attention, which was in short supply at the time. I didn't understand then that she was doing the best she could. I see things much differently now."

His poor Olivia, the neglected daughter who had tried so hard to be perfect.

"I shouldn't have written that in my journal," she went on. "I'm sorry I did and I'm even more sorry that you read it."

"It hurt. A lot," Caitlin said, her voice muffled. "I always loved and admired you so much. It hurt to read how much you resented me."

"Please don't hate me for something I should never have written. You were the very best thing that could have happened in our family. My mom started laughing again. I did, too. You brought so much love and joy and *life* to Sea Glass Cottage. We needed it desperately."

Caitlin sniffled but he wanted to think she was hugging Olivia a little more tightly.

"What happens now?" Caitlin finally asked, drawing away from Olivia.

He had a million things he wanted to say to her but none of them seemed right.

"I have no idea how to be a dad," he admitted, wondering if she could hear the little tremor in his voice. "The very idea scares the hell out of me. But if you're willing, I would like to try."

She gazed at him for a long time, until he was afraid she would reject him and tell him she didn't want a relationship with a guy who was so stupid he believed a girl when she told him he wasn't the father of her baby.

After a moment, though, she smiled. "I don't know how to *have* a dad, either. I guess it would be okay if we tried to figure it out together."

This time he went with his gut and he hugged her. It was more than a little awkward but at least she hugged him back.

It was a start.

"First things first," Olivia said briskly. "I think we need to go tell Mimi. She has to know, before anyone else."

His daughter's eyes widened as if she hadn't given that any

330

thought. "Yeah. I guess you're right. Jake already knows, though. He knew about the DNA stuff all along but I know he won't tell anyone."

"Is Jake Cragun your boyfriend?" Cooper asked. "A dad should probably know these things."

"No!" she exclaimed, but she blushed as she said it, making him wonder.

For a moment, she looked so much like Natalie, his heart ached for the friend he had loved, who had so much potential. If she hadn't taken the road she did, to drugs and addiction, if she had married him when he asked, could they have been happy together?

He wasn't sure. He suspected she had been right about that, at least, that they would have made each other miserable. He had loved her as a friend but had never felt anything like what he was beginning to feel for Olivia.

He was in love with her.

As if he needed one more shock in this tumultuous day, one more tangled emotion to work through. Still, the truth of that seemed to push through everything else. He was in love with Olivia Harper. He didn't know how it had happened. He only knew the thought was like a bright beacon to hold on to in the midst of all this chaos.

"I can meet you at Sea Glass Cottage," he said.

Her mouth worked and he thought she would tell him no, but she finally nodded. "You should probably be there, I guess. All right. We can meet you there."

She turned and she and Olivia walked out of his office, leaving him feeling as if he had just ridden a tidal wave to shore on a flimsy piece of plywood.

3 2

OLIVIA

She and Caitlin decided to hook Cait's bike on the rack of her SUV and ride together to Sea Glass Cottage. As she drove away from the fire station with her niece sitting in the passenger seat next to her, Olivia's thoughts seemed to run in an endless, jumbled loop.

Cooper and Natalie.

Natalie and Cooper.

They shared a child.

How could she not have known Cooper was Caitlin's father?

She couldn't seem to process all her tangled emotions. Shock, of course, was center stage, but she was also aware of a certain sense of…betrayal.

These last few weeks, she had opened her heart to him, had told him things about herself no one else knew.

If she had known he was Caitlin's father, that he had once

slept with her *sister*, would she have allowed herself to be so vulnerable with him?

Probably not, she admitted. She gripped the steering wheel.

How foolish she was not to learn from her past mistakes. She should have known it was all too good to be true.

"You really didn't know."

She shifted her gaze from the road to Caitlin and found her niece chewing her bottom lip, looking nervous and excited at the same time.

Caitlin was thrilled to be able to claim Cooper as her father. As she looked at the girl's pink cheeks and bright eyes, so much like Natalie's, Olivia was suddenly ashamed of herself.

None of this was about *her*. How selfish of her to put her own feelings first, to focus on how this bombshell would impact *her* life, instead of being happy for her niece that she had answered a vital question about her very existence.

Olivia's growing feelings for Cooper and the heartache she could see coming were the least important factors in this equation, as were any feelings he might have in return.

Caitlin was at an age where she desperately needed a father. Olivia knew that from hard, painful experience. She could remember how she had ached for fatherly guidance during those hard teenage years and would have given anything for it.

His presence in Caitlin's life now might make all the difference for her niece.

"I honestly didn't have a clue."

"I can show you the DNA results, if you want to see for yourself."

Olivia shook her head. "I don't need to see any DNA results to believe you. I know you wouldn't lie about this. I would be happy to look at them, if it's important to you. I'm sure your grandmother will, too."

"Are you…pissed?" Caitlin asked when they were almost to the house.

She jerked to look at her. "Why would I be?"

Caitlin chewed her lip again. "You didn't like my mom much. That's what you wrote in your diary."

That diary. She wanted to find it and burn it right now. "You don't have a sibling, so you don't know how…complicated that relationship can be," she said, choosing her words with care. "I loved my sister. You have to know that. She was my hero for a long time."

Her eyes burned, remembering how she used to follow Natalie around, reading the same books so they would have things to talk about, walking the way she did, using the same words to describe things. She had adored Nat, who had been beautiful physically but also funny and creative and kind to her annoying pest of a kid sister.

"And then she started to make choices that complicated everything for Juliet and me. I understand a little better now why she made some of those choices, but at the time, I didn't have a clue. So, yes, I resented her. I was lost and grieving for my father and I suddenly felt like I was losing my sister, too."

"And then you really did," Caitlin said, her voice more subdued.

Olivia nodded, her heart pinched with sorrow, as she pulled into the driveway of Sea Glass Cottage. "I may have said in the journal that I hated Natalie but that was never true, any more than I thought you were a brat. I hated her choices but she was my sister to the end. She's *still* my sister and I'm so very glad that the best parts of her live on in you. I love you. I hope you know that."

She squeezed Caitlin's hand and felt something inside her calm when Caitlin turned her hand over and gripped hers.

"I love you, too. But you're wrong when you say I was never a brat. I've been worse than that since you came back to help Mimi. I'm really sorry."

She hugged Caitlin, determined to work harder to keep a strong and healthy relationship with her niece, moving forward.

Poor Natalie. Her sister never had the chance to know the amazing girl she and Cooper had created.

The day had been a revelation and had given her so much more insight into her sister and the demons she had been fighting, first because of an assault that was never her fault and then the guilt she must have carried over Steve's death. All the resentment she had carried over the years toward her sister, the anger and hurt, seemed a terrible waste of energy now.

She wished she had been more compassionate, more understanding. She wasn't sure if it would have helped in the end. Nat's choices were her own and couldn't entirely be blamed on things that had happened to her.

It was too late to fix her relationship with her sister but not too late for her and Caitlin to create tighter bonds.

"I'm nervous to tell Mimi," Caitlin said as they walked toward the house. "Do you think she'll be mad?"

At the fear in her niece's voice, Olivia stopped on the sidewalk and hugged her again. "Of course not, honey. I think mostly she'll be sad that she didn't have answers to give you about your father, so you had to go searching for them on your own."

Outside the temporary ramp into the house, Caitlin held tight to the railing while a sea breeze rippled her hair. "I have to say one more thing to you before we go in."

"Sure."

"I'm sorry I was rude earlier, asking things that were none of my business. But I would like to know. Are you and my dad dating? It would be weird to have my aunt as my stepmom but... I'd be okay with it. Just so you know."

She could only think it was a very good thing she wasn't taking a drink of water at that because she would have spewed it all over her niece. Stepmom. Good grief. She and Cooper had only kissed a few times. *Stepmom* was jumping about a hundred steps ahead.

For one wild moment, she imagined it. A future with him, here in Cape Sanctuary. Building a life together by the sea, surrounded by friends and family.

Her heart pinched again at the sheer impossibility of dreams that were destined to remain only that.

"We're...friends. That's all."

She wanted more. She wanted that future. When she was a girl, she had a terrible crush on him. Cooper had epitomized what she thought she wanted in a man when she was younger. He was cute, smart, kind to a gawky girl who didn't know how to talk to guys but somehow never had a problem confiding in him.

Now that she was a woman and had connected with the grown-up version of Cooper, everything she had come to know only reinforced that he was exactly right for her.

"But he's a nice guy, right? I would hate for my dad to be a jerk."

That would be tough, to spend all this time looking for her father and have him turn into someone she didn't want to know. Lucky for Caitlin, Cooper would be an amazing dad. She had seen him with his nephews and had no doubt.

"Your father is a man of character and strength. He's loyal. He's courageous. He's protective. He's kind. Also, he's a lousy liar, but don't tell him I told you that."

Caitlin gave a nervous little laugh.

"You won the dad lottery, Cait. Any young woman would be lucky to have Cooper as her father."

Some of her niece's anxiousness seemed to ease and she smiled. "Thanks," she said, just as he pulled up in front of the house.

After all these years apart, Cooper would always be in her life now, she realized somewhat grimly. She could go back to Seattle but she would never be able to escape him completely.

They were bound by her niece. Through all of the important events of Caitlin's life, she would have to see him. Graduations, weddings, baby blessings.

Somehow she was going to have to figure out a way to handle that without making a complete fool of herself.

JULIET

Rarely in her life had she ever found herself completely speechless. Usually she could manage *something*, even if it was only a long, drawn-out *okay*.

Right now as she gazed at her daughter, granddaughter and Cooper Vance, Juliet couldn't come up with a thing.

Otis seemed to sense her shock. He wriggled a little and nuzzled her hand. She petted him while she tried to process the stunning news.

Cooper Vance was Caitlin's father.

How on earth had she not *realized*?

"Are you…sure?" It wasn't much of a sentence but at least she had found a few words to string together.

Caitlin nodded. "Yes. That's why I ran to my room when we first got home. I wanted to show you the results I printed out earlier."

She thrust out a piece of paper. "See, right there. It says I share a significant portion of DNA with Melody Vance Baker, which indicates we're close relatives. And there's her picture in my connections. If Chief Vance had taken a DNA test, it would be even more conclusive."

Cooper shifted, looking uncomfortable. "I believe her, Juliet. It was…always a possibility in my head, I suppose, but I believed Nat when she told me Caitlin wasn't mine."

How could she not have known the two of them had been

together? They had never seemed romantically inclined toward each other.

Was this one more way she had been a completely oblivious mother?

He had said it had only been once, before he left town. Maybe that was why she had never picked up a shift in their relationship.

"No matter what she told me, I should have known," Cooper said. "Or at least verified. I should have taken responsibility."

He was uncomfortable because he didn't know how to face her, the boy who had knocked up her daughter, she realized.

"I'm sorry, Juliet. I know what you must be thinking of me and there's nothing I can say in my own defense."

It was completely inappropriate, but for an instant, Juliet wanted to laugh. He hadn't ruined her daughter's life. If anything, Caitlin was the very best thing to come out of that tragic time.

As if she could ever think less of him, anyway. This was the boy who used to eat dinner at her table at least once or twice a week, who always helped wash up afterward.

Who had risked his own life to save Steve's.

"The hard truth is, I've been a deadbeat dad all these years without knowing it, leaving you to bear all the responsibility for raising my child. On the way here, I was thinking I have some savings. Some stocks and things. I need to pay you back child support or something for all the years I should have been here taking care of Caitlin."

Her words suddenly came back to her in a rush. "You will do nothing of the kind," she exclaimed.

"I have to do *something*. A man takes care of his responsibilities."

He was always such a stubborn boy, always determined to do the right thing.

Oh, Natalie. How could you do this to your dearest friend?

"You didn't know you had a responsibility because my daughter told you that you didn't. You believed her. We all believed her. If you had any inkling, I'm certain you would have been here."

He was a victim, too, denied the joy of being a father for fifteen years, she realized suddenly. Why hadn't Natalie told him the truth? She thought she might suspect the reason. Cooper had been on the cusp of starting his life away from Cape Sanctuary, something at the time he had desperately needed.

By joining the military, Cooper was trying to escape the hard family life he'd had here. Would he have gone on to become a special forces pararescue specialist, as he had dreamed? Doubtful. He would have stayed here to take care of his child.

Natalie had loved him, had known what he needed maybe even more than Cooper had. Perhaps she hadn't wanted to give him one more responsibility, when he had spent his entire childhood caring for his mother and his baby sister.

Or maybe, knowing now what kind of life Natalie was living by then, the drugs and the partying, it was possible her daughter genuinely hadn't known who had fathered her baby.

Juliet petted the sweet little dog, her heart aching with sorrow for all of them.

"I shouldn't have accepted what she told me," Cooper said again. "I have no excuse, really. But now that I know, I intend to step up. If it's all right with you, I would like to start building a relationship with Caitlin."

"Naturally. Of course you will. I would have been disappointed in you if you had said otherwise."

Caitlin look thrilled, which made Juliet's heart ache all over again. She had known her granddaughter wanted a father. That was natural. Juliet should have realized how much Caitlin had *needed* a father. The longing in her eyes as she looked at Cooper was raw, vulnerable, nervous, as if she were afraid to hope.

"Caitlin is fifteen. She'll be sixteen in September. She's old enough to decide how much or how little she wants you involved in her life."

"Agreed," he said, looking relieved.

"Much," Caitlin said in a small voice that made Juliet want to hug her.

"You're part of this family now," Juliet told him sternly. "That means I expect you for Sunday dinners when you can make it, an invitation that will of course include your sister and her boys."

He nodded, looking overwhelmed and, she thought, touched. He had always been such a sweet boy, so grateful to be welcomed into their home.

She didn't like to think ill of the dead but his and Melody's mother had been a weak, selfish woman who had given little love and no structure to her children. That he had turned out to be such a good man was a testament to his own strength of character.

"Thank you, but I'm willing to take a rain check on the invitation for now. I'm afraid you won't be up to cooking one of your big Sunday dinners for some time yet."

"I'm stronger every day," she said. How long that would last, she didn't know, but at least if her MS took a sharp downward turn, she would find comfort in knowing Caitlin would have a father and a new aunt Melody to watch over her, along with Olivia.

"Anyway, Olivia can help me."

"I would love to," Olivia said, "but I'll be going back to Seattle soon."

"Not that soon."

Olivia forced a smile that Juliet realized was not genuine. How did she feel about this new revelation? There had been a few times within the past two weeks when she had wondered if there was something going on between Cooper and Olivia. She had hoped so, anyway. How would knowing Cooper was Caitlin's father impact Olivia?

"You're doing well," Olivia said. "Better than the doctors expected. If your plan is still to return to the garden center part-time this week, there's no need for me to stay longer. Especially now that you have Melody to help you at work."

Olivia didn't look up after she spoke. If she had, she might have seen that Cooper and Caitlin both wore matching expressions of dismay at the news.

"I can help you, Mimi," Caitlin said. "With the cooking or the garden center or whatever you need."

Though Caitlin still looked upset about Olivia leaving, overall Juliet thought there was a lightness about her she hadn't seen in weeks.

"Thank you, honey."

Cooper rose. "Speaking of Melody, I should go tell her the news that she has a new niece and that her boys' babysitter all these years has really been their cousin."

"That's right! I have new cousins! How cool is that?" Caitlin looked both astonished and pleased.

He reached down to kiss Juliet on the cheek. She wrapped her arms around him and held him close. "If I could have chosen anyone in Natalie's life to be my granddaughter's father, you would have been at the top of the list," she said quietly.

They were words she had to say, for his sake as much as her own.

He looked humbled and she thought she saw suspicious moisture in his eyes. "Thank you for saying that."

"It's the truth. You've always felt a little like a son to me. Now you truly are."

He gave her a ragged-looking smile, hugged her again, then turned to hug Caitlin, too.

"I'll see you later, Chief Vance."

"You can call me Cooper for now," he said.

"Okay. Bye, Cooper."

And then he turned to Olivia and the stark emotion in his eyes totally stunned Juliet.

There was *definitely* something between the two of them.

"Can you walk me out?" he asked her.

Olivia looked as if she wanted to say no. After a moment, she nodded and followed him, but not before Juliet, looking closely, saw the misery in her eyes, too.

Olivia was in love with Cooper.

And she was running away, going back to Seattle.

Juliet didn't have time to dwell on that or what she could do. The instant the door closed behind them, Caitlin rushed to her and wrapped her arms around her.

"Are you mad, Mimi?"

"Mad? Why would I be mad?"

"Because I went looking for my dad. I don't want you to think...to think you weren't enough for me. It wasn't that. I love you so much."

"Oh, honey. Of course I'm not mad! I completely understand that you wanted answers. I'm only sorry I didn't have them for you."

Caitlin laughed. "That's exactly what Olivia said you'd say."

"She's pretty smart, that aunt of yours."

Juliet could only hope she was smart enough not to walk away from a good man like Cooper Vance.

33

OLIVIA

As she followed Cooper to the front porch of Sea Glass Cottage, she saw that, as predicted, the afternoon had turned stormy, with dark, ominous clouds on the horizon.

"Hell of a day." He stopped at the railing and looked up at the sky, but she knew he wasn't talking about the weather.

"I believe that's the understatement of the century."

She still couldn't seem to process everything that had happened, from finding out Natalie had set the fire that killed their father to this latest shocking news about Caitlin.

Cooper looked stunned and a little lost, as if everything he thought he knew about his world had been tossed off the cliffs and into the Pacific.

"I have a kid. I have no idea where to go from here."

"You have a *great* kid. Caitlin is an amazing girl. She's creative and funny and kind. You two are lucky to have each other."

He ran a hand through his hair, his usual calm nowhere in evidence. "I have a *daughter.*"

Did he think saying it enough times might make it feel more real? "I'm sorry you missed so much of her life. Natalie should have told you."

She still had no idea why her sister had chosen to keep that information from her best friend. It was a question they would likely never answer, especially if Caitlin hadn't been able to learn more through the journals Natalie had left behind.

"I've been thinking about that. I was so determined to leave Cape Sanctuary. She knew all about that, knew I wanted so much to become the man your dad wanted me to be and I didn't see a way to do that here. Nat was my best friend. She knew my dream was pararescue."

"You wouldn't have done that if you had known about Caitlin, would you?"

"No. Or I would have tried harder to convince her to marry me, anyway, and tried to take her along." He gazed out at the darkening sky. "I guess history doesn't really matter. It's done. My job now is to build a strong relationship with my child."

"Juliet will help you figure out the best way to move forward with Caitlin."

"I don't want to change things. She has a wonderful home here. I would like to be part of her world but I would never want to completely uproot her life."

She forced a smile. "The good news is, you're already here in Cape Sanctuary with the fire department. Imagine how much more difficult this would be if you were still stationed all over the world."

"But you won't be here."

She looked out at her mother's flowers, their heads bobbing in the increasing wind that seemed to chill her to the bone. "No."

"Do you have to leave?"

His words cut through her and she gripped her hands together tightly. "My stay here was always temporary," she said. "My mom is healing quickly. She's anxious to return to the garden center. She doesn't need me like she did right after the accident."

"She might not need you as much, but I don't think Juliet wants you to leave."

"I have a job waiting for me in Seattle. Clients for my company. Friends. A life. Mom understands that."

"Sure. I get that. I just wish you could stay."

She caught her breath at the low intensity of his voice. What did he mean? Her gaze flew to his and she saw emotions there she couldn't decipher.

She wanted so much to be brave right now, to find the strength to ask him why he wanted her here. Because they were friends? Because of Caitlin? Fear tangled the words.

"Everyone here will be fine," she said briskly. "You don't need me to help you navigate this new relationship with Caitlin. Juliet will be here."

For a crazy moment, she thought he would take her hands, pull her to him and kiss her. She could imagine the words he would say. *What if the reasons I would like you to stay have nothing to do with Caitlin? Or Juliet, for that matter? What if I'm in love with you and can't imagine my life without you?*

Instead, he gave a slight smile that she thought held traces of pain and nodded. "I hope you know I wish you all the very best in Seattle. I'll miss you."

He leaned in and kissed her cheek, and then with one last solemn look, he headed down the steps toward his pickup truck.

She wanted to call him back, to say everything inside her, but she couldn't seem to untangle the words from her fear, and so she watched him drive away as the sky began to spit cold raindrops that plopped against the sidewalk and the flowers and her heart.

★ ★ ★

She stood for a long time on the porch, fighting tears and the terrible sense of her own inadequacy, wishing things could be different between them.

Finally, knowing she couldn't stay here all day with the rain beginning to blow in and soak her clothes, she walked inside the cottage, hoping her mother didn't ask questions she wasn't at all prepared to answer.

Juliet and Caitlin were going through Natalie's journals and hardly looked up, much to her relief.

"I'm heading over to the garden center," she announced. "I probably won't be back in time for dinner. Can you warm up some of that soup we had the other day?"

"I can take care of it," Caitlin said. Her belligerence seemed to be gone for now. Olivia hoped they were past that and could go back to the way things used to be. Except nothing stayed the same, she knew, and they could never really go back.

Grabbing an umbrella, she headed toward the garden center and stayed busy until closing taking care of paperwork and organizing files for her mom's return.

Right after close, Doug Carlson popped into her office, the college kid she had met that first day back. She had become fond of him over the past few weeks. He was earnest, if a bit distracted by his own grow operation.

"Your mom is really coming back soon?" he asked.

"That's the plan. It might take her a few weeks to ease up to full speed, but you all seem to have things under control and I know everyone will help her."

"I'm happy to work as many shifts as you need until she's back to her old self. Even overtime, if I have to."

"Thanks, Doug. I appreciate that and I know my mom will, too. I'll be sure to let her know when she's working up the schedule over the next few weeks."

"She's a nice lady, your mom."

"Yeah. I'm pretty lucky in the mom department."

"Too bad about her MS, you know, but she doesn't seem to let it get her down."

She stared at him, certain somehow that she must have heard wrong. He did tend to mumble his words, as if he didn't remember how to talk without a bong nearby.

"Sorry. Her what?"

He blinked at her. "You know. Her multiple sclerosis. My mom has it and they go to the same clinic. Dr. Hall. He's a great guy."

"I didn't know your mom has multiple sclerosis." She felt as if she had entered some alternate universe. None of this was making sense to her.

"Yeah. She's had it most of my life. Over the past few years, it's gotten worse. That's why I left school and came home, only a few classes away from becoming a pharmacy tech. I might go back someday but she needs me right now. She can't drive on her own now because she can't see too well, so I take her to appointments. I do the shopping, pick up her meds. That kind of thing."

All this time, she had thought he was just a pot-smoking college dropout living at home and working part-time while he tried to figure things out. Now she felt terrible for making assumptions, for not digging deeper.

Of course, he was still completely wrong about Juliet.

"I'm sorry about your mom but you must be mistaken about Juliet. Maybe she was taking a friend or something."

Doug looked doubtful. "It was about a month ago or so, during Dr. Hall's MS clinic. She was in one of the rooms, in a hospital gown. I was pushing my mom's wheelchair down the hall when a nurse slid open the door to one of the rooms and I happened to look in. I wasn't snooping on purpose—it was a total accident. I don't think she saw me, though."

"If it was just a fleeting look, you were probably mistaken."

Her shock and denial must have finally filtered through to Doug. His eyes widened and he suddenly looked horrified. "Oh man. You didn't know. I shouldn't have said anything. Juliet will kill me. I just figured, you're her kid. You would know about her MS. Forget I even opened my big mouth. Who knows? I could be totally wrong."

Could it be possible? Could Juliet have kept something as significant as a serious medical diagnosis from Olivia?

She *had* broken her hip and Olivia hadn't found out for hours. This was vastly different, though.

"Just forget I said anything, okay?" he repeated.

She forced a smile for Doug. "Don't worry about it. It's all good. Thanks for everything today."

He waved and shuffled out of her mom's office, leaving Olivia alone with shock waves still rippling through her.

She wanted to think it was a terrible mistake, an unfortunate case of mistaken identity. But the longer she sat there, the less that theory made sense. Doug might not be the most reliable witness but he wasn't stupid. Yeah, he was probably stoned a lot on his free time, but not when he was driving his mother to a doctor's appointment. Surely he would recognize his own boss.

Why else would her mother be there? Maybe the doctor saw people for a multitude of things. Headaches, maybe.

Except he said it was an MS clinic. Why would Juliet be there for something else during an MS clinic?

Was it true? Did her mom have multiple sclerosis? If she did, how long had she known? And why would she keep something like that from Olivia?

This day was turning into the most surreal of her life. First finding out about Natalie's history and her involvement in the fire that killed her dad, then discovering Cooper was Caitlin's father, now this, if it was true.

She wanted to go back to Sea Glass Cottage, climb into her bed and pull the covers over her head for a few months.

With great effort, she forced herself to work another half hour on social media postings for one of her clients for an urgent event the following week, then turned off her laptop, stowed it in her bag and headed out of her mom's office toward home.

The storm had intensified while she had been holed up. She hadn't realized. As she walked the short distance to home, the wind blew so hard off the ocean, wet and cold, that she could hardly stay upright.

It was after ten and the lights of Sea Glass Cottage were off, the house quiet. After the tumult of the day, she might have expected to find Juliet and Caitlin in the sunroom, heads close together as they talked and laughed and watched the storm, one of Juliet's favorite things to do.

Maybe they were both exhausted. Olivia certainly was. Even Otis didn't come running, as she might have expected.

He was probably curled up next to her mother. The dog had fallen hard for Juliet, which didn't really surprise her. Everyone did.

Perhaps she ought to leave him here when she returned to Seattle.

The thought sent a shard of ice through her heart. How could she even think it? She loved him beyond words. He had brought so much joy and light into her life.

But at least here, he wouldn't have to be alone all day while she went to work and then all evening while she was stuck at her phone and tablet, taking care of her clients. Juliet could take him to the garden center with her during the day. Otis would love frolicking in the plants, greeting customers, helping her mother.

He even loved her mom's two cats, who had finally come to tolerate him.

She couldn't leave him. She absolutely adored Otis and couldn't imagine how cold and lonely her apartment would seem without him. But was she being selfish to take him back to a place where he spent twelve hours a day alone in her apartment?

She didn't have to decide this now, she thought as she set her laptop bag down on the table without bothering to turn on a light.

"Hello."

Olivia gasped at the disembodied voice suddenly emanating from the dark room. Now she did flip on the lamp and found her mom sitting in her favorite recliner with Otis and one of the cats on her lap.

"Mom! You scared me to death."

"Sorry. I didn't mean to. We fell asleep out here and only woke up when you opened the door. I guess I thought you must have seen me."

"No. No, I didn't." She pressed a hand to her still-pounding heart.

"You're just getting home. It's so late! You put in a long day, honey."

Yes, and she felt it in every single one of her muscles. Only half of her exhaustion was physical. Maybe less than half.

"I was trying to finish the month-end reports for you before I leave, and then while I had the chance, I scheduled some social media posts for some of my clients, to run next week."

"You love doing that, don't you?"

She shrugged. "It's fun when you find something you're good at. I never realized I could be so creative. Plus, I love that every project is different. There's no chance for me to get bored."

"Unlike your regular job."

Her mom had said it. She hadn't. But it was true. She was coming to dread returning to work and facing the same routine, day after excruciating day.

"It's a good job that pays the bills."

"I can't understand why you don't leave and focus on building Harper Media. You love it and you have such a gift."

"Do you have any idea how expensive the Seattle real-estate

market is? I would be living in a cardboard box on the street if I didn't keep my day job."

"Or you could come home and live here. You can do your freelance work from anywhere. Sea Glass Cottage is certainly big enough. We could even finish that apartment in the garage your dad always wanted to build so you could feel a little more independent."

The idea had immediate appeal. She could stay here. Work on her relationship with Caitlin and with Juliet. See where things led with Cooper.

She loved Cape Sanctuary. These past few weeks of being home had reminded her of the good people here and how much she loved the sense of support and community here. The idea was so very tempting. She could go home now, put in her two weeks' notice, get out of her apartment lease and pack everything up and come home.

And then what?

She looked at her mom. It was completely impossible.

She had built her entire life away from Cape Sanctuary since she left as a college freshman. She didn't belong here anymore.

What if she failed, if she threw all her energy into building Harper Media and ended up falling flat on her face?

And Cooper. He would be focused on Caitlin, as he should be. It would be so difficult to be close to him, to allow her feelings to grow until she'd be left with only a broken heart.

She would have traded a solid portfolio and comfortable retirement for possibilities that might never happen.

No. She couldn't do it.

"I have a good job that pays well and has amazing benefits. I would be a fool to walk away for something that could disappear tomorrow."

"Or that could take off beyond your wildest dreams. Life is about taking chances, honey."

"I can't leave my job, Mom."

"People leave their jobs all the time. It's a paycheck, not your identity. Anyway, the risk is great, but the reward might be so much greater, too. Why are you so afraid?"

The words seemed to slice through her, cutting her to the bone.

She was.

The attack on that barista had shown her the truth with painful clarity. She was always so worried about things that might go wrong that she was often paralyzed into inaction. While she had cowered under that booth, she had played a hundred different scenarios in her head about how she might stop the attack, but had done nothing because all she could see after every possible course of action were negative outcomes.

That was the same reason she knew she had to push Cooper away. She was only looking ahead to her own possible heartbreak.

But what if she took the chance? What if instead of focusing on her fear of pain, she embraced the possibilities instead?

She wasn't thinking clearly. She couldn't make this decision right now, after the emotional, tumultuous day that felt as if she'd lived a week in about twelve hours.

"Let's forget about me for a minute, Mom. Why don't we talk about you?"

Juliet frowned. "You're trying to change the subject."

"Maybe I am. Maybe I don't want to talk about my career path right now. Just like you apparently haven't wanted to talk to your only remaining child about the fact that you have multiple sclerosis."

Juliet gave an involuntary gasp then went deathly still. She stared at Olivia, her eyes wide.

"How...? You didn't... You don't know what you're talking about."

Until that moment, she hadn't really believed what Doug had said, certain he must have somehow made some kind of egregious error, confusing Juliet for someone else. As she watched the color seep from her mother's features, heard her fumble for words, she knew it was no mistake.

"It's true," she breathed. "You *do* have multiple sclerosis. Mom. Why didn't you tell me? How long have you known?"

Juliet was quiet for a long time, her features pale and still but her eyes distressed. "I wanted to tell you," she whispered. "I just… I didn't want you to worry."

She was so stupid, Olivia thought. She should have realized. She had sensed something was going on but she hadn't pushed.

So many things began to make sense. Juliet had been secretive about her health, insisting on preparing her own medicine dispensers. That must be why, because she was adding the medications she must take for her MS.

"How long have you known?" she asked again.

"Four years."

"Four years. You kept a secret like this from me for *four years*?" She struggled to comprehend the depth of what felt like a vast betrayal.

"I would like to know how you found out," Juliet said, instead of answering her. "Only a few of my dearest friends know and I'm certain they would never…"

"Other people know but you couldn't be bothered to tell your own daughter. Does Caitlin know?"

Her mother made a face. "Are you kidding? If I ever told her I have multiple sclerosis, she would never leave my side. You know how protective she is. How did you find out?"

She couldn't believe that seemed to be her mother's primary concern, not how betrayed Olivia felt that her mother hadn't told her something so significant in her life.

"Your secret wasn't as safe as you thought. Apparently Doug Carlson takes his mother to the same multiple sclerosis clinic as you and saw you there last month being treated. He casually mentioned it to me. I told him he must be mistaken. How stupid of me. He wasn't mistaken. I'm just the idiot whose mother doesn't think she's strong enough for the truth."

If possible, Juliet looked more stricken. "It wasn't like that. I promise. Oh, honey. I found out about the MS just as you were starting your new job. You had just moved into your new apartment and had started dating Grant and you seemed…happy. I didn't want to be a burden to you. I didn't want you to feel like you had to come home and take care of me."

"What about since then? It's not like you and I never speak. Grant and I aren't together anymore. I've been at my job for four years. My apartment is no longer new. You could have mentioned it anytime since then. It's not that hard to pick up a phone. Or forget about over the phone. We've lived in the same house for three weeks. You don't think it might have come up during this time I've been here, while I left everything to come home and take care of you?"

Otis apparently didn't like her tone. He jumped down from her mother's lap and scurried over to her, rubbing against her leg until she picked him up.

"I should have told you. I'm sorry. I don't have an excuse. The truth is, I prefer to forget it myself and pretend I don't have MS. I know that probably sounds stupid to you but that's how I've been able to cope with it. It can be a terrifying diagnosis."

Olivia didn't know that much about MS, other than she'd had a friend at work who had been diagnosed at a relatively young age. She knew it was a chronic autoimmune disorder affecting the central nervous system and that symptoms and outcomes could vary widely.

"I've been in remission most of that time. I have a few episodes here and there but mostly things have been okay. A little dizziness here and there and some trembling and double vision when I'm tired, but most of the time I don't even notice."

She definitely needed to do more research, she thought, then suddenly remembered why she was even here in Cape Sanctuary. Her mother was healing from a broken hip and concussion.

"What in the *hell* were you thinking, to climb a twenty-foot ladder when you have MS?"

Juliet winced. "Not one of my smarter decisions. I told you, I prefer to forget I have it, most of the time."

"So you're in denial."

"I'm not. I know I have it. I take medication every day and I've completely changed my diet since I was diagnosed. Overall, I think I'm healthier than I've ever been."

"Then why the secrecy?"

"I don't know if I can explain it. It's just... I refuse to give people another reason to pity me."

"Who pities you?"

"Everyone! In the years since your father died, everyone in Cape Sanctuary has given me the identity of that poor young widow who lost her husband so tragically. And then when Natalie overdosed, it became so much worse. I have hated that. I want them to see me as *more*. As a person first, with opinions and causes and emotions. The last thing I want is for people to think of me as the poor widow with MS. Anyway, it's not impacting my life or the garden center in any significant way, so why do people have to know my business?"

Okay, that rationale she could understand, especially knowing how fiercely independent her mother could be.

When her friend in Seattle had told Olivia she had MS, she had asked her not to tell anyone else about her diagnosis, saying she feared the information might impact her standing at work and could influence whether or not she received promotions or other career opportunities.

"Henry," she exclaimed suddenly as another thought occurred to her.

Juliet swallowed hard. "Excuse me?"

"Does he know?"

After an extended pause, her mother shook her head.

The break between them was wholly her mother's fault, because of this, she suddenly realized.

"You broke things off with him without telling him. That's the reason. It has nothing to do with any age difference between you, does it? It's because you have multiple sclerosis?"

Juliet didn't answer for a long time. When she did, her voice sounded strained. "Lilianne was a beautiful, kind, athletic woman. My friend. Her life was filled with joy and art and kindness. Her death, on the other hand, was anything but. It was long, horrible, drawn-out. And Henry was there for her, every single step of the way. For five long, dreadful years, he cared for her. I can't do that to him again. I...I love him too much. He deserves someone young and healthy, vibrant and strong."

Olivia stared, aghast. "How can you arbitrarily make that decision for him? He deserves to be with the woman he loves. If you've never told him, don't you think he deserves all the information so he can be the one to make that choice?"

Juliet huffed out a breath. "I know what he would say. He would say it doesn't matter. He's too honorable to say otherwise."

"Or too honest. Maybe it truly *wouldn't* matter to him."

"You don't know what you're talking about," Juliet said, her usual way of shutting down a discussion she didn't want to have.

Only Olivia wasn't fifteen years old anymore, trying to be the perfect daughter. She wasn't finished giving her opinion yet, that her mother was being stupid to throw away something wonderful without giving him a chance.

"Think about what you're doing. What's the difference between you keeping the truth about your diagnosis from Henry and Natalie keeping the truth about Caitlin from Cooper?"

"They're not the same thing at all," Juliet protested.

"Aren't they? You're unilaterally making decisions for him without giving Henry the right to choose for himself. You have to tell him."

"That's easy to say, not so easy to practice. What if I tell him the truth, he says it doesn't matter, and then he changes his mind down the road, once he faces the reality of my diagnosis?"

If she had been in her mother's shoes, with a potentially life-changing disorder, would she have done the same thing? Walk away from someone she loved to protect them?

Possibly.

Her mother was acting from a position of fear. Exactly the same reason she was running from Cooper. She couldn't think about that now.

"Weren't you just telling me life is about taking chances? That the risk is great, yes, but only because the reward is so much greater, too."

Juliet glared. "That's not fair. You're not supposed to throw my own words back at me."

"Henry is a good man. You know he is. If he truly loves you, he would want to know this. If you truly love him, as you said, you owe him the chance to make that decision for himself."

Wind rattled the windows and a branch from one of the trees outside scratched against the glass. Juliet said nothing for a long moment, her features distressed. Then she sighed. "I do love him."

"Then you need to tell him."

She looked out the window, then back at Olivia. "I probably shouldn't wheel down the hill in the rain. Would you mind giving me a ride?"

"Now?" She disguised her shocked laugh with a cough. "The truth will still be the truth in the morning, when it's not raining."

"I need to go now. If I wait, I'm afraid I'll lose my nerve."

Her anger at her mother for not telling her warred with an unwilling admiration. She should learn a lesson here. Juliet was throwing her heart on the line, taking a chance.

"All right," she said. "Sure. Let me grab an umbrella."

Her mother didn't waver as Olivia wheeled her to the car and helped her in.

"What if he's in bed?" Olivia had to ask after she had backed out of the driveway and headed down the street.

"He won't be," Juliet said with confidence. "Henry is usually a night owl. And Jake was over earlier tonight and told Caitlin his dad isn't sleeping well. He hasn't seen Henry's insomnia this bad since right after his mom died."

Poor man. He had been shut out of Juliet's life and had no idea why.

Sure enough, there were several lights on at the Craguns' elegant midcentury modern house. She glanced at her mother, hoping she hadn't been completely wrong to push her into this.

"Are you sure you want to do this tonight?"

Juliet gave her an exasperated look. "Are you kidding me right now? You're the one who just lectured me vehemently about how I need to be honest with him. Don't make me doubt myself more than I already do."

"You're right. You're absolutely right. Don't listen to me. I'll wheel you up to the front door, then wait in the car."

"I'm going to walk with the crutches. That's why I brought them. He doesn't have a ramp into his house."

"It's rainy and wet, Mom. What if you fall?"

"Fine. You can walk with me to make sure I don't."

She helped her mom out as lightning slashed across the sky, followed quickly by a drumroll of thunder.

"Do you want me to ring the bell?" she asked when they reached the door.

"No. I've got this. You don't have to wait. Henry can give me a ride home or I'll call a ride share service."

"I don't mind waiting."

"I don't want you to. Go back home."

Home.

The word seemed to resonate through her soul like that thunder shaking the night.

Cape Sanctuary was her home.

Yes, it had been a place filled with painful memories. But there was also so much she loved here. Today had reminded her of that in a hundred different ways, from the outpouring of support for the Gallegos family to the sheer drama of a storm rolling across the ocean.

She didn't want to leave.

She had friends here, family, loved ones.

She wanted to build her life here. She wanted to do as her mother counseled and take a chance on Harper Media—and on Cooper.

Could she borrow some of Juliet's strength? The greatest risk also carries the greatest reward.

Cooper would be the very best of rewards, the man she loved, if only she could find the strength and courage to face him and tell him how she felt.

She was tired of cowering. She wanted to reach for what she wanted.

34

JULIET

This might be the craziest thing she had ever done.

Juliet made sure that Olivia was back in her vehicle before knocking softly on the door. Lightning crackled through the night, illuminating the beautiful, elaborately designed gardens around his home.

Henry Cragun was a man who nurtured the things he loved.

He didn't answer the door for so long, she wondered if she was going to have to text him and tell him she was waiting on his porch. Maybe he was ignoring her. Olivia hadn't driven away yet, which might be a good thing, if he didn't answer.

As soon as she thought that, the door opened suddenly and Henry stood there, wearing his reading glasses, his hair mussed as if he had been lying on the couch.

He needed a shave and had dark circles under his eyes, and she wanted suddenly to kiss them away.

Now those eyes darkened with alarm. "Juli. What's wrong?

What are you doing here? Has something happened to Olivia or Caitlin?"

"No. Nothing like that. May I...may I come in?"

Looking wary, he stepped back and held the door for her. Olivia still hadn't driven away and Juliet made a little shooing motion behind her back to her daughter, then walked carefully inside on the crutches.

Now that she was here, she didn't know where to start.

"It's been quite a day at Sea Glass Cottage," she finally said. "Did Jake tell you?"

"I got the impression he had news after he came back, but he said it wasn't his story to tell."

In truth, the news was Cooper's and Caitlin's to share but she doubted either of them would mind her telling Henry, especially since his son already knew. "She found her father. Apparently Jake helped her take a DNA test through one of those genealogy websites and she was able through that to find relatives here in Cape Sanctuary."

Surprise registered in his beautiful dark eyes. "Really? Who is it? Do you know him?"

"Cooper Vance. Can you believe that?"

"Wow. That's a shocker."

"I know! He was Natalie's best friend but I never suspected for a moment they were ever more. For Caitlin's sake, I couldn't be happier. He's going to be a terrific father."

"That's very exciting. But are you telling me you came all the way down the hill in the rain in the middle of the night to tell me Cooper Vance is Caitlin's father?"

Oh, this was much harder than she'd dreamed it would be. "No. I... Could I sit down? I'm still not as strong as I would like to be on these."

He looked momentarily abashed that he hadn't considered her crutches. He gestured to his living room, where soft, plaintive-sounding jazz music played and a mystery novel by an author they both enjoyed rested on the arm of the sofa.

She would prefer to do this standing but wasn't sure her legs would hold her.

Once she sat and rested the crutches beside her, his sweet old dog Rosie came over and rested her head on Juliet's lap. Grateful for the moral support, she petted the dog for a moment to gather her thoughts before she faced him.

"It has…come to my attention that I have been…unfair to you. At least that's what my daughter very firmly lectured me about tonight."

"Oh?"

His tone was not encouraging at all. If anything, he was going out of his way to be the opposite. She sighed. She deserved nothing else.

"Olivia insists I owe you the truth about…about why I told you I didn't want a relationship."

He said nothing, only continued looking at her.

"I don't want to bury the lede, so I'm going to start by telling you that I…love you."

He stared at her, not saying anything, though he seemed to make an involuntary movement toward her. She held up a hand.

"Wait. I…I need to tell you the rest. I love you so much that I felt like I was doing the right thing for you by pushing you away. Olivia tells me that I was really being afraid and that the right thing would be telling you the truth so that you can decide for yourself."

"The truth?"

Oh, this was hard—which was probably the reason she hadn't told him, all these years.

"Four years ago, I was diagnosed with multiple sclerosis. I've been lucky. It's been mostly in remission since then. I've been on various medications and the one I'm on seems to be doing a good job of controlling my symptoms for now. My doctor tells me that while my particular case is mild currently, obviously there are no guarantees. It could progress tomorrow and I could permanently need that wheelchair I've been using the past few weeks."

He sank onto the sofa next to her, still watchful and silent. Why didn't he say anything? Had she made a terrible mistake?

"I'm sorry I didn't tell you. It's just… I know how hard things were for you, caring for Lilianne. You were so wonderful with her. Sweet and loving and patient."

She could feel hot tears at the memory of her dear friend and willed them away for now.

"Her cancer became so much a part of your lives. I couldn't do that to you again. I wanted you to have someone young and healthy and strong. That's why I…told you I couldn't have a relationship with you."

"Because you have multiple sclerosis."

"Yes. But Olivia made me see I had to be honest with you, no matter how hard, so that you could choose."

She looked down at Rosie, afraid to meet his gaze. "So there you have it. You don't have to decide anything right now. You can…think about it. Weigh the options. I can give you some information about MS so you can make a truly informed decision. But if you decide you're…you're willing to take a chance on a future with me, I would…would want that very much."

Her voice trailed off and she finally lifted her gaze to meet his. The blazing emotion in his expression stole her breath.

"Are you done?"

"I… Yes. I think so."

"Good." He leaned over, wrapped her in a tight embrace and kissed her so fiercely, she had to reach for the arm of the sofa to keep from falling backward against the cushions.

The kiss was raw, wild, and so full of life and promise and joy that those tears spilled over and trickled down her cheeks.

Oh, she wanted this. A future with him. But she was so afraid to hope. "Henry, stop. You haven't read any of the information yet. You need to be sure."

He gave a strangled sort of laugh. "Juli, I've known about your MS all along."

"You have not."

He left her for a moment, turning to the built-in cabinets on either side of the sofa. The top was bookshelves but the bottom was cupboards, and he reached into one and pulled out a stack of books.

All of them were about multiple sclerosis, including several she had in a drawer of her own nightstand.

She stared, not understanding. "How? You *can't* have known!"

"Who did you tell when you were first diagnosed four years ago?"

She blinked, trying to remember that frightening time that seemed a lifetime ago. "No one. Well, okay, Lilianne. But I made her promise she wouldn't tell anyone."

His face twisted into a sad kind of smile. "She broke her promise to you a few weeks before the end. She was worried about you and made me promise to watch out for you. She seemed to think you would be too stubborn to ask for help, even when you needed it."

Oh, Lili. She had known Juliet so well. She gave a small laugh, even as she felt more tears trickle down. "I miss her so much."

He rubbed his thumb against her tears. "So do I. But here's the thing. She didn't want me to spend the rest of my life mourning her. She made me swear. She wanted more than anything for me to keep living. She hated that the damn cancer was winning but said it was more important than ever that I squeeze all the joy and happiness out of life that she would have to miss out on now. She said I owed her."

Juliet sniffed, feeling as if her heart was going to break and overflow at the same time.

"We both owe her," Henry said. "I fought falling in love with you. I fought it hard. I told myself your friendship was enough for me, that I wasn't strong enough to let myself love someone again, especially after I read about what you might be facing down the road."

She slid away from him. "I understand, Henry. I do. It's too much."

"I didn't say that." He came closer and pressed his forehead to hers, their gazes locked.

"And then I realized that your MS doesn't matter to me. I love you and I want a life with you, no matter what."

"You can't be sure. We don't know what might happen."

"I know that whatever time I have with you will be worth anything that might come. Remember that bare patch of ground at Hidden Creek? Together, we created something amazing. Is it perfect? No. It will always have a few problem areas that will need special care. But the result is a beautiful thing that brings beauty to the world."

Henry loved her, was willing to embrace a future with her, no matter what might come. How had she been so blessed to be loved so deeply by two wonderful men?

"You really knew, all this time."

"I've been waiting for you to say something. I thought for sure you would tell me after your accident. You're not planning on climbing any ladders again, right?"

"No. I promise. I'm a woman who learns from her mistakes."

"Good. I hope that also means you won't shut me out ever again."

"Never," she promised.

As he kissed her again while the storm raged outside and his sweet old dog stretched out in front of the hearth, joy and relief flooded through all the cold, empty places in her heart.

3 5

COOPER

He had a daughter.

Hours later, Cooper still hadn't adjusted to the news. None of it felt real, like some surreal dream that came out of nowhere. He had a feeling he would be pinching himself to make sure he was awake for a long time to come.

Caitlin was his and Natalie's, created in a moment that should never have happened but one he would never again regret. He had a child and felt as if his entire worldview had now changed.

Melody had been shocked, of course, but once that wore off, her reaction had been exactly as he'd expected, sheer delight.

"I have a niece. And it's someone we already love," she had exclaimed, looking dazed and happier than he'd seen her in a long time. "What an unexpected miracle."

She was right. Finding out the truth about Caitlin felt like a gift, one last precious piece of the friend he had loved and lost.

He couldn't explain all the emotions in his chest as the reality began to filter through.

He couldn't wait to get to know his daughter in the coming days. At the same time, his happiness in discovering his connection to her was tempered by the knowledge that in finding Caitlin, he had lost Olivia.

He had wanted to tell her his feelings earlier when they were out on the porch of Sea Glass Cottage, then had realized how totally unfair that would be to her.

She had a life in Seattle. When his own life had suddenly become so much more complicated, how could he ask her to give up everything to come back here, the place she couldn't wait to leave?

Lightning flashed outside, followed by a clap of thunder. Normally he loved these dramatic storms over the ocean, but right now he yearned for a little calm in his world, a chance to catch his breath and figure out where to go from here.

Jock, his retired fire dog, wandered to the front door and stood beside it with a worried kind of expression. Cooper might have thought the dog was afraid of the storm, but Jock was mostly deaf and had never been bothered by them before, as far as he knew.

"What's up? You don't really want to go out in this, do you?"

The dog sat on his haunches, continuing to look expectantly at the door.

Jock always went out to the fenced backyard of the small house Cooper rented near the fire station, so why was he suddenly so interested in the front door?

Puzzled, Cooper went to the back door and held it open, despite the cold wet wind that blew inside. "I'm not going out in that, but if you need to, have at it."

Jock didn't budge, stubborn thing.

"Come on," he said. When Jock still just looked at him, Cooper shut the door and headed back toward him.

"We're not going for a walk right now," he started to say, but just as he muttered the last word, the doorbell rang.

"How did you know someone was here?" he asked the dog.

And who the hell was at his door so late? He really hoped it wasn't someone else with some other revelation that would rock his world.

Jock just looked between him and the door, as if wondering why he didn't answer it. Finally Cooper pulled open the door and was astonished to find Olivia Harper standing there, hair drenched, looking bedraggled and wet and so beautiful she took his breath away.

Her face was pale in his porch light, her eyes huge in her face. She looked at him uncertainly, and he could see she was upset.

"Olivia. Come in. What's the matter?"

She stepped inside and stood dripping on his mat. "I shouldn't have come. This was a mistake."

She reached for the door handle as if intent on leaving, but Cooper and Jock did a pincer move. Cooper closed it behind her, and his smart, wonderful dog approached her from the other side, then sat again, almost on top of Olivia's wet shoes.

She looked down at the dog, gave a raw-sounding little laugh and reached to give him a pat.

Why was she here? What had happened?

"You're soaked through. Did you walk all the way here in the middle of this storm?"

"No," she said, her voice small. "I was…standing outside in the rain for a few minutes before I found the courage to ring the doorbell."

He pictured her as he had seen her a few weeks ago outside the door of The Sea Shanty, her mouth trembling and her eyes haunted as she tried to convince herself to face the crowded tavern, nervous after that attack she had witnessed in Seattle.

What could she possibly fear inside his house?

"Let me find a towel for you." He grabbed a fresh one out of the dryer off the kitchen and brought it to her, warm and fragrant. She stood holding it as if not quite sure what to do with it. She was shivering and he couldn't bear to see it, so he finally took the towel from her and started drying her face, her hair, her arms.

"You're upset. What's happened?" he finally asked, when she remained quiet, as if trying to gather her composure.

She gave a raw-sounding laugh and took the towel from him. "What *hasn't* happened today? This has been quite a day. And in other news, my mom has multiple sclerosis. She's known for years but I just found out tonight."

More shock rippled through him as he pictured the strong and resilient Juliet, keeping such a secret from her daughter. "Oh, Liv. I'm sorry."

"Maybe I shouldn't have told you that. It's her diagnosis, after all. Her business, as she so plainly told me tonight. On the other hand, you're her granddaughter's father and she said herself you're family now. There have been too many secrets in the Harper family. If she didn't want you to know, too bad. She'll have to deal with it."

Was that why she had come here? To tell him about Juliet, because she needed a friend to confide in? He was touched and honored that she had turned to him, even as he ached to wrap her in his arms.

"MS is a serious condition but it's not a death sentence. There are new treatments being developed all the time. Your mom is tough. She'll deal with whatever comes her way with dignity and strength, like she's done everything else in her life."

She lowered the towel from her face and gave him a tremulous smile. "You're right. She will. Thanks. I needed that reminder."

"Glad I could help. Would you like something dry to change into?"

She looked down at her clothes, still dripping. "No. Sorry. I won't be here that long. I just came to…ask you something."

So she hadn't come about Juliet. Or at least not *only* about her. "Sure. Ask away."

She swallowed, her eyes nervous again. After a pause so long even Jock started to look anxious, she released a long breath. "Earlier today, you said something and I was too afraid then to ask what you meant."

"Oh?" he asked, suddenly wary. He had told her many things he had never shared with anyone else.

"When we were out on the porch of Sea Glass Cottage, you... asked if I had to go and you said you wanted me to stay. I should have asked you why but I didn't. So I'm...asking you now. Why do you want me to stay in Cape Sanctuary?"

He had a hundred reasons. Thousands. He wasn't sure he could put them into words. "Because you're my friend and I care about you. And because your mom needs you and so does Caitlin," he finally said.

"Oh."

She looked crushed suddenly and he knew he had said exactly the wrong thing. He could do better. If he could jump out of airplanes and bust people out of vehicles with the Jaws of Life, surely he could find the right words to tell Olivia Harper he was in love with her.

He grabbed her hands, seeking the peace he found whenever he touched her. Her fingers were cold and trembling, but she didn't pull away, and he felt calm determination flow through him. "Those are all important things. But the truth is, I don't want you to go back to Seattle because I need you here. Because the thought of not having you in my life makes me want to go into The Sea Shanty and start knocking down that crappy paneling with my bare hands."

"Does it?"

She looked astonished and maybe a little alarmed. He couldn't blame her. He was seriously screwing this up. He had to tell her. All of it.

"I don't want you to leave because I want to see where this goes between us. I'm crazy about you, Liv. Every time I'm with you, I fall in love a little more."

She blinked, gazing at him as if she wasn't sure whether to believe him. Finally, she smiled, eyes suddenly radiant.

"Oh," she breathed. "That's a good reason."

"The only one that matters," he murmured, then tugged her toward him, wrapped his arms around her and lowered his mouth.

As she settled against him, damp and still cold, joy crackled through him, strong and powerful. She kissed him fiercely, with a heat and passion that left him light-headed. She was so much more than he deserved, but he wasn't about to let her go now.

"Please stay," he said gruffly. "I didn't feel like I could ask earlier, with everything that has happened and everything I've done, but I'm begging you now. It's not easy for a guy like me to admit to being scared of anything, but the thought of not having you in my life straight-up terrifies me."

"Oh, Cooper." She smiled, a radiant, take-his-breath smile he didn't know how he could ever live without. "I don't want to leave Cape Sanctuary. I want to stay here, with my mom and Caitlin and Mel and her boys. And, just like you, I want to stay here so we can see where things go between us."

If he had his way, he knew exactly where they would go. He wouldn't let her out of his arms or his life ever again.

"Because I'm crazy about you, too," she finally said in a rush. "It helped that you said it first but I probably would have gotten around to it eventually. I'm in love with you, Cooper. You might find this surprising but I kind of have been since I was twelve years old."

"You have not," he exclaimed.

"Ask Caitlin. She has the diaries to prove it. You were everything I ever wanted in a man back then and you still are."

He wasn't. He was so unworthy of an amazing person like

Olivia Harper, but he couldn't wait to spend forever trying to be better.

"What about your job?" he asked a long time later, after they were cuddled together on his sofa under a blanket, his gas fireplace on, while the storm raged outside.

She lifted her shoulders against him. "I want to see where I can take Harper Media. I've been too worried about failure to throw my whole energy behind it before, but I have a million ideas and want to see what I can do. I'm done being afraid."

He hugged her close, overwhelmed all over again that she was here with him and that a lifetime of possibilities stretched out ahead of them.

She would do amazing things, he had no doubt. And he would be here to support her in whatever she tried.

Epilogue

CAITLIN

Thirteen months later

"What a beautiful day. Isn't your aunt a lovely bride?"

"She is," Caitlin said, pressing her cheek against her grandmother's as they watched her dad twirl Olivia around the wooden plank dance floor that had been laid down in the beautiful gardens at Sea Glass Cottage, overlooking the ocean.

"I can't tell who's prettier. My aunt or my new stepmom."

"It's a toss-up," Mimi said with a smile. "Especially as she is the same person."

Olivia and Cooper did make a great-looking couple, she had to admit. More than that, they just seemed perfect together.

She thought of the journey they all had been on over the past year and some of the changes. It hadn't always been easy. At first, she had been a little jealous of Olivia, she had to admit, until she realized she was being stupid.

Olivia had been supercool about stepping back and urging her and her dad to spend time alone so they could get to know each other. She also had been the one who had encouraged Caitlin to become a junior EMT, something she never would have done on her own but which she'd unexpectedly come to really love—and not only because it gave her a great opportunity to be with her dad.

She wasn't jealous now of the two of them. Her father, she had discovered, had a huge heart, with plenty of room for her and for Olivia—and for the kids she suspected he and her aunt would someday have down the road.

"The bride might be beautiful," she said now to Mimi, "but she gets it all from you."

"I couldn't agree more," Henry said from Mimi's other side. Her grandmother rolled her eyes but she smiled, looking pleased. In reality, Caitlin thought Mimi really did look younger and prettier than she ever had. Marriage obviously agreed with her.

So many changes over the past year. Henry and Juliet had married at Christmastime, a beautiful ceremony at their church followed by a reception inside the largest greenhouse at Harper Hill Home & Garden, bedecked with garlands and Christmas trees and poinsettias by the hundreds.

Caitlin and Olivia hadn't been the only people who cried watching their joy together, these two who had both lost someone they loved dearly but who had found happiness again.

Henry never stopped holding Juliet's hand, which Caitlin found the sweetest thing. He and Jake had moved into Sea Glass Cottage while Olivia and Cooper were now renting Henry's house down the hill, though she knew they had plans to build their own house. She split her time between both houses, feeling lucky to know she was loved by people in each.

The dance with Olivia ended and her aunt started dancing with Henry, which made a lump rise in Caitlin's throat. She was pretty sure Olivia was a bit sad her own dad wasn't there on her wedding day to dance with her. Yay for Henry for step-ping in. His calm presence in their lives seemed to make every-thing better.

"May I have this dance?" She looked up to find her dad there, looking handsome and distinguished in his Air Force reserve officer uniform.

"I'll step on your toes," she warned.

"I'm willing to risk it." He held his arm out and she took it, a lump in her throat as they danced together to a song she par-ticularly liked.

When she started on the quest a year ago to find her father, she had no idea how important he would become in her life. The more she'd come to know him over the past year, the more she'd come to love him.

Her mom may have made a lot of mistakes in her life, mis-takes that ended in tragedy for her. But she had certainly picked the best possible man to be Caitlin's dad.

"You're good with this whole wedding thing, right?"

She rolled her eyes. "Dad, you can stop asking me that any minute now. I've told you a hundred times, I'm thrilled for both of you. You two belong together. You make each other happy and I'm totally cool with it."

He hugged her close and she tried not to sniffle a little. Would she ever find a guy who looked at her like her dad looked at Olivia? Instinctively, she searched the crowd until she found Jake, tall and handsome, now dancing a little awkwardly with Mimi, which made her smile.

When the music ended, somehow she and Cooper were close to the other couple, and before she knew it, they all traded part-ners and she was dancing with her best friend.

Jake had grown a lot in the past year. She knew she wasn't the only girl at school who had noticed. He'd gotten taller and had filled out. She didn't like the breathless feeling she got when-ever he was around, which was all the time since they lived in the same house. For now, anyway, until he went away to college in a few months.

"How are you doing?" he asked as they moved around the dance floor.

"I'm good, Uncle Jake. How are you?"

He made a face. "Fine, except you know I really hate when you call me that."

She knew, which was why she teased him by doing it often. Technically, she wasn't wrong. Since his dad was her step-grandfather, she figured that made Jake her stepuncle.

But he was so much more to her. He was her best friend, who always had her back. He was also, though she wasn't ready to tell him yet, the guy she loved with all her heart.

Someday, she and Jake would be the ones dancing together at their wedding with fairy lights in the trees and ocean waves crashing below and family all around. Jake had never even kissed her but she somehow knew it, without the tiniest sliver of doubt.

She wasn't quite seventeen yet and wasn't ready to even *think* about taking things to the next level with Jake. Now that she knew who her dad was and had come to know her mom a little more—and, okay, maybe even forgive her a little—she knew the next step. Now it was time to go out into the world and figure out who *she* was.

Once she did, she knew the time would be right for her and Jake. For now, she was happy here, in this beautiful town by the water, surrounded by people she loved.

★ ★ ★ ★ ★